Suffer

the

Little Children

MORE BY THIS AUTHOR

The Anniversary
The Travellers
A Running Tide
The Testament of Mariam
Flood
This Rough Ocean
The Secret World of Christoval Alvarez
The Enterprise of England
The Portuguese Affair
Bartholomew Fair

Praise for Ann Swinfen's Novels

'an absorbing and intricate tapestry of family history and private memories ... warm, generous, healing and hopeful'
VICTORIA GLENDINNING

'I very much admired the pace of the story. The changes of place and time and the echoes and repetitions – things lost and found, and meetings and partings'
PENELOPE FITZGERALD

'I enjoyed this serious, scrupulous novel ... a novel of character ... [and] a suspense story in which present and past mysteries are gradually explained'
JESSICA MANN, *Sunday Telegraph*

'The author ... has written a powerful new tale of passion and heartbreak ... What a marvellous storyteller Ann Swinfen is – she has a wonderful ear for dialogue and she brings her characters vividly to life.'
Publishing News

'Her writing ...[paints] an amazingly detailed and vibrant picture of flesh and blood human beings, not only the symbols many of them have become...but real and believable and understandable.'
HELEN BROWN, *Courier and Advertiser*

'She writes with passion and the book, her fourth, is shot through with brilliant description and scholarship...[it] is a timely reminder of the harsh realities, and the daily humiliations, of the Roman occupation of First Century Israel. You can almost smell the dust and blood.'
PETER RHODES, *Express and Star*

Suffer the Little Children

Ann Swinfen

Shakenoak Press

Cover images
Portrait of Queen Elizabeth I
Contemporary drawing of whipping a beggar

Cover design by JD Smith www.jdsmith-design.co.uk

For

Michael & Sally

Chapter One

Autumn, 1589

*T*hey were here again today. A hasty passer-by might mistake them for a bundle of rags thrust into the angle between the outside wall of the playhouse and the bottom of the staircase which led up to the more expensive tiers of seats. I knew better. I had been coming every afternoon this week to practise a duet with Guy Bingham, comic actor and musician in James Burbage's company of players. Or more properly, Lord Strange's Men. And every day they were here. When my duties at St Thomas's Hospital were finished in the late afternoon, I walked across the Bridge, up through the City and out again at the north through Bishopsgate. The Theatre lay beyond Petty France, almost into Moorfields, though even here a few new houses were being thrust up along the edges of the open ground, in defiance of all the regulations intended to restrict the size of London.

The rags stirred and a dirty hand was thrust out.

'Shilling for bread, Master? Spare a shilling for bread?'

It was the usual beggar's whine, somehow both obsequious and threatening. The amount demanded was outrageous. You could buy twelve standard loaves for a shilling.

'You shall have a groat,' I said, reaching into the purse at my belt. I was not so well paid as an assistant physician that I could give a shilling to every beggar in London, though a groat would not go far amongst the five of them.

As I dropped the coin into the dirty palm, the fingers closed round it, quick as a man-trap, and the hand disappeared under the rags. It was the oldest boy, of course, who was some kind of a leader. He looked about nine, but was so gaunt and ill-nourished that he might be twelve or thirteen. The youngest, who was perhaps three or four, and

1

who never spoke, could have been either a boy or a girl. There was a fierce girl, a little younger than the leader, who glared at me, as usual, through a matted tangle of hair so dark she might have been a gypsy. Or perhaps she was a cast-off bastard of one of the Lascar sailors who sometimes swarmed about the ships down by the Custom House. The other two – one boy, one girl, brown haired and freckled – were probably about seven and sufficiently alike that they must have been twins. Something of a miracle, then, to have come into the world of the London streets as a twin and yet survived. The girl kept a constant watch over her brother, who was nearly bald, his scalp covered with the unmistakable sores caused by ringworm. The first time I had seen them, I had offered the boy a salve, but they had shrunk away from me as though I had suggested skinning him. Both he and his sister kept a wary eye on me now.

'A'nt you got no more'n a groat?' the eldest boy whined.

I gritted my teeth. I had heard him speak like any other child when he did not know I was listening, but the whine was a carefully cultivated part of his profession.

'Nay,' I said firmly. 'No more coin than a groat.'

For all I knew, every penny they earned might pass straight into the hands of some adult beggar who was controlling them. I had never seen them with an adult, but their position was carefully chosen. Some thought had gone into it. Round by the playhouse entrance for the penny groundlings they would have little chance of earning anything, but here the more prosperous members of the audience would pass on their way in and out, and the pickings would be better. I knew that the company had played a comedy this afternoon – soon after midday, because of the cold weather and early dusk – and people were more likely to be generous when cheered by a comedy.

'However,' I said, unbuckling my satchel, 'I've brought you these.'

I handed out five spiced buns, still warm from the bakeshop, a paper cone of roast chestnuts, and a rather greasy pie, which had stained its paper wrapping, so that I hoped it had not leaked into my medical supplies. Out of the deep pocket in my physician's robe I drew a cheap pottery flagon of small ale, stoppered with a rag and a wooden bung.

'You'll get a farthing, if you return the flagon to the Saracen's Head in Camomile Street,' I said, jerking my head back in the direction of Bishopsgate.

I was about to tell them to share out the pie fairly when I saw that the elder girl had pulled a knife from a sheath at her belt and was cutting it into five slices. They were as even as she could make them.

'Thank you, Master.' The boy spoke gruffly, as though the words came with difficulty, but at least he had abandoned the whine.

All the children fell upon the food as if they had not eaten for a week, which perhaps they had not. I watched them with sympathy. I knew what it was to starve.

'What's your name?' I asked the boy, when every scrap of food had gone and they were passing the ale from hand to hand. It was so weak it would not even harm the little one.

He flashed me a suspicious look, but then seemed to decide I deserved something in return for the food.

'I'm Matthew and that's Katerina.' He pointed to the elder girl. 'Them two's Jonno and Maggie. We don't know the baby's name. Found him in the churchyard of St James Garlickhythe, so we call him Jamey.' He clamped his jaws shut. Clearly he thought he had said too much.

That settled the question of the youngest child's sex. Hearing his name, he beamed at me. He had a full set of teeth and was hardly a baby, but since he never seemed to speak, perhaps he was simple-minded.

'And where will you sleep tonight, Matthew?' I said. 'It's growing very cold. I think there may be a frost.'

This, it seemed, was a question too many. He frowned. 'We got a warm place. We'll stay here till the players leave. The big man sometimes gives us sixpence.'

'That would be James Burbage,' I said. 'He owns the playhouse.' It would be like Burbage to give the children sixpence. He was a big man in every way and would probably give them sixpence even if the takings had been poor today, but he might not stop to think whether they would be allowed to keep it.

'Well, I hope you can sleep warm tonight,' I said, and nodded a farewell to them. They seemed a little less hostile now, yet I was not deceived. These street urchins were feral, regarded by the City officials as little more than animals. Christ's Hospital provided refuge for orphans and abandoned children, but waifs like these would no more cross its threshold than that of Newgate Prison, its near neighbour. I turned away and followed the wall of the playhouse round to the common entrance, the shortest route to the stage and tiring rooms.

3

'Still out there, are they, Kit?' Guy handed me his second-best lute. My own lute had been taken by my father's creditors while I was in Portugal, so I was always grateful for the chance to play with Guy.

I nodded.

'The same five. I gave them a groat and some food. Even discovered their names.'

'Aye, that's best. Food in their stomachs is better than any chinks.'

Guy himself had known times of great poverty. Like all the players he could see through the rags to the scraps of humanity beneath, however unattractive.

'What are they called, then?'

'The two older ones are Matthew and Katerina, the twins are Maggie and Jonno. The smallest is Jamey.'

'So it is a boy.'

'Aye. Difficult to judge, through all that dirt.'

'I'm surprised they told you. The food must have loosened their tongues.'

'They wouldn't tell me where they sleep.'

He shrugged. 'Plenty of places around here. Stableyards of the inns. Tenters' sheds out on Moorfields. Some of them just sleep in shop doorways, and are kicked out by the apprentices in the morning.'

All of this was true. Matthew had said they had somewhere warm to sleep. That sounded better than a doorway. We were drawing near to the time of year when some of the apprentices kicking out the recumbent beggars in the morning found they had a stone cold corpse on their hands. Despite Christ's Hospital for children and Bridewell for adult vagrants, the London authorities could not cope with its great underbelly of the poor as successfully as the old monasteries had once done.

'I've written out the next section,' Guy said, handing me a sheet of closely handwritten music. 'Would you take the upper part?'

I hooked a stool toward me and settled down to tune the lute. It was a fine instrument, but I still sadly missed my own.

'Katerina, did you say?' Guy looked up from his own tuning. 'Sounds foreign.'

'She looks foreign too.' I grinned. 'Like me.'

'Nay. You just look Spanish or Portuguese. She's something other.'

'Lascar, perhaps. But she swears as fluently in English as any other London beggar.'

He laughed. 'Right. I'll give you the beat.'

4

We had played through the new section once and Guy had made some minor changes, when Simon Hetherington came out from the tiring house and sat down cross-legged on the stage between us.

'You should watch yourself with this fellow, Kit. He'll have you on stage with him in our new play before you know what has happened.'

I grinned down at him. At one time Burbage had tried to recruit me as a boy player, at the time when Simon himself was still playing women's parts, but I had firmly refused. Working as assistant to my physician father at St Bartholomew's had been enough for me, quite apart from my less well known work for Sir Francis Walsingham. The players knew something of my code-breaking now. Apart from Simon, they knew nothing of my other work. Simon himself had recently been raised to second romantic lead, after Christopher Haigh, though sometimes he must be content to hold a pike beside a king's throne or play the fool opposite Guy. In a company of players you must be prepared to take on any role.

'You know I could never appear on a stage, faced with all those eyes and gaping mouths,' I said, sweeping out my hand to indicate the tiered seats and the flat ground below us, where the groundlings would stand.

The lute gave out a soft note of sympathy as my elbow knocked it.

'That was what you said when you were a lad of sixteen.' Simon gave me a teasing smile. 'Surely you no longer fear them.'

I shook my head and laughed. 'I haven't changed.'

'Oh, but I think you have,' he said quietly, with a look that made my stomach clench. I looked away and shuffled the music, which I had propped up on a chair painted to look like a throne.

'Come, you are keeping us from our practice,' I said briskly. 'Are you not off home?'

'I'll wait for you,' he said, stretching out to lie on the stage with his hands behind his head.

Half an hour later, Guy carried the lutes back to store in the tiring house and Simon and I left the playhouse. We both had lodgings in the same building over the Bridge in Southwark, convenient for me, now that I was working at St Thomas's Hospital, south of the river, but not so convenient for Simon. He had moved there while he was on loan to Philip Henslowe's company at the Rose and kept the room on because it was far better than anything he could have rented for the same money near the Theatre.

'Before we go,' I said, 'I want to see if those beggar children are still here.'

'I heard you talking to Guy about them. You seem very interested in the little rascals.'

I shrugged.

'I think it a sad state of affairs that children so young should live and starve and probably die on the streets of London, when there is food enough and money enough in the city to keep them fed and clothed and safe.'

We walked round to the place where the children begged, but there was no sign of them, apart from the screwed up greasy paper which had contained the pie.

'Ah, well,' I said, 'I hope they do have a safe place to sleep tonight. It will be very cold, I think.'

We had both pulled our cloaks tight around our shoulders, and I was glad of my physician's gown over my doublet and breeches.

'I've been thinking a good deal about the street children,' I said as we reached the north end of the Bridge. 'Especially since I've been working at St Thomas's.'

'You have charge of the children's ward there, have you not?'

'Aye, and the lying-in ward endowed by Sir Richard Whittington for unmarried mothers. Many of them cannot keep their babes, so we take them to Christ's Hospital. I'm coming to know it very well.'

We stepped on to the Bridge. The crowds were thinning after the hurly-burly of the day, but many were hurrying in both directions, to cross the river before the gates were closed. Most were travelling south, in our direction, those who worked in the City but lived cheaper in Southwark. As we often did, we paused at the break in the houses about halfway across and leaned on the parapet, looking down river towards the bustle of ships at the Legal Quays, preparing to set sail on the turn of the tide. Beyond them the grim bulk of the Tower rose, and further still I could see the long ferry making its way down to Greenwich. The grey waters of the Thames, unsavoury by day, lay at this moment of slack water in soft ripples like a silk scarf, catching glints from the setting sun as if it were laced with thread of gold.

I turned and braced my back against the parapet, screwing up my eyes against the low glare of the sun, sinking behind Westminster.

'I must have walked past Christ's Hospital a thousand times when my father and I lived in Duck Lane,' I said, 'every time I went through Newgate. I never gave it a second glance. I knew Greyfriars had been turned into a home for abandoned children, but I had no idea that it was – well – so vast. There is the church, of course, which you can see from the street, but there are quadrangles like the inns of court, and dormitories, a refectory, all the usual kitchen offices – brewhouse, bakehouse, dairy. They have a school, and teach the children their letters. The little ones are called 'petties' and have their own teacher. For the older ones there is a grammar school, a music teacher . . . They even teach the girls to read and write.'

'I didn't know,' Simon said. 'But what of the babies you take there? They are too small even to be petties!'

'Oh, the babies are sent out to wet-nurses in the country. From the start, the governors thought it would be better for their health. When they are weaned and old enough, they come back to the Hospital. I am surprised the governors cared enough to make such wise provision.'

'I'd heard tell that it was a great gift to London from the boy king Edward, but it hasn't put a stop to the child beggars, like ours,' he said. 'Though was it not a few City benefactors who set it up? Not the king himself.'

'Aye, and put those collecting boxes in all the churches. It seems the numbers are supposed to be limited to five hundred, but they already have seven hundred living there.'

I hitched myself away from the parapet and began to walk on toward the Great Stone Gate. We would need to hurry or we wouldn't reach our lodgings.

'So there wouldn't be room for those children, would there? Even if you could persuade them to go.'

I gave a rueful grin. 'Nay, I think to Matthew and his friends it would seem no better than a prison. Hurry! They have already closed one side of the gate.'

Seeing the guards approaching the other gate, we broke into a run.

The house where we lodged stood on Bankside, facing the river, and not far from the whorehouses where the Winchester geese plied their trade. The first of their customers would have come over the Bridge with us, others would take a wherry across the river after the gates were closed. Further along there was a bear pit and the Rose playhouse. Southwark was an odd place, very different from the City itself, but if you could endure the stench of the tanneries and dye-works, it was a lively place. Londoners flocked here for entertainment of every kind.

'Burbage has been talking lately about moving us south of the river,' Simon said. 'He has had a few fallings-out with the owner of the land on which the Theatre is built. And he thinks more people are coming over here now, instead of going out to Bishopsgate.'

'That would mean less walking for you,' I said, pushing open the heavy front door.

He grinned. 'Aye. I'd save on shoe leather.'

It was dark inside the house, but our landlady, Goodwife Atkins, must have heard us, for she came bustling through from the kitchen at the back of the house carrying a candle lantern. I fished a candle stump out of my satchel and lit it from hers. Simon never remembered these small domestic details, but depended on me to light him up the dark stairs to his room, which was on the floor below mine.

'A man came asking for you, Master Hetherington,' the landlady said. 'Early afternoon. He left a message.' She fetched a folded paper out of her apron pocket and handed it to him. It was crumpled and grubby, but might have suffered from contact with Goodwife Atkins's cooking, which was of the greasy variety.

'I thank you.' Simon looked puzzled, and peered at the paper in the poor light, then motioned slightly toward the stairs with his head.

'Give you goodnight,' I said to the landlady and led the way upstairs.

The house was one of those which had been added to over the years simply by building first one extra storey and then another on top of the original house. Land was in short supply in London and now Southwark was suffering from the same problem. Simon's room was on the second floor, mine was on the third. There were even two rooms high up under the sloping roof space above mine, reached by a ladder from the landing outside my room. I had never been inside them, but Simon had. They were so low, he said, that he could not stand upright. One was occupied by a little wisp of a woman, old and frail, who earned a few pennies spinning white warp. A water carrier had the other. He was a big man, as he needed to be to carry the huge water casks on his back from house to house. He must crawl about the room on hands and knees, or that is what it sounded like, over my head.

'Come in while I light my candle,' Simon said when we reached his room.

As usual, his room was filled with untidy piles of clothes, dirty plates and tankards, rough pages of play scripts. I had long ago abandoned any attempt to reform him. My own nature, and the nature of my profession, have instilled in me a passion for order.

Simon lit a candle standing in a holder on his clothes coffer and peered at the paper, which was roughly sealed with a lump of unmarked wax.

8

'It looks like Tom Kyd's writing.' He prised the wax off with his thumbnail and ran his eye down the message.

'It's about Marlowe,' he said.

I frowned. I had no love for Marlowe, who took every chance he could to insult me.

'What about Marlowe? I thought he was back in Cambridge.'

Or on some errand for Sir Francis Walsingham, I thought, but did not say.

Simon looked shocked.

'He's in Newgate Prison. Arrested for a fight in which a man was killed. He is charged with murder.'

Chapter Two

Simon had gone very white and his hands shook. 'He will be hanged,' he whispered. Marlowe had sought Simon's friendship with an intensity I found disturbing, and I knew he resented the easy friendship I shared with Simon. I think somehow that made Simon feel responsible for him, which was an unenviable burden, for the man was violent, untrustworthy, even – so I had heard it hinted – a man who denied the existence of God.

I had no love for Marlowe, but even so I would not wish him hanged. That he had been involved in a brawl came as no surprise. He had a vile temper, was puffed up with pride and quarrelsomeness. And he had been in trouble before.

'Was it Marlowe himself who killed the man?' I asked.

Simon shook his head. 'It was some dispute in Hog Lane between Marlowe and an innkeeper from Bishopsgate called William Bradley, which grew into an armed fight. Another man struck the fatal blow, one Thomas Watson. It seems there was some previous trouble between Bradley and Watson, involving Edward Alleyn and his brother. But if Kit Marlowe is accounted an accessory to murder, then surely he will hang.'

'When did this happen?' I asked. 'Today?'

While Simon and his fellows were performing some light-hearted comedy? And I was supervising the delivery of a premature baby by one of the hospital midwives. It was a girl and despite her untimely birth she seemed healthy and like to live. One fragile soul born into the world. One soul rent from it, bloodily, at the point of a sword.

'Nay, not today.' Simon shook his head. 'Tom says the fight was a week or more since. We had not missed Marlowe. Sometimes he is about the playhouse every day, pressing Burbage to buy one of his plays. Sometimes he is off in Cambridge, though I think the term is not yet started.'

'And sometimes he is abroad,' I finished, 'working for Sir Francis, though I had not heard that he was on any mission at the moment. Matters are very quiet in Seething Lane at present, for Sir Francis has been ill.'

'If we had known about this, something might have been done. He's been at least a week in Newgate.'

'He will not suffer like the poor prisoners,' I said. 'He will have a gentleman's room, with a decent bed and a fire. He can buy food.'

Simon gave a rueful smile. 'You know Kit Marlowe! When does he have two sixpences to rub together? Or if he does, they're soon spent on wine. It seems he was thrust into the Limbo dungeon, manacled, until someone else paid the fee for him to be moved to one of the upper cells.'

'What does Tom Kyd say? Is he asking you to do something?'

He thrust the paper at me and I tilted it toward my candle to read it. Kyd was asking for help in raising money to have Marlowe released on bail until he stood trial.

'Would they let him go free until the trial?' I said doubtfully, thinking that I'd as soon trust an adder as Marlowe. 'On a murder charge?'

'Look what he says there.' Simon pointed. 'Kit and this other fellow went and handed themselves over to the Constable. They claim they were attacked first and struck out in self-defence.'

The note did indeed say that. It was undoubtedly the wisest action for them to have done, to surrender to the authorities.

'You cannot help with money, Simon. You haven't any.'

Like all the players, Simon lived very much hand to mouth. He had enough foresight to set aside the money to pay his rent, but like the others he veered constantly between times of plenty and times of dearth. With winter coming on, the playhouses would be closed. There would be no work and no pay for the players, unless they were hired for performances at one of the Inns of Court, or a gentleman's house, or at the royal Court itself. For the last few years Burbage had been speaking of buying an indoor playhouse for winter. It would hold only a small audience, but it would be more select and he could charge more. He had hoped to take over the boys' theatre at Blackfriars, but nothing had come of it, and the players still had nowhere to perform in winter.

'It is too late tonight for you do anything,' I said. 'Tomorrow, you should go to Burbage.'

He nodded. 'He might stand the bail money, though I know he thinks he has already put too much money in Marlowe's pocket.'

'Perhaps Sir Francis might do something,' I said hesitantly. I was reluctant to approach Walsingham with such a request, for he had been ill for weeks now. When he came into Phelippes's office at Seething Lane, where I had my own desk, he was gaunt as a famine victim, like the survivors of our Portuguese expedition. His skin had a greyish pallor and his eyes were deep sunk above jutting cheekbones, as some internal sickness sucked the life out of him. His wife Dame Ursula and his daughter Frances flitted about the house like ghosts, for they knew that he was dying. Even little Elizabeth, Frances's daughter, was subdued and had lost her merry laugh.

'If Marlowe had been caught up in some trouble while working for Sir Francis, then I am sure he would have paid the bail money,' I said, 'but this is some drunken street brawl amongst violent men. He may feel it is not his affair.'

'But you will ask?' Simon looked hopeful.

'I will ask, but I think you and Kyd should approach Burbage first.'

'Walsingham is much the wealthier man.'

'Do not be deceived,' I said. 'Ever since he paid for his son-in-law Sidney's lavish funeral, *and* paid off all his debts, I do not think Sir Francis is wealthy at all. He has also spent nearly every penny he owned to maintain his intelligencing service for the safety of England and the Queen. It is not the Queen who pays.'

'I did not know that.'

'Hmm,' I said. I was sure I had told Simon this before, but perhaps not. 'I am off to my bed. Will you be up in the morning before I leave for the hospital?'

Like all the players, Simon saw no need to leave his bed betimes, unlike those of us in regular employment.

'Knock me up as you go out, will you? Then I will find Kyd and we'll go together to see Burbage.'

'Very well. Give you good-night.'

I took my candle and headed up the last flight of stairs, realising that I was suddenly very tired. I closed the door to my little room and leaned back on it, letting my satchel slide to the floor. I braced myself as my dog Rikki leapt from my bed and flung himself against my chest as if I had been gone for weeks. While I worked in the hospital during the day I left him with the gatekeeper Tom Read and his old wolfhound, but I was training him to stay quiet in my room in the evening, for the night watchman at St Thomas's was a surly fellow, whose own dog was a vicious brute, taught to attack on command. I would never trust him with Rikki.

'Hush now,' I said, as Rikki tried to lick my face. 'I haven't been gone above two hours.'

My room was freezing. Frost flowers were already patterning the window glass and the hearth was, of course, cold. I could leave it unlit, but by the middle of the night I would probably be too cold to sleep, and that meant an exhausting day tomorrow, when I was due at Seething Lane after the hospital.

I hung my satchel, my cloak, and my gown on the pegs I had hammered into the wall and prised off my boots. In my stocking feet I went to the window and drew the curtains across it, two bits of heavy woollen stuff I had bought in the market. They were faded and ragged at the hem, but helped to keep out the cold and draughts from the window. Then I knelt in front of my small hearth and laid a fire of kindling. With my tinderbox I soon had it burning through and added pieces of sea coal until there was a good blaze going. Sea coal fills the London air with filthy smoke, but it cannot be denied that it gives a good heat. My room began to warm through and Rikki settled comfortably, with his stomach stretched out in front of the fire.

As I climbed the stairs I had thought of nothing but getting into my bed, but now that I had the fire going I did not want to waste it, so I poured some wine into a small pot and set it close to the fire, adding a cinnamon stick, a bay leaf, a curl of orange peel (carefully saved) and a few peppercorns. Recently I had purchased a small hanging cupboard, like the one where my father had kept his medicines. Mine I used for food. There was a colony of mice in the building, growing fat on the food scraps left lying about by Simon and some of the other tenants. I had no wish for them to move and take up residence with me.

The new season's apples were on sale at every street corner since the fruit harvest, and I had bought myself a supply. I munched one now as I sliced bread and cheese and stirred my wine as it warmed through. The room filled with the comforting scent of the spices and when I drew up a stool near the fire to eat my supper, I was warm enough to unbutton my doublet. I fished the cinnamon stick, peppercorns, orange peel, and bay leaf out of the wine, to be used again, poured it into a pottery beaker, and grated a little nutmeg over the top. Nutmeg is expensive, for it is believed to ward off the plague, but a single nutmeg will last a long time if you are sparing.

The smell of food roused Rikki, who placed his chin on my knees and fixed me with a pleading look.

'You can't be starving, lad.' I scratched him behind his ears. I knew that Tom Read filched a good bowl of scraps from the hospital kitchen every day for the two dogs, who probably lived as well as any gentlemen's dogs in London, but I could not resist that look. I spread a hunk of bread with a little dripping I had saved the last time I had cooked myself a chop, broke it into smaller pieces and put it into a chipped bowl I had salvaged from a rubbish heap. Rikki fell on it with the same enthusiasm as the beggar children.

During the weeks earlier in the year when I had lived at the Lopez house, I had eaten lavishly. After our voyage of starvation, I was ravenous, and Sara Lopez constantly pressed food on me. As a result, I had gained weight, and filled my doublet more than I could have wished. I feared I might not be able to continue passing for a boy. Since coming to live in Southwark, I had been careful to eat less. In the morning I took nothing but a cup of ale and a slice of bread. St Thomas's gave all the medical staff a good dinner, and I was happy to eat it, for it saved me money and meant I had one substantial meal a day. In the evening I often had no more than an apple or a piece of cheese, but tonight I had felt chilled and saddened. Perhaps by the sight of those ragged beggar children. Perhaps by the thought of Marlowe in Newgate Prison. Perhaps also by the thought of Walsingham, who had played such a large part in my life since I was sixteen, and who was slipping away from us.

When I had finished eating I tidied away all the food into the cupboard and made up the fire so that it would keep the room warm for a few hours. Then I locked and bolted my door before I undressed and donned my night shift. I did not expect to be disturbed, but I was always careful.

Before getting into bed I drew aside the window curtains. There was a faint glow from off to the right – probably a torch in a sconce outside one of the whorehouses. Otherwise it was very dark and very still. I could almost hear the crackle of frost in the air. I hoped those children would keep warm. When I knelt by my bed to pray, it was in a wordless jumble of thoughts, for these days my faith was confused. Phrases from the Jewish prayers of my childhood were interwoven with the Christian prayers I heard every Sunday in the parish church. I prayed for the children, for the souls of my parents and my little brother, for my lost sister. I prayed for Walsingham in his pain and sickness. I prayed for my friend Sara and her family. I prayed for Simon and the other players. I prayed – for the first time in my life – for that rogue Marlowe, whose way with words was little short of miraculous, even though the man was despicable. Last and least, I

14

prayed for myself, that I might continue to live my deceitful life undetected.

My knees were aching as I rose and climbed into bed. Until recently I had owned only two thin blankets, but a few days ago I had bought a secondhand feather bed. It was thin, but provided some welcome additional warmth. Rikki leapt on to the bed and curled up against my back. I blew out my candle and watched the pattern of the firelight on the ceiling before I dropped into a deep sleep.

The next morning Rikki and I clattered down the first flight of stairs at dawn. When I thumped on Simon's door, there was at first no response, but I kept up my banging until a sleepy voice groaned in response, then I was down the stairs and out of the front door.

I nearly went flat on my face, for the steps were icy and Rikki was tugging at his lead, eager to relieve himself against one of the scraggy trees which had found a foothold here and there along the river's edge. This morning they were transformed. Like one of the sugar confections spun for a nobleman's banquet, they sparkled in the first low rays of the sun coming up the river from Greenwich. Hoar frost had hung every twig with diamonds. Not all the leaves had yet fallen and every surviving leaf was rimmed with frost as if it had been dipped in sugar crystals. The road here was little better than an earth track, though where it tended to bog it was patched with rough cobbles. Along the centre it was worn down with the feet of men and horses, and carts had carved deep ruts, but, along the edges and in clumps on the roadway, grass grew, tired and withered at this late season of the year, but now – like the trees – transformed into sprouting shards fragile as glass, which crunched and shattered under my feet.

Rikki found this change in his familiar world exciting, and kept wanting to dash off and investigate the new smells, cleaner smells, I suppose, than the usual street smells of Southwark, which can be unsavoury. The brisk walk along the river to St Thomas's left me feeling invigorated, my cheeks glowing from the cold, and my lungs full of clean frosty air. This early in the morning the tanneries and dyeworks had not begun to pollute the air, and with house fires smoored down for the night the sea coal smoke had cleared away. It would not be too troublesome even later in the day, in this clear frosty weather. When fog gathered over the Thames it trapped the smoke in a smothering pall over the City and Westminster and Southwark, caused old men and small children to die because they could not draw breath. It was the curse of London.

When I had left Rikki with Tom in his snug lodge, I went first to the lying-in ward to check yesterday's premature birth. As always the ward was warm and clean. Mistress Maynard, governess of the nursing sisters, was strict with those under her command, though her iron discipline concealed a kind heart. The patients had already breakfasted on barley gruel with thick cream, wholesome bread baked in the hospital bakehouse, and our own small ale brewed in our own brewhouse. Those whose babies had already come into the world were feeding them, others were dozing or talking quietly. Mistress Maynard would allow no raised voices or foul language. It must have been quite a trying time for some of the Winchester geese.

Not that all the women were prostitutes. Some were foolish girls who had been promised marriage and then abandoned. Mellie White, whose baby had been born the previous day, was a fourteen-year-old servant girl raped by her master. She was small and scared.

'What will become of me and the babe, doctor?' she pleaded, raising blue eyes swimming with tears. 'I cannot go back there. I dare not. Though my term of service is not completed.'

'Of course you shall not go back there.' I sat down on the end of her bed and turned back a fold of the blanket in the wicker cradle which had fallen over the baby's face. She was a good colour and breathing naturally. Mellie was not sure of her due time, but the baby was certainly early. Even so, she seemed just as likely to live as a full term child.

I looked up at the girl, who was plucking at the edge of her blanket.

'Our deputy superintendent will speak to him, your late master. By the time he's finished with him, there will be no question of you working out your service. And no risk of his doing to another girl what he did to you. If you wished, you could take him to court.'

She looked frightened and shook her head.

'Oh, I could not!'

Master Ailmer, the deputy superintendent, was the one who ran the hospital, for the superintendent's role was purely honorary, and the governors keep but a distant eye on St Thomas's. He was not always an easy man, sometimes interfering, but admirable at his job. And he would put the fear of God into Mellie's master.

'But I must find work,' the girl said, her voice thin with anxiety.

'Have you no family who could take you in, at least until you are strong again?'

She shook her head mutely.

'Mellie? That's an unusual name.'

16

'I was baptised Emilia, but I had a little sister who could only say Mellie, so that's what I came to be called.'

'So you have a sister.'

She shook her head. 'All dead.'

Well, it was not such an unusual story. When disease swept London, whole families could be wiped out in days. It did not even need to be the plague. It could be the sweating sickness, which killed in hours, though it had not been known of late. Or a long drawn out weakening and death from the bloody flux.

'I will talk to the governess of the sisters,' I said. 'Sometimes there is work in the hospital. Sometimes she knows of a vacancy for a maid or an apprentice. I know you were a house maid. Do you have any particular skills?'

'I can cook,' she said. 'I often helped the cook at . . . at that last place.'

'Then perhaps there might be a position at a bakery or a pie shop, or in the kitchen of an inn or an ordinary.' I looked down again at the baby, who was stirring and pursing her lips as if she was hungry, but she was not awake yet.

'What are we to do with the babe?' I asked gently. 'Do you want to keep her?'

A look of distress came over Mellie's face and the tears welled up and ran down her cheeks.

'Before,' she said, clutching her hands together, 'before, I wanted nothing to do with it, after that filth . . . after what he did to me. But now she is here, and she is so small, and so pretty, and . . . she is part of *me* as well. I don't know what to do. Could I keep her? Do you think I should keep her?'

I feel my chest tighten in sympathy. I had never borne a child and if my life continued as it was, I never would, but I could feel that terrible force pulling Mellie toward her child. Yet she was hardly more than a child herself. She must make a new start, in a new place, and put the horror of her past behind her. How could she do that, with a child?

'You must think about it very carefully,' I said, 'and you need not decide yet. But I think it would be best for both you and the child if you do not keep her.'

The tears were falling faster now. 'Then she would go to Christ's Hospital?'

'Aye. And it is a fine place. A good place. She will be fed and sheltered and given a safe home. She will even go to school and later she will be found an apprenticeship.'

Her eyes widened. 'I never went to school. Nor I didn't have an apprenticeship, though my Pa, before he died, meant to 'prentice me.'

I was conscious I must not try to influence her too much. 'Think about it. Look, she's waking.'

I lifted the baby out of her crib and she opened wide unfocussed eyes at me. As I continued down the ward to visit my other patients, I was aware that Mellie was feeding her and crooning over her, the tears still falling.

The other mothers in the ward were all doing well, though two of them were very near their time and might be delivered today or tomorrow, so I left them to the care of the nursing sisters and went through the door at the far end which led into the children's ward.

While Whittington's lying-in ward was devoted to one purpose only, the children's ward was another matter. St Thomas's was both a hospital caring for the sick poor and also a hospice for the weak and enfeebled, the destitute poor. Although Bridewell took in what were known as sturdy beggars – healthy vagrants both men and women – and put them to useful work, St Thomas's here and St Bartholomew's north of the river served a double purpose. Many of our people were not sick, or at least not of a treatable illness. In the almshouse attached to the hospital we housed and fed the aged and infirm, the blind, the simple-minded, in short those citizens who could not care for themselves.

Sometimes we took in whole families. It was the task of the almoner to decide who should be admitted and who not, and if it seemed to him that a whole family was incapable of caring for itself, they all came under our wing. What this often meant was families with too many children to feed, or families where both parents were dead and the children had come into the care of a grandparent who could no longer provide for them. After the late wars against Spain, in which thousands of soldiers and sailors had died, their widows struggled to feed themselves and their orphaned children. So it was that I had divided the children's ward into two rooms with screens – one side for the sick children, the other for those who were merely destitute. In the past they had all been thrust in together, but I was sure the merely poor and hungry should be separated from those who were ill. We would find places for those children who were old enough to work, the younger ones would go to Christ's, the permanently enfeebled would move to the almshouse.

It had seemed a good plan at first, but you had as soon try to herd wild birds as children. The pauper children quickly grew strong on St Thomas's diet of plain but nourishing food, so they were soon running about, in and out of the whole ward. As the sick children began to recover, they were little better. Even in the women's ward I could hear a rumpus, which barely subsided when I entered the children's ward. Mistress Maynard generally deputed two of her younger and gentler sisters here, reserving the older and more experienced ones for the often unpleasant and disturbing duties of the men's wards, where surgeons had frequently to be called in to amputate limbs damaged in the cruelly hard labour of these Southwark men. Today two young girls were trying, and failing, to keep order amongst the children. They were much the same age as I, but my physician's gown and my title of doctor gave me an authority they did not possess.

'What is all this hullabaloo?' I demanded, attempting to sound as fierce as Mistress Maynard. It was difficult not to smile, for I had caught young Davy – one of the paupers – turning handstands down the centre of the ward. Someone (I hoped it was not the sisters) had pushed back the screens, so that the children in both halves of the room could watch.

'You will be waking the babies in the next ward with your noise,' I said, 'and then Mistress Maynard will be after you, and no dinner, I warrant.'

That sobered them. For those who had known the pain of an empty belly it was no idle threat.

'Back to your bed, Davy,' I said severely, and he complied somewhat sheepishly. Despite his antics, he had a rattle in his chest which gave me cause for concern.

The two sisters rushed to replace the screens and restore some order to the tumbled bedding. I had some sympathy for the children, especially for those well enough to be up and about, but I could not have my truly sick patients disturbed. Fortunately there was only one serious case at present, a girl, Ellyn, with suspected consumption, whose condition worried me. The others were recovering from childish ailments of one kind and another, except for a lad who had been knocked down by a carter. He was badly bruised and the knock on his head had left him unconscious for two days, but now he was mending fast.

I pulled up a stool to Ellyn's bed and checked her heartbeat, which was steady, then laid my ear on her chest to listen to her lungs.

'Deep breaths, Ellyn,' I said.

The rustling which I had heard when she was first admitted, coughing and spitting blood, had gone. The sound of her breathing was normal. I smiled at her.

'Good. You are much better. Do you feel better in yourself?'

19

She gave me a quick nod, but her face was pinched and pale below a thick mass of copper red hair. She reminded me in some ways of Mellie in the other ward. There was a kind of undercurrent of fear in her demeanour.

'Now, Ellyn,' I said, sitting back and clasping my hands between my knees. 'When you came in, you would tell us nothing, but you were spitting blood and that worried us. You are old enough to know the signs. What are you? Twelve?'

'About that, I suppose, sir.' It was no more than a whisper, and almost the only time I had heard her speak. Usually she kept her mouth tight closed.

'Well, you will know that is a sign of consumption, which is a very serious illness, but I am glad to say that you do *not* have consumption. So why were you spitting blood?'

She did not answer, but glanced around fearfully, as if she expected to be threatened.

'Open your mouth,' I said. 'Nay, wider than that.'

The child had certainly had a chest infection which had made her cough, but I had thought of another explanation for the blood.

Reluctantly, she did as she was told. I tilted her head toward the window in order to see better. My guess had been correct. I released her chin and laid my hand on hers.

'Someone has been drawing your teeth. Two of your new molars are gone.'

She began to weep silently and hung her head as if she were ashamed.

'Who did this to you, Ellyn? You are too young and those teeth too new for them to have been rotten.'

'My Ma said I had to,' she whispered.

'Did your Ma pull them?'

She shook her head. 'My Pa. He's a blacksmith. He *was* a blacksmith, but he lost his place.'

'So he used his blacksmith's pliers?'

She nodded. 'Ma held my head, so I couldn't pull away.'

Christ's bones, it was a miracle they had not broken her jaw.

'They're going to sell them, your parents, to the men who make false teeth?'

She nodded again. 'They took two of my brother's as well, but he didn't bleed as much. And I was coughing already. When I didn't stop bleeding, Ma left me here.'

I could feel anger rising up through me like a burning flood. 'Why did you not tell us? I could have given you a salve for your mouth.'

'Pa said, if I told anyone, he'd beat the hell out of me.'

The words, repeated in that soft young voice, made me shiver, despite the heat of my anger.

'Did he? Well, do not worry, Ellyn. I will not let him lay a finger on you.'

I was not sure how I would manage it, but I was determined. Before he was done, the brute would probably draw all her adult teeth. She had grown all but those at the very back and they were new, white and undamaged. He would be able to sell the set for a good price, if he found the right buyer, probably as much as he would earn in a year as a blacksmith. And there was a boy, too. At the moment I could do nothing about him, but I might be able to persuade the deputy superintendent not to return Ellyn to her family. Her own mother had gripped her head while the man drew the teeth! I shuddered. There would have been a lot of blood, for some bleed more than others when teeth are drawn.

I left Ellyn and checked the injured boy as well as the other sick children, then went through to the paupers' section. They all turned on me such expressions of angelic innocence that I wondered what further mischief they were planning when I left. Davy looked most innocent of all, which did not bode well. It did these children no good to be cooped up here, once they had been brought back from the brink of starvation. They needed something to occupy them, work or play.

There were some simple workshops at St Thomas's for those of the paupers who could manage a little light work, and their children would join them there, plaiting straw for the wide-brimmed hats country people wore all summer, and for baskets, or chewing scraps of leather to make embossed ornaments for the cornices of rich men's houses. Many of the blind did this. The cleaner women who were free from disease might help in the bakehouse or brewhouse, where children could fetch and carry.

St Thomas's had once been an abbey, around which a number of famous workshops had grown up, producing beautiful carving and cabinet work, stone carving for the embellishment and repair of churches and monastic buildings, and stained glass which was famed throughout England. There were even famous printing presses. The paupers were mostly unable to carry out the skilled work, but could do menial tasks. From time to time a carpenter or mason who had fallen on hard times might find work here, and children who had come in with their families tended to stay with their families, until they could be found work elsewhere.

There were, however, other children without families, and Davy was one of them. He had been found in a ditch near one of the tanneries out along the road into Kent and brought in to us a few weeks ago, looking like a plucked partridge, with no flesh on him to stop the sharp angles of his bones poking under his skin. He could tell us very little about himself. He thought he had been born in England, although he had recently come from Calais with a vagabond troupe of acrobats who had found him somewhere and trained him up in their skills. With them he had travelled in the Low Countries, before crossing to England. They had been intending to perform at Bartholomew Fair, but had been diverted by an offer to perform at a yeoman's wedding in a village near Canterbury. Having missed the Fair, they had wandered about Kent, performing at country markets for the ha'pennies thrown at them, until they had turned their steps toward London. Then one night a quarrel had broken out between two of the men about the division of the money. Knives were drawn.

Davy would say little more except that he had crawled away and hidden under a bush for the night. In the morning he found one of the men dead of stab wounds and everyone else gone.

'So I scarpered,' he said. 'Didn't want nobody fixing the killing on me, so I asked the way to London, where we was going anyway.'

He had no money and no food, and made it only as far as the ditch beside the tannery.

However, now he was almost restored to health, we needed to do something with him, once the trouble in his chest was cleared.

I sat down beside his bed. We had given him one of the hospital night shifts, but his own clothes were neatly folded on a stool. They were garishly coloured and threadbare. The hospital laundry had washed them, but they would not last much longer.

I put the case of Christ's Hospital to him. He was perhaps nine or ten years old, but with a knowing air that came from a rough and unforgiving life on the road. Was it too late for him to benefit from what Christ's Hospital had to offer?

He listened while I described how Christ's Hospital could give him food and clothes and a roof over his head until he was able to be apprenticed. From the expression of wary unbelief on his face, I saw that he thought I was describing the folk tale Land of Cockaigne.

'I an't taken in, Master,' he said when I had finished. 'An't no such places. You fixing on putting me in prison?'

'Of course not.' I found I was growing weary of this. I knew Christ's Hospital could give these abandoned children some hope in life, but Davy – like Matthew and the other beggar children – had been dealt such blows in their young lives that they had learned to trust no one. No wonder they did not believe me. Probably I would be able to place Mellie's baby there. Fresh into the world, she could grow up lapped in safety and love, but these children were as intractable as the hardened and cruel adults amongst whom they had lived.

'I could take you to see it,' I said finally to Davy, 'then you can decide. You would no longer need to work for every crust of bread you eat.'

He looked at me slantwise out of the corner of his eyes and I knew that he suspected I was planning some kind of trap. I could not spend any longer here with him now. Although I had overall supervision of these two wards, we all of us – physicians, surgeons, sisters – must be prepared to work anywhere in the hospital as need arose, and I had promised to help on the men's wards today, which were overcrowded.

I bade farewell to my young patients, who looked rather more pleased than sorry to see me go.

'Let them play a little,' I murmured to the more sensible looking of the young nursing sisters, 'but keep them away from the sick children. And use some of the clove salve on Ellyn's gums. She's had two teeth drawn by force.'

There was a standing agreement between Walsingham and the governors of St Thomas's that when I was needed for his work at Seething Lane I was to be released for however long the need might last. Often I was reluctant to go, for the work of the hospital was never-ending, new patients coming in every day – and sometimes at night as well. Moreover, I had been given much more responsibility at St Thomas's than ever I had had at St Bartholomew's, where I was always perceived as my father's assistant. Now I held the position of a full physician, although I was paid only the salary of an assistant, since I was neither a Fellow nor licensed by the Royal College of Physicians. With my new position and new responsibilities had come an even stronger conviction that this was the work I should be doing, not acting as code-breaker and intelligencer for Sir Francis.

However, today I was glad to walk out into the fresh air again, where it was still frosty and clear. There had been some emergency surgery in the men's wards, which I had followed up with physical care, but we had lost one patient, a stone mason who had been working on repairs to Greenwich palace when a crane had collapsed, dropping a block of stone on him. His chest was crushed so there was little we could do for him, apart from give him a strong dose of poppy syrup to ease the pain. He had barely been able to swallow it and had died in great agony. I was thankful that I spent more of my time seeing new life into the world than watching helplessly as a life was snatched from under my hands.

I fetched Rikki from Tom Read, and as we crossed the Bridge toward the City, my thoughts turned to the other case, Marlowe's case, and another man hastened out of this world untimely. Even if it were true that this unknown victim was the aggressor (and I was sure Marlowe would gladly lie to escape from a dangerous situation), was it really necessary to kill him? I wondered whether Simon and Tom Kyd had been able to persuade James Burbage to put up the bail money. I would say nothing to Walsingham until I had spoken to Simon.

As usual I went round to the stableyard at Walsingham's house, where the back stairs led up to the rooms used for the intelligence service. It also gave me the opportunity to visit my favourite horse in the stables, the piebald Hector, who hid his qualities of intelligence and speed under a somewhat ugly exterior. That is, many people thought him ugly, but I knew and loved every patch of grey and black, even the black patch around one eye that gave him something of the appearance of an equine pirate. Beneath his deceptive colouring were his powerful haunches, his beautiful lines, and his elegant head. Nothing could conceal the clever gleam of his bright eyes.

I had brought two of my new season's apples which he ate with relish, though he always politely accepted the withered offerings at the end of the apple season. Giving him a final pat I nodded to the stable lad Harry, then bounded up the stairs with Rikki at my heels, feeling suddenly invigorated after those awful scenes in the men's wards.

Phelippes looked up as I entered the office, peering at me for a moment with a distracted air as if he had no idea who I was. I knew that look. It meant he was absorbed in cracking a new code and was turning over combinations and permutations in his mind, quite oblivious to his surroundings.

'Ah, Kit,' he said, coming back from wherever he was inside his head.

'You needed me?' I reminded him.

'Nay, there is not a great deal to do at the moment, though I should be glad if you were to look over this with me afterwards.'

'Afterwards?'

'It is Sir Francis who wishes to see you.'

'He's here?' I perched on the edge of the table I used as a desk. I lowered my voice. 'How is he?'

Phelippes shook his head and a look of distress came into his eyes. 'Not good.'

It hung in the air between us, though neither of us voiced it. He is dying, and what will become of us, and all of this, when that happens?

'Do you know why he wishes to see me?'

'Something about the College of Physicians, I believe.'

I felt a sudden stirring of panic. Had the fellows of that distinguished institution decided that I was not fit to practice? I had no proper training in their eyes, not having attended either Oxford or Cambridge, not even a foreign university like Portugal's Coimbra, where my father and Dr Nuñez and Sara's husband Dr Lopez had studied. I could have told them that Coimbra was far in advance of the English universities in medicine, with its application of Arabic medicine, but of course I would not dare, even if I had the opportunity.

Instead I had learned my medicine with my father, both the theoretical knowledge with the use of his medical textbooks and his instruction – he had been a professor at Coimbra – and the practical experience, working as his hospital assistant from the age of fourteen. All of that probably counted for nothing in the eyes of the College and its fellows. They could, if they wished, have me dismissed from my post at St Thomas's. If I lost my position and my work for Sir Francis ended with his death, how should I live?

I looked at Phelippes in dismay. 'What does the College want with me?'

'Best go and see. Leave Rikki with me.'

Rikki, who was familiar with this room, had already made himself comfortable in front of the fire. I slipped down from my perch, brushed down my gown and straightened my cap. I hoped that it would only be Sir Francis waiting for me in his office.

In answer to my tentative tap, Walsingham called 'Enter', and I found he was not alone. Drawing up a second chair to the fire was Dr Hector Nuñez, who had clearly arrived just ahead of me.

'Come in, come in, Kit.' Sir Francis smiled at me. 'Hector, will you pour us all some wine?'

'Of course.'

Dr Nuñez patted my shoulder as he passed me on the way to the court cupboard where Sir Francis kept his glasses and wine. I realised it was the first time I had known Sir Francis to ask someone else to serve wine in his office. Perhaps he did not trust the steadiness of his hands. Was the wine intended to console me for bad news?

I took the glass proffered to me and looked from one to the other of them. Dr Nuñez acted as one of Walsingham's channels of foreign intelligence via his trading network, but we did not often see him here in Seething Lane. What could be afoot?

'Do not look so worried, Kit.' Walsingham took a sip of his wine. I noticed that his hand was trembling. 'Dr Nuñez and I have been discussing your future.'

My heart sank. Now that my father was gone, these two men had in some sense assumed responsibility for me.

Walsingham smiled. 'You need not look as if we are about to scold you, Kit. You have done so well in your work as a physician, despite my demands on your time, that we think you should take the next step.'

I looked at them in confusion, but before I could speak, Sir Francis raised his hand to stop me. 'We think you are ready to take the examination at the College to obtain a licence to practice as a full physician.'

Chapter Three

I looked at Sir Francis in astonishment. This was the last thing I had expected. I took a sip of my wine in order to give myself time to think. How could I be a licensed physician without a university degree? I turned a puzzled face to him.

'I am afraid I don't understand. What examination? I have no university degree in medicine.'

'Nay, you have not.' He smiled. 'But it is well recognised in both hospitals where you have worked that you are a skilled physician. You will remember that at one time the governors of St Bartholomew's offered to send you to Oxford, but you were unable to take up their offer.'

I nodded. I had pretended it was a family problem, but in truth I had known that I could not have shared my tutor's lodging in close company with other students without them discovering that I was a girl.

'It is still possible for a candidate to become a licensed physician by passing the College examination,' he said. 'Of course, such candidates are normally graduates in medicine from a university either here in England or abroad, but I understand from Dr Nuñez that you have read widely, not only in the standard texts studied here, but also in Arabic texts.'

Dr Nuñez shifted uncomfortably. 'Best not to mention that in the College. They are very conservative in their views. Arabic medicine is not regarded with favour there. Stick to Galen and his followers.'

'But,' I said, for they were getting ahead of me, 'what sort of examination?'

'It would be an oral examination,' Walsingham said, 'like the examinations at Oxford and Cambridge, so I suppose you will have little experience of that.'

Having been taught by my father from an early age, I was well accustomed to being tested regularly on my studies, but it is one thing

27

to be tested by a loving father, quite another to face an examination by a group of strangers who have no particular wish to see you succeed.

'Can you tell me anything more?' I asked nervously.

'Let Dr Nuñez explain,' he said, 'for he will know far more than I, having been a censor himself.'

'Censor?' I said.

'It is what the College calls the examiners,' Dr Nuñez said. 'The censors are Fellows of the College, elected on an annual basis. I am not one at present, but I can guide you through the entire process. The examination is conducted by the President and four censors, in Latin, which I know will not give you any trouble.'

I nodded. My father had taught me Latin from the age of four. For any scholar, not just physicians, it is an international language, allowing communication throughout the known world.

'The subjects of the examination?'

'It falls into three parts: first part, anatomy and physiology; second part, pathology and disease; third part, therapeutics. You will be given certain texts to study in detail, then recalled and tested on your knowledge of the contents. It is the third part where you will need to be careful – no whisper of anything so outlandish as Arabic medicine.'

'There is no practical examination?' I was confused. 'No testing of how a candidate examines, diagnoses, and treats patients?'

Dr Nuñez laughed. 'Nay, Kit, nothing so practical and mundane as that! This is a body of men who pride themselves on carrying forward the ancient body of medical knowledge. It is the *texts* which matter.'

I was beginning to feel a stirring of excitement. I could do this, I knew I could do this. I am blessed with a powerful memory by nature, and it had been strengthened by my father's training. Also, I had read all these texts, though I had also supplemented my reading with the despised books of Arabic medicine and with practical experience.

'I no longer own any medical texts,' I said mournfully. 'When my father's creditors seized our possessions, they took all our books and I have not been able to afford to purchase replacements.'

'I can lend you everything you need,' Dr Nuñez said. 'Come to see me tomorrow and we will find what you had best borrow. I can also help you practice for the examination by posing the kind of questions they will ask.'

'Also,' said Sir Francis, 'I will write a letter to the President supporting your candidacy, with evidence of your work in the hospitals and as a physician with the army on the Portuguese expedition. I expect the St Bartholomew's governors will be willing to support you as well.'

Despite myself, I could not stop tears filling my eyes. With a licence I would be recognised as a full physician, with no questions about my competence.

'You are both so kind.' I could hardly get the words out.

Dr Nuñez reached over and patted my hand.

'Since your father died, we know you have been without the support of a family. Sir Francis and I have both watched how hard and how well you have worked these last few years. We are both old men. We want to help you before it is too late.'

I looked down at my hands. Sir Francis was many years younger than Dr Nuñez, but it was he who would go first. I felt the soft plop of a tear on my wrist. I was glad it was growing dark in the room, that they might not see.

'And of course,' Dr Nuñez said cheerfully, 'I am being entirely selfish. Once you are licensed, I will be able to pass over to you most of my private patients, and live the life of a gentleman of leisure.'

'Oh please!' I said in panic. 'Not Lord Burghley!'

They both laughed.

So it was decided. Sir Francis would write to the College and encourage the governors of St Bartholomew's to do the same. I would go to Dr Nuñez's house in nearby Mark Lane the next day to collect the text books and thereafter he would test me once a week until I was summoned for the examination. I walked back along the corridor to Phelippes's office in a daze.

'Well?' he said, as I sank down on my chair. 'It was not a telling off, was it?'

He was trying to hide a smile.

'You knew! They want me to take the examination to be licensed to practice by the College of Physicians.'

'You will have no trouble with that. Think of some of the missions you have undertaken for Sir Francis.'

I laughed. 'Of course, you are right. This is not nearly so alarming. At least, I do not think it will be.' The thought of those five men, solemn in their robes, was nevertheless worrying, but I pushed away the thought.

Before I left, I looked at the new code Phelippes had been puzzling over. He had nearly finished it, but I saw a way round one of the difficulties. Donning my cloak and whistling to Rikki, I ran down the stairs and out into the darkening streets in a strange mood, part exhilaration, part apprehension.

Back at my lodgings I saw from the street that there was a light in Simon's room. I was not sure whether I should take that as a good sign or a bad one. If he and Kyd had secured Marlowe's release on bail, they would surely be celebrating at an inn. On the other hand, if he was still chasing Burbage or anyone else for the bail money, he would not be back here.

I thumped on his door and went in when he called, Rikki running ahead of me to lick Simon's hand where it dangled off the edge of his bed. He sat up, rubbing his eyes. He did not look worried, merely tired.

'Well?' I said, seizing a stool and sitting down.

'I fell asleep. Did not get much sleep last night, then you woke me before the birds were up.'

'You asked me.'

'I know. Then we had to play that fool comedy again this afternoon. I'm no comic actor, I do not understand how Guy can take pleasure in it. So I fell asleep when I got home.'

'You know that what I am asking about is Marlowe.'

He grinned. 'I thought you did not like him.'

'I do not. However, *I* do not wish *him* ill.' I left it to Simon to take my meaning.

'Burbage said he might put up the bail money, though he was reluctant and grumbled a great deal.'

'I am not surprised. So he's out of Newgate then, Marlowe?'

'Not yet. In the end, Kyd suggested going to the Alleyns, who arranged for the forty pounds bail to be paid. It has to go before a magistrate or a minor court or some such thing. Watson, who struck the blow that killed Bradley, remains in Newgate. Marlowe will be released in a few days, on the first of October.'

'Then he must be very grateful to you.'

'I hope so. I have not seen him. Kyd visited him in Newgate this afternoon to bring him the news, while we were playing the comedy.'

'When does he go on trial?'

'Not till December.'

'Then you have saved him many weeks in prison.'

'Aye'

I could not think why he looked downcast, but the solution with Simon was often to feed him.

'Come,' I said, 'let us take some supper at the Lion. I also have some news to tell you.'

We settled happily over our trenchers of the Lion's best offering, beef with onions – plenty of onions, the way I liked it. Unlike many inns, the Lion baked its own bread. Simon seized a whole basket from a passing pot boy and began to tear off lumps to dip in the gravy. I sipped my ale and watched him. My news could wait.

When Simon had devoured his beef and onions and was wiping up the last fragments with more of the bread, I was glad to see that he no longer looked so tired and gloomy.

'So,' I said, 'I can see that you have not eaten all day.'

He grinned at me, and drank half his tankard of ale in one long draught.

'We had no time for a meal before the performance, what with chasing up Burbage, then back to Bankside in search of Edward Alleyn or his brother John, then hurrying to Newgate. Turned out, we had to take the surety for the money all the way to the court at Westminster. When we arrived, there was such a crowd everywhere – petitioners, lawyers, court officials – I knew I could not wait, so I left Kyd to make the arrangements and caught a wherry back to Old Swan Stairs. Ran all the way to the Theatre and just reached it in time.'

'So how did you know that he is to be released on the first of October?'

'Kyd sent a lad with a note, saying what the conditions were and that he was on his way to tell Marlowe. When Marlowe is released, Kyd will take him to his own lodgings so he can keep an eye on him. They've shared before.'

I did not envy Kyd the task, but I kept my tongue behind my teeth.

'It all seems to have gone well,' I said, 'so why do you look as though you have lost sixpence and found a penny?'

He gave me a rueful grin and waved to the pot boy to bring more ale. 'Just tired and hungry, I suppose.'

'It is more than that.' I knew Simon as well as a brother. Something else was troubling him.

He shrugged, and waited until the pot boy had deposited two fresh tankards of ale and cleared away the debris from our meal.

'Burbage wants me to go on playing the comic roles, and I hate them! I was supposed to be following Christopher in the romantic leads, but he gets them all, and I am always a "friend", or a "confidential servant", or some such. And then there's Richard as well. His father is bound to favour him.'

This was a little unfair, though I did not say so. Richard Burbage, a few years older than we were, was growing into an exceptional actor. But his father showed no family favouritism. His concern always was for the best performance of the play, whatever it might be. In that he could be ruthless. Though I felt he had somewhat misjudged Simon, if he thought him suited to comic roles. Perhaps he was merely trying to develop his talents, all of them, but it might not be wise to point this out, with Simon in his present mood.

'I thought Richard inclined more toward tragic roles,' I said.

'He does, but there are not so many in our book of play scripts. What your London citizen wants is damnable fool comedy – some horseplay, some dirty jokes, a good belly-laugh, and he is happy.'

He kicked the leg of the table in frustration, narrowly missing my shin.

'Well, if Marlowe writes some more of his unpleasant pieces, then there should be plenty of gloomy roles for Richard.'

'Aye, but will Burbage buy them and stage them? He has to give the audiences what they want.'

He bowed his face over his ale. Then, because he was Simon who could not be gloomy for long, and because he really did care about me and my life, so different from his own, he said, 'What is this news you have to tell me?'

So I explained the proposal of Walsingham and Dr Nuñez that I should take the examination to become a licensed physician. At once his face lit up.

'But that is wonderful news, Kit! You will be able to have your own private patients amongst the rich. No more scraping to stretch every penny.'

'Dr Nuñez says he will pass some of his patients to me.'

He gave a low whistle and raised his tankard to toast me.

'Too soon to celebrate,' I said, 'I must pass the examination first, and these censors will not be eager to license a Stranger who does not even have a degree from a foreign university.'

'You must just believe in yourself. Remember what I have told you about playing a part, when you were on a mission for Walsingham? It is like appearing on stage. You must think yourself into the skin of the character.'

'I cannot see how that applies here.'

'But of course it does. You must see yourself as a successful candidate, a licensed physician, and you will pass the examination with ease.'

I laughed. 'Perhaps you are right. I hope it may be that easy! I must practice speaking Latin again. Can I practice with you?'

I was teasing him. He had attended St Paul's school and had a good grammar school education, but I do not suppose he had uttered a word of Latin or opened a single Latin author since the day he left school and joined Burbage's company.

'It's a bargain,' he said, 'as long as, in return, you agree to appear on stage in our next performance.'

'We'll shake on that,' I said.

We left the Lion in a much happier humour than we had arrived and walked the short distance to our lodgings, slithering on the icy roadway, which had grown worse since the morning. Rikki ran ahead, as eager as we to reach the warmth and comfort within doors.

As we climbed the stairs, I asked, 'Were the children there at the playhouse today?'

'The beggar rascals? Aye. I gave them a penny.'

'All five of them?'

'As far as I could see. You are taking a mighty interest in them.'

I paused on the landing outside his door.

'With all that is done in London, it is not enough,' I said. 'Why are there so many children wandering the streets and sleeping in doorways or under bushes in churchyards? Why do we turn away, wilfully blind to the cruelties inflicted on the helpless young?'

He looked at me soberly. 'You have had a bad case at the hospital?'

'Would that it were just one case! Only today . . . there is a little maidservant, barely fourteen, a child raped by her master, who gave birth to another unwanted child yesterday. A foundling boy trained to be wandering acrobat, then abandoned and nearly dying in a ditch. A girl – she cannot be more than eleven or twelve. Her parents – her *parents* – have been drawing her teeth to sell. We thought she was consumptive. All the blood, you see, as well as a chest infection. I cannot let her go back to those monsters.'

'Can you prevent it?'

'I am not sure. I shall speak to Superintendent Ailmer tomorrow.' A deep sigh rose up from my lungs unbidden. 'Those three – no, four, if you count the newborn babe – all in one day, as well as those starving beggars.'

I reached down and ran Rikki's silky ears through my fingers. Hearing something in my voice he had pressed himself comfortingly against my side.

'The baby, at least, you will be able to give a home in Christ's Hospital,' Simon said.

'I hope so. The girl must agree, and she is torn. I can understand why. All her family is dead. It would be someone for her to love.' I could hear the break in my own voice. 'But what sort of future would that mean for her? She must find work, and who would take her on, with a newborn baby?'

33

'You cannot solve all the world's problems, Kit, nor care for all the lost and abandoned children.'

I gave him a wan smile. 'Nay. Only the ones who come my way.'

I turned toward the last flight of stairs.

'Give you good night,' he said.

'And you. I will leave you to sleep in the morning.'

'I should hope so indeed.' He was grinning as he closed his door.

It would be some days yet before any decision would need to be made about the three children who caused me most concern at St Thomas's, but I feared that once Ellyn had recovered from her severe chest infection (and she was on the mend) her parents might come to claim her, not from affection, I was sure, but as a source of income from the sale of more of her teeth. I had no idea what kind of family they were, but if the father had once been a blacksmith they did not come from amongst the lowest scrapings of Southwark's alleys. As a craftsman in a respectable trade, he would at some time have had a position in the community.

It was common enough for the London beggars to be accompanied by maimed or disabled children, not always their own. If they did not have a crippled child to arouse sympathy in the breast of some rich lady marked for appeal, it was easy enough to break a child's limb or cause some disfigurement. Nothing too unpleasant, for a disfigurement too grotesque would be more likely to cause a mark to turn away in horror at the sight of some child blighted by God for the parent's sin.

I did not think this was the case with Ellyn's parents. They would not be beggars, not yet at any rate. They would consider that they were engaged in legitimate business, selling what was theirs, for under the law, the child is the property of its parents, just as the wife is the property of her husband. An apprentice, too, was the property of his master, though the guilds offered some protection to apprentices, since they were the source of future journeymen and master craftsman. If a master was found to have treated his apprentice badly, the apprentice was no longer bound and the master could be disciplined with greater or less severity, depending on the offence. However, as for parents who abused their children, I was not sure that the law offered much protection to the victims.

Next morning, I put the case to Superintendent Ailmer. Although he was merely the deputy superintendent, he liked the title of Superintendent and it was as well to yield to this small vanity in order to gain his support. Besides, he worked hard and conscientiously, while the gentleman superintendent merely drew the stipend and was never seen at St Thomas's.

'You are quite sure of the truth in this case, Dr Alvarez?' he said, steepling his fingers before his face and regarding me across the desk. I had not been long at St Thomas's, but I believed I had earned his respect.

'Quite sure,' I said. 'You may see for yourself that the teeth have been drawn. The gums are not yet healed. She was bleeding profusely when she was left here. Merely dumped on the doorstep like a foundling, as it were. No caring parent came with her. I think that tells us something.'

'Hmm.' He opened the admissions ledger which he had sent for from the almoner's office when I had put the case to him. 'Ellyn Smith. Not a very revealing name. I see there is no address given.'

'Her name is Ellyn. And it may well be Smith. The father is an out-of-work blacksmith. These crafts tend to run in families. They may be a long line of blacksmiths.'

I leaned over the desk and studied the register upside down. Ailmer pointed to the blank where the address should have been written.

'She may have been too ill to give it when she came in. Or she may have been too frightened. I wonder . . .' I looked up at him. 'If the parents thought we might realise what had been done to her, they may have threatened her, told her not to give the address. They certainly made her so terrified that she was afraid to say what had happened to her until I worked it out for myself.'

Ailmer closed the book and rested his palms on it.

'If we have no address for the child, we cannot return her to her home.'

'What I fear is that they may come for her, if they believe she has survived. She might not have done, it was a serious chest infection. With all the blood, I was afraid at first that it might be consumption.'

'I assume that what you are saying is that we should not return the child to her parents,' he said.

'In all conscience,' I said, 'I do not think we can.'

'I am not sure that the courts would quite see it that way. In any case, what is to become of her? She is old enough – eleven or twelve, you say? – old enough to go for a maidservant.'

'Aye, she is, but she will not be strong enough for such work for some time. It can be heavy work, and long hours.'

'What, then?'

'I wondered whether we could ask Christ's Hospital to take her in. She has, after all, been abandoned here by her parents, and we have no address. They are meant to take in abandoned children.'

He gave me a tight smile. 'I believe you are become a lawyer as well as a physician, Dr Alvarez, making a case out of cobwebs. At all events, is she not a little old?'

'We can but ask,' I said, seeing that he was coming round to my way of thinking. 'I have had some dealings with the staff at Christ's. They are kindly folk. I believe they will help if they can. Do I have your permission to raise the matter with them?'

'Very well, but do not make any final arrangement without coming to me again.'

'Of course. There is another child, the baby born early two days ago.'

'It has died?'

'Nay, not at all. I think she will live. The mother is hardly more than a child herself, a victim of rape.'

He passed a hand over his face. 'I remember that one. I have sent for the master. He will not get off lightly, if I can help it. She was an apprenticed servant, to all intents and purposes, although there was no formal agreement. She should therefore have been protected.'

'The girl, Mellie, is in two minds about giving up the baby, but I am hoping she will let the little girl go to Christ's. She cannot start her own life afresh while caring for a child at the same time.'

'And the baby will fare better. Otherwise they may both end up in the gutter, or in one of the whorehouses.'

I nodded. 'The baby is very small. They will both need to spend some time here until they are stronger. Then we shall see.'

'Well, that is a straightforward case, Dr Alvarez, which I can leave to you and Mistress Maynard. Is that all?'

'Aye, thank you, Superintendent.'

I rose, bowed and left his office, feeling I had achieved all I could hope for. It seemed that Ailmer was willing, like me, to bend the rules in the case of Ellyn. All that I must do now was to persuade Christ's Hospital that she was not too old to be taken into their care. But Davy – what could be done for the little acrobat Davy?

On my way to the playhouse that afternoon, I turned aside to Dr Nuñez's home in Mark Lane. I felt some guilt as I knocked on the door. When I was younger, I used to come here with my father to attend Jewish services in the makeshift synagogue provided by the Nuñez's great hall. I had not attended since my father's death. I did not even know whether the services were still held. Dr Nuñez had never made any reference to them. Perhaps he understood that for us, the younger members of the immigrant Marrano community, already baptised Christians, the old faith was slipping away. Once or twice Sara's daughter Anne and I had discussed it. Living in Christian England, obliged by law to attend our parish churches every Sunday, finding our friends amongst the English, meant that our ties with the old country and the old faith were loosening, for Anne even more than for me. Her mother had been born in England, and so had she. For myself, I had no desire to return to Portugal. As time passed I had begun to think of myself more and more as English, not Portuguese, especially now that my father was gone.

Beatriz Nuñez followed the maid who opened the door to me and gave me a quick hug. Her husband had become almost a second father to me and although I saw Beatriz less often, she was always kind to me.

'Come in, Kit. Hector has been looking out the books for you and he has them laid out in his study.' She beamed at me. 'So we are to have another Fellow of the College, are we?'

I laughed. 'Nothing so grand, I fear, Mistress Nuñez. I am to try for a licence. To become a Fellow is far above my aspirations.'

'Well, well, we shall see. In time, who knows? This way.'

I knew the way to Dr Nuñez's study, for I had been here on Walsingham's business before, but I let her escort me. I liked the Nuñez house. They were surely as wealthy as Ruy Lopez, wealthier probably, for Dr Nuñez had his own fleet of ships trading in spices, but this home had none of the florid ostentation that Ruy so loved. It was spacious and extremely comfortable, with cushioned chairs and thick but modest tapestries on the walls. There were rugs on the floor, probably obtained as part of Dr Nuñez's trading, but there were no displays of silver and Venetian glass and jewels, no useless ornamental objects such as Ruy liked to flourish before his guests. It was truly a home, where you were not afraid that you might break some priceless object with a careless elbow.

'Ah, there you are, Kit,' Dr Nuñez said. 'I have been busy, you see!' He gestured at several piles of books laid out on his desk, then laid his hand on one.

'These, I think, will be the most useful.'

He passed them to me.

'The standard edition of Galen in four volumes. The College still places him above all others. Modern authors who disagree with Galen's teachings are regarded as little better than religious heretics. Here is a recent reprint of Celsus, Galen with annotations, if you like. It was first printed about a hundred years ago, but is still regarded as a useful commentary on Galen.'

He picked up a slim volume with celestial symbols depicted on the cover. '*Fundamentals of astrology*. You will not be expected to know this in detail, but best to be able to show that you have read it.'

'Paracelsus?' I asked hopefully. Paracelsus believed in experience and experiment, rather than the slavish adherence to the theories of second-century Galen.

He shook his head. 'Not Paracelsus. Too controversial.'

I looked wistfully at a large volume standing separately in the centre of the table and ran a loving finger along its spine.

'Not Vesalius?'

'Definitely not Vesalius! What, the anatomy of human corpses! Be content with Galen.'

'Well,' I said, with a touch of stubbornness, 'you know best. I will parrot the ancients and do my best to sound convinced, but afterwards, however the examination goes, I may return to Paracelsus and Vesalius and the Arab texts?'

'Of course. Simply avoid making a parade of it. The wise man always practices discretion.'

He loaned me an extra satchel to carry the heavy tomes, so I went on my way burdened like a donkey with two saddlebags. We agreed that I should return in a week to be tested on the first volume of Galen.

I continued on my way to the playhouse, but made some purchases in Wormwood Street – more spiced buns, which were filling as well as tasty, a dozen apples, and another pie, rabbit this time, for it was larger than the mutton pie and the same price. The beggar children were in their usual place. I handed out the food first, then gave Matthew a groat again.

'I'll ask one of the lads to fetch you some ale,' I said. 'I could not carry any more today.'

'What's all that, then?' Matthew eyed my two satchels, clearly weighing up whether they were worth stealing, while he munched his way through his slab of pie.

'This one,' I said, patting my own satchel, 'is for my salves and other medicines. I am a physician, you see, and always carry a few things with me, in case they are needed.'

'What about the other one? A'nt seen you with that before.'

'It belongs to a friend and is full of books. Medical books, written in Latin.'

'Oh, books!' He spat contemptuously. 'Not worth nothing.'

In fact they were worth a good deal, but I was not going to tell Matthew that.

'If you are a doctor, why are you always going to the playhouse?' he said. 'Play's over for today.'

'I know that. I am here to play music with one of my friends who is one of the players' company.'

'Can you really play music?' It was the girl Katerina. She had never addressed me voluntarily before.

'We are playing music for two lutes,' I said. 'I can play the lute and the virginals and several different sizes of recorder.'

None of which, sadly, I still owned.

'Katerina used to play a pipe,' Jonno volunteered, 'but it was pinched.'

'Do you like music, Katerina?'

She shrugged. 'Well enough.'

'People used to give us pennies when she played,' Jonno said. 'More'n we get here.'

'Perhaps you can get another pipe,' I said, but the girl just gave me a scornful look, as if I were soft in the head.

Once inside the playhouse I found one of the lads of all work, who ran errands and sold playbills and fetched and carried. Some hoped to be taken on as boy players, some merely glad to earn what they could. I gave him enough to buy a flagon of small ale for the children.

'When you have brought it back, you shall have a penny for yourself,' I said and he ran off.

Guy and I practised for about an hour, and I told him that I was to take the examination for the College.

'You will soon be too grand to speak to us, poor players that we are,' he said, putting on his sorrowful clown's look, which reminded me uncomfortably of the Commedia dell'Arte puppets I had encountered earlier in the year.

'Don't talk nonsense,' I said, rather crossly. 'You are all my friends. It is nothing very grand, but it would mean I could take private patients of my own and not depend on St Thomas's for every penny.'

'Have you told them?' he asked. 'For surely, once you are licensed, they will be obliged to pay you a full salary.'

'I suppose they will.'

I had not thought of that. It might be wise to say nothing at the hospital. It might not please Superintendent Ailmer if he found he must pay me a full physician's pay.

'Is Simon still here?' I asked, as I fitted my borrowed lute into its case and took up my heavy burden again.

'Nay, his part was only in the first two acts today. He has gone off to Newgate to see that fellow Marlowe.'

Guy, like me, did not care for Marlowe, who had no time for Guy's musical and comic talents. Their dislike was mutual. When in company they eyed each other like hostile dogs.

I sat down on my stool again and let my satchels slide to the ground. Rikki who had risen eagerly to head home, slumped down and laid his chin on his paws with a sigh.

'Guy, what do you think of Simon as a comic actor?'

He shrugged. 'His heart is not in it, but he does his best. Why?'

'He thinks Burbage is passing him over for the young romantic leads, which is what he wants to play.'

'It seems only yesterday he was still playing the women's parts. He cannot expect to claim the best roles all at once. Christopher Haigh is good, you know.'

'And Simon isn't?'

'Oh, the boy has talent, but he's still young.'

'Nearly twenty. The same as me.'

Guy laughed. 'Indeed, a great age! Burbage is giving him the chance to try everything. That's what a player should do, if he wants to be sure of always having work. Now me, with my monkey's face, I've never been able to play the young heroes, so I've needed to work hard at what I can do. Simon will do well, he must just be patient.'

I gave a dubious grin. 'Patience is not his best quality. And he is not happy at present.'

'This new fellow from Warwickshire – you've met him – Will. He's been writing light romances with more than one young man in them. He likes to play games with pairs of lovers and mistaken identities and all those devices. We played one of his earlier this year, but that was when Simon was away in the Low Countries. I think Burbage is planning to stage it again and Simon will have a better part. Not so roistering as our audiences mostly like, but it is a good piece, some clever twists and turns.'

'That's good to hear,' I said, picking up my satchels again. Rikki jumped to his feet. 'I'll give you good day then, Guy. I may not be able to come as often to play with you now I must study for this examination, but I will come when I can.'

Rikki and I made our way out into the street. The children were gone.

'I don't like the look of that sky,' I said to Rikki. I had been half aware while we played that it was growing darker, but I now saw that deep purple clouds were rolling in from the west and a sharp wind was blowing. They looked like snow clouds, though it was surely too early in the year for snow. A heavy thunderstorm, then. I quickened my pace. I did not want to risk Dr Nuñez's books in the rain, even inside a satchel.

Too many things seemed to be crowding into my life. Simon to reassure with Guy's words about Will's play. Marlowe to avoid. The examination to be studied for. And above all, the children whom no one seemed to care for. Somehow soon, perhaps tomorrow, I must find time to visit Christ's Hospital and raise the matter of finding a place of sanctuary for Ellyn.

Chapter Four

On my way to Christ's Hospital the following afternoon, I turned aside, south of St Paul's, into Knightrider Street and paused across the road from the rather forbidding building which I knew was the home of the Royal College of Physicians. Although distinguished Fellows like Dr Nuñez spoke of it familiarly as 'the College', it had been granted a Royal Charter some seventy years earlier by old King Harry, and so was the Royal College. Though I suppose he must have been young King Harry as long ago as that. Living and working amongst physicians ever since my father and I had come to England, it was inevitable that I heard of the disputes and struggles for precedence amongst all the practitioners of medicine in London.

The physicians were reckoned (and reckoned themselves) the most distinguished. Far superior to surgeons, who were sneered at as mere 'sawbones'. However, the surgeons covered a wide spectrum of ability, the most capable were respected even by physicians. The bottom of the heap were the apothecaries. Some were charlatans. Some – a few – were truly skilled, with a wide range of knowledge of herbal cures. The poorer folk of London would always visit an apothecary for a case of minor illness, not serious enough to take them to hospital. Even many of the middling sort would find it difficult to afford the services of a personal physician. Such as I could become, if I were licensed.

Although I felt honoured by the suggestion that I should take the College examination, I was not sure that I wanted to be a private physician. I loved my hospital work and my father had taught me from an early age that it was the duty of a physician to devote his life to the service of the sick, to preserve life and allay suffering. I knew I did not want to follow in the footsteps of Ruy Lopez, husband of my friend Sara. He had come to London many years ago with a degree in medicine from Coimbra and had been glad to be employed as a physician to the poor at St Bartholomew's – the position my father had later occupied. But that was not good enough for him. He had gained a license from the College, then been elected a Fellow, had abandoned his hospital work for private practice, leaving behind his humble St Bartholomew's house for the grand house in Wood Street. Then, the crowning glory, he was appointed principal physician to Her Majesty the Queen herself. No physician could rise higher, although recent events had shown that his ambitions did not stop there. He was greedy for money. And, had the recent ill-judged expedition succeeded, he might have won great estates and public office back in a restored Portugal, free of Spain.

Nay, I had no wish to emulate Ruy's rise through the ranks of the medical profession. If I were to pass the examination, why then, I would be grateful, and I would be glad to relieve Dr Nuñez of some of his work, for he had begun to display the fatigues of age, but I would never abandon my hospital work, whether it was amongst the children and whores of Southwark, or the injured and sick soldiers and sailors I had cared for in the past. That was where my heart lay.

As I turned away and headed north again toward Newgate and Christ's Hospital, I reflected that my life might change a great deal over the next few months, not only my work as a physician but my work in Walsingham's intelligence service. It was clear that Phelippes was worried about the future, as he was right to be, for he had no other profession than his position as Walsingham's senior assistant. And what of Arthur Gregory, with all his exceptional skill in forging seals for intercepted enemy despatches? What did the future hold for him? He had a wife and a very new baby. He must be as concerned about what would become of them all as Phelippes was.

I had noticed a change in the whole atmosphere at Seething Lane. In the past, when one of Sir Francis's 'projections' was coming to a crisis, or when there was yet another assassination plot afoot against the Queen, there was an air of tension about the place, but it was a kind of controlled excitement. Our skills were pitted against the enemy's, but we were confident that we would triumph. So far, we had done so. Now there was a different kind of tension. Sir Francis drove himself as hard as ever, but sometimes even his great courage could not overcome the weakness of his failing body and he would be forced to retire to bed, clearly in almost unbearable pain. If she could, Dame Ursula would carry him off to their country house at Barn Elms. He would continue to run affairs from his bed, but his grip on the reins was slackening. Phelippes had mentioned that a few of our less reliable agents were drifting away, seeking work elsewhere. The danger was that they might even turn traitor, for some were of doubtful loyalty to England and the Queen. If they did, they could carry with them much intelligence that would be useful to the enemy.

'What of Robert Poley?' I had asked Phelippes just a few days ago. Although Poley was a Walsingham agent, during the summer he had been suspected of being part of conspiracy to blow up Drake's house in the middle of London and cause panic on the streets. The other conspirators had been caught, but Poley had slipped through the net, not difficult for a man who knew every trick of the intelligence service.

'He has been seen in France,' Phelippes said, 'some weeks ago, but nothing since. He is being watched for at all the main ports, but he is slippery as an eel and can easily move back and forth across the Channel. We cannot be certain that he was truly involved in that plot, or was infiltrating it as he has done before.'

'But without your knowledge,' I said, unwilling to give Poley the benefit of the doubt.

Phelippes nodded his agreement.

Apart from this almost imperceptible decline in the intelligence service, there was a new element which made me uneasy. The Earl of Essex was a constant visitor to the Walsingham family in the Seething Lane house. There was a whisper going around amongst the stable lads (who knew everything before anyone else) that the Earl was courting Sir Francis's daughter. It was three years now since Frances Walsingham's husband, Sir Philip Sidney, had died of his wounds while on campaign in the Low Countries, supporting the free Hollanders in their fight against the Spanish forces of King Philip. It could well be that Sir Francis might want to see his only surviving child safely married, with a secure future, before he died, but I shuddered at the thought that the poor girl, who was only three years older than I, might be married to that arrogant, selfish, stupid man. I had seen enough of Essex on the Portuguese campaign to make a very fair assessment of his character. He was also notorious for his womanising. It might seem a great match for the daughter of a simple knight to be married to one of the greatest noblemen in England, and the spoiled favourite of the Queen, but for myself, I pitied her.

It was bad enough that Essex should be constantly in the family's quarters, but lately he had taken to poking about in the offices of the intelligence service, constantly asking questions and probing his long nose into affairs which were no concern of his. One day I had arrived at our office when Phelippes was not there, nor was Arthur in his adjacent cubbyhole. I had found the Earl going through the secret papers on Phelippes's desk. I knew enough of Phelippes's habits to be sure that any important decoded despatches would be locked away before he left the room, so the papers were either of little importance or else were still in code. Nevertheless, the Earl blustered and shouted some abusive remark at me which I ignored, taking my place quietly at my desk until he left. When I told Phelippes about it, he was worried.

'We cannot complain to Sir Francis, Kit,' he said. 'My Lord is a guest in the house.'

'In the house, perhaps,' I said, 'but not in these offices. He has no business here.'

Phelippes simply shook his head in resignation, but I had observed Essex closely over many weeks during the Portuguese expedition, and I had seen how his posturing and ill-conceived bravado had caused the deaths of many men. I did not trust him.

I pushed these uncomfortable thoughts away from me as I approached the impressive gatehouse of Christ's Hospital. It seems that after the taking down of the monasteries, Greyfriars had been in a ruinous state, with lead and tiles stolen from the roof, pigeons nesting in the church and rats infesting the monks' dormitory. A few whores and vagabonds had taken to sheltering there at night, but they were briskly evicted when it was decided to convert the old monastery into an orphanage for abandoned children. It was remarkable that it had not already been demolished, like St Bartholomew's, just the other side of the city wall, which had nearly been pulled down almost immediately, before some good citizens had stepped in to save the hospital and part of the church of St-Bartholomew-the-Great. Greyfriars, on the other hand, had been cleaned, repaired, reequipped, and made ready for its new inhabitants in a remarkably quick time and it now ran with great efficiency. A gateway had even been knocked through the adjacent part of the city wall so that sick children could more easily be carried to St Bartholomew's. I had treated some of these children while I served at Barts, though I had only recently visited Christ's Hospital itself.

Uncertain who was the best person to approach about the possible admission of the child Ellyn Smith, I decided I would seek out the matron, Mistress Wedderbury, as she was the one with whom I had had most dealings, in bringing to her the unwanted babies from St Thomas's. Like the two dozen or so sisters who cared for the children, she lived in the hospital, with comfortable quarters of her own.

'You see, the child is perhaps a little older than you would normally admit,' I explained, sitting in Mistress Wedderbury's small parlour, where she received visitors and sometimes children in need of scolding or comfort.

'About eleven or twelve, you say.' She cocked her head to one side. Like Mistress Maynard at St Thomas's, she was built on ample lines. And like Mistress Maynard she was strict in discipline toward the sisters she directed, but many a child must have found comfort in that wide lap. She wore an old-fashioned gable hood, such as her mother or grandmother might have worn, which – instead of seeming ridiculous – somehow gave her an air of dependability and wisdom.

'Aye,' I said, 'but small and undernourished for her age. She is still suffering from a chest infection and the brutal removal of two of her back teeth has left her mouth very painful. We can give her little but gruel and soup to eat for the moment, but we would not bring her to you until she is quite strong again.'

'Do you truly believe she has been abandoned by her parents, Dr Alvarez?'

I shrugged. 'I have no way of knowing. But I fear for the child, should she return to them. If they continue to wrench out her teeth, I fear she could die of the shock. She is such a slight little thing.'

I gave her a grim smile. 'I am afraid this case has made me very angry.'

She nodded with understanding.

'We see some terrible cases here, you know. Especially the children who have been forced to beg for adults, usually not their parents. They are often cruelly misused.'

I nodded, wondering whether I should mention Matthew's little group of beggarly waifs, but I decided that it was better to concentrate on the case in hand.

'And are you sure that the child wishes to leave her family?' she said. 'She is old enough to have an opinion of her own.'

'I have not discussed it with her yet, for I did not want to raise her hopes if it was quite beyond any possibility for her to come here. It is clear she is terrified of her father, and her mother can be little better, for she forced Ellyn to submit and held her head while the teeth were pulled.'

'I think there will be no problem admitting her, for we do sometimes take in children of that age. But not if she wishes to return to her family. It may seem unlikely to you and me, Dr Alvarez, but the ties of blood can be very strong, even where there is cruelty and abuse.'

I felt a great rush of relief. 'I will discuss it with her, Mistress Wedderbury, as soon as she is a little stronger,' I said. 'Now there is the case of this other child.'

'The baby born before its time?'

'Aye. The mother, as I have said, is but a child herself, and cannot decide whether to give her up. She clings to the child. I know in her heart she wants to keep her, even though her head tells her that the baby would be better off here.'

'Aye, we both know that it would.'

'I am sure it is not something you would normally countenance.' I hesitated.

'What would that be?'

'I think if the mother could come here, see Christ's Hospital, she might be readier to give up the child. At the moment, it is no more than a name to her, however much I may sing your praises. I do believe she has never been outside Southwark, never even crossed the Bridge, strange as that may seem. All of her family died of the plague when she was seven years old and the parish placed her as a maidservant with the master who has now raped her and got her with child. To such a girl, never allowed outside the house except to fetch and carry in the neighbouring streets, Christ's Hospital in the City of London must be as remote as the Kingdom of Cathay!'

She allowed herself a small smile. 'It is not quite without precedent, for a parent to see us before parting with a child. It would usually occur where a family with many children has fallen on hard times and can no longer support them all – the father injured and unable to work, or a widower left with a motherless brood. We are not altogether without compassion, you know, for such families.'

'I do know,' I said. 'So I may bring her to see you?'

'Indeed, when both she and the new baby are strong enough. Do you know what will become of this girl, if she gives up the child?'

I shook my head. 'She has been a general maidservant for seven years and she tells me she can cook. If she is not burdened with a child, it should not be too difficult to find her a position.'

Mistress Wedderbury offered me a glass of wine to conclude our business and we arranged that I would return with the children when they were recovered sufficiently to leave St Thomas's.

As I crossed the courtyard to the gatehouse, a procession of the older children in their long blue tunics and flat caps crossed in front of me, coming from the grammar school after their lessons and heading toward the refectory. There were even a few girls amongst them, walking together at the front, followed at a slight distance by a much large group of boys. The children bowed and curtseyed, and I bowed in return, with a deeper bow to the grammar school master who brought up the rear. These were the fortunate poor of London. I had heard that even on occasion one of the boys proved clever enough to be sent to

Oxford and enter the church. A true wonder, compared to Matthew and his group of strays, living on the edge of danger and starvation.

As I left Christ's Hospital, I glanced across at Newgate Prison. Somewhere in there was Marlowe, but he was to be released the next day. I hoped he would not haunt the playhouse, as he had done before, for he seemed to take a perverse pleasure in taunting me, calling me 'Jew boy' and detailing the unpleasant things he would like to do to all Jews. When I had first encountered him, at one of Raleigh's gatherings in Durham House, I thought that he was driven to bait me merely by his hatred of Jews, but lately I had begun to realise that it was more complex than that. He must have noticed my easy friendship with Simon, which stretched back to the time we had met at the age of sixteen, and it was clear that he was jealous of it. Whenever he was about, he would monopolise Simon, dragging him off to join in his own wild pursuits, like this latest one which had led to a man's death. He also put it into Simon's head that he should dress like a gentleman. Marlowe himself was a dandy, though where he found the chinks to buy an entire wardrobe of velvet and satin doublets I did not dare to think. Simon could certainly not afford such clothes, but Marlowe was continually egging him on to live well beyond his means.

By the time I reached St Thomas's, the daylight was fading.

'Nights drawing in,' Tom Read said, buckling Rikki's lead to his collar. 'Don't seem no time since the summer and already you can feel winter round the corner.'

'October tomorrow,' I said. 'I hope it may not be a bad winter, though weatherwise folk are predicting one.'

'Aye. I'm thankful they let me have a coal fire in here.'

On the ground floor of the gatehouse, Tom had his snug daytime quarters with its own fireplace, where he could prepare food if he needed to, though mostly he was fed from the hospital kitchens.

'The fire here warms my chamber above, see,' he said. 'No fireplace there, but the chimney runs up the wall and I push my bed up against it. And the night watchman generally keeps the fire up, when he sits here between his rounds.'

'Thank you for keeping Rikki,' I said. 'I didn't want to take him to Christ's Hospital with me.'

'He's no trouble.' Tom rubbed the top of Rikki's shaggy head. I saw that I would need to clip some of his fur soon, for it was tumbling over his eyes.

'Adam was asking for you,' Tom said. 'Pleased with himself. They've raised his wages at the glass workshop. Says he's going to get some training in working the glass, 'stead of just doing the rough labour.'

'That is good news,' I said. 'I am sorry I missed him.'

I nodded farewell to Tom and set off to my lodgings. Adam was one of what Simon called my waifs and strays, but as a large former soldier and blacksmith he bore little resemblance to the children under my care. I was glad to hear that he was settling in at the glassworks attached to St Thomas's. They produced the finest church glass in England, marvellous in its colours and fine detail.

Rikki pulled me along the road, eager to get home, but I was in no great hurry. Several hours ploughing through Galen lay ahead of me, a task I approached with little enthusiasm.

The next few weeks passed uneventfully. The children under my care made good progress, except for Davy, whose lungs were showing signs of severe infection, while in the evenings I continued my studies of the old-fashioned medical texts, committing their diagnoses and treatments to memory, while inwardly rebelling. In studying the inaccurate anatomical drawings I forced myself to draw a curtain over the well-remembered images planted in my brain from pouring over the precise diagrams in my father's copy of Vesalius. I was beginning to realise that this examination would prove more difficult than I thought. Not because I could not recite the appropriate passages from Galen and Celsus, but because I would have to restrain myself from crying out my objections to their mistakes.

My father had not even believed in much bleeding of a patient, or the use of clysters, though both were not only common practice but fashionable. Dr Nuñez had once told me ruefully that many of his rich patients did not believe that they had received proper treatment unless they were bled, even where he did not think it appropriate. My father, working almost entirely at St Bartholomew's, had rarely had this problem, but I saw that it might be one I would encounter if I took on private patients. Purging, too, was considered by many to be beneficial, a thorough cleansing of the inner man, but my father had taught me to use it with restraint, only in cases of food poisoning, or other forms of poison. For me, purging would always be associated with the first time I had encountered Poley, then a prisoner in the Marshalsea. I was obliged to purge him of bad oysters when my father had been absent, assisting Dr Nuñez at Lord Burghley's house.

Once a week now I presented myself in Mark Lane, to be tested by Dr Nuñez on my knowledge of the prescribed texts, our conversations being conducted entirely in Latin. I found my fluency in the language, which I had not used much of late, came back to me quite quickly. Dr Nuñez, however, made no concessions to our friendship, but barked out the questions, criticised, pulled a long face when I did not answer quite as he wished, shook his head, glowered. All in all, he made me feel that the examination itself could not be much worse than this.

Afterwards, he would remove his Fellow's gown and cap and his wife would bring us spiced wine and cake. I sometimes found my hands shaking so that the cup clattered against my teeth following a particularly trying ordeal.

Toward the middle of November, after one of these sessions, I said, 'I am beginning to regret ever undertaking this. Who would wish to undergo such an ordeal?'

He gave me one of his particularly sweet smiles. 'A horse or a dog or an apprentice. Train them sternly, and when the time comes, they will acquit themselves at their best.'

I grunted. 'I assume I am the apprentice, not a horse or a dog.'

'In the taking of this examination, yes. As a practising physician, you are no apprentice, but as far as the College is concerned, you are nobody until they approve you. Do not worry. I have made you jump through the sort of hoops the worst of the censors might present you with, but I believe the current holders of the post will give you little trouble. You answer well and clearly. You must just try to look a little more enamoured of the subject.'

'Hmph,' I said, taking a bite of one of Beatriz's excellent saffron cakes. She loved to do much of the fine baking herself. I swallowed a mouthful of wine.

'I will try to look more engaged and forget what nonsense it all is.'

'Not all of it.'

'Perhaps not all,' I conceded.

'Sir Francis sent me a note this morning,' he said. 'He has been told that you are to report to the College on the twenty-eighth to receive the texts on which you will be examined. Then you must report again at seven on the morning of the thirtieth for the examination itself. It will take all day.'

Now that it was becoming a reality, I felt sick, and beads of sweat broke out around my neck, to trickle down my spine. No escape, then.

All this time I had hardly seen Simon or the other players, and had sent word to Guy that our music-making must wait until after the examination. Every minute when I was not working at the hospital, I spent pouring over Dr Nuñez's books. Rikki had grown irritated for lack of walks and I had spent a fortune on candles.

That evening as I walked toward the Bridge, with Rikki at my heels, I suddenly heard someone calling my name.

'Master Alvarez, is it not?'

I stopped and turned on my heel. Rikki tugged impatiently at his lead, but I signalled at him to lie down, which he did with resignation. It was that time at dusk when it is not quite dark, but sight is blurred and the torches and lanterns set up outside the principal buildings were only just being lit. There was something familiar in the man hurrying toward me, but I could not at first place him.

'Ah,' he said, 'it is indeed you. I was not quite sure. You are taller, I think, than when I saw you last.'

At that moment a servant stepped out of a house fronting on to the street and hung a lantern on a bracket beside the door. As he moved out of the beam of light and back inside, it flowed across between the stranger and myself. I recognised him now. It was the steward from the Fitzgeralds' house in Surrey, where I had once carried out a spying mission for Sir Francis, passing myself off as a tutor in music and mathematics to the Fitzgerald children. The Fitzgeralds were known Catholics and I had left their house abruptly, after discovering that they were passing letters to the French embassy. Poley had been present there too, though keeping out of sight, and there had been a Catholic priest.

'Master Alchester!' I said, as the name came back to me. 'How do you fare? I have not seen you this long time.' I bowed. And hoped never to see you again, I thought. I had liked the steward, Edwin Alchester. Indeed, uncomfortable as it was, I had liked all the Fitzgerald household, with the exception of fifteen-year-old Cecilia, who was a little too knowing for her age, and had made a clumsy attempt to seduce me, believing absolutely in my boy's disguise.

'It is good to see you,' Alchester said. 'I was sorry you were called away so suddenly by your father's illness. He is well, I hope?'

I shook my head. 'My father died in the spring.'

'Ah, indeed, that is sad news. But will you not take a sup of ale with me? Unless, of course, you have urgent business elsewhere?'

Only with Galen, I thought. Well, why should I not take a drink with the man? I did not know whether he shared his master's faith or clandestine practices, but he had always been pleasant to me. Indeed, Sir Francis had himself decided not to pursue the Fitzgeralds, feeling that it was more useful to allow the channel for letters to continue so that we could keep a watch on it. As far as was ever discovered, Sir

Damian Fitzgerald never engaged in any serious treasonable activities, and soon afterwards that particular route for correspondence was given up.

'I should be glad to join you,' I said, and we turned aside together to the nearest inn, where he insisted on treating me not only to a tankard of excellent beer, but also to a chop and baked onions.

'You seemed in haste when I saw you first,' he said apologetically. 'I hope I have not kept you from something of importance.'

I laughed and dropped my chop bone to Rikki, who had been leaning rather pointedly against my knee.

'Nay,' I said, 'only some dull study of Galen.'

'Galen? The physician?'

'Aye. I am not only a musician and mathematician. I work as an assistant physician at St Thomas's, over in Southwark.'

'Indeed! You are a very talented young man!'

'I was trained up by my father, but now . . . friends . . . have urged me to take the examination at the Royal College of Physicians to obtain a licence to practice as a fully qualified physician. I have just heard this afternoon that the examination is to take place on the last day of the month.'

'Hence your study of the master.'

I nodded. Now was not the time to speak of Galen's flaws and my interest in Arabic medicine.

'And you, Master Alchester, what are you doing in London? Are you no longer with the Fitzgeralds?' I thought he looked tired. His hair was greyer than when I had last seen him and, although he still moved with dignity, his shoulders had developed a slight stoop.

'Oh indeed, I am certainly still with the family. We are come to the London house for a few months. Mistress Cecilia was married here in September, to Sir Jacob Digby.'

'Please convey my congratulations to her,' I said, suppressing a smile. 'I am afraid I know nothing of Sir Jacob.'

'He is a gentleman of about fifty,' Alchester said, 'who lives very quietly on his estates in Gloucestershire. It is his second marriage.'

'And she must be – what? – eighteen?'

'Aye.' He made no comment on the disparity in their ages, but I could read his opinion in his face. Well, perhaps a husband old enough to be her father might keep her in order, or perhaps not.

'She will enjoy having an establishment of her own, I am sure. And what of young Master Edward? He will not have much fishing in London!'

Alchester laughed. 'Indeed, I think he misses the country. He has been attending Westminster school since the summer, as a paying pupil. His father hopes to send him to Oxford in three or four years' time.'

That was interesting information. A declared Catholic could not attend the university. Perhaps the family had converted to the English church. They had certainly complied with the law and attended their parish church when I was with them, and their local rector had been Edward's tutor at home. Their Catholic masses they had held in secret.

'Sir Damian and his lady are well?'

'Indeed, indeed. Though there has been an addition to the family.'

I must have looked startled. Lady Bridget was surely past child-bearing. Seeing my expression, Alchester laughed.

'Nay, not another child for the Fitzgeralds themselves. A ward. A little girl, five years old. Sophia Makepeace. Her father was a dear friend of Sir Damian's from boyhood. The little girl's mother died in childbirth and now the father is dead, leaving the child as ward to Sir Damian. The wardship agreement was very carefully drawn up and sealed with every protection of the law.'

I nodded. If the position of a ward was at all questionable, the Crown could claim the wardship and all kinds of troubles might ensue.

'So is this new addition to the family a trouble to you?'

He smiled. 'Not at all. She is a dear child, very lively and clever, but she is the heiress to great estates in Derbyshire. The next heir – some distant cousin of her father's – has tried to dispute the wardship, and that is another reason we have come to London, so that Sir Damian may consult the best lawyers. He must ascertain that the child may remain safely and securely in his care, for this other claimant is a man not to be trusted. Sir Damian fears that if he should gain control of the little girl, she would never reach her majority.'

'That is a very serious case indeed,' I said. 'And has all been made certain?'

'It seems so, but we will probably stay in London until the spring, while Sir Damian makes quite certain of the case and takes care of other matters concerning Mistress Cecilia's dowry and various land transactions.'

'And do you enjoy London, Master Alchester?'

He shrugged. 'I do not care for the dirt and noise. I miss the country. But there are entertainments in London, certainly. My time is not so fully occupied here as at home. It is a much smaller household to supervise, and my hope is that my assistant is managing the Surrey estates without too much difficulty. I have even managed a visit to the playhouse! It was the first time. My lady Bridget urged me to go. It was a just a light comedy, at the Theatre, out beyond Bishopsgate. Do you know it?'

'Aye. And they do perform serious plays as well, although the cold weather will soon close the playhouses. The audiences do not attend once the weather is too cold.'

I pushed back my stool.

'It has been good to see you again, Master Alchester, but I fear I must return to my studies.' I held out my hand to him. I spoke truly, for I did like the man and felt guilty about my deception of the whole family. Perhaps it could be forgotten at last.

He shook my hand and we both rose and went out into the street together. It was quite dark now and the gates at the far end of the Bridge would be closed. I would need to take a wherry across the river.

'Perhaps we might meet again,' he said, as we pulled our cloaks close against a penetrating wind which was blowing upriver. I realised he was probably lonely in London, without his usually busy life and no doubt lacking any acquaintance outside the family.

'Indeed,' I said cheerfully, 'though I fear I shall be poor company until this examination is over!'

'I wish you every success in it.'

'Afterwards, aye, let us meet. I may always be found at St Thomas's Hospital in Southwark. Anyone may show you the way.'

We parted with mutual good wishes, and I ran down the steps to the wherry mooring at Old Swan Stairs, Rikki following, eager to be home and out of the cold. The wherry man was hunched under his canvas tilt-cloth, rubbing his stiff hands together, and greeted the prospect of a fare with relief. In this bitter cold so early in the winter, the wherrymen would be fearing that the river might freeze and rob them of all trade. When the Thames freezes, wherrymen starve.

Chapter Five

*E*arly on the morning of the twenty-eighth, I went, as bidden, to the Royal College to collect the texts on which I was to be particularly examined. They were awaiting me in the gatekeeper's lodge, wrapped in soft leather and fastened with a book-strap.

'Master Christoval Alvarez?' the gatekeeper said, in a somewhat patronising tone.

No danger here of being addressed as 'doctor'.

'That is my name,' I said, with dignity and ignoring his implied sneer. I held out my hand for the books.

He looked at me as though he trusted me little and liked me less, but handed over the parcel of books with a grudging air. I hurried away, for I had to walk all the way back across London and then over the Bridge before I could reach St Thomas's in time for my usual arrival. Superintendent Ailmer had granted me a free day to take the examinations in two days' time, but I had no wish to be accused of slacking beforehand. When I made the request, explaining why I needed a day away from my duties at the hospital, I could see him weighing up the prospects both in favour and against my gaining a licence. On the one hand it would enhance the reputation of the hospital if I succeeded. On the other, he would be obliged to pay me a full salary. Would it be worth it? I saw the calculation in his eyes.

Now, as soon as I was out of sight of the College, I unwrapped the parcel to check which texts they had given me. Volumes One and Three of the same edition of Galen as the one Dr Nuñez had loaned me, and Celsus, but a different edition, a more recent one. I would need to check whether there were any amendments. That would mean a tedious evening's work tonight.

I stowed the books in my satchel and hurried on. There was a great deal to do today.

It proved to be even busier than I had feared. One of the Winchester geese was brought in by her friends, bleeding profusely. She had visited one of the rogue abortionists who inhabited the back lanes of Southwark. The abortion had failed, but the dear God only knew what terrible injury had been inflicted on the woman.

'She tried everything,' one of her friends confided, a blousy wench called Bessie Travis, whom we had encountered before. She was one of the leaders of the Southwark prostitutes, and a formidable woman. 'Raspberry leaves boiled in hot water and drunk morning and night, dog's turds smeared on her belly, oil of olives – a pint of it she drunk, and that cost a pretty penny, I can tell you. Nothing worked. So she went to that old hag in Butcher Lane. I told her. I said, "She won't do you no good. Nearly killed Jane Fletcher, she did." But would Meg listen? Not she!'

For a moment the hospital and Bessie Travis dipped and swam, as memory engulfed me.

I picked up the bottles lying near my mother's hand. Seeds of flos pavonis. Leaf of leonurus cardiaca. Root of the rare American cimicifuga racemosa. Tincture of stachys officinalis. All the bottles were empty. Even then, I knew what they signified.

She could speak no more, for her body arched and heaved, and suddenly a great bloody mass burst out between her legs. She screamed and retched.

Terror swept over me. I did not know what to do. I did not know what to do. I seized a bolster from the bunk and wedged it under her head, then ran for my father. I seemed to hunt for hours, running up and down companionways, along the decks, until I found him at last in the captain's cabin.

'Come,' I gasped. 'You must come. Mama.' The words froze on my tongue.

I clutched my father's sleeve in both hands. If I could hold on to him, perhaps the horror would stop. Time would slip back. Everything would be as it had been, only a few hours before.

When we reached my mother she was breathing still, but the floor was awash with blood and she could not speak.

'What did she take, Caterina?' My father took me by the shoulders and shook me so I could not speak.

'Abortifacients,' I managed to say at last, breaking away from his grasp and pointing at the empty bottles. Tears were running down my face and soaking the front of my tunic. Jaime's tunic, ragged and filthy.

'But why?' His cry was terrible to hear. 'Why?'

I hung my head. I could not meet his eyes. 'She was raped,' I whispered. 'Over and over, they raped her in the prison. She told me she was with child. While we were still in the prison. And now, she said . . . now all she could say to me, was that she wanted to kill the baby.'

'She has killed herself as well!' he wailed, taking my mother in his arms.

I drew a deep breath and tried to steady my voice. Bessie was staring at me, her mouth agape. I feared I had come near to swooning. I must not allow it to be seen.

'Why did Meg not come here to the hospital?' I said at last. 'She could have the babe in safety and we would hand it over to Christ's if she was so anxious not to keep it.'

'Ha!' She tossed her head and smiled sardonically at me. 'That's very well for you to say, a man working in a clean hospital, with your wages and your meals and a roof over your head. How long do you think we can go on working, great with child? And if we don't work, we don't eat!'

She flounced off, certain of the strength of her argument, and who was I to contradict her? In endowing the lying-in ward for unmarried women, Sir Richard Whittington had not provided for their keep when they were unable to work before their children were born. And I could hardly tell Bessie I was as much a woman as she was. We had saved Meg's life for the moment. I was not sure whether the unborn child would survive the brutal treatment it had received, or if it did survive, whether it would be severely damaged.

This emergency had caused a great disruption in the ward, but at last it grew quiet. Meg, who had been howling like a stuck pig, had been bathed, treated to staunch the bleeding, and given poppy syrup to ease the pain of the abortionist's cruel efforts. She was asleep now, and I took the opportunity to speak to young Mellie.

She was sitting up on a stool beside her bed, dressed in day clothes. Not the torn dress in which she had come to St Thomas's, for it seemed she had to fight her master to escape and come to us. He had half ripped the gown off her back. As had been the practice at St Bartholomew's, we kept here a store of clothes for the poor, who often arrived in filthy rags. These garments were donated by charitable citizens, and we generally had a good supply of outgrown children's clothes, or doublets that no longer fastened across a shopkeeper's expanding waist, or handed-down servants' gowns that were a little too shabby to suit their mistress's idea of respectability. Mellie was wearing a blue gown which was somewhat too loose, but she had tied a spotless white apron tightly over it, cinching in the waist. Her face had filled out and her skin, which had been waxy and pale, now had a healthy bloom of youth to it.

She would be ready to leave any day now. She sat looking down into the wicker cradle and singing softly, perhaps a lullaby her mother had once sung to her, when she was a cherished daughter in a loving family. I leaned over the cradle and saw that the baby's eyes were open and fixed on her child mother. It seemed a cruel thing to tear them apart, but was it not the best way for them both?

'You are both looking well, Mellie,' I said, sitting down on the edge of her bed. 'You will be ready to leave us soon.'

She raised frightened eyes to me. This time at St Thomas's – prolonged because of her own weak state and the baby's early arrival – had meant peace and safety to her, something she must not have known since she was seven years old. She stretched out a protective hand toward the baby.

'I cannot give her up, Dr Alvarez, I cannot!'

'I know it is hard.' I felt my own stomach twist in sympathy. 'I have spoken to the matron at Christ's Hospital, Mistress Wedderbury. She is a kind and loving woman, no one better to care for young children. She has said you may come to visit Christ's with me, to see the kind of home they give the children in their care. You would not need to hand your child over to strangers, not knowing what will become of her, where she will live, who will care for her. Will you come with me to see?'

She looked at me doubtfully. 'I may bring Hannah with me? You would not let them make off with her, behind my back?'

'Nay, Mellie, I swear to you. That will not happen.'

'And may I bring her with me?' She was insistent.

'Very well.' It seemed cruel to deprive her of any of these last hours with her child.

'Doctor Alvarez,' she said hesitantly, 'was Hannah properly baptised? I cannot truly remember what happened.'

'She was baptised,' I assured her. 'As soon as she came into the world. When a baby is born weak and sickly, or very early, as Hannah was, the midwife is licensed to baptise the child, so that it shall not die before being received into the Christian faith. It is a wise precaution, but in Hannah's case it has proved unnecessary.'

She frowned. 'It does not seem a proper christening to me. In a church, at the font, with the priest and godparents. I went to the christening of both my little sister and my brother, and it was properly done.'

She had not mentioned a brother before.

'You may have a church christening if you wish,' I said, 'and if you will feel that it better serves Hannah's soul. It could be held in the hospital chapel here, or in the church at Christ's Hospital.'

'Will you stand godfather?' she demanded.

This was an awkward question. If I lied before God about my sex and my dubious and wavering faith, would I imperil the baby's immortal soul?

'There must be other friends you could ask to be godparents,' I said.

She gave me a bleak look, as if I had betrayed her somehow, and shook her head.

'Only the cook at my old place, Goodwife Edwards, but if I asked her, that might give me away to . . . that man.'

She would never speak the name of the master who had raped her.

'Well, we shall see what can be done.' Perhaps if I made a compromise with God, that I would serve as a *godparent*, not a godfather, I would not imperil the child, though I feared the Almighty must see through my temporising. I was probably already in poor favour with Him, for it is held to be blasphemy for a woman to masquerade as a man, defying the natural hierarchy and assuming a position she has no right to.

'Two days from now,' I said, 'I am to take an examination at the Royal College of Physicians, but the day after – that will be the first day of December – I will take you and Hannah to see Christ's Hospital and meet Mistress Wedderbury. Until then I want you to walk about the hospital as much as you can, to regain your strength, for it is a long way from here, as far as Newgate. I do not want you to overtire yourself.'

Clearly she had no idea of the distance, this Southwark child.

'What is an examination?'

'It means I must answer a lot of questions about medicine, to some very important and grand doctors, who are the best in England.'

She shook her head and said scornfully, 'They cannot be better doctors than you are! You saved that woman's life this morning, the one who was bleeding all over the floor.'

'I thank you for the praise,' I said, with a sad smile. 'But do not forget what I said about walking as much as possible.'

'I have already been helping the sisters,' she said. 'Before you come in the morning I help to clean the babies and change their dirty clouts, and I sweep the floor, and I help to carry breakfast to the mothers who are still abed.'

I had not known this. It seemed the nursing sisters were using her as an unpaid skivvy, but perhaps it was no bad thing. It would give her occupation and help to restore some sense of worth to her, after the way she had been misused.

'That is good,' I said. 'Perhaps one day you may become a nursing sister yourself.'

'I should like that!' She grinned at me suddenly, and seemed for the first time the carefree child she should be. 'Perhaps I could work here?'

'Not yet, I'm afraid. The Superintendent would not employ someone so young, but perhaps, one day.'

The other girl I hoped to take to Christ's Hospital, Ellyn Smith, was almost ready to leave St Thomas's as well, but I did not want to take both girls there at the same time. Better to deal with one case at a time. As for that imp Davy, his condition had grown worse for a time, as though the exposure and starvation he had experienced had caused some lingering damage to his lungs, but he was gradually getting better. I had had an idea about his future, but I needed to take advice first.

Before I left St Thomas's that afternoon, I sought out Mistress Maynard in the room where she issued her instructions to the nursing sisters and kept a supply of bandages and simple salves. She was also in charge of the clothes issued to the poor patients when they were discharged.

'I understand you are to take Mellie to visit Christ's Hospital,' she said. 'I hope you will be able to make her see that it will be best for the babe.'

'That is my hope also,' I said, 'but I wanted to see you about something else.'

I sat down on the chair she indicated.

'I have encountered a group of child beggars,' I said. 'Whether or not they are being controlled by an adult, I cannot be sure. There are five of them, always together: a boy about three, boy and girl twins perhaps seven years of age, and an older girl and boy. They are maybe nine or ten but could be older. They are so undernourished it is difficult to tell.'

'In the streets round the hospital, are they? I cannot say that I have noticed a group like that.'

'Nay, I should explain. I do not know what part of London they may come from, but their favourite place to beg is by one of the entrances to the Theatre, out beyond Bishopsgate. People coming and going at the playhouse give them a few pennies.'

'Ah, well, of course I would not have seen them.'

It was clear from her expression what she thought of playhouses.

'The Theatre is very respectable.' I felt a need to apologise for my friends. 'It is Master Burbage's company. Lord Strange's Men. They perform sometimes before the Queen herself.'

'One of these beggar children is sick?' It seemed she relaxed a little. There was nothing wrong with the warmth of Mistress Maynard's heart.

'Not at present, though the middle boy has a bad case of ringworm, which he will not let me salve. With winter coming on, they may well fall ill. As far as I can tell, they are homeless, though Matthew – the boy who is their leader – says they have somewhere warm to sleep. I fancy it may be a barn in Moorfields.'

'How can I help?'

'These vagrant children,' I said, 'they are suspicious of all authority. I think it unlikely I could persuade them to take refuge at Christ's, and I fear what will become of them. It seems likely we will have a hard winter this year. They wear nothing but rags, so I wondered whether you could spare any clothes from our store? In different sizes, to fit the children. The appearance is of no consequence, as long as they are warm. I realise they are meant for patients here, but this may prevent these children becoming patients.'

'Certainly!' She sprang to her feet. For a large woman she could move quickly when she chose. 'Come with me, doctor, and we will see what we can find.'

With a key from the bunch she wore at her waist, she opened a cupboard door in the hallway beside her room. As was to be expected, where anything was under Mistress Maynard's care, the clothes were arranged meticulously on the shelves within according to size – men's to the right, women's to the left. She soon selected full suits of clothing in sizes I judged to be about right for the five children, including woollen caps and cloaks. Our one difficulty was shoes. I had no idea what sizes would fit, but she chose what seemed right for their ages.

'If they do not fit, you must measure them and we will do better,' she said. 'Many of these beggar children go barefoot, poor mites, and in winter they are like to perish of frostbite.'

She closed and locked the cupboard, while I attempted to make the clothes into manageable bundle.

'Now, doctor,' she said briskly, 'you cannot easily carry them like that. We have been sorting the blankets for winter and some were so frayed they were set aside to be sold for shredding, but some are good enough to provide a little warmth. Come with me.'

She led me into the back reaches of the hospital, where I had never been before. In one of the storerooms there was a pile of old blankets from which she selected three with frayed hems and a few small holes, but otherwise in fair condition. Between us we made everything into a large bundle, held together with a short length of rope. She looked at it dubiously, then at my physician's gown and cap.

'Surely you cannot walk through the streets carrying this, doctor. It would not be suitable for a gentleman. I'll send one of the lads to carry it for you.'

'Nay,' I said with a laugh. 'It is a little awkward, but not heavy. I shall do well enough.

It was indeed awkward, as I discovered before I was halfway across the Bridge, trying to dodge through the crowds. By the time I was nearing Threadneedle Street, I was hot, despite the cold wind, and not a little cross, but I struggled on, Rikki staying close to my heels. The journey was made the more unpleasant because I had the uneasy sensation that I was being followed. Any agent of Walsingham's soon develops this sensitivity and learns a number of skills for dealing with it. I stopped, on my way, to buy food for the children and at each stop – at the pie shop, the bakery, the fruit stall – I was able to direct a glance casually behind me, yet I could see no one I recognised.

It would not have surprised me to pick out Poley in the crowd, for the latest news that Phelippes had was that he was back in England. Poley had long ago guessed my sex and used his knowledge as a weapon against me. He might do so again. By threatening to expose me to Walsingham and make my disguise public knowledge, he could endanger not only my employment but my life. Now that I was well established at Seething Lane, as one of the most skilled code-breakers and an agent who could be useful from time to time, Poley might feel I could be forced to smooth his path back into the service. I shivered at the thought and Rikki, who was quick to understand my moods, growled softly, the hair on the back of his neck stirring.

I paid for a dozen apples and stowed them in my satchel, taking the opportunity to glance again behind me. Apart from a large burly workman I had noticed before, the crowd in the street seemed to have changed since I had last looked. The workman was a stranger to me, probably simply headed, as I was, toward Bishopsgate. I decided I was imagining things, picked up my bundle, and went on my way.

The workman was still following when I reached the gate, but I lost sight of him soon after, when I had turned left toward the Curtain playhouse and beyond it the Theatre.

There seemed to be a great bustle going on. Round the side of the playhouse where the children begged, three large handcarts were lined up, the first of which was already filled with the large wicker coffers in which the players stored their costumes and properties. Guy came round the corner with a lute case in each hand and a tenor recorder gripped precariously under his arm. I dropped my bundle and managed to catch the recorder before it fell, while Guy tried to fend off a too-enthusiastic greeting from Rikki.

'What's afoot?' I cried. I did not like the look of this. Had Burbage's company been turned out by their landlord?

'Do not look so stricken, Kit.' Guy face crinkled in a happy smile. 'It is good news.'

'Good news? I looks as though you are moving house!'

He placed the two lutes in the second cart and wedged them in carefully with a length of drapery, then relieved me of the tenor recorder. When he was satisfied that the instruments were safely stowed, he leaned his back against the side of the cart and folded his arms.

'Rather let me say, Kit, that it appears that it is you who are moving house. Is that all your worldly possessions?' He pointed the toe of his boot at my bundle, which had begun at last to come apart.

'Nay.' I laughed. 'It is a few warm clothes and blankets for the vagrant children that I begged from St Thomas's. I hope they are still here.'

'Aye, though I think they have missed your bounty. Some of us have been obliged to feed the brats, now that you have roused their expectations.'

'I'm sorry.' Though I suspected Guy was not as put out as he pretended. 'I have been very occupied, studying for this examination.'

'Ah, and are we to pull our forelocks to you now, a full physician?'

'Not yet. The examination is the day after tomorrow. I confess, Guy, that I do not look forward to it with any pleasure.'

He shrugged. 'It will be no worse than it is for us when we try for a part. At least you know you will continue to work and eat, however it goes. Not so with us.'

'You have the right of it,' I said, feeling somewhat ashamed that I should let the examination loom so alarmingly over me. For the players every performance was a kind of examination. If they failed, they might lose their place, and then they would not eat. 'But tell me what is afoot here – what is this good news of yours?'

Two more of the players arrived, carrying another costume basket between them, Christopher Haigh and the new player from Warwickshire, who took some of the smaller parts and was writing new pieces for the company. Simon said that at first he had such a strong country accent Burbage would not give him a speaking part, but he had a good ear and now spoke almost as well as a Londoner. It seemed he had quite a skill with words as well. I remembered now: he was called Will, with some outlandish surname.

'Our good news,' said Guy, smiling broadly, 'is that Master Burbage has secured the great chamber of the Cross Keys to be our winter theatre. We shall be able to continue to play all through the cold weather.'

'That is fine news indeed! The Cross Keys in Gracechurch Street?'

'That's the one. And,' Guy drew the word out and his eyes sparkled. 'And we are to play for Her Majesty at Twelfth Night!'

'Her Majesty!' Simon had come up behind me and thumped me on the shoulder. 'What do you think of that, Dr Alvarez, our distinguished physician?'

'It is truly wonderful,' I said, catching their excitement. 'What will you play?'

'It is not decided yet. Master Burbage must discuss it all with the Master of the Revels first. We heard the news only this morning.'

'Now, then, Kit,' Guy said, 'can I not persuade you to join me in making music for Her Majesty? You would have the chance to see the Queen herself.'

I smiled and shook my head. Guy did not know, though Simon did, that I had once been summoned to Greenwich, to an audience with the Queen. Not even the prospect of another encounter could persuade me to appear in a play. Besides, the Queen might value me less as one of Walsingham's agents if she caught sight of me amongst a company of players.

'Those children will not find it so easy to beg at the Cross Keys,' I said. 'The innkeeper will turn them away.'

'Aye, he will,' Simon said. 'It will mar his trade to have beggars at his door. It's a respectable inn.'

'Even with a company of vagabonds like you playing there?' I said. 'I am surprised the neighbours have not raised an objection, as the people at Blackfriars did, when Master Burbage wanted the boys' theatre for your winter playhouse.'

'It is not *that* respectable an inn.' Guy grinned. 'The neighbours are accustomed to the busy coming and going of customers. We shall be as quiet and discreet as mice by comparison. Master Burbage has abandoned the Blackfriars plan.'

'Hmm,' I shook my head. 'You would do better in Southwark. But I am glad you have found winter quarters.'

I picked up my bundle and walked on to the base of the stairs, where the children were huddled as usual. I wondered whether they had overheard our conversation. Matthew, I suspected, had sharp ears and must keep all his senses alert to safeguard his little band. Although these children lived on the streets of London, they were like wild deer, ready to flee at any sign of danger.

'God be with you,' I said as I stopped a few feet away and looked down at them. They were braced back against the outer wall of the playhouse, as if they hoped to draw some warmth from its cold plaster. I thought they looked more frail than ever. The girl Katerina had a hacking cough and all their noses were running. The ringworm sores on Jonno's scalp were red and crusted where he had been scratching them. All in all, they were not an appealing sight. Certainly the innkeeper of the Cross Keys would not welcome their presence.

At my mention of God, I was met with blank stares and no response. At last Matthew said accusingly, 'You a'nt been here in weeks.'

Immediately I felt guilty. While I had been working hard with Dr Nuñez I had not visited them once, though I had sent occasional parcels of food with Simon. I did not remind them of this, but merely said cheerfully, 'I am afraid I could not come, but I am here now, so come and look what I have brought you.'

I had never before seen them move from their tightly packed group in the corner, but as I began to untie the bundle their curiosity became too much for them. Even Matthew in the end got to his feet and came reluctantly over to peer at what I had brought. As the dusk was drawing in, the players had brought out torch stands, the better to see to their packing, and on the edge of their flickering light I spread out the clothes I had brought. It was the two girls who came close and began to finger the thick woollen dresses.

'For us?' Maggie breathed, looking up at me in wonder.

'Aye,' I said. 'Undershifts for you all. Gowns and stockings for you and Katerina. Tunics and hose for the boys. A cloak and a cap each. I don't know whether the shoes will fit. I could not be sure of your size.'

I looked down at the two pairs of dirty feet, caked with mud, but where the skin showed, red and cracked. There would be painful chilblains under the mud.

Katerina reached out and stroked a dress which had once been a merry scarlet, but was now faded in patches, except where an apron had once protected it.

'For me?'

I picked it up and held it out to her.

'For you. There should be a shift here in your size. This is it.' I turned to Simon. 'Could the girls dress in the tiring room?'

Before he could answer, Katerina backed away, clutching the dress and shift.

'I a'nt going in there!' She looked horrified. 'Come with me, Maggie.'

Maggie grabbed the green gown which was clearly meant for her, and a confused handful of stockings. I handed her a shift as the girls slipped away behind a clump of bushes.

'Jamey,' I said persuasively, 'look what I have for you.'

The little boy turned in confusion from me to Matthew and back again.

'Aye,' Matthew said. 'Go to the gentleman. He's got clothes for you.'

While I dressed Jamey in hose and a thick tunic which reached to his ankles, the two older boys rummaged through the pile and ran off to the bushes to dress. I hoped they would discard their dirty rags, but they might simply put the clean clothes on over the top of them. I made sure Jamey was stripped of his old garments, which were jumping with lice, though he seemed somewhat astonished to find himself stark naked, even for a few moments. Once he was dressed, I fastened the small cloak round his shoulders and pulled the woollen cap over his matted hair. He was not clean, but at least he would be warm. I thrust the old rags at Simon.

'Burn these, will you?'

He looked at me in amusement. 'Aye, I will, but I suspect you will find most of the lice will have migrated to you.'

His words had me immediately scratching, though it was probably no more than imagination.

The girls came back into the edge of the light, suddenly as shy as any normal little girl, who does not need to beg and fight simply to stay alive. Katerina, with her long black hair, was almost pretty.

'You do look fine,' I said, and was rewarded with unexpected smiles. 'Now, find your cloaks and caps, and see whether any of the shoes will fit.

Maggie shook her head. 'A'nt never worn shoes.'

'Well, try them anyway. Your feet will be much warmer. They may feel strange at first, but you will grow used to them.'

In the end, the shoes fitted fairly well for all the children except Matthew, whose feet were larger than I had reckoned. Perhaps he was indeed older than I had supposed. Guy had finished packing the instruments into the cart and came over to see how we were faring. He clearly found the whole business amusing, but he was a kind man.

Looking at Matthew's feet, he said, 'I think we might have a pair of shoes that would fit you, lad. They were a good pair once, worn by the boy actors, but they are scuffed now. We thought to throw them out, but you can have them.'

He rummaged through one of the costume baskets and came back with a pair of stout brown shoes which were indeed scuffed about the toe and somewhat down at heel, but they fitted Matthew.

'Where are your old clothes?' I asked.

Matthew pointed to the clump of bushes. 'A'nt going to throw them away!' He was accusing. 'Them'll do for bedding.'

Well, I could not expect perfection. I shook out the three blankets which had served to wrap the bundle, and folded them up.

'These will make better bedding.' I handed them to him, then I emptied my satchel of the food I had bought. There were some cooked sausages that Rikki had his eye on, but I shook my head to give him a stern warning.

While the children were eating, I took out from my satchel a small pot of salve and handed it to Maggie. 'This is for Jonno. Rub it into his scalp night and morning. Can you do that? It should get rid of the ringworm, and in time I hope his hair will grow back.'

When I had tried to give them a salve before it had been rejected in fear, but Maggie trusted me enough at last to take the pot, though I could not be sure she would use it. The children were warmer now, with one good meal in their bellies, but what would become of them if they lost their begging place?

The players had finished packing up the three carts until they would hold no more, and set off to trundle them down through Bishopsgate and into Gracechurch Street to the Cross Keys. Guy had gone to keep a careful watch on his instruments, but Simon had stayed while the children were dressed and fed. Master Burbage, too, remained, after seeing the costumes and properties carried off.

67

'This is excellent news, Master Burbage,' I said, 'that you will have an indoor playhouse for the winter.'

'Indeed, indeed!' He rubbed his hands together and beamed at me. 'And well placed, too, in the middle of the city. Even could we continue to play here, few Londoners will brave the walk out so far in the cold weather. We should do very well.'

'Better than those ragamuffins,' I said, nodding toward the beggars.

'Aye,' he said soberly, shaking his head. 'They will have no pickings here now.'

'Nor at the Cross Keys neither.'

'There is little we can do about it.'

'I would try to have them admitted to Christ's Hospital,' I said, 'but I fear they would run from me. As soon try to cage a hare. They would not even go into the playhouse to dress.'

'I wonder whether they have ever entered a building,' he said.

'They shelter somewhere at night, but my guess is that it is a barn or stable.'

'It is to our blame that children like this exist in London,' he said sadly. 'They are as wild as stray dogs or the rats which infest the docks. It seems there is nothing to be done about them.'

The children had finished the last scraps of food when Matthew stood up from where he had been squatting on the ground and came over to us.

'Master,' he said, looking at Burbage and trying, it seemed, to speak politely, 'is it true you are going away?'

Simon and I exchanged a glance. Matthew must have been listening to our talk earlier.

'We are going into winter quarters, lad,' Burbage said kindly. 'We have one last performance tomorrow, then we will close up the playhouse and take up residence at the Cross Keys Inn, Gracechurch Street.'

'I thought that was what the other man said, the little man with the odd face.'

Simon turned away to hide his smile at this description of Guy.

'So there won't be no people coming here, as might give us pennies?'

'I'm afraid not.'

'I know Gracechurch Street,' Matthew said, 'and the Cross Keys.'

It was clear Burbage was uncomfortable. He was a tolerant man, but he was also a man of business, and the players' profession is an unchancy one. He could not encourage the beggars to follow the players to their winter theatre.

'It would not be a good place for you to – er – for you to practice your trade,' Burbage said. 'I fear the innkeeper would drive you away. He cannot have you worrying his customers.'

Matthew raised his chin and for a moment he looked like a young soldier. 'Never fear, Master,' he said, and his voice was cold. We won't be hurting the Cross Keys' trade. We'll find us another pitch.'

He turned on his heel and marched back to the others.

'That was bravely done,' Simon said softly.

Burbage shook his head. 'There is nothing for it. They must find another pitch. It's a pity I could not have had the training of him when he was younger. There is something about him . . . he would have made a fine player, but it too late now.'

Burbage went to lock up the playhouse as Simon and I prepared to walk home to Southwark, but first I went back to Matthew.

'I do not know where you will go, Matthew, after the playhouse is closed for the winter,' I said, 'but if ever you need help, you may find me at St Thomas's Hospital in Southwark. Ask for Dr Alvarez.'

'Or come to me at the Cross Keys,' Simon said. 'Master Hetherington.'

Matthew nodded, but did not thank us. He might be a waif of the London streets, and a beggar, but he had his pride.

'We shall miss the gate,' I said. 'We'll need to take a wherry. Come along, Rikki.'

'I wonder what will become of them,' Simon said. 'Look, it's beginning to snow.'

Chapter Six

I wore out two candles that evening, which I could ill afford, reading painfully through the two editions of Celsus, checking whether there had been any material changes in the newer edition, on which I was to be examined. After many hours' work, with the first lightening of the sky over the river outside my window, all I had discovered were some typographical corrections, where the first printer had made some mistake in the Latin, transposing two letters or omitting another. My head ached and I felt a bubbling impatience with all these ancient writers and transmitters of the ancients.

More than ever I believed that the observation and practical treatment of disease was where the physician's true vocation lay, not in repeating the bookish theories of past centuries which modern enquiry had proved false. I admitted – as I had admitted to Dr Nuñez – that not all of the ancient knowledge was wrong, but there were times when even the old country wives' remedies were more effective, having been arrived at through practical trial and error. I laughed quietly as I finally closed the volumes. I could not quite go along with Bessie Travis's belief on smearing dog's turds on a woman's belly to bring about an abortion. That was one I had never encountered before.

'Come along, Rikki,' I said. 'We are going for a long walk to clear my head before the day's work, or I do not know what strange practices I may employ.'

Rikki was familiar with the word 'walk', and sprang eagerly to his feet. We made our way quietly down the stairs, so as not to wake the other inhabitants of the building, and I pulled the door closed as softly as I could, for it was inclined to stick. Outside, standing on the steps, I caught my breath, for the air was bitterly cold after the warmth I had built up in my room with keeping in the coal fire all night. It must have snowed more during the hours of darkness, for a thin covering lay over the frozen ground below, and footing was slippery on the roadway. Not another soul was to be seen, so I let Rikki off his lead and he bounded ahead, rushing aside to investigate every promising smell.

I turned left and headed west along Bankside, past the Clink Prison, past Paris Garden with the bear baiting and bull baiting, and the straggle of mean houses which eventually petered out. No one had been this way since the snow had fallen and I enjoyed the crunching under my feet as I impressed my mark along the snow-covered grassy verge of the roadway, which made for easier walking than the road itself. This road running parallel to the river was poorly made up and badly rutted from the carts which came this way from the Southwark markets to the palace of Lambeth and its cluster of attendant buildings, where the river bent south, opposite Westminster.

As I walked along briskly, with Rikki circling around me as if he were herding sheep, I began to feel better, drawing in great lungfuls of the cold, clean air. Along this stretch of the riverside there were no buildings and no insidious smoke. The air felt almost as clean as the air at my grandfather's *solar*, back in my childhood days in Portugal. My headache began to ease. After a few minutes I found a stick to throw for Rikki, which he chased like a puppy, as if he had forgotten his days as a working dog in Amsterdam and his rather sober life here with me since he had come to London. I wondered whether he yearned for a more active occupation.

Even on the river there was little stirring, though I saw one of the grain barges coming down from Berkshire or Oxfordshire, making, no doubt, for Queenhithe. No one was rowing. They had hoisted a patched brown sail and allowed the favourable wind and the flow of the river to carry them slowly along. The helmsman was the only one in sight. He raised his hand in a salute to me, and I returned it. When the barge had gone past, I stepped down to the edge of the water and saw that ice was beginning to form along the bank. It was thin as yet. When I poked it with Rikki's stick it shattered into shards like glass, but it was a worrying sign. Ice in the river, and not yet December.

Further along, where the ground on my left dipped below river level and the road lay along a kind of causeway, the marshy land was pooled between clumps of rushes, and the pools were frozen hard, for here there was no river current to stir the water. Amidst all this ice and snow, I wondered where Matthew and the others had spent the night.

In the end, I walked almost to Lambeth and turned back reluctantly. I was half tempted to keep going into the country and forget the ordeal I must endure the next day, but long training in obedience to duty turned me back, however much I rebelled within. Just before I reached home, it began to snow again.

The walk had made us both hungry. Usually I ate little in the morning, but today, while I heated some left-over broth in a pot over my fire and set an egg and a piece of bacon to fry, I fed Rikki some of the scraps I bought every few days from the neighbourhood butcher. He gobbled them up as if he had not eaten for days. After my large breakfast I even sliced some stale bread and toasted it on a long-handled toasting fork before the last of my fire. I buttered it lavishly and wondered whether I was becoming a true Londoner. For reasons which are a complete mystery to me, born Londoners are called 'Cockneys' and 'eaters of buttered toast'. Why, I could not understand. Sometimes, even now, I find the English unfathomable.

Dr Nuñez had impressed on me that during the last day before the examination I must close my books and set them aside, so that my mind would be fresh and clear. I remembered that my father used to give the same advice to his students in Coimbra. Two such experienced men must know what was the best way to approach an examination, but it would be difficult to stop myself having a quick look at my books in the evening. However, I kept myself busy all day, which was not difficult, as we had two new births and six new admissions to the children's ward, all with winter chest infections. The woman Meg was still in a bad way, and I feared she might yet lose the baby, which I would try to prevent, however much she might wish it.

By the time I left the hospital in the early evening, I was tired. The lack of sleep the previous night was starting to tell on me and I began to think I would follow advice and avoid any more study. I arranged with Tom that I would bring Rikki to him very early the next morning, before I left for the College.

'Good luck to you, Dr Alvarez.' He gave me one of his gap-toothed grins. 'We hope all goes well, me and Swifty.'

The ancient wolfhound, hearing his name, opened his eyes and thumped his tail, but did not get up.

'I thank you both,' I said, returning his grin.

Outside the gatehouse I was surprised to find Simon.

'So,' I said, 'you have had your last performance at the Theatre.'

'Until the spring, Aye.'

He turned to walk with me away from the hospital.

'Now,' he said, 'as you have this terrible examination tomorrow, on every aspect of you medical knowledge, conducted *in Latin*, and as I am in the chinks for once, Master Burbage having paid us, I am going to treat you to a meal at the Lion. You shall eat well, but not heavily, and you shall drink a little good wine, but not heavily, then I shall escort you home, where you will go to your bed early.'

'You have become very dictatorial,' I said.

'As you are honorary physician and sometimes musician to Lord Strange's Men, I feel it is my duty to see that you do not disgrace us.'

'Very well,' I said with a laugh, 'but see that you do not spend all your chinks. You will need them to see you through the winter.'

'As for that,' he said airily, 'I shall be working all winter – for the first time ever, I may add – so I shall grow quite rich.'

'I never yet met a player who was rich.'

'Times change,' he said. 'Whatever you may say, we are become quite respectable. We are no longer wandering vagabonds. We have our permanent playhouses. We have our noble patrons. The Queen herself enjoys a good play, well acted. And some of our new playsmiths are giving us fresh works that are worth performing, not like some of the silly stuff we have had to mouth and play of old. You may not like Marlowe, but he is a fine poet. And this new fellow, Will, for all his country ways, is an excellent wordsmith.'

'Oh, I do not doubt that you players are rising in the world. When can we expect your knighthood? But I never yet knew a player who could keep two shillings in his purse from one day to the next. Spendthrifts, every one!'

With that he began to chase me toward the Lion, until he slipped on a patch of ice and went down hard, Rikki standing over him and barking loudly.

'It is all right, Rikki, he wasn't going to attack me.'

I stood over Simon, my hands on my hips.

'Are you hurt?'

'My bum hurts. Give me a hand.'

I hauled him to his feet. He stood, checking that each limb was intact.

'That was a near thing.'

I nodded. A broken or even a sprained limb would have put an end to his winter employment.

'Better be more careful on the ice. Would you like to take my arm?'

I offered my elbow solicitously, as if he were a delicate maiden.

'Very witty.' He examined his palm, which was slightly grazed. 'Come on, I'm even more in need of that supper.'

We continued on our way, but with more circumspection.

I supped well, but not heavily, and I drank a little good wine, but not heavily, then we walked home together. Although I went early to my bed, I tossed restlessly, unable to sleep for fear I should oversleep in the morning and fail to arrive at the College in time. Half in and half out of sleep, I found the much conned passages from Galen and Celsus dancing through my brain. Sometimes the words tumbled into nonsense and I sat up in bed, my heart pounding in panic.

At last I abandoned any attempt to sleep. I got up, dressed carefully with clean linen, and combed my hair. I realised I should have had my hair cut, but it was too late to think of that now. My stomach was churning too much for me to eat even a morsel. I carefully wrapped the College's books in their original thin leather and buckled them into my satchel, for on looking out of the window I could see that it was snowing again, the flakes driven slantwise across the pale beam of light shining out from my candle. Rikki stretched and yawned when I poked him awake, and we crept out of the house even earlier than the day before.

There was no lightening of the sky this morning, and by the thickening of the snow it appeared that it would be one of those days which remained almost as dark as night, clamped down under a heavy ceiling of cloud. Rikki and I slithered our way along to the hospital, and by the time we arrived my shoes and the bottom of my gown were caked with snow and more was crusting on my shoulders and cap.

The night watchman was just going off duty at St Thomas's and gave me a brusque nod.

'Tom's not astir yet,' he said.

At the gatekeeper's lodge I had to pound on the door to rouse Tom, who came at last, yawning till his jaw cracked. He took Rikki's lead and invited me in to thaw by the fire, but I shook my head.

'I am afraid of coming late to the College,' I said. 'It will be slow walking in the snow. It's already nearly a foot deep.'

Before I set off, I slipped into the hospital chapel for the dawn service, for it was Sunday, and today of all days I needed the comfort of prayer to see me through the anxious hours ahead. I was surprised that a Sunday had been chosen for the examination, but perhaps there were difficulties in bringing all these distinguished gentlemen together. As soon as the short service was over, I set off on the long walk.

Indeed the journey to Knightrider Street was a trial. The gate to the Bridge was not yet open, so I took a wherry across the river. The wherryman had to break a crusting of ice around his boat before he could set out, and break more ice on the far side before he could come alongside the landing place. I gave him a double fare for all his extra work, then made my way cautiously up the ice-covered steps at Old Swan Stairs. Walking through the streets of the City was even worse, plodding through the drifted snow, which no one had yet attempted to

74

clear, while more snow continued to drift down. By the time I reached Knightrider Street my hands, feet and face were frozen, but the rest of me was sweaty with exertion. I would not make a very pleasing spectacle for the President and censors.

That day passed in a strange blur of fierce questions fired at me, with no time to think, only the response of recited passages from the authorities. I seemed somehow to be outside myself, the answers proceeding from someone else's mouth, like an automaton, or one of the puppets I had watched at Bartholomew Fair. Two hours, I believe, was devoted to the first part, anatomy and physiology, or perhaps it was nearer three hours. I was then permitted a short break – or perhaps it was more for the benefit of the examiners – when I was given a pint of ale and a pie, and shown to the privy by a College servant.

I came back for the second session a little calmer. The different parts of my body had regained the same temperature and my heart was not pounding so fast. The examiners were stern and unbending, but seemed fair, and I felt I had acquitted myself well enough. The second examination was in pathology and disease. I must be careful here not to reveal any of my modern practices in diagnosis. Galen, I thought, only Galen.

Those hours passed also in a kind of trance, in which I imagined myself not in hospital confronted by patients, but sitting in my lodgings with the textbooks in front of me, so that I could read the answers off the printed page. Toward the end I was becoming very tired, for I was required to stand throughout, in one spot, facing the examiners in their cushioned armchairs across a wide table. My legs began to feel numb and I feared I might develop cramp.

Another break, and the final examination: therapeutics. There was a large window in the wall to my right, and out of the corner of my eye I had seen snow driving against it all day. By now it had begun to build up on the sill in a drift which rose almost halfway up the glass. There had been two candles on the table from the morning, the day was so dark, but before the third session started a servant lit sconces all along the walls. It gave the room a strangely theatrical look and I remembered what Guy had said, about an examination being like trying for a part in a play. Simon's advice was to think myself into the part, the part of a successful physician, like one of these distinguished men who filed in and took their places again.

I raised my chin. I would not look defiant, but I would not look humble either. I would be polite, dignified, but assured. And I would not breathe a word of Arabic medicine.

It was over at last, and my knees were nearly giving way beneath me. I was normally on my feet all day, but not locked into one position. The examiners closed their books and the President addressed me, switching, for the first time that day, to English.

'That concludes the examination for a licence to practice, Master Alvarez,' he said. 'We are aware that you have not attended university, but you come warmly recommended for your work by both Sir Francis Walsingham and the governors of St Bartholomew's. Your father, to whom you served as assistant, was highly respected. Lord Burghley himself has spoken to me of his skill. You have acquitted yourself well today, but we will need to deliberate on this, for we rarely license a physician without a university degree. I will write to you at St Thomas's when we have reached a decision.'

Then to my astonishment, all five of these distinguished doctors filed round the table and came to shake my hand and bow. When they had gone, I felt dizzy with relief. Outside, it was snowing hard. Hang it! I thought, I will take a wherry home.

A night trip by wherry on the river is always a strange, dreamlike experience, and tired as I was, both in body and mind, it seemed even stranger than usual. Once again the wherryman had to break his boat free of the ice, and as I sat there waiting for him to get underway, I began to shiver. I realised the room in the College had been very warm, with a huge fire burning and the walls hung with thick tapestries to keep out the cold, though I had scarcely noticed it at the time. Outside it was much colder than it had been even before dawn that morning. The scar on my left palm, where I had burned my hand a few months before, began to throb. My fatigue also drained me of warmth, so that my teeth were chattering before the man finally managed to pull his boat clear of the jetty. Out on the river, away from the shelter of the buildings, it was even colder. The wind had shifted to the east and blew straight upriver, bearing all the cold of the German Sea and the Baltic with it. The tide was also rising, so that the wherryman had to work hard, in the teeth of both wind and tide. At least he would be kept warm by his labours. I had half a mind to offer to take an oar, but he would not have been pleased.

Once we were out on the river, the black waters seemed to stretch out endlessly. I have noticed that when you are on the river, and especially at night, it seems much wider than it does from either bank, and by day. There was not much water traffic tonight, and we moved in our own small circle of light, cast by the lantern hanging from the top of the hoop that supported the tilt canvas. Within that circle, flecks of reflection danced on the water like silver pennies, but just a few feet away, beyond our light, all was black. I could not push away the thought that it would be a very easy thing for the boat to overturn. So far I had not seen any floating slabs of ice, but they were not unknown when the weather turned this cold. The snow continued to drift down, settling on the boat, but vanishing into the darkness of the river.

In the distance, closer to the Bridge, there were a few other lanterns showing from wherries, and warm candlelight shone from the windows of the houses lining the Bridge. Upriver, toward Westminster, I could make out a solitary boat, while along the Strand, the great houses of the rich showed a careless profusion of candles, though even their light reached only to the fringes of the river. A sudden burst of music flowed down toward us from one of these mansions, for sound carries well over water, and especially at night, it seems.

'Someone holding a ball,' the wherryman said, with a touch of sarcasm in his voice. 'All very well for them as don't have to work for their living.'

'Aye,' I said. 'Well enough for some. But why did we hear it suddenly, like that?'

'Some fool threw open a window, because they was too hot. Ha!' he said, looking down at his hands which were cracked and painful, as I could clearly see in the light of the lantern.

'I can give you a salve for that,' I said, pointing toward his hands. 'And you should wear gloves.'

'Can't grip the oars so well. Doctor, are you?'

'Aye, at St Thomas's.' I peered into my satchel. I should have a pot of the salve with me, I always carried it in winter – made of calendula and honey in a base of olive oil blended with beeswax.

'Here.' I set it on the boards at his feet. 'Rub that into your hands tonight, and then every time you go out on the river.'

'Not some fancy lady's stuff, is it? All perfume and no use?'

'Nay.' I laughed. 'Do I look like a ladies' physician? I prescribe it for the workmen we see at St Thomas's, out in all weathers like you. Builders and plasterers and draymen. It won't cure the problem completely, but it will help.'

He paused in his rowing and looked at me doubtfully. 'What's it cost, then?'

'Nothing to you, if you keep rowing and get me home out of this snow. I'll soon make up more at the hospital.'

'Right.' He grinned suddenly, which made him look a much younger man. 'Home it is! Pepper Alley Stairs, for the hospital?'

'Aye, I must collect my dog, then home to my lodgings.'

After that he put on a spurt of speed, and I turned my back on the fearful darkness of the river, looking ahead toward Pepper Alley Stairs, close to the south end of the Bridge. By the time I had paid him three times the normal fare – what with his struggles against wind and tide and ice – we were great friends.

'If I need more of this salve,' he said, 'can I get it at St Thomas's?'

I paused, perched precariously at the bottom of the slippery steps.

'Aye. Ask for Dr Alvarez.'

'God go with you, doctor, and I thank you.'

'God with you,' I said.

At the gatekeeper's lodge, Rikki greeted me as if I had been gone a month, and I was almost too tired to fend off his enthusiastic leaps. Tom fastened his lead and passed the end to me.

'Message came for you,' he said, 'from Master Thomas Phelippes at Seething Lane. Would you call there as soon as convenient.'

I ran a weary hand over my face.

'Tomorrow I shall be at Christ's Hospital, then in the wards the rest of the day. Was there a note?'

'Nay, just a lad brought the message. He only said "when convenient", he didn't say as you must rush there at once.'

I nodded. 'Well, I will go tomorrow, when I have finished here.'

'There was someone else looking for you.' Tom hesitated. 'Didn't much like the look of him, to tell the truth.'

'Who was that?'

'Didn't leave a name. Wanted the doctor who looked after the children. Big fellow. Workman, I'd say. Hands like – I dunno what. Like them claws on the end of the cranes, down at the docks.'

'I can't say I like the sound of that,' I said, with a weak laugh.

'Nor I. You be careful, walking home, doctor.'

'I will,' I promised. 'When was he here?'

'Oh, hours since. Not long after midday.'

'He'll be well away by now then. Besides, I have Rikki to guard me.'

'Aye, he's a grand fellow.'

I bade Tom goodnight and started on the last part of my journey home. It was not far, and the wind was now coming from behind me, but the snow found its way down the back of my neck and the wind tried to strip off my cap. Earlier someone had partially cleared the road, but it was filling up again with snow. Rikki and I ploughed our way grimly home. When I had left the College I thought I would want to discuss my day with Simon, but now all I wanted was a fire and bed.

Luckily, the fire caught quickly, I found myself some bread and cheese and draped my wet clothes over the furniture. It was almost too much effort to change into my night shift, but at last I was in bed, with Rikki curled up against my back. We warmed each other. Well, the examination was done, for good or ill. I could no longer affect the outcome. With that comforting thought, I soon fell asleep.

The next morning I looked out on a morning entirely white. Snow had transformed the City. Lying across the river it sparkled like some confection at a rich man's sugar banquet. The sky was clear of cloud and the sun was already casting shards of brilliant golden light horizontally up the river, for I had slept past dawn. Every roof and pinnacle of London glittered in the low slanting light, while the dozens of church spires thrust up from the cityscape like swords of glass. Away to the right, past the Bridge, the Tower stood like a giant square cake, every battlement sugared over. The ships anchored three or four deep between the Bridge and the Tower were sheathed in ice. If you approached them, you would hear their rigging chiming like bells on the harness of a drayman's horses. Almost opposite me, but a little to the left, Paul's Tower rose, squared off like a castle turret, for the spire destroyed by lightning had never been rebuilt.

Beautiful indeed it was, but when I stepped outside I could hardly draw breath, for it felt as though the very air would turn to ice in my lungs and make of me a frozen statue. For once Rikki seemed unwilling to come with me. I thought for a moment that I should leave him behind in my room, but it would soon be bitterly cold, once the fire had gone out. He would be much more comfortable and safe in Tom's lodge.

We walked to the hospital as quickly as possible over the frozen snow. At some time during the night it must have stopped snowing and then a hard crust of frozen snow had formed over the top of the softer snow beneath. It made walking treacherous, so that even in the short distance between my lodgings and the hospital I saw three men stumble and catapult forward into the snow.

Tom welcomed Rikki in, but barely opened his door, to keep the heat within doors.

'Don't expect no deliveries today,' he said through the narrow gap in the door. 'No carter would be fool enough in this weather.'

Up in the children's ward I found Mellie already dressed and waiting for me.

'We cannot leave yet,' I said. 'I must see to my patients in the lying-in ward first. And you cannot go out like that. Find Mistress Maynard and tell her that I say you must have some thick woollen stockings to wear over those you are wearing now. A sturdy pair of boots. She will show you how to oil them. A jacket to wear under your cloak. A thick cloak with a hood as well as a woollen cap. And gloves.'

Mellie stared at me.

I laughed at her expression. 'You have been snug in here, like a contented cat before the fire. Wait till you go outside. Then you will see why you need so many clothes. Are you quite sure you want to take Hannah? It is bitter cold for a young baby.'

She looked uncertain but stubborn. 'You promised. But I do not want her to come to harm.'

'Ask Mistress Maynard what she can give you for Hannah to wear. Then she must be wrapped in several shawls. And Mistress Maynard will show you how you may carry her strapped to your chest in another shawl, under your cloak.'

'I've seen women carry babies that way.'

'Aye, well, there's a knack to it. You won't want her to slip and fall, will you?'

'Nay,' she said, and ran off to find the governess of the nursing sisters. That should keep her occupied until I was ready to leave.

The patient giving me most concern in the lying-in ward was still Meg. She had developed a nasty uterine infection, no doubt caused by the dirty implements of the abortionist, and she was weak and feverish. She was a good deal more subdued than when she had first arrived. I instructed the senior nurse to bathe Meg's private parts with Coventry water in which healing herbs had been infused, then to apply a salve for which I gave her the list of ingredients, containing the same herbs. I could only hope that Meg's blood did not become tainted, spreading the infection throughout her body. I thought wryly that Galen, whom I had recited so meticulously the day before, would have recommended extensive bleeding to rid her of the fever, and some of the nursing sisters would expect me to prescribe it, but Meg was so weak already that I knew she would not survive bleeding. I had been given a fairly free hand in these two wards since I arrived, for St Thomas's was short of money and short of physicians, but these sisters had worked under my predecessor, the much loved but old fashioned Dr Colet. Whispers might get back to Superintendent Ailmer that I was not carrying out the correct procedures. I had better be proved right and bring this patient to a full recovery.

When at last I was finished with my patients, Mellie appeared at my side, looking about twice her normal size and as round as a barrel of beer. All being well, she should not suffer from the cold. The only bit of Hannah that could be seen was the tip of her nose. I lifted my own cloak down from its peg, fastened it firmly around my shoulders and threw the hood up over my cap. Mindful of how my scarred palm had ached yesterday, I also pulled on a pair of gloves.

'Very well,' I said, 'we are ready to start.'

The full effect of the cold did not strike us until we crossed out of the hospital gatehouse and the wind caught us. Although Mellie was so reluctant to hand her baby over to Christ's Hospital, I could see that she was excited by this adventure, crossing the Bridge for the first time in her life and venturing into the City. Had she not been so burdened with layers of clothes and the baby strapped to her chest, I do believe she would have skipped.

We did not speak as we crossed the Bridge, though Mellie dawdled from time to time, admiring the fine merchants' houses built on either side, especially the great Nonsuch House. I was thankful the cold weather had driven away the hucksters and acrobats, or I should probably never have managed to get her to the far end.

'I hadn't no idea it was so beautiful,' she breathed as we stepped off the Bridge, 'right next to Southwark, and I never knew.'

'Well, you will see many fine buildings as we walk through London, Mellie, but you must not linger, for Hannah will get cold, and we will be late for Mistress Wedderbury.'

'Oh, I won't stop,' she promised, and gave a skipping step to keep up with me, 'but I never saw the like!'

A little later she demanded, 'What is *that!*'

We had reached Cheapside. 'That is the Great Conduit,' I said. 'Water comes along underground channels from the north of London, and is piped to the conduit. Anyone may come and fetch water from it. Or pay for a water-carrier to fetch it for them. Like him.'

We watched as a man lowered his tapered water barrel off his back and began to fill it from the spout on the conduit.

'Don't you have to pay?'

'Nay, the water is free to all Londoners, but you must pay if you want someone to carry it for you.'

'I used to have to fetch buckets of water from the inn, where they had a well. A farthing a bucket, the cook had to pay. Heavy it was, too, and tasted funny.' She gave me a pleading look. 'Can I taste that?'

'Very well, but be quick.'

She picked up one of the tin cups chained to the edge of the bowl, having watched a woman drink from it, and was about to drink herself.

'Wait, Mellie!' I said. 'Wash the cup first, very carefully, before you drink.'

She looked at me as if I was mad, but humoured me, rinsing the cup before she drank.

'It's good,' she said. Then wonderingly, 'And it's *free!*'

'Come on,' I said, smiling and touched by her excitement, 'we must hurry.'

All the way along Cheapside she chattered as I had never heard her do before, admiring the stalls selling goods of every kind, lining both sides of the street, and – behind them – the tall houses of rich merchants. At one point she stopped and grabbed my arm.

'Oh, look, Dr Alvarez, how those lions on the front of that building shine like gold!'

'They are gold,' I said, 'that is Goldsmiths' Row, where the goldsmiths have their businesses.'

This was almost too much for her and rendered her speechless for at least two minutes. I found I was enjoying this odd tramp through the London streets. I was so accustomed to thinking of myself as an outsider, one of those whom the native Londoners called 'Strangers' or in my case (if like Marlowe they were being unkind) 'a Portingall', that it was strange indeed now to find myself the Londoner in the eyes of this Southwark child. I began to point out more of the sights to her, as if she were a visiting ambassador. When we reached St Paul's, she stopped dead again.

'That can't be St Paul's.' She shook her head in disbelief and looked at me accusingly when I named it. 'I've been seeing St Paul's all my life, across the river. This is much too big.'

'Biggest church in England,' I said. 'One of the biggest in the world. It looks smaller from Southwark because it's far away, and there are all these buildings in between.' I waved my arm in the direction of the close-packed buildings crowded on the slope down from St Paul's to the river. 'If we had more time, I'd take you inside, but we have a little further to go.'

We trudged on. The piled snow had slowed us all across London. Householders and shopkeepers were supposed to clear the area before their premises, but not everyone complied with the regulations of the Common Council, and those who did shovel away some of the snow often ended by throwing it in front of their neighbours, while some of the draymen and carters might clear a way for themselves on the road by casting the snow back toward the houses. Along the major streets of London there were posts erected in front of the buildings to prevent damage from passing vehicles, and this usually provided a safer passage for people on foot than walking in the roadway, but today it was blocked every few yards by heaps of snow. In the road the snow had been packed down by the vehicles driving to and fro, till it was slippery and stained with horse dropping. Neither way made for easy walking.

At last, however, we reached the Newgate area.

'That,' I said, pointing, 'is the gate in the old City wall called Newgate. Beyond it is St Bartholomew's Hospital, where I used to work, before I came to St Thomas's, and I lived nearby, in Duck Lane.'

'Was that like St Thomas's?' Mellie asked.

'Very like,' I said. I thought, but did not say, that it was very different too, working under my father. I missed the companionship of those days, and wondered how Peter Lambert was faring. I enjoyed the responsibility I was given at Thomas's, but there was much that I regretted losing.

'Now, *that*,' I pointed to the left, 'is Newgate Prison and the Sheriffs' courthouse, which I hope you may never seen inside. And *this*,' I gestured with my right hand, 'is where we are bound. Christ's Hospital.'

'It is very big,' she said in a small voice.

'That building is the church, just like any other parish church. Then there are the buildings where the children sleep and eat, and the school, and all the buildings to supply Christ's – bakehouse and brewhouse and dairy. There are two separate schools, one for the little children who are just learning to read and write, one for the older children, which is a grammar school, for learning mathematics and Latin and logic and grammar. And they study music and drawing as well. Those who do not attend the higher classes of the school may be taught a trade. Some are learning to make very beautiful tapestries.'

I realised that in my enthusiasm I was saying too much and confusing her. Hannah was not likely to be reading the Roman poets in grammar school, or learning to make tapestries for some years yet. I had been so taken with all that Christ's Hospital achieved that I let my tongue run away with me.

'We go in here,' I said, leading Mellie toward the gatehouse. 'Then we will go and seek out Mistress Wedderbury in her parlour. She will be able to show you around and explain everything to you.'

As we crossed the courtyard, a file of the older children crossed from the school to the refectory, as they had done on my previous visit. I tried to imagine how they would look in Mellie's eyes. They must seem as gaudy as those exotic birds brought from the Indies, like the parrots some of the seamen sold down on the docks, the boys in their long blue tunics trimmed with bright brass buttons, over canary yellow stockings, the girls in matching blue gowns, with a glimpse of yellow stocking showing as they walked.

'Who are those people?' Mellie whispered.

I saw that some of the children were stealing sideways glances at her. They must have wondered what she was doing here, for she was just too old to be one of the poor orphans for admission. In all her bundling of warm clothes they would not see Hannah, nor would they suppose that such a young girl could be the mother of Christ's child. But nay, some of these children could well have come from the dark alleys of London where such child mothers were not unknown.

'Those?' I said. 'Why, those are the boys and girls who live here. There never seem to be as many girls as boys, but you see that there are even some girls who attend the grammar school.'

'My Hannah would dress as fine as that?' She looked wistfully after the procession as it entered one of the large stone buildings, the one I took to be the old Greyfriars refectory.

'Aye, she would, when she comes to that age.' Some of the children must be of an age with Mellie. One or two of those boys might enter university and follow a profession in the church or law or medicine.

I turned to look at Mellie and saw that tears were running down her cheeks.

*

84

Chapter Seven

Mistress Wedderbury showed just how skilled she was from the moment we entered her parlour. She hugged Mellie, but carefully, because of the baby, took her cloak and made her sit down in a cushioned chair beside the fire to dry out her wet boots and skirts. Then she asked very hesitantly whether she might be allowed to hold baby Hannah – having taken the trouble to discovered to baby's name from me in advance, and even remembering it. If one considered the number of children for ever passing through her hands, it was quite a feat.

I retreated to a quiet seat by the window and watched her with amusement and admiration. She rang a small hand bell and a servant girl brought in a tray with spiced wine (very weak) and gingerbreads, just what would appeal to a girl of Mellie's age.

'As my hands are full with little Hannah,' she said, 'will you serve us all, my dear?'

Mellie sprang up at once and passed round pewter mugs of wine and plates of gingerbread. When she sat down again I saw that she did not fix Mistress Wedderbury with the anxious and jealous look she sometimes turned on the nursing sisters when they held Hannah. And when the matron asked her about how Hannah was feeding and how much she had grown since she was born, she talked eagerly and without any reserve.

'When we have finished our refreshments,' Mistress Wedderbury said, 'I will take you to see all of the children's quarters – the dormitories and refectory, and the hall where they can play when the weather is bad. We cannot disturb the lessons in the schoolrooms, but we might take a peep in the windows.'

'Dr Alvarez says that you have your own bakehouse and brewhouse.'

'Aye, we have. And a dairy and laundry. We even have our own tailor to make the children's uniforms.'

'I saw them. They are very beautiful.' Again that wistful look. Then she brightened. 'I can bake bread, and brew ale. And I can cook too. At . . . at my last place, I used to help the cook. She had troubles with her hands. They would swell up and get very stiff, so sometimes I had to do all the cooking.'

Mistress Wedderbury shot me a quick glance which I could not quite interpret.

When we had finished the refreshments, Mistress Wedderbury rose, still holding Hannah, who was asleep, curled into her shoulder.

'It seems a pity to take little Hannah out into the cold,' she said. 'I keep a cradle here.' She nodded toward a corner where I had not previously noticed a beautifully carved wooden cradle with brightly coloured blankets. 'Shall we leave her here in the warmth, while we look around? My girl Moll will keep a watch on her and call us if she wakes.'

I did not believe that Mellie would agree, but she hesitated only a moment. 'She will need feeding soon, but if we can be called . . .'

'She will find us at once, I promise you that.' Mistress Wedderbury tucked Hannah as carefully and gently into the handsome cradle as if she were her own child. Mellie gave the baby a quick glance, but seemed satisfied.

Our visit to the various part of Christ's was swift but thorough, taking in both the girls' and boys' dormitories, the refectory (where the dishes from the children's meal were being cleared away), the kitchens, and the church. We looked through the windows of the grammar school and of the petty school where the smallest children were conning their letters from horn books. Then, since Mellie seemed interested in the other outbuildings, we ventured into the heady warmth of the bakehouse and the sleepy malted scent of the brewhouse.

'It is not a washing day today,' Mistress Wedderbury said, 'though I can tell you that we have a great deal of washing!'

Seeing the huge laundry tubs and rows of buck baskets, I could imagine that washing for so many children, teachers, nurses and servants must be like caring for an entire regiment.

When we returned to the parlour, Hannah was just beginning to stir and whimper, so Mellie lifted her up to feed her. I thought how well the baby looked, who had been such a tiny scrap when she was born, and how skilled and motherly Mellie had become, despite her youth. Mistress Wedderbury was also watching her keenly. She glanced across at me as she had before, so that I wondered what was passing through her mind.

'So, Mellie,' she said, 'now that you have seen Christ's Hospital, what do you think of us?'

Mellie raised her face from the baby and looked back and forth between us, her eyes filled with distress. 'It is a beautiful place.' Her voice caught in a half-suppressed sob. 'I wish I might have come here when my family died. I was seven. Would you have taken me in?'

Mistress Wedderbury leaned forward and placed a plump hand on the girl's shoulder. 'Indeed we would, but that was the decision of the parish. They will more often place young girls in service. Boys are not so useful at that age!' She laughed and gave me a roguish look. 'That is why we always have more boys than girls. The founders felt there was need for more places for boys. But if your parish had come to us, then we would have taken you.'

Tears were running down Mellie's cheeks, at the thought of that lost happiness.

'I do not want Hannah to end as I did,' she whispered, 'but I cannot bear to give her up.'

'I know that it is very difficult, my dear, but how should you be able to find a new position, with a young baby? That will be difficult, nigh impossible.'

Mellie was crying in earnest now, and wiped her eyes on one of Hannah's shawls before laying her back in the cradle.

'What am I to do?' She looked at me imploringly. 'Dr Alvarez, what am I to do?'

There was something in the matron's look that prompted me to say, 'I think Mistress Wedderbury has something else she wants to tell us.'

The woman smiled broadly and sat back, planting her capable hands on her knees.

'Indeed I have. One of our kitchen maids has just left us to be wed, and at the moment we have not filled her position. I think, from all you have said, that you enjoy kitchen work, Mellie.'

The girl looked at her in amazement. 'You mean – I might work here? In the kitchens here? And keep Hannah?'

'Do not leap ahead too fast. First, you would need to prove to our senior cook that you are capable, and I warn you, he is a very demanding master. Second, there is the question of Hannah. It is our practice to send all the infants out to wet nurses in the country. This has been the policy of Christ's from its foundation, as it is felt that the clean air of the country is better and more nourishing for the little ones than the pestilential airs of London. So you might be required to send Hannah into the country until she is weaned.'

Mellie seized on that word 'might'. 'But I might be able to keep her with me? I understand that when you take in a foundling, of course there is no mother to feed the babe, so it must be put to a wet nurse, but I can feed Hannah myself, and no one can look after her so well as I.'

'But you would be working.'

'I could manage!' Mellie looked around, suddenly wild at the hope which seemed to be offered, only to be snatched away. 'Dr Alvarez, what do you say?'

Now I was caught on the proverbial horns of a dilemma. I wished Mistress Wedderbury had discussed this with me first, so that I might have been prepared.

'I cannot interfere with the practices of Christ's,' I said. 'I think you are being offered a wonderful chance. You will have work that you enjoy in a place where you will be safe.' I saw her understand what I meant. 'And whether Hannah goes to a wet nurse or stays with you, then you will provide for her in a way you could not on your own.'

She nodded, though her eyes were brimming again. My heart was wrenched. This was a hard ordeal for a girl so young.

'As for whether Hannah goes into the country for the first year or two of her life,' I said, 'that must be a decision made here.'

I caught Mistress Wedderbury's eye, and added, 'However, I do believe that a baby should be nursed by its own mother if possible.' I did not say – for fear of frightening Mellie – that I knew children put out to a wet nurse did not always survive.

The matron nodded, clearly satisfied with what I had said.

'If you wish to take the position, Mellie,' she said, 'we might make a trial of keeping Hannah here. I can make no promises. If it interferes with your work in the kitchens, she must go into the country, to one of our nurses, and she will return when she is weaned. But if we can make some arrangement to the satisfaction of all, especially our head cook, then she may stay here. On those terms, do you wish to take the position?'

Mellie gulped, looked at Hannah, looked at me. I smiled and gave a slight nod.

'Aye,' she said, 'I will take the position. And I thank you, Mistress Wedderbury.'

It had all happened much faster than I had expected. Instead of a simple visit to view Christ's Hospital, the day had turned into a great change in Mellie's life. When Mistress Wedderbury asked whether I considered Mellie sufficiently strong to undertake kitchen duties at once, I agreed that she should start, but only work half days for the first two weeks. That seemed to be satisfactory. Mellie would have a room in this same wing of the building as the matron, and because she would have the baby with her, at least at first, she would have a room to herself, to avoid disturbing the other girls when Hannah needed to be fed in the night.

Mellie seemed stunned at everything that was happening. I was somewhat stunned myself. Once everything was settled, and it was agreed that Mellie should remain at Christ's Hospital at once, I said I must be going.

'You stay here in the warm with the baby, Mellie,' Mistress Wedderbury said. 'I will see Dr Alvarez to the gate.'

Once we had descended the stairs to the courtyard, I turned to her.

'Did you have all this planned in advance? I wish you might have warned me.'

She began to walk briskly toward the gatehouse.

'I knew we should be needing a new kitchen maid and that the child had some experience, but I needed to look her over first. The more I saw of her, the better I liked her. She is well spoken, clean and tidy. She served the wine and gingerbread neatly – and jumped up to do so as soon as she was asked.'

'Ha!' I said. 'So that was a test!'

She smiled sweetly. 'She has a real interest in kitchen work, and if she can bake and brew, she will be an asset. But above all I watched her with the baby. I could not be a party to tearing those two apart. It is not one of our usual cases. The baby is not some poor unwanted scrap, left in a doorway. We may feed them and shelter them and school them, but the most important thing we can give these children is love. And Mellie is giving that child unbounded love.'

She paused, resting her palm on the stone of the gateway arch.

'Do you know, doctor, we had an interesting case here just a few weeks ago. We had apprenticed one of our boys to a carpenter. I remember when the lad first came to us. He wasn't a baby, but a dirty little beggar child of four. He didn't want to come, but one of the constables had found him being used by a villain of a vagrant who had broken his leg to make him a pitiful sight. The vagrant, who was no kin, was sent to Bridewell to be set to useful work, and the lad was brought to us. He screamed and fought. Didn't want to leave that filthy beggar, who was the only living soul he knew. Well, we had his leg set at Bart's and he lived here for seven years, till he was apprenticed, but it turned out his new master beat him and half starved him, so he ran away and came back here.'

She smiled.

'He clung to me, crying his heart out. Said he only wanted to come *home*. This was his home now, you see. Before he left us, he had not paid much heed to his schooling, he wanted an apprenticeship, but now he swore that he would work hard at his studies.'

'And has he?' I asked, fascinated by this tale.

'Aye, he's clever enough. All he lacked was application. The master of the grammar school has hopes he will now do well. But you see, the most important fact about this whole story is that here the lad had what he had nowhere else. Love.'

I nodded. 'I agree. We all need it, do we not? Not only the little children.'

It was beginning to snow again. 'Come,' I said, 'you must go within doors. Please send me word about Mellie and what is decided about Hannah. I will bring the other child, Ellyn Smith, in a few days' time.'

I bowed and we parted.

The snow grew heavier as I made my way back to St Thomas's, so that I was wet through and very cold by the time I arrived. I was also very hungry, for I had had no time for a meal. Fortunately I had not too much to occupy me for the rest of the afternoon, as I had remembered Phelippes's message, requesting me to call on him. Once I was finished for the day, I collected Rikki and headed back across the Bridge to Seething Lane. For the last few days I seemed to have spent all my time walking back and forth across the river.

Phelippes looked more worried than I had seen him since the months leading up to the Armada attack, more than a year before. He had lost weight and his eyes, behind his thick spectacles, were red from lack of sleep.

'Good, Kit,' he said, 'I am glad you could come.' Then he did something I had never known him do before. He rose from behind his desk and crossed the room to me. Taking both my hands in his, he gripped them. 'We are in a bad way here.'

'How is Sir Francis?' I asked, with a sinking heart, all too aware what must lie behind this.

'Ill. Very ill. I fear the service is beginning to fall apart.' He let go of my hands and wandered over to the window, while I took off my cloak, shaking it to rid it of snow, and hung it up. Rikki had lain down so close to the fire I was afraid he might singe his fur.

Phelippes removed his spectacles and pinched the bridge of his nose.

'I told you, last time you were here, that a number of our agents have disappeared. Simply slipped away. I very much fear what they may be about. For some men, loyalty to England and the Queen has little to do with their work as intelligencers. They are more concerned with who will pay the highest fee for information.'

'You do not really believe any would desert to the enemy.' I said. 'Do you?'

'I do not know, Kit. Even here in England–'

'What?'

'We both know that Sir Francis does not have much longer. When he goes, there will be a struggle between those who wish to step into his shoes.'

'You have some knowledge of this?'

He sighed and sat down at his table. 'I do not know whether they are true, these rumours that the Earl of Essex is courting the Lady Frances.'

'Ah,' I said, enlightened. 'You think he may hope, by marrying Sir Francis's daughter, that he may inherit Sir Francis's position.'

He nodded, looking at me blearily with his short-sighted eyes. He passed a hand over his face, then put his spectacles on again. His look sharpened at once.

'My lord of Essex is one contender.'

'He is still about the house?' I said. 'Still trying to search our papers?'

He gave a tight-lipped smile. 'It requires all my ingenuity to keep them from him.'

'One contender, you said. Who are the others?'

'The Cecils, certainly. Lord Burghley and his younger son, Sir Robert Cecil, who is become of late his right-hand man.'

'Of course,' I said slowly, 'but if it is a question of Sir Francis's official position, First Secretary to the Queen . . .' I looked over my shoulder, as if we might be overheard, though that was impossible. 'The Queen makes a great favourite of Essex, but surely she would never entrust him with affairs of state! Sir Francis and Lord Burghley have been her stalwart supporters throughout her reign. Essex could never replace one of them. Surely!'

'Lord Burghley is growing old and infirm,' Phelippes said. 'Sir Robert is cast in the same mould as his father – clever, and an astute judge of political affairs. But his physical infirmities . . . Her Majesty

91

has ever loved handsome men about her, and Sir Robert is a cripple. A man like Essex, handsome, vigorous . . . he despises Sir Robert.'

'Then he makes a foolish mistake. Perhaps a fatal mistake. But was it about this that you wanted to speak to me? Or do you need work with deciphering?'

'Nay. Sit down, Kit. There is little more than a thin trickle of despatches coming in, but there is something in particular. Word of fresh treason. And a case where I believe you can be of assistance.'

'You know that you may always rely on me,' I said, 'as long as I can be excused my duties at the hospital. What is this fresh treason?'

'It was Nick Berden who ferreted it out. You remember that he employs a gaggle of street boys and masterless men who bring him information and sometimes work with him to apprehend ill-doers?'

'Aye,' I said, rubbing my thumb over the burn scar on my palm. 'Nick has heard some whisper?'

'That is where his men serve him so well. They haunt the mean ale houses and drinking shops in the back streets, those that are frequented by idlers and vagabonds, runaway apprentices and masterless men. The scum of London. It is in such places that crimes are plotted – a man will slit you an enemy's throat for the price of enough beer to drink himself senseless, or a gang of house-breakers will plan an attack on a rich merchant's premises. And in such places, when men think themselves secure in dark corners, and drink has loosened their tongues, those loose tongues may blab more than they should. That is where the sharp ears of Nick's men come in.'

He drummed his fingers on the table.

'They have heard of another conspiracy against the Queen. A paid assassin this time, not some crazy Catholic priest, ready to die in the glory of killing Her Majesty, blessed by the Pope.'

His lip curled and I saw that he was clenching his fists.

'Nay, this time it is a paid killer sent by Philip of Spain.'

'Is that all you know?' I said, frowning. It was little enough to go on.

'There is more. The attack is planned for the Christmas season, it is said for Twelfth Night, when there are to be particularly extravagant entertainments for the Court at Whitehall Palace.'

I caught my breath. Simon's company would be at Whitehall for the Twelfth Night Revels.

'As far as Nick's man could ascertain (for he could not hear every word), the killer will go in the guise of an entertainer, but what kind of entertainer, that we do not know. He might be a player, a musician, an acrobat, a juggler, a trainer of performing animals . . . anything.'

'A puppeteer,' I said, remembering.

'Or a puppeteer. Although those you found at Bartholomew Fair have been despatched back to Italy.'

''Twas unfortunate they could not be prosecuted.'

'Unfortunate indeed, but they were under the protection of their ambassador, and pleaded that the puppet used for the explosion was stolen from them. The Queen decided to let them go, rather than cause a rupture with the ambassador.'

I nodded. 'I know. It was still unfortunate. But why do you think I can be of particular use in this present case?'

'You know that group of mo . . . players, do you not? The company that plays out at the Theatre in Shoreditch?'

I pressed my lips together. He had very nearly said 'mountebanks' instead of players. 'I know Lord Strange's Men,' I said, somewhat stiffly.

'That is what I thought. And they are to perform at the palace on Twelfth Night.'

Was there nothing that was unknown, here in Seething Lane? From time to time it made me very uneasy. Could it be that Nick's unsavoury crew of men were watching me as well? Sometimes it felt as though every London street was full of watchers.

'Aye,' I said, 'I understand that they are to perform then, but have not decided on the piece.'

'Until we know more, there is not a great deal we can do. Nick's men will be listening out for anything further. I want to catch the fellow before ever he goes to Whitehall, but if we fail in that, I will be arranging for Nick to be present in some capacity or other, and also a few of the most reliable of his men. I want you to do two things.'

'Aye?'

'First, see whether you can discover anything by asking questions – discreetly – of your friends. What other entertainers will be there. Are any known to them. Any foreigners. Any thing out of the ordinary.'

He paused. 'Of course, it might not be a foreigner. It could be a treasonable Englishman. Not a priest, as far as we can tell, but a trained assassin.'

'If it is a trained assassin,' I said slowly, 'he will not be looking for a glorious martyr's death, like others we have encountered. He will hope to do the deed, but escape unharmed. That will make him subtle, experienced, all the more difficult to detect and arrest.'

'It will.'

'I can try to get what information the players may have, but it may be that they will know little of the other entertainers. They do not move in the same circles as acrobats and sword swallowers.'

I spoke crisply, and he had the grace to look apologetic.

'You said there were two things you wanted me to do.'

'I want you to be in Whitehall Palace on Twelfth Night,' he said, 'mingling with the players, keeping your eyes and ears open. It will be easier for you than for Nick, as you are known to these players. Can you do that?'

'I suppose I might,' I said reluctantly. Why did everyone seem to conspire to force me into an appearance with the players? 'I might be able to help with the costumes, or checking the properties, but they have their own men to do that.'

He waved his hand, brushing aside this objection.

'In addition, of course,' he said, 'should there be any kind of accident, it would be convenient to have a physician on hand.'

'Indeed,' I said dryly.

The sort of injury inflicted by a professional assassin was likely to be well beyond any physician's competence, not just mine. 'I will be sure to carry my satchel of medical supplies.'

'Aye, do that.'

If he noticed the irony in my voice, he ignored it.

'Good. That is all I can tell you for the moment. We have about six weeks until Twelfth Night, so I hope we may learn more, and catch this rogue long before. I will send you word of anything Nick manages to discover, and I would like you to call in here once a week.'

I glanced at the table where I worked at code-breaking. How peaceful those very early days now seemed, when all I was required to do was puzzle out some new cipher, or translate a despatch written in French or Spanish. I was not quite sure how I had come to be much more active as an agent. Somehow Walsingham and Phelippes between them had slipped me gradually into a different role.

Just as I was getting up to leave, Arthur Gregory came in, bearing with him not only snow on his shoulders and boots, but a very blast of icy air which seemed to emanate from his clothes. His cheeks and nose were red with the cold, despite a scarf which he had wound high around his neck.

'Ah, good day to you, Kit,' he said, beaming. 'I feared I might miss you.'

'I was just leaving.'

'I have been out buying fresh wax for the seals. Had to tramp all round Stationers' Row before I could find all the kinds I needed.'

Arthur was meticulous in his work and always took care to match the wax of his replacement seals on enemy despatches to the original wax. Until I came to work at Seething Lane I had not realised that there could be so many shades and textures of sealing wax. They all looked the same to me.

He set down his parcels and unwound his scarf.

'So, Kit, and how did you fare in the examinations yesterday? Have you recounted everything already to Master Phelippes?'

Out of the corner of my eye, I saw Phelippes give a guilty start. He had quite forgotten my examinations, I knew. He was like a hunting dog on the scent, his nose always down following some trail or other, not to be diverted by other issues.

'I think it went quite well,' I said. 'At least I managed to answer all the questions they asked me, but they have not made a decision yet. I think they do not like that I have not attended a university.'

Arthur shook his head and Phelippes grunted. As far as I knew, neither of them were university men. Arthur had been a journeyman engraver, making plates for the illustrations of printed books, before Walsingham had employed him to carve forged seals. Phelippes was more of a mystery to me. He was a clever man, fluent in several languages and certainly a gifted code-breaker, but I knew nothing of his earlier life. He kept such matters to himself.

'Well,' said Arthur, 'the College would be foolish indeed not to give you a licence. Everyone knows you for an excellent physician.'

'There will be no speaking to you, Kit, when you are a full physician,' Phelippes said. 'We must pull off our caps to you.'

I grinned at him. It was rare indeed for him to tease anyone.

I had donned my cloak and Rikki was getting reluctantly to his feet, when Francis Mylles, Walsingham's chief secretary came in.

'Here is another,' said Arthur, 'who is becoming too grand for present company.'

'Oh?' I said. 'And what has Francis done?'

'Bought a manor house from Sir Francis,' Arthur said.

I stared at Mylles in astonishment, for I would never have supposed that he was rich enough to aspire to owning a manor house. Moreover, why would Walsingham wish to sell it?

'Francis?' I said. 'Can this be true?'

Mylles looked embarrassed and made some little business of setting down the pile of papers he was carrying on to Phelippes's table before he answered.

'Aye, it is true, Kit. Sir Francis wished to sell off some of his smaller properties and asked if I might care to buy one. He has sold a few he no longer wants to hold and charged me a very reasonable price. Said it might serve partly as a pension, after so many years' service with him.'

He looked suddenly very sad.

I sat down again and stared down at my clasped hands. So that was the way of it.

'He is disburdening himself of landed property,' I said, 'and turning it into coin.'

Phelippes took off his spectacles and polished them on his handkerchief.

'Aye. I think he wishes to set his affairs in order, so that Dame Ursula and Lady Sidney are not burdened with too extensive a holding in land. With coin he can provide annuities for them.'

I nodded. 'I am glad you were able to buy the manor, Francis. He would be glad that the land and the people of the manor would come into the hands of a man he has known and trusted for so many years.'

Indeed, I meant what I said, though I found it difficult to imagine the quiet secretary as the lord of a manor. But such are the changes of our times. Men born quite humble may rise to any height. Yet the thought of Walsingham meticulously preparing for his death cast a dark cloud over me.

As I turned from the Seething Lane house in the direction of the Bridge, I almost collided with a man walking in the opposite direction. As we bowed and apologised, I realised that it was Edwin Alchester.

'Good e'en, Master Alchester,' I said.

'And to you, Dr Alvarez.' I saw that he was looking over my shoulder, and must have realised where I had come from. 'Is not that the home of Sir Francis Walsingham?'

'It is,' I said, with a slight sinking of my heart. Would he now connect Walsingham with my brief period in the Fitzgerald house, and deduce that I had been sent there to spy on them?

'You will remember,' I said, somewhat hastily, 'that I have an interest in mathematics. Sometimes I am called upon to help with the decipherment of codes for Sir Francis. I first began it as a game with my mathematics tutor, Master Harriot, and sometimes Sir Francis finds me useful.'

I realised I was talking too much, and I remembered that I had seen Poley arrive surreptitiously at the Fitzgerald house while I was there. Poley knew very well that I worked for Walsingham. Could he have mentioned it to the Fitzgeralds?

However, Alchester showed no sign that he was disturbed by my connection with Walsingham and walked a short way with me, talking pleasantly of London and all that the family had been doing. The matter of Cecilia's dowry in lands and coin had been settled, and Sir Damian's lawyers had confirmed that the wardship of Sophia Makepeace was flawless. The distant cousin could have no claim on the inheritance while she lived.

'It seems we shall remain in London until after the Christmas season,' he said. 'Sir Damian and Lady Bridget have been attending Court and are invited to some of the Christmas festivities at Whitehall Palace. Usually we live quietly in the country, even at Christmas, so it will be a pleasant entertainment for the family. Cecilia and her new husband will return to London for the season, and young Master Edward will have a holiday from his school.'

Festivities at Whitehall again, I thought. I seemed to be haunted by it. The thought crossed my mind – though I immediately dismissed it – that Sir Damian, as a Catholic, might somehow be implicated in the plot Nicholas Berden had discovered. It was too fanciful an idea. Sir Damian, as far as we knew, had never been involved in any violence. He had merely allowed his house, briefly, to be used as a conduit for letters to the French embassy. Moreover, if it was true that he had ambitions for Edward to attend university, then he must conform to the English Church. Any reckless action now would destroy Edward's prospects for ever. I had not known the Fitzgeralds well, but I believed that their strongest allegiance was to family rather than to faith, or they would not have allowed their children to be educated by an Anglican vicar.

'It is not long until Christmas now,' I said. 'You will find that London celebrates Christ's Nativity with all kinds of festivities, not only at Whitehall.'

He laughed. 'Well, I shall certainly not be attending Whitehall!'

'Let us meet and dine,' I said, feeling somewhat sorry for his loneliness away from everyone he knew down in Surrey. 'Some time next week? Send me a note at St Thomas's. If you have no objection to such company, I will introduce you to friends of mine who are members of Lord Strange's Men. There are some fine musicians and poets amongst them.'

He looked a little startled at the suggestion of such rakish company, but he rallied, saying that it would be an honour. Wednesday, he thought, he could be free of duties, but he would send a message to confirm.

We parted at the entrance to the Bridge, he turning back to continue into the City, where, he said, the Fitzgeralds owned a town house near Goldsmith's Row in Cheapside. I must have passed it with Mellie that morning. My walk with her through London now seemed a week away. I whistled to Rikki, who was investigating something indescribable in the gutter, and we set out once more across the Bridge.

My day had been so full that it was only then that I remembered that in two days' time Kit Marlowe was to stand trial for his part in the killing of a man back in September. If he was guilty, he might hang. And if that were the case, my friends amongst the players would have little heart for entertaining the Fitzgeralds' steward. Simon believed Marlowe would be exonerated, claiming he and his friend Thomas Watson had acted in self defence, but sometimes Simon was apt to be too optimistic, in particular where Marlowe was concerned.

Well, there was nothing I could do to affect the outcome. All I wanted now was to reach home, out of the snow and wind. I could see that Rikki felt the same. Near the southern end, Nonsuch House is built across the whole width of the Bridge, with a roadway like a tunnel running through it to allow the passage of people and vehicles. It can be very dark on a dull day, particularly at that hour, as now, when the sun is setting but the Nonsuch household has not yet lit the torches in the sconces along the walls. In broad daylight I never give the tunnel a second thought, but the feeling that I had experienced in recent days, that I was being followed, had made me nervous, so that I quickened my step, and Rikki trotted to keep up with me. There were few people about. Those in work had gone home for the night, while the cold weather had driven away the performers and hucksters as soon as the crowds thinned. Yet, unmistakably, I heard the echo of footsteps behind me in the tunnel.

By the time I reached the Great Stone Gate, I could feel a trickle of sweat down my back, despite the cutting wind and the snow, which continued to fall, though not so heavily. It occurred to me that I would only have heard following footsteps in the tunnel, which was clear of snow. Outside they would be muffled. I bade a cheerful good-night to the guards on the gate, who knew me well by sight. They shouted a greeting back, which I hoped would be heard by my pursuer, if there *was* a pursuer, and not just some phantasm conjured up by I knew not what nervousness.

It was quite a short walk to my lodgings once I was out of ear-shot of the guards, who might have provided some assistance should I need it. I wished I was wearing my sword. I did not normally wear it to the hospital and I had not thought to take it with me on either of my trips into the City today. I felt for my father's dagger, which I always wore at my belt, and loosened it in its sheath.

I was almost home when the attack came.

I did not hear him so much as sense a sudden swift movement behind me. Or perhaps there was a shift in the pattern of light and shadow cast by the torches burning on either side of the door to the neighbouring whorehouse. Whatever it was, I whirled round, drawing my dagger, just as the man leapt toward me and made a grab for my arm.

It was the same heavy built workman I had seen before, following behind me when I last walked up to Bishopsgate.

'I'm armed,' I shouted, breaking away. 'Keep your distance.'

Rikki jumped in front of me, snarling. The man hesitated. In the light from the torch I could see the shine of the dog's teeth as his lip lifted. He had saved me once before, in the Low Countries, and taken a sword slash for it. I prayed this man did not wear a sword. One of his degree would not be permitted by law to carry one, but that does not stop the lawless.

All I could see in his hand was a dagger like mine.

'What do you want?' I said. I could not stop myself sounding breathless. 'I carry no coin. This satchel contains nothing but medicines, the tools of my trade.'

'I know who you are,' he spat out. 'And what you are. A doctor at St Thomas's where you are holding my daughter. She's a useless wench, but she belongs to me, and I want her back.'

Understanding broke. This great rogue could easily be an out-of-work blacksmith. It was also the man Tom Read had described, with hands looking like the grabs on the end of the cranes at the docks. I could see them now. He could probably do me far more damage with those hands than with a dagger. This must be the father of Ellyn Smith, and with those brutal hands he had torn out her teeth. Well, he was never going to do it again, if I could help it. I would try pretending innocence.

'I am not sure I understand you.' I tried to make my voice polite, and to suppress the tremor which ran through my whole body. 'There are many sick children in the hospital, but the admissions and departures are none of my affair. Those are handled by the almoner and the superintendent. My duties are confined to the sick in the wards.'

For a moment he looked uncertain. Then he glared at me.

'Ellyn Smith, that's my daughter. Weeks, she's been in there. I want her back.'

'Oh, it is Ellyn, you are talking about.' I thought if I could keep him speaking long enough, he might calm down, or I might manage to sidle into the whorehouse for help. 'Ellyn has been a very sick child. We thought it might be the consumption, with her infected lungs, and spitting blood. She was very weak. It took a long time for her to begin to recover, she was so undernourished.' I thought he might not understand the word. 'She looked as though she had eaten little for many weeks.'

'Poor men cannot feed their families.'

I did not like his tone, which was a kind of aggressive whine. What he said was hardly borne out by his own robust build. Still, it is common enough in some families for the man to eat all the meat, while the woman and children must make do with nothing but black bread.

'But surely Ellyn has no family,' I said artlessly. 'She was left abandoned on the hospital doorstep. If you are indeed her father, why did you not come with her? Why have we seen nothing of you, all this time she has been lying so ill?' I feared I was baiting him. I must be careful.

He made another sudden movement toward me, his arm rising convulsively, thrusting the dagger toward me, but not quite touching me. I raised my own dagger, to show I was not afraid to use it. Rikki's snarl rose in pitch and he began to bark loudly. The man hesitated, looking from the dog to me.

'He is trained to fight,' I said.

A look of fear showed in his eyes and I smiled. 'He has taken on three men armed with swords before now.' This was a slight exaggeration, but near enough the truth. One of the men had only had a dagger. 'He will not hesitate to tear your throat out. His coat is very thick. Do not think you can do him much harm with that little table knife of yours. You are one against two.'

I watched the conflict in his eyes. He was a big man, surely accustomed to winning most fights, but even big men are afraid of large dogs like Rikki when they display the considerable size of their bared teeth. Rikki was heavily muscled and looked larger than ever with the fur on his neck standing up. On my own, I might seem an easy target, but the man had not managed to take me unawares, and I had the dog. I was armed. I was clearly fit and strong. And I must be half his age. Moreover, from certain smells that reached me as he breathed heavily, he had been drinking. He would not be quick on his feet.

As he paused, Rikki's growl rose to a high pitch, and he barked again. Behind me, I heard a window thrown open. There was a shout, and another from the whorehouse. The man took one step back. Rikki took a step forward, and I followed him.

Then several things happened at once. From the house behind me someone shouted, 'Shut that noise! I'm sending for the Watch.'

The door of the whorehouse was flung open, casting a flood of light across the three of us.

The man took another step back and his feet shot from beneath him on the ice, so that he fell backward into the snow piled up at the side of the door.

A large woman surged forward from the door, bearing a large piss pot, which she flung over the sprawling form of the blacksmith. Bessie Travis, in the full glory of her working clothes, trimmed with scarlet feathers and false fur, her face whitened with lead and her lips painted in a terrifying scarlet grin.

'Saw you through the window, doctor,' she said. 'Thought you could do with some help.' She shook the last dregs from the piss pot over the blacksmith, who was swearing worse than any soldier I had ever known, threatening vengeance, and trying to scramble to his feet, despite the slipperiness of the ice.

By now quite a crowd had gathered – lodgers from the neighbouring house, including several men I recognised from the building works near the bear garden, half a dozen whores and their clients, and a few passers-by who had been drawn by the noise.

Rikki was sniffing the stained snow as the blacksmith scrambled away into the dark.

'Thank you, Bessie,' I said. 'That was timely and appropriate.'

She gave a great raucous laugh. 'I enjoyed that. Bothering you was he?'

'He's a nasty piece of work,' I said. 'I hope he doesn't come back and make trouble for you.'

'I eat rogues like that for breakfast,' she said. 'Oh, look! He's dropped his wee penknife.' She picked up the blacksmith's dagger and tucked it into her belt. I feared it might shear through her flimsy robe – if one could call anything so transparent a robe.

'Show's over, my dears,' she called to the crowd. 'But there's a warm welcome inside.'

Some of the men shambled off, others laughed and slipped through the door.

'And won't you come in, my duck?' she said to me. 'I've some pretty young girls. Good clean girls.'

I shook my head. 'Thank you for the offer, Bessie, but I've had a long day. Rikki and I just want to go home.'

She flung a heavy arm around my shoulders and bussed me on the mouth. 'Another time, then, my duck.' And followed her clients indoors.

By the time I reached home, I was half shaking, half laughing. It was likely I had had a narrow escape, but the vision of Bessie emptying the piss pot over the blacksmith would stay with me forever. I had probably also had a fairly narrow escape from being dragged bodily into the bawdy house, which would soon have put an end to my masquerade. I could still taste Bessie, a mixture of strong beer, some sickly lip paint, and – could it be? – tobacco? Did Bessie smoke a pipe? Nothing would surprise me.

I leaned back against the closed door of the building and began to laugh.

'Kit?'

It was Simon, leaning over the stairs, his face, lit below from a candle, looking anxious.

'Has something happen? Is something amiss? You sound hysterical.'

I started up the stairs, snorting a little as I tried to suppress my laughter, which was getting somewhat out of hand.

'Nothing is amiss,' I said, as I reached him, 'but aye, you could say something has happened. Invite me in for a bite and a sup, and I will tell you of a mighty contest.'

Once we were inside his room, he looked me up and down quizzically. Rikki was pacing about restlessly, his ruff of fur still standing up about his neck.

'Will you stop waving that dagger about?' Simon said. 'If it is all the same to you, I should like to keep my nose intact. A small thing, I know, but we players have our little vanities.'

I had not realised I still had my dagger in my hand. I sheathed it and hung up my wet cloak, then I took off my boots and set them beside the good fire Simon had lit on his hearth. Rikki was calmer now that he was in familiar territory and stretched out in his favourite place before the flames.

'Will a sausage or two suffice?' Simon asked. 'Fresh today from that butcher over near St Thomas's. I believe his meat is clean. Cut us some bread. It is in the cupboard.'

As a result of my urging, Simon had bought himself a hanging cupboard like mine in which to keep his food and had the grace to admit that he was now less troubled with mice. I fetched the loaf, which was reasonably fresh, and a chunk of hard cheese.

'Can you make us some spiced wine?' I said. 'I seem to have spent much of the day out in the snow and I am frozen, blood and bone.'

Simon was threading the sausages on to a toasting fork and shook his head. 'I've no wine, but I do have the spices you gave me. Will spiced ale suit you instead?'

'Aye. Anything to drink, as long as it is hot and spiced.'

We soon had our meal assembled, which we ate off our knees. I now had a table and two chairs in my room, so that I could entertain a friend to a meal sitting in a civilised fashion, but Simon had progressed only a little since I had once visited him in the rooms he shared with Christopher Haigh up in Shoreditch. At least now he did not allow his dirty dishes to accumulate more than a day or two.

'So,' he said, his food finished and his warm ale pot cupped between his hands, 'what is it that has been happening? I have not even seen you since you took your examinations. Did they go well? I thought you would come and tell me this morning, before you went to the hospital.'

'You were abed and snoring,' I said. 'As usual. They went well enough, but the lords of physic still need to sit in judgement on me, a mere Portuguese and a physician without a university degree.'

'Come,' he said, 'you have lived in England almost as long as in Portugal.'

'Not quite.'

'Well, I think of you as English.'

I looked down into my ale pot. It was perhaps the most heartening thing he had ever said to me.

'When will you know their verdict?'

'They did not say, only that the President would write to me.'

'But that was yesterday. What has happened today to make you wield a dagger, yet laugh like a Bedlam fool?'

So I told him first of my visit to Christ's Hospital and what had happened there, then my summons to Seething Lane, though I did not, for the moment, mention the Twelfth Night festivities. I would need to think out my best approach, and I was too tired tonight.

'Do you remember how I once had to play the part of a tutor to two children in a Catholic household, down in Surrey?

'Aye, I remember. I told you to play it like a part on stage.'

'Well, I ran into the Fitzgeralds' steward, Edwin Alchester, as I was coming home this evening. It is the second time I have seen him. The family is in London for the winter.'

'Was that risky?'

'I do not think so. I always liked the man. He saw me coming from Walsingham's house, so, to account for it, I reminded him about my interest in mathematics and said I sometimes helped with some deciphering.'

'He did not guess that you sometimes do . . . other things for Sir Francis?'

'Nay, it did not seem so. I promised to dine with him next week. I thought I would introduce him to some of Lord Strange's Men. He is lonely in London, poor fellow.'

Simon raised his eyebrows, looking at me over the rim of his ale pot. 'Will he not think us the verriest vagabonds? Him a steward to a respectable family?'

I smiled. 'I think not, as long as you are on your best behaviour.'

I finished my ale and set down the pot on the floor. Simon refilled it from the pan, splashing a little on the floor boards. Rikki opened his eyes, but decided it was not worth getting up for.

'Then,' I said, 'after I reached Southwark and was nearly home, I was attacked by a huge blacksmith with a dagger, who is the brutish father of one of my patients.'

Simon leaned forward, frowning. 'So that is why you were waving your dagger about! Christ's bones, Kit, surely that was nothing to laugh about!'

'I was rescued, and saved from having to fight for my life, by an Amazon in dyed feathers and war paint, armed with a full piss pot. As a reward, I was then nearly abducted into the bawdy house.'

I began to laugh again, until Simon shook me by the shoulders and demanded the full story. I gave it to him, in all its colourful details, until we were both laughing so much our sides ached.

'Thank you for the meal,' I said. 'I must go to bed now and think how I am to convey little Ellyn Smith to Christ's Hospital without that brute seizing her and carrying her off. It must be tomorrow, to be sure of escaping her father.'

'Perhaps we can help,' he said, as he lit me a candle to carry up to my door. 'Create a little distraction while you get her on board a wherry.'

'Aye, a wherry, that would be the best way. Give you good night, Simon.'

'And you. Best be careful passing the whorehouse tomorrow morning.'

'Never fear,' I said. 'At the time I go to my work they will be like you, snoring in their warm beds.'

He punched me lightly on the shoulder and I ran up the stairs, sheltering the candle flame with my cupped hand.

The following morning I slipped a note under Simon's door on my way downstairs. I had been giving much thought to the problem of taking Ellyn all the way to Christ's Hospital. Simon was right. The safest way would be by wherry. It is not so easy to be followed and attacked in a wherry as on the street. Also, now that the blacksmith had shown his hand, he might try to abduct his daughter from St Thomas's. He had probably spent the money he had got from selling two of her teeth and saw her as the source of further funds. As Superintendent Ailmer had pointed out, in law Ellyn was her father's property and we might be on shaky ground if we did not hand her back to him. Before, when there had been no sign of any family, she could be regarded as an orphan and therefore rightfully a suitable child for Christ's. On the other hand, the hospital's founding principles had been to provide a home for orphans, foundlings, and the children of poor men who could not support them. The blacksmith had said he could not feed his family. Would that be evidence enough that he could not support his daughter? Certainly the child had come to us as thin as a starveling bird in winter.

In my note I asked Simon whether he and some of the others from the playhouse could help me smuggle the child out of the hospital and on to a wherry that very afternoon. The sooner she was safe in Christ's, the better. Also, I realised that the next day was set for Marlowe's trial, and many of the players would want to attend. It must be done today, to be sure of removing Ellyn from the danger of being seized by her father, so I asked Simon to meet me at the gatehouse at noon.

All that morning I found myself looking over my shoulder, fearful that the blacksmith might break into the children's ward, even though I had warned Tom Read and several of the hospital servants to detain him if he tried to enter the hospital. I had also spoken to Superintendent Ailmer and gained his permission to remove Ellyn to

Christ's. As the circumstances had changed since we had discussed Ellyn before, I told him of the father's attempt to attack me the previous night. The tale of the vengeful whore with a piss pot even raised a smile on that austere face.

'I think we may claim that we are acting in the best interests of the child,' he said, after a few moments' consideration. 'If you can convey the child to Christ's Hospital, she will be safe from interference there. And if the man makes threats against you again, or tries to invoke the law on his behalf, refer him to me.'

I thanked him with a solemn face, but wondered exactly how I could refer a large, angry, dagger-wielding man to Ailmer, and how he proposed to protect me in such a situation.

The other person whose help I needed was Mistress Maynard.

'I will be taking Ellyn out of the hospital at midday,' I said, 'and a group of friends will help me to get her on to a wherry, but it would be best if we could make her look as little like herself as possible, in case the blacksmith is lying in wait, hoping to seize her.'

'We need to conceal that red hair of hers,' she said. 'I will braid it up on top of her head myself, and find a large cap to cover it. That foxy hair is the most noticeable thing about her.'

'I agree.'

'I wonder–' she fiddled with the bunch of keys at her waist. 'Perhaps she would be even safer if we dressed her in boy's clothes, just until you reach Christ's. A tunic and long hose, her hair hidden under a cap, a coarse cloak. She could pass for one of the pauper lads we have through here every week.'

'Do you not think they would be shocked, at Christ's?' I thought how bizarre this whole adventure was becoming. My own disguise had started in the same way, as an attempt to divert our gaolers from the knowledge that I was a girl.

'I know Mistress Wedderbury,' she said comfortably. 'It would take more than this to shock her. I will make up a bundle of girl's clothes that Ellyn may carry with her, so that she may change as soon as she is safely within the walls of Christ's.'

'In that case,' I said, 'I think it is an excellent idea.'

'Could you send her to me, Dr Alvarez, as soon as you visit the ward?'

I nodded. These formidable women! I could easily imagine Mistress Maynard herself stepping in to tackle the blacksmith, though she might wield some other weapon than a piss pot.

Before returning to my work, I found one of the boys who ran errands for the hospital and gave him a note to take to Mistress

Wedderbury at Christ's, saying that I would be bringing Ellyn that afternoon. Once in the children's ward, I told Ellyn to go to Mistress Maynard's room, and explained that I would be taking her to Christ's at midday. I made no mention of her father, for I did not want to frighten her.

Her small face brightened at once. The swelling cause by the tooth-pulling had gone down. Once she was able to eat solid food again, she had begun to put on a little weight, though I suspected she would always be slight. She had a fine dusting of freckles over her nose, almost invisible, but her hair, now that it was washed and combed and trimmed neatly, fell over her shoulders in a rippling wave of glorious red. She was as foxy-haired as the Queen herself.

'Shall I see Mellie at this place?' she asked.

I had not realised that she knew Mellie. Although the two wards were adjacent, the patients rarely mixed. But of course Mellie had been helping the nursing sisters before she left and might well have come into the children's ward. Ellyn was close to her in age, unlike the other mothers in the lying-in ward. It was not surprising that the two girls had become friends.

'Aye,' I said. 'Mellie is working there now, as a kitchen maid, and for the moment she has the baby with her.'

'Good,' Ellyn said. 'That is as it should be, if a mother loves her child.'

She looked down at her feet and I wondered what thoughts were passing through her head about her own mother.

'Quickly now,' I said gently. 'Mistress Maynard will be waiting. I will come for you at midday sharp, and you must be ready.'

She ran off. My strictures were quite unnecessary, for it was several hours till midday, but I knew that if the blacksmith did manage to get into the hospital, he would come to this ward, but would be unlikely to find Ellyn if she was with Mistress Maynard.

By noon my fears about the blacksmith had not been realised. I hoped that after his humiliation last night he had taken himself off to one of the sleazy ale houses in the back alleys of Southwark and had there downed so much drink that he was still sleeping it off. However, I could be sure of nothing. The blacksmith might be waiting even now, just outside the hospital gate. Had Simon been able to act on my note? All the players were late risers, especially when they had no performance at two o' the clock. The previous evening Simon had mentioned that they were still busy adapting the Cross Keys to serve as a winter playhouse and would not stage a performance until the following week. This temporary holiday might make it difficult to gather up the players to meet me.

Prompt at midday I went to Mistress Maynard's room on the ground floor, not far from the superintendent's office, and there found a young lad with a freckled nose and a large cap, whose eyes were shining with excitement.

'Will he serve?' Mistress Maynard asked, but her smile was complacent.

'He will serve very well,' I said. 'I think I shall call him Eddi. Come then, Eddi. Time we were on our way.'

Ellyn caught up a large bundle and turned to bid Mistress Maynard farewell. The matron leaned down and kissed her on the cheek.

'God go with you, child,' she said. 'Here, young lads are always eating. You can munch this as you go.' She handed Ellyn a large bun studded with currants.

'Excellent,' I said. 'Wait until we are out in the street, then it will help to partly hide your face.'

I paused a moment at Tom Read's lodge, but he shook his head. 'No sign of him,' he said, and we passed out through the gatehouse.

To my relief, there was quite a crowd of the players there – Simon and Guy, of course, but also Christopher, Dick Burbage, and the new man from the country, Will, who was smiling at all this to-do. Even some of the company's young lads had come along to see the fun.

'As well we came,' Simon said quietly to me as I met them. 'Look over there. I think one of them may be your friend of last night.' He jerked his head to indicate the other side of the street, where a group of rough men were standing together and watching us. One of them was the blacksmith.

Ellyn had not yet noticed them. If she did, she might be so frightened that she gave everything away, so I took care to stand so that I blocked her view. At the moment she was eating her bun, engrossed in watching Guy, who was juggling half a dozen objects, balls, knives and a skittle, which had drawn quite a little crowd.

'I don't know why he runs the risk,' I said to Simon, momentarily diverted. 'That knife could damage his musician's hands.'

'I do not think it is very sharp. Besides, I have never seen him miss.'

'This is Eddi,' I said, laying stress on the name. 'Will you walk with us to Pepper Alley Stairs?'

'Aye. The lads will run about and confuse matters. Guy will stay here and entertain. The rest of us will walk with you as if we were all bound together somewhere – the bear baiting, perhaps. There is a show this afternoon.'

I nodded. It seemed as good a plan as any. However, on the streets of London a brabble may break out at any time between two groups of men, a brabble may develop into a brawl, and a brawl into murder, as it had with Marlowe.

I leaned down to Ellyn. 'Give me your bundle. Then run ahead with the lads to the river.'

She nodded happily. One of the players' boys grabbed her by the hand and they ran off together with the other lads. The rest of us followed, strolling along slowly, as if we were in no hurry. Guy performed a few hand-flips and a cartwheel, and then began plucking comfits from under the chins of some servant maids who had stopped to watch him. Out of the corner of my eye, I could see the blacksmith and his fellows hesitating, unsure what to do. He must have recognised me and was now torn between following me or waiting by the hospital, where he might hope to gain entrance once I was gone, and so snatch his daughter. So far, it seemed, he had not recognised her.

'I have already bespoken a wherry for you.' The quiet voice in my ear belonged to Will. He still had a trace of that country accent, but Simon was right, he spoke almost as well as a Londoner.

'I thank you,' I said. 'You must think this a great to-do over one child.'

'Not at all,' he said. 'We must see the little maid safe. Simon has told me what her parents did to her.' He looked truly distressed. 'We should never permit such cruelty to a child. I have three children of my own.'

I was surprised at this. He looked too young, but perhaps Englishmen marry younger in the country than here in the city.

'I am afraid we see much cruelty to children in London,' I said. 'They are forced to beg in the streets or work very young as servants, where they are beaten and misused. And where I come from, even the Inquisition did not hesitate to torture children.' The words came out of my mouth unbidden. I never meant to speak them, yet there was something about this quiet man that called them forth.

'You are Portuguese?'

'Aye.'

We came at that moment to the river bank, close beside the upstream side of the Bridge, and there was the wherry Will had hired for us, with a gaggle of young lads chattering to the wherrymen. If one of them was wearing an overlarge cap, no one seemed to notice.

'Dick and I and two of the boys are coming with you,' Simon said, 'that's why Will hired a two-man wherry. It will help to disguise the true reason for the journey upriver.'

'An excellent plan,' I said. 'I do thank you, all of you.'

'A merry afternoon's pastime,' Christopher said. 'Time drags slowly when we have no performances.'

'I believe,' said Will quietly, 'that your friend the blacksmith has decided to follow us after all.'

I shivered, but forced myself not to glance round. 'Let us get into the boat, then.'

We urged Ellyn and two of the players' boys into the wherry. I followed, then Simon and Dick Burbage. Will and Christopher waved us off, then made a great business of chasing after the other two boys and dragging them back to the Bridge. They might have been two masters rounding up their wayward apprentices. It was cleverly done, but of course they were all players. Deception came naturally to them.

'Where to, master?' the older wherryman asked Dick, as clearly the most senior in the party.

'Blackfriars Stairs,' he said. 'No need to hurry. We are out for the pleasure of a trip on the river.'

The wherryman looked at him sceptically, for it had begun, for the first time that day, to snow. Still, there was no accounting for the folly of landsmen.

Once we had pulled away from the landing stage, I risked a glance back over my shoulder and caught my breath.

'Those men are after Christopher and Will,' I said, gripping Simon's sleeve.

Simon and Dick both looked back. I felt sickness rise in my throat. The players were surely in danger from that rough crowd. I found myself praying that they would not feel honour bound to fight. Young men in London are as quarrelsome as fighting cocks and the two of them stood no chance against that mob.

'They're giving them the slip,' Dick said.

He was right. Christopher and Will were running toward the Bridge, chasing the boys ahead of them. They slipped in front of a tottering cart drawn by an ancient mule, which followed them on to the Bridge, blocking the entrance to Old Stone Gate, so that the blacksmith and his friends were frustrated, trying to push past and being threatened by the carter with his long whip. He had stopped to confront them and even from the river it was clear that a shouting match was taking place. I did not care if it now came to blows, our friends were comfortably out of the way. There was no knowing why the blacksmith was pursuing them, unless he believed they knew how to get hold of Ellyn. He had seen them with me, and I was now out of reach. Or perhaps it amounted to no more than natural aggression.

The wherrymen began to row in a leisurely way, taking Dick's words literally, that there was no need to hurry, but I was growing impatient. Soon Ellyn's father would be on the other side of the river, where we were headed ourselves. Could he have guessed our destination? I did not think he had recognised Ellyn, in her boy's clothes, with her hair hidden, but perhaps I was wilfully deceiving myself. It would not normally be easy to follow the progress of a wherry from the shore, but there was less traffic than usual on the river, no doubt due to the gathering snow clouds, and ours was the only two-man wherry in sight.

The tide was coming in, which meant it was easier to row up river. I leaned forward and spoke to the older man – they were clearly father and son. 'We are in a hurry now,' I said, 'with the snow starting. There will be an extra sixpence if you can get us quickly to Blackfriars.'

The man gave me a knowing look. He must have witnessed the events onshore.

'Aye, master,' he said, 'we can get you there quicker.' He leaned to his oars and set a faster rhythm, which the younger man, after an awkward jerk in the movement of the boat, quickly copied.

The three children, clustered in the bows of the boat, were chattering excitedly as we picked up speed. For Ellyn, unaware that her father had been close by, the whole journey was an adventure. For the players' boys, it meant a holiday from rehearsals and helping to build the stage at the Cross Keys. The three of us sitting in the stern were silent, Simon and Dick having been infected by my anxiety.

The snow began to fall more heavily, blotting out our view of the shore. Dick reached behind him and tugged at the tilt canvas until he had pulled it forward over the supporting hoop. It gave a little shelter, but the wind was blowing across us from the north and driving much of the snow under the tilt. In my hurry to leave the hospital I had forgotten my gloves, so that my hands began to turn blue. I thrust them inside my cloak under my armpits to try to warm them.

'There's a small canvas behind you,' I called to the children. 'Pull it up to keep out the snow.'

'We don't need it!' one of the boys shouted, and they all laughed.

'They want to prove that they are hardier than we are,' Dick said with a grin. 'Let them endure the snow if they will. They will learn sense when they are older.'

Because of the snow, we could not see how far we had travelled along the shore, so the journey upriver seemed to continue for hours, but at last the wherrymen, who must have some instinctive sense of where they are on the river, turned toward the City bank. At once the wind started to blow the snow directly in our faces, so that we all three ducked and pulled the hoods of our cloaks as close round our heads as we could.

There was a slight bump as we hit the landing stage at Blackfriars Stairs. The younger man shipped his oars and jumped out to cast a mooring rope around a post. Then he thrust out a leg and drew the boat close to the jetty with his foot.

'Take care!' he said. 'There's ice on the boards.'

'Aye,' I said to the children, 'take care, for no one will be able to fetch you out of the river before you freeze to death and float away to Muscovy.'

The boys giggled at this and began to show off as they climbed out, so that one slipped and fell on his knees. We all cried out in alarm, but he scrambled to his feet, ran to the stairs, and disappeared from sight as he climbed up into the snow. I passed Ellyn's bundle to the young wherryman, then stepped across to the jetty with great care. Dick was paying the wherryman, and I reached for my purse, but he shook his head.

'Later,' he called. 'Let us get out of this weather first.'

Simon and Dick followed me, and we thanked the wherrymen. They can be a curmudgeonly breed, but they had rowed valiantly in dreadful weather.

'We'll be going home ourselves, master,' the father said. 'There will be no more fares today, I'm thinking.' They began to gather up the oars and everything movable that might be stolen from the boat.

When we reached the top of the stairs, we found the three children huddled in a doorway, having lost their taste for braving it, out in the snow.

'Eddi and I go up to Christ's Hospital from here,' I said. 'I thank you all for your help and your company, but you need not come with us.'

'We will walk with you as far as Newgate,' Dick said, 'then I will take the boys back to the Cross Keys where we can warm ourselves and dry our clothes. Why do you not join us there, when your business is done? We are all in need of a hot meal.'

113

'Very well,' I said. 'I do not think I shall be long. What will you do, Simon?'

'I will come with you to Christ's,' he said. 'One extra, in case.'

I nodded. We would say nothing further in front of the children. The wherrymen passed us, carrying their gear, and we turned north, into the wind.

Despite the blizzard, it was warmer work trudging up St Andrew's Hill and the Wardrobe than it had been sitting still in the wherry. The snow was already piling up in the streets, with hardly a soul about. After crossing Carter Lane, we waded up narrow Creed Lane and Ave Maria Lane, where the snow was up to our knees and the children became very quiet. At last we emerged from Warwick Lane into Newgate Street, cold and wet, with breastplates of driven snow. Snowflakes clung to my eyelashes. I had lost all feeling in my toes. And there, to my astonishment, was an old friend, the chestnut seller, out here even in this weather, although I could see that he was preparing to go home.

'Wait!' I called. 'I would buy some chestnuts before you leave.'

'Why, 'tis you, master! I a'nt seen you these many months.'

'I have left Bart's,' I said. 'I work over the river now, at St Thomas's.' I felt in my purse with my numb fingers. I would have enough. 'A poke each for the children,' I said, 'and one for the prisoners.'

'Ah, they've missed you, master, and your gifts of hot nuts.'

'Two for the prisoners, then,' I said recklessly, feeling a stab of guilt. Before long I would be eating a hot meal at the Cross Keys, while the sad prisoners confined to the worst part of Newgate would have no heat and no bedding but dirty straw, and only such food as the charitable passers-by might give them, of whom there would be few on such a day as this.

The chestnut seller doled out a generous helping of the roasted nuts to each of the children, who burned their fingers in their eagerness to peel and eat them. The rest of the chestnuts I took over to the grid where nothing could be seen of the prisoners but their bony hands stretched imploringly out into the snow.

'I hope they share them out fairly,' Simon said, 'though starving men may fight over scraps.'

I shook my head. 'I cannot know. I hope they share them, and all do not go to the strongest and fiercest.'

'We'd best be on our way,' Dick said. 'Come along, lads. I will see you both shortly.'

114

With that, we went our several ways, Dick and the boys towards Cheapside and the middle of the City, Simon, Ellyn and I turning to cross the deserted Newgate market to the gatehouse of Christ's Hospital.

'Ellyn is almost at the end of her strength,' I murmured to Simon. 'She has been very ill, though she is well recovered. It is the struggle through the snow which has proved too much for her.'

'Come, Eddi, or Ellyn, whatever your name is,' Simon said. 'If I squat down, come behind me and put your arms about my neck. I'll carry you the rest of the way on my back.'

Ellyn did as she was bid and although it was not far I could see she was glad to be carried. She leaned her cheek against the back of Simon's neck and was nearly asleep when we reached the gatehouse.

The gate, which had been open every other time I had visited, was firmly closed, and snow was beginning to pile up against it. I pulled hard on the bell chain and heard the muffled sound of the bell in the gatekeeper's lodge. It was followed by the sound of footsteps on stone slabs and the grate of bolts being drawn. A man holding a candle lantern peered out at us.

'Dr Alvarez, is it? Come within. You are expected.'

The three of us stepped in under the gateway, out of the wind and snow.

Sanctuary.

Chapter Nine

Simon lowered Ellyn carefully on to a stool beside the gatekeeper's fire. She was so nearly asleep that she came close to toppling off, but Simon put an arm around her shoulders to steady her. She blinked and yawned.

'Are we here?' She yawned again.

'Aye,' I said. 'We are here. Now we all need to thaw out.'

I turned to the gatekeeper, an elderly man with a kind face and an extraordinary bush of white hair, which sprang out from his head in all directions. When he was young he must have had a mop of curls any maiden would envy.

'Can you send word to Mistress Wedderbury that we are here? We have had a trying journey in this weather and the child would be best in bed.'

He gave me a puzzled look.

'We was expecting a girl, Dr Alvarez.'

I laughed. There had been so much to worry me that I had forgotten how strange Ellyn's appearance would seem.

'This is a girl, Ellyn Smith. See! Ellyn, take off your cap.'

Obediently the child pulled off the baggy cap and revealed a head covered with tight plaits, from which the pins were beginning to fall out. I knelt beside her and began to undo the plaits, which must have been pulling painfully at her scalp all afternoon, though she had not once complained. As the last strands came free, the red mane tumbled down to her shoulders.

'There,' I said. 'That is better. Let your hair dry by the heat of the fire.'

The gatekeeper was looking askance at Ellyn's boy's clothes, but I said briskly, 'It was necessary for a little subterfuge on our journey. Ellyn has girl's clothes here in her bundle. Mistress Wedderbury will understand.'

'I am afraid Mistress Wedderbury is not here,' he said, shaking his head. 'She went out late this morning to see a lace-maker in Little Eastcheap who wants to take on one of our girls as an apprentice. Then the snow came on so bad, she must have decided to stay until it should ease a little.'

'It has not eased at all,' Simon said. He was standing with his back to the fire and steam was rising from him like smoke. 'I should say that it is growing worse.'

'You need not worry,' the man said. 'Before she left, Mistress Wedderbury said as how, if you was to come before she was back, then I was to fetch her girl, and she would take the child to her mistress's rooms.'

He went to the door of his lodge and called out instructions to someone. I could hear running feet on the dry paving under the gatehouse, muffled as soon as they reached the snow of the courtyard.

'Move over,' I said to Simon, giving him a poke in the ribs. 'I am wet through as well.'

He moved to give me a share of the fire, so we stood there steaming like two pillars of smoke as a cloaked and hooded figure hurried in. When she threw back her hood, I recognised the girl who had served us when I had brought Mellie to see Mistress Wedderbury.

'Is this the lass?' the girl said, taking in Ellyn's long hair and her odd clothes.

'Aye,' I said, 'and she needs to change into her dry gown in this bundle.' I handed it to the girl. 'Now, Ellyn, are you strong enough to walk across the courtyard and up some stairs, or do you need one of us to carry you?' I was exhausted myself after our battle through the snow, but I was prepared to carry her if need be.

'I can walk,' she said stoutly, slipping down from the stool. Indeed, the warmth seemed to have revived her.

'Come with Moll, then,' the maidservant said, and held out her hand. 'We will soon have you in dry clothes, and I have a pan of thick soup warming on the fire. What do you say to that?'

'I say "aye",' Ellyn said, and smiled at her. She turned to me. 'Will you come, Dr Alvarez?'

'Nay, my pet,' I said, taking her hand. 'I must walk back all that long way across London in the snow before dark, but Moll here will look after you. I will come to see you, and Mellie too, in a few days.'

She seemed content with that and went off happily enough with the girl.

'We must be on our way,' Simon said the to gatekeeper. 'I thank you for the warmth of your fire.'

117

'Nay,' he protested. 'Let me give you a stoop of ale afore you go out into that storm again.'

He brought out a flagon and ale jars, and – although it delayed us a few minutes – we were glad of the ale in our stomachs as he let us out into the blizzard once more.

By the time we reached Cheapside, I was beginning to wonder whether we should have begged a cot for the night at Christ's Hospital. At St-Mary-le-Bowe, I was certain of it, but it was too late. There was no going back now. We plodded on, our heads down, like two old worn-out cart horses.

'At least,' Simon muttered, as we passed the end of Wallbrook, 'there will be no thieves and cut-throats about in this. They will have the good sense to remain within doors.' His voice was muffled, because he was clutching his hood closed over most of his face.

I merely grunted in reply, cursing myself again for forgetting my gloves, so that I could not do the same with my hood. I needed to keep my frozen hands tucked under my cloak and would beg a pair of gloves off the players before the final walk home.

At long last we reached Gracechurch Street and turned north, heading into the wind, but then, to our relief, the inn sign came into view, half covered with snow and swinging wildly on its brackets. Two enormous crossed keys, picked out in gold. We fell through the inn door like two statues moulded from snow, such as children love to make.

'Fire!' Simon croaked. 'Hot food!'

'Spiced wine,' I added, 'before we fall dead at your feet.'

Then they were all there, the players, laughing and stripping off our cloaks and boots, which we were too numb to do for ourselves. James Burbage himself dragged a settle almost too close to the fire for comfort and thrust us down on it. I feared the chilblains that would be the penalty for this proximity, but by now my teeth were chattering so hard I did not care. Someone found a blanket and threw it over our knees. Someone else thrust a pint of Hippocras into my hand, but my hand was so numb I could not hold it.

'Steady, that's good wine. Don't waste it.' It was Guy, gripping his hand round mine and raising the ale pot to my lips. 'It is just cooled down enough to drink. I tested it myself.'

'D-Drinking m-my wine, were you?' I said.

He patted me on the shoulder. 'Only a sip, and in your own interests. Get that inside you, lad.'

The pewter rim of the ale pot rattled against my teeth, despite Guy's steadying hand, but the taste and the warmth of the Hippocras as it slipped down my throat began to make me feel human and alive once more.

'Did you ever know such a winter?' I said, when I could speak again.

'Aye,' James Burbage said. 'When I was a young man, back in '65 it would be, the Thames froze over. We had all kinds of games and sport on the ice. The Queen herself, and the Court, held archery contests, and she rode in a carriage upon the frozen river.'

I shuddered at the thought of nothing but a layer of ice between oneself and the dark depths of the Thames.

'I pray it does not freeze over this winter,' I said.

'There has been ice along the river banks,' Christopher Haigh said, sitting down on the floor and clasping his arms about his knees.

'Aye,' I said, 'I know. But not out in the centre. And I do not remember snow like this before.'

'We shall be snug in our winter playhouse,' Burbage said complacently. 'You may all thank me for that.'

'Christopher,' I said, 'what happened to you and Will, after we took boat? Did those ruffians catch you?'

'Nay,' he said. 'We were well away before they broke free of the cart. It sounded as though a fight broke out there, but we didn't wait to see.'

'Chased the boys halfway here to the inn,' Will said, 'before the snow came on, and we had to slow down, for you could not see the fingers of your hands before your face.'

'Aye,' one of the boys piped up. 'Master Haigh and Master Shakespeare chased us away, but we would have put up a good fight against those men. They stopped us.'

'Sometimes,' I said, 'the wise man knows when it is better to save his strength for another day.' These London lads, I thought, they would rather fight than eat a good dinner, which started me thinking again of food. I could not remember when I had last eaten.

Then the innkeeper and his maidservants came in and began laying out a supper for us. From his deference and eagerness to please Master Burbage, it was clear that he expected to do well out of providing the company with a playhouse. Many of the audience would drink here before the play, and others would dine afterwards. It should be profitable for all.

Supper was a good thick mutton stew, with a dish of turnips and leeks on the side and a syllabub to follow, all washed down with plenty of strong beer. By the time we had finished eating and the young boys had been sent to bed, I wondered whether I could stay awake long enough to walk back to Southwark.

'Time we were gone,' I said to Simon. 'This supper has saved our lives, but we need to brave the storm again.'

'Nay, you cannot.' It was Guy, who had gone to the window and folded back the shutter. 'It is worse than ever out there. The Great Stone Gate will be closed by now and no wherries will be abroad, even if they are not frozen in.'

'But I must make my way back to Southwark!' I said. 'I have patients to see in the morning.'

'Guy is right,' James Burbage said. 'You will do no good outside in this weather, Kit. There is no chance of reaching Southwark tonight. You must spend the night here with us at the Cross Keys and go over the Bridge in the morning, after the gate is opened.'

There was no arguing with the sense of this. All the players had decided to stay overnight at the inn. Only James Burbage had taken a room here while the stage was building, the others lived in lodgings scattered about the City, or out beyond Bishopsgate near the Theatre, or in Southwark, like Simon. None of them proposed battling through the storm to reach home.

The innkeeper had rooms to spare, but would probably want paying for them. Christopher took one, and a few of the older players did likewise, but the rest of us begged some straw palliasses and bedded down where we were, on the floor of the parlour. It was not what I had intended when I set out at midday, and I hoped that Tom Dean would not object to keeping Rikki overnight without notice, but there was nothing to be done about it. The innkeeper found us a blanket each, over which I laid my cloak, even though it was not quite dry.

I have spent worse nights. Compared with sleeping under a bush in the Low Countries, or on the stony ground of a Portuguese forced march, it was quite comfortable. It was not without disturbance, for a few of the players snored, but I was so exhausted after our battle with the storm that I slept through most of it.

No one slept late. I was the first up and made a dash for the privy before I could be noticed. I found the kitchen and begged a manchet of bread and a pot of small ale before I set out. When I returned to the parlour, the others were stirring, yawning and stretching, complaining of stiffness from their hard beds.

I opened the shutter to see what awaited outside. The storm had abated, but the snow lay deep, while the wind, which still blew with some vigour, swept clouds of spindrift off the surface, so that the air was filled with the sparkle of diamond-bright fragments. It would have been beautiful, had it not been so deadly. I wondered how many beggars and other poor folk had died in London that night.

'Will you be walking back to Southwark, Simon?' I asked.

He shook his head. 'We are going to the Old Bailey, to the Justice Court, to give what support we can to Marlowe.'

Of course. I had forgotten. This was the day of Marlowe's trial for the killing of that man in the street brawl.

'I hope the verdict will be favourable,' I said. 'It was not he, was it, who struck the fatal blow?'

'Nay,' said Guy, 'it was Thomas Watson, but he could be accounted an accessory to murder, which carries the same punishment. It was Marlowe who was fighting with William Bradley first, before Watson arrived. He will only escape a guilty verdict if the judges accept that it was done in self defence. There are witnesses to say it was.'

'And we go to give witness to his good character,' Simon said.

I wondered how they could do that, in conscience, for Marlowe was known for his violence and hot temper, but I held my peace and pulled on my boots, which were dry, although they had stiffened as they dried. I would have blisters long before I reached home.

'Can anyone lend me a pair of gloves?' I asked plaintively. 'I came away without mine yesterday, and I'd fain not make another journey in this cold without a pair.'

'I have a pair you may borrow,' Guy said. 'Somewhat rubbed and too large for you, I'll wager, but they should serve.'

They were too large, but better too large than too small. I thanked him, and before setting out smoothed into my cracked and painful hands some of the same salve as I had given the wherryman. It stung a little, but I knew it would prove helpful. Then I donned my cloak and Guy's gloves, caught up my satchel, and bade them farewell. When I pulled open the outside door, a pile of snow as high as my waist fell inside. Everyone cried out.

'Are we snowed in?' Dick asked, pushing past me and leaning out through the door frame. 'Nay,' he reported. 'It has drifted high into the doorway, but even so it is still deep enough elsewhere to make for hard going. We will all of us be soaked to the hips, whether we go to Southwark or the Old Bailey.'

'Then I had better go and be done with it,' I said. I stepped past him and set off on the journey home.

Despite the deep snow, the morning's tramp from Gracechurch Street to the Bridge was as nothing compared with our struggle the previous night in the dark and the storm. I was soon caked with snow as high as my knees and above, but no fresh snow was falling. And, although the wind still blew from the north, it had lessened, and was now at my back. My hands and feet and face were very cold, but the struggle to walk through the drifted snow warmed the rest of me, so that I was like a half-cooked pastry, hot and cold in patches.

I did not spare time to return to my lodgings but went straight to the hospital, arriving after my usual time, but not as late as I had feared. Rikki, leaping out of the gatehouse lodge, clearly thought he had lost me for ever.

'Tom, I am sorry,' I said. 'I was trapped north of the river after leaving Christ's Hospital, and snow bound at the Cross Keys in Gracechurch Street.'

'Nay, don't fret,' he said. 'Rikki was restless, but Swifty and me, we were glad to have him safe out of the snow. That were a storm and a half, weren't it? Worse places to be snow bound, I'll wager, than a great inn like that.'

'I slept on the floor,' I said pointedly, 'not in one of the fine chambers.'

Rikki was eager to come with me now, but perforce I must leave him again and go to my work.

I reported first to Superintendent Ailmer, giving him a full account of the events of the day before, from the time the blacksmith and his band of roughs had been lingering outside the hospital.

'My friends distracted them, and in her boy's clothes the blacksmith did not recognise Ellyn, though I think he guessed something was afoot.'

'And did you reach Blackfriars Stairs before the snow?' he asked.

'Nay, we were caught in the blizzard on the river, then must walk up Ludgate Hill to Christ's.'

I recounted how we had been received at Christ's, then our fight through the snow to the Cross Keys.

'We were warmed and fed there, at Master Burbage's expense,' I explained. I wanted him to understand all that was owed to the players. 'Otherwise, I think we might have died in the storm. By then we were snow bound, and I have had to make my way back to Southwark through the drifts this morning.'

He seemed satisfied enough by all I had done, so I went briefly to tell Mistress Maynard that all was well with little Ellyn, who had become a favourite during the time she had been with us.

'Ah, God bless the little chick,' she said. 'I hope she will be safe and happy now, away from that monster of a father.'

'He is likely to come here still, seeking her,' I said. 'Master Ailmer has agreed that a little deceit on our part may help to protect her. As far as we know, Ellyn Smith left the hospital of her own accord. We assume that she has gone home.'

She smiled. 'Near enough the truth to serve. She did leave the hospital of her own accord. Let him search the streets of Southwark for her, and leave us in peace.'

It was not until I had been home for an hour or two that evening that I heard Simon come into his room below. I called to Rikki. We clattered down the stairs and I thumped on Simon's door.

He was pulling off his sodden boots, for the snow was as deep as ever.

'Well,' I said, 'what happened in court?'

'He was cleared of any wrong-doing,' Simon said with a grin. 'There were enough witnesses of the brawl to say that Marlowe and his friend were attacked first. Then Watson drew his sword and in the scuffle the attacker was killed. Marlowe was party to the brawl, but did not wield the weapon. The judges gave them a dressing down for brawling, but accepted the plea of self defence. Watson has been sent back to Newgate, but it's believed he will receive a pardon.'

He had his back to me while he finished speaking, pouring us a measure of ale each. As he turned and handed me mine, he looked at me sideways and, I thought, seemed a little ashamed.

'We had no need to give testimony as to Marlowe's character. He had a good lawyer to speak for him. I *think*, though I cannot be sure, that the lawyer had bribed the witnesses to say what they said.'

I sat down on the end of the bed and sighed. 'I am not surprised. All the time one hears of it. Even if Marlowe did not thrust his own sword into the man, I wonder who really provoked the brawl.'

I took a sip of my ale, and as I did so, the thought came to me, that if my encounter with the blacksmith had come to blows, I might have been the corpse, or I might have been the killer. Would a judge have accepted my plea of self defence?

'So, have you been celebrating Marlowe's release?' I asked.

'We went for a few drinks,' he admitted, 'but I did not stay as long as some others. After our adventure last night, I wanted to make my way home safely before dark.'

'Have you supped? I have a good-sized pie, and a fresh loaf I bought on my way home from the hospital, and some apples.'

'I'd be glad of it,' he said. 'I will bring the rest of my cheese. What you left of it after your own brawl the other night.'

'We live in exciting times, do we not?' I said. 'Brawls and blizzards. And you ate more of that cheese than I did. But bring it anyway.'

Once we had eaten and were settled in front of the good fire I had built up on my hearth, Simon stretched out his legs and gave a sigh of contentment.

'A little different, this,' he said, 'from where we were at this time yesterday.'

I nodded. 'I hope never to walk through a blizzard like that again. I really feared that we might not survive.'

'It is hard on the poor,' he said soberly. 'Even those with a roof over their heads, if they cannot afford firewood.'

'Aye, you could freeze in your own bed,' I said. 'And I cannot rid my mind of those children.'

'Your beggar waifs?'

'My beggar waifs. Where have they gone? Where can they beg, now they have lost their place by the playhouse? The adult beggars will drive them away from all the best spots.'

'Unless an adult owned them, but was keeping out of sight.'

'I was never sure. Usually they only use one or two children, don't they? To elicit sympathy. Somehow I had the feeling those children had banded together themselves.'

'Perhaps the city constables have caught them.'

I shook my head. 'In that case, they would have been handed over to Christ's, at least the younger ones, and I would have heard about it. Nay, I think they must still be out there.' I paused, then said quietly, 'Unless they have perished in the cold, like the robin and the thrush I saw lying in the snow on my way home tonight.'

He gave me a curious look, weighing me up, which I found disconcerting.

'You are very distressed about these children, Kit. And about all your sad cases in the hospital. You cannot take every lost and abandoned child under your wing.'

'I know that very well,' I said crisply. That look of his had unsettled me. 'I need to talk to you about something quite different.'

Simon was aware of my other work, apart from my profession as a physician. I had trusted him with a little information about what I did for Walsingham's service. Not just the code-breaking, but the other missions on which I had been sent. I would need to say even more this time.

'You are looking very mysterious, Kit. What can it be?'

'It is no trivial matter.' I drew breath. 'Thomas Phelippes has had word that there is to be another attempt on the Queen's life.'

He gave a low whistle. 'I thought we were free of that at last. Her enemies must know by now that she is well guarded. The business in the summer when you burned your hand, that was intended to cause terror and panic on the streets of London instead. Those conspirators must have guessed that they could not come near Her Majesty.'

'It may be that news has spread that Walsingham is very ill, almost certainly his final illness. The service *is* Walsingham. Without him, it is like to fall apart. Already it is weakened and faltering.'

'I did not realise.'

'Aye, well, it is not part of your world, but Spain and France have their own intelligencers, even if they have nothing to match Sir Francis's organisation. They will have sent word of how matters stand here, in despatches back to their masters.'

'So does Phelippes know anything more about this new plot?'

'In some ways he knows a great deal. Not the source of the threat, though it is probably Spain. However, we know that it is a paid assassin, someone who will have skill and experience. Not one of those Rheims trained priests, who come equipped to convert or assassinate, as they are bid.'

'A professional assassin! Do such men exist?'

'Aye,' I said wryly. 'They do.' Sometimes I wondered at Simon's sheltered world of players and playhouse. Some of their very plays contained assassins. Did he think it was all make-believe?

'What else does he know?'

'This is why I need your help. The man will come in the guise of an entertainer. And he will make his attack during the Twelfth Night Revels at Whitehall palace.'

He shot upright, no longer lounging at his leisure.

'Do you mean *these* Twelfth Night Revels? Next month? When we are to perform before the Queen?'

'Aye, those very revels. There may even be some danger to you and the other players. We do not know what means he will use. A dagger or a sword would be fatal to the Queen, but unlikely to hurt anyone else. On the other hand, if he were to use a pistol, or gunpowder, that would be a different matter.'

'God's bones!' Simon sprang to his feet and began to pace about. 'The Revels! What kind of entertainer, do you know?'

'That is the first thing I need your help with. Can you discover who else is to perform? If any are known to you or the other players, can you say for certain that they are not the assassin? And of those unknown to you, can you make enquiries? Find out everything you can?'

'Certainly I can do that.' He returned to his chair and sat down, leaning forward with his hands on his knees. 'You say that is the first thing you want of me.'

'Aye. There is also this. Phelippes will post Nicholas Berden and some of his men about the palace of Whitehall, to keep watch and try to prevent a disaster, but at the moment they will not know what manner of man they are looking for. He also wants me to be there, as part of your company, to watch out for anything suspicious and to work with Berden. He thinks I will be better placed that way, since your company will know many of the other entertainers.'

'I am not sure whether that is true,' he said gloomily. 'These Twelfth Night Revels, the Court sets much store by them and puts the Master of the Revels on his mettle to provide more and more exotic entertainments every year. So there will be many entertainers who have never been seen in London before. It is very clever, whoever planned this. Just the very occasion where a stranger will not be out of place. Guy says there may be anything from a Turkish sword swallower to an Egyptian with a performing crocodile! The Revels has always at least one play, to round all off in a decent fashion. That will be our task. Followed by music and a formal dance. Sometimes the courtiers will join in our dance, even the Queen herself. That might be the moment when he would choose to strike.'

He looked at me and gave a sideways grin. 'Perhaps you will need to play the lute with Guy after all.'

'If I must do so in the Queen's service,' I said grimly, 'then I will do so, but I will take no pleasure in it. Is there not some other role I might fill? Caring for costumes?'

'What do you know about caring for costumes? Goodwife Blakely is in charge of all our costumes, with a girl to help her. She is very skilled, and can mend a tear or sew on a button between scenes. She would laugh you to scorn.'

'Well, if I must play the lute, I will do so, but do not think I will ever do so at a public performance.'

'I can tell you,' he said, 'that performing for the Court is a great deal more alarming than performing in the playhouse.'

'That is very reassuring,' I said.

While we had been speaking, I had become aware of a noise downstairs. Our landlord's voice and another man's, which sounded agitated, although we were too far away to hear the words.

'What is that?' Simon said, getting up and throwing open my door, the better to hear.

'Dr Alvarez?' It was the landlord, calling up the stairs.

I joined Simon by the door. 'Aye? What's to do?'

'Gentleman to see you. One Master Alchester. Do you know him?'

'Aye,' I called. 'Send him up.'

I turned to Simon in surprise. 'It is the Fitzgeralds' steward, Edwin Alchester. What can he be doing here? I did not tell him that I lived here, only that he could reach me at St Thomas's.'

We could hear the sound of hasty steps as the steward climbed the stairs. He arrived breathless at my door, pressing his hand against his side. His cap was askew, his grey hair in a tangle beneath it, his boots and hose soaking from the snow, his eyes filled with fear.

'Master Alchester!' I said. 'Come within. What is amiss? You are distressed.'

He nodded, still too breathless to speak, and allowed himself to be led into my room and seated on the chair Simon had just vacated. Simon threw a log on to the coal in my fire, so that it would blaze up quickly, and I poured Alchester a mug of ale.

At first he could not drink, but struggled to calm his breathing, for he had run up those steep stairs far too fast for a man of his age. To give him time to gather his wits, I said, 'This is Master Simon Hetherington, one of Lord Strange's Men. You remember that we were to dine with them next week.'

He nodded and took a sip of the ale, which seemed to restore his powers of speech.

'Forgive me for seeking you at home, Dr Alvarez,' he said. 'I went to St Thomas's first, in the hope that you might still be there. When I found that you had left, I did not know what to do. Then I met a gentleman coming in by the gatehouse, a Superintendent Ailmer.'

'Aye?' I said encouragingly. Let him say truly what he wanted.

'When I explained my business, he said that he judged it right to give me the address of your lodgings. I beg you will forgive me, when you hear why I have come.'

'It is clear to see that it something serious.' I sat down again in my chair and Simon pulled up a stool. 'Tell us what we can do to help.'

'It is the little maid,' he said. 'Sophia Makepeace.'

I turned to Simon. 'She is Sir Damian Fitzgerald's ward. A young heiress.'

As a thought struck me, I leapt to my feet and reached for my satchel of medicines.

'She is ill? She needs a physician?'

'Nay!' He shook his head violently. 'I would it were that simple.'

To my astonishment, I saw that his eyes had filled with tears. The child could not have died, else why should he come to me? I sank back on to my chair.

He drew a deep breath. 'Forgive me. I must tell it all clearly. Because of the weather, the child has been confined indoors, not able even to play in the garden behind the house, and she is a lively little thing, accustomed to riding her little pony at home with us in Surrey, or to playing with the dogs. A little hoyden, she is.'

He said it fondly, and I saw that the child had quite won him over.

'When we saw that the snow had stopped this morning, she begged to be allowed to play outside, but my lady was worried she might take a chill, for it was still so cold. Sir Damian went to Westminster on business yesterday and did not expect to return for two or three days. Mistress Cecilia's new husband went with them. He is staying with us, and Mistress Cecilia also. They came to London to order new furnishings for their house in Gloucestershire. Then this afternoon, I accompanied Lady Bridget to the Royal Exchange, where she wished to visit the shops.'

I nodded. It was all taking a great deal of time to come to the point, but I supposed he had some reason for all this.

'While we were at the Royal Exchange, my lady met a friend who had come there by horse litter. It was decided that my lady would accompany her friend home and stay to supper, then be conveyed home by litter. I was sent back to the house in Cheapside with her parcels. When I arrived, the house was very quiet, but Master Edward came to me and said he was worried.'

'Just a moment, Master Alchester,' I said. 'Before you reached the house, the only members of the family who were there were Mistress Cecilia and Master Edward?'

'Aye. And the little one. It seems that after my lady left, little Sophia begged Mistress Cecilia that she might be allowed to go out and see the snow giants the apprentices were building at the end of Cheapside. She could just make them out from her window. Mistress Cecilia said she might go, with her nursery maid to accompany her. Master Edward was very angry and told his sister she should not allow it, but it seems she told him she was a grown woman now and a married woman, and she knew better than he.'

I could hear Cecilia's voice in my head. She would enjoy lording it over her younger brother, although he was right that the child should not go wandering about Cheapside with no one but a young maid, who was probably not much more than a child herself. I also had the suspicion that Cecilia might not care for another girl usurping her place as the daughter of the family, even if she was now a married woman. She might not be much concerned about the child's safety.

'By the time I reached home,' Alchester said, 'they had been gone above two hours. Edward was very worried. Cecilia affected not to be, but I could tell that she was beginning to be frightened. I had just opened the door to go searching for them myself, when the maid stumbled in.'

He passed his hand over his face and I saw that it was shaking.

'The girl had been beaten. Her cap was gone, her collar ripped half off, her face bruised and bloody. She said they had been set upon before ever they reached the snow building. Two rough men who grabbed them both and carried them off, tying a cloth over her eyes so that she could not see. When she tried to scream, they stuffed a rag in her mouth. They were dragged away, and when the blindfold was removed, she thought they were in the back premises of some ale house.'

'Why did she think that?' Simon interrupted. He was listening keenly, leaning forward.

'She says there was a strong smell of beer, and she could hear voices some way off that sounded like the crowd in an ale house. She is not a stupid girl, merely young. Sophia was there also. Not injured, but very frightened.'

'But the maidservant managed to escape?' I said.

'After a time, they covered her eyes again and carried her away from the ale house, if that was what it was. She said she knew at once that Sophia had been left behind. She was put in a cart and driven away, then suddenly tipped out in the street and heard the cart drive away. Although she pulled off the blindfold at once, she had no idea where she was, not being a London girl. All she knows is that it was a narrow alley, deep in snow. She struggled out to a wider street, where she found a woman who told her she was in Lothbury and pointed out the way back to Cheapside.'

'And that was all?' I said. 'She did not know where Sophia had been taken?'

He shook his head. 'Nay, but they had stuffed a paper into the breast of her gown. She cannot read, so she gave it to me.'

'Do you have it here?' Simon asked.

'Aye.'

He reached into the purse hanging from his belt and drew out a dirty scrap of paper, which he handed to Simon, who brought it over to me. I tilted it toward the light of the candle and together we leaned over it, trying to make out the smudged letters, hastily scrawled with thin ink and a broken-nibbed quill.

If you wish to see the child again, you must pay the price. Five thousand pound in gold or the child's throat is cut.

Chapter Ten

Simon and I looked at each other in horror. I did not know what to say, or why Edwin Alchester had come to me.

'Have you sent word to Sir Damian?' I asked.

'Aye,' he said, taking back the note with a trembling hand. 'I sent one of the London servants at once, on horseback. But the roads are so blocked it will take him some time to reach Westminster. I have not been able to tell my lady, for I do not know her friend's address.'

'Is the maidservant badly injured? Is that why you have come to me?'

'She is more frightened than injured. She will have some bad bruises on her face and neck, and they twisted her arms when they first caught her, but it is nothing that the housekeeper cannot see to.'

He gave me an anxious, apologetic look.

'I came to you because . . . You will remember that when we met the other day, you were coming from Sir Francis Walsingham's house. You said . . . You said you sometimes helped with the breaking of codes.'

'Aye,' I said cautiously, wondering where this could be leading.

'I thought perhaps his men might have information about who these ruffians might be. Might help us to find them.'

I hated to dash his hopes, but it was only right to be honest with him. 'Sir Francis's service occupies itself with threats against the Queen and the state of England from abroad. It does not concern itself with English criminals whose crimes are more–' I could not think of the right word. 'Who commit crimes against other Englishmen.'

A look of despair came into his eyes, but before he could speak, Simon began to pace about the room again.

'Does Sir Damian *have* five thousand pound in gold? Forgive my asking, but surely this is important.'

The steward shook his head. As part of his duties, he would have a good idea of his master's income and assets.

'Nay. Nothing like. His wealth is principally in land. As well as the estate in Surrey, he also owns a number of smaller manors in different parts of the country. One of them he has just settled on his daughter, as part of her dowry, together with a substantial amount of coin.'

It occurred to me, as he spoke, that Sir Damian might have needed to offer a considerable dowry to persuade a Protestant aristocrat to accept in marriage the daughter of a suspected Catholic.

'Given time,' Alchester said, 'Sir Damian could realise the sum in gold, but it might take weeks, and what will become of the little maid in the meantime?'

'We must think first of her safety,' I said. I was thinking furiously. 'Was the maidservant able to tell you how far they had walked before they were set upon?'

'Only past three or four houses, she said. I think these men must have been watching our house, awaiting their chance. The two girls had gone just far enough that their cries would not be heard by any of the household.'

He was probably right. And even if the servant had managed to scream before they gagged her, most Londoners are loath to come to the aid of anyone attacked in the street. It is a brave soul indeed who would risk his own life to save a stranger, especially a mere servant girl. I suppose London is no more lawless than any other great city, but I never walked abroad without my dagger. Nevertheless, the snatching of a rich child within sight of her own home in the hours of daylight spoke of considerable boldness. I wondered whether these men had kidnapped the child for their own gain, or at the bidding of someone else.

'After they were captured,' Simon said, 'had the girl any idea how far they were taken before they came to this ale house? If it was an ale house.'

Alchester shook his head. 'She could not be sure. I do not suppose she has a very clear idea of time. I pressed her for an answer, but all she could say was that it might have been a quarter of an hour.'

'If you are blindfolded and terrified,' I said slowly, 'it is likely that the time would seem longer than it really was.'

'Whether her guess is accurate or not,' Simon said, 'we should first search all the taverns and ale houses within a fifteen minute walk of the place where they were captured.'

'Do you suppose they will still be there?' I said doubtfully. 'It must have taken the maid an hour to find her way home again. And that was how long ago?' I looked at Alchester.

'It must be another hour by now,' he said. 'I sent word to Sir Damian, and questioned the girl. Then I thought of you and went from Cheapside to St Thomas's before coming on here.'

Simon and I exchanged a glance. That would have taken more than an hour. Outside it was full dark by now. Even the moon was hidden behind snow clouds. Further snow threatened.

Alchester rose to his feet with a groan and pressed his hand against the small of his back. 'I thank you, Dr Alvarez, for your time, and you also, Master Hetherington, but I must go back to the Fitzgeralds' house to see what need be done. My lady may be home by now and I should to be there to assist her, for I fear Sir Damian may not reach us until tomorrow.'

'Nay, stay a little,' I said.

I had an idea. Nicholas Berden and his men. They would be of far greater use than any constable or city official, however distinguished the Fitzgerald family might be. For a stolen pauper child, like Ellyn, the officials would not lift a finger, but they might institute a search for an heiress like Sophia. Berden's men, on the other hand, would have their ears open to every whisper in the dark underworld of London. There was a much better chance that they would hear something of what had occurred.

'I know someone who might be able to help,' I said. 'I will come with you and try to reassure Lady Bridget. Have you a servant I could send with a message, to fetch help?'

His face lost a little of his despairing look. 'Of course. But I cannot impose–'

I brushed his words aside as I pulled on my boots and cloak. Rikki looked at me expectantly. I could leave him here, but perhaps I should take him with me. He had shown the other night that I was safer with him at my side.

'I am coming with you,' Simon said. 'I will fetch my cloak as we go downstairs.'

'You are both most kind,' Alchester said, with a tremor in his voice. I felt a surge of pity for him. This was a terrible burden which had been thrust upon him in the absence of his master.

I locked my door, and we started down the stairs.

'What I do not understand about this whole affair,' Simon said, as he came out of his room, fastening his cloak, 'is how Sir Damian is meant to hand over the five thousand pounds in gold. No place is mentioned. Nor any means of contacting these ruffians.'

'That too I wondered,' I said.

'You are right.' Alchester followed us out of the front door and we turned right in the direction of St Mary Overy Stairs. 'I have been so concerned about finding the child that I had not thought how the money is to be paid.'

We trudged past Bessie Travis's whorehouse, where the torches were again burning cheerfully, and I remembered something Alchester had told me about the child Sophia Makepeace. I did not yet mention it to Simon, for I was anxious not to add to the steward's worries. Sophia was the heiress to great estates, but there was another claimant, a distant cousin. Was it possible that this other claimant, having been defeated, as Alchester said, at law, might take matters into his own hands? I could not be sure what the legal position was, but it was possible that, if the child disappeared, he might be able to claim the inheritance. In that case, the demand for five thousand pounds might be no more than a blind, to distract the Fitzgerald family from the true purpose of abducting the child.

Sophia Makepeace might already be dead.

We took a wherry from St Mary Overy Stairs to Salt Wharf, and walked up to Cheapside from there. The Fitzgeralds' house was quite new, probably no more than twenty years old, with herringbone brick between the timbers instead of lath and plaster, four storeys high, elaborately carved on all the exposed timbers. It spoke money, but perhaps a merchant's money rather than a landowner's. I knew little of the Fitzgeralds' past history, but had always assumed they belonged to the landed class, like most of the old Catholic families. The merchant families were, almost without exception, Protestant. Perhaps the house was a recent purchase. Or perhaps it had replaced an earlier one. All over London, men who could afford it were pulling down old houses and building anew. Those who had not the means for such a radical solution to their aspirations for better housing simply defied the regulations and added an extra storey or two on top of their existing homes, like the house where Simon and I had our lodgings.

The Fitzgerald house was in an uproar when we arrived. Lady Bridget had returned home to find her husband's ward kidnapped, her steward disappeared, and her children quarrelling violently. To say that she was astonished when her steward walked into the parlour with two strangers would be to understate the case. For it was clear that at first she did not recognise me. After all, it was more than three years since I had spent barely two weeks in her house, and she had had very little to do with me at the time. As it was, she was now hysterical, being ineffectually comforted by her lady's maid, while Cecilia shouted at her brother in a manner which I thought her aristocratic new husband would not have approved. It was Edward who recognised me first.

'Master Alvarez!' he cried, running across the room to us. 'Can you help us? My fool of a sister–'

Cecilia looked at me and coloured slightly, but then she sneered and said, 'The music tutor? What use is he?'

'My lady,' Alchester said, ignoring her, and addressing Lady Bridget, 'this is Dr Alvarez. He is a physician at St Thomas's, but he also works for Sir Francis Walsingham. He believes he may be able to help. And this is Master Simon Hetherington, his friend.'

I was relieved that he did not mention Simon's profession, which would certainly have condemned us in the eyes of the two ladies. At the words 'Sir Francis Walsingham' I saw a look of fear in Lady Bridget's eyes, but she was too distracted by the present disaster to pay it much heed.

'What do you mean, *Doctor* Alvarez?' Cecilia demanded. 'It is that tutor we had, who ran off in the night with some excuse about his father.'

I gave her the slightest possible bow I could, without an open insult. 'Nevertheless, Cecilia,' I said, 'I am indeed *Doctor* Alvarez. Before we discuss anything further, can you supply me with paper and ink? I need to send word to the man who, I believe, can help. One of Sir Francis's chief men.'

I took some pleasure in addressing her by no more than her Christian name, as when she had been my pupil. She opened her mouth – quite certainly to abuse me – but her mother said sharply, 'Be quiet, Cecilia. If Dr Alvarez can help us, we are grateful.'

The maid found me paper, ink and quill, and I scrawled a quick note to Nick Berden. Alchester summoned a boy to carry the message to Berden's lodgings in Tower Ward. It was getting late, so I hoped he would be at home.

'May we speak to the nursery maid?' Simon asked. 'And learn what she can tell us?'

The girl was sent for. She must have changed her clothes, for she was neatly dressed, but the bruises on her face were large and painful looking, and from her red and swollen eyes it was clear that she had been crying. Cecilia seized her by the arm and shook her.

'This is the fool who let those men seize Sophia! All this is her fault.' And she struck the girl hard on the side of the head.

I walked over to them and prised Cecilia's fingers from the girl's arm.

'You will do no good by striking her,' I said, containing my anger with difficulty. The girl looked no older than Mellie. 'It was you, Cecilia, was it not?, who ordered this child to go with a younger child out into the streets of London, unprotected. At your age, a woman grown, surely you must have known the dangers?'

She stared at me defiantly, then turned and ran out of the room. I was glad to see her go, for her presence only served to make the present situation worse. I led the nursery maid to a stool and made her sit down, which she was reluctant to do in the presence of her mistress, then I crouched down beside her.

'Now,' I said, 'tell us everything you can remember.'

She was a sensible girl and now that Cecilia was gone she was less frightened. She gave her account clearly, but added little to what Alchester had already told us.

'Think very hard,' I said. 'For a short while, when you were in the ale house, you were without the blindfold. Can you describe the men? How many were there?'

'Just two,' she said, 'but they were very big men.' She looked round at Simon, Alchester and me. 'Much bigger than any of you.'

'What sort of men were they? Gentlemen? Of the middling sort?'

'Oh, nay, sir! They were workmen. Rough workmen. Not a gentleman's servants.' She thought for a moment, clearly trying to decide why she had said that. 'Their hands were dirty.'

'Good girl,' I said. 'You have sharp eyes and an excellent memory. How did they speak?'

She frowned for a moment. 'One was a Londoner, I am sure of that. The other, he had a funny way of speaking.' She looked beyond me at Lady Bridget. 'Do you remember that stable lad, my lady, who broke his leg? One of the men spoke like that.'

I looked over my shoulder at Lady Bridget and raised my eyebrows in query.

'He was from the north,' she said slowly. 'Yorkshire, I believe. Do you remember, Alchester?'

'Aye, I remember the lad. It was Yorkshire.'

I turned back to the girl. 'See how well you are remembering. Two men. Big. Workmen with dirty hands. One a Londoner. One from Yorkshire. Can you remember what they looked like?'

She gave me a tentative smile. 'The London man was bigger. Only a little. He had thick arms and black hairs on the back of his hands. His hair was black too. He didn't have a beard, not a real beard, but he had not shaved for a good while.'

'His age?'

She shook her head. 'I cannot tell ages very well, sir. Younger than Master Alchester, but older than you.'

That covered a very wide range of years, but I let it pass. 'And the other man, was he black haired too?'

'Nay, he was brown haired, but he was starting to go bald at the front, although he was younger than the other man. He did have a beard, just a small one, not very thick.' She shivered suddenly. 'He was the worst. The other man was rough, but this one, I think he liked hurting me.' She touched her bruised face carefully with the tips of her fingers. 'He was the one who did this.'

'You have done very well,' I said, 'and I have a salve made from arnica root that will make those bruises disappear more quickly.'

I reached into my satchel. The girl looked confused.

'Dr Alvarez is a physician,' Edwin Alchester said in explanation.

When I had treated the girl's bruises she was sent away to her bed, and Master Alchester rang for a servant to bring a hot posset for Lady Bridget, who was beginning to tremble in the aftermath of shock. The lady herself, belatedly recalling her duties as a hostess to her unexpected and unconventional visitors, told him also to bring us wine and marchpane. Although marchpane seemed a strange thing to be eating in the midst of all this distress, we obligingly ate and drank what we were given. Rikki had been left in the hall when we arrived, but slipped into the parlour behind the servant and hid behind my chair.

It seemed hours before the messenger boy returned, although I am sure he went as fast as he could through the snow to Tower Ward. And with him came Nicholas Berden. I have rarely been so glad to see someone. He was soberly dressed, like a moderately successful merchant, a *persona* he can assume along with many others. I had hoped that he would come at once, but hardly dared to be confident of it.

'This is Master Nicholas Berden,' I said, introducing him to the company in general. 'He is one of Sir Francis Walsingham's most trusted men.' I did not use the word 'agent', having no wish to alarm Lady Bridget any further. 'Master Berden himself employs a number of men who are very skilled at searching London. If there is any whisper anywhere about what has happened to Sophia, they will hear it.'

Nick was invited to sit down. We were becoming quite a democratic little party, all notions of status quite forgot. In the normal course of events, I do not suppose Lady Bridget would have dreamt of sitting down with a player, a junior physician and a spy, but the emergency had levelled all ranks. The steward poured Nick a glass of wine and I repeated in detail everything the nursery maid had been able to remember. At the end of my account, he nodded briskly.

'Now,' he said, 'what I need is a description of the child herself. My lady?'

Lady Bridget had sent her personal maidservant away when the wine was brought in, and now sat somewhat forlornly in a high backed chair, twisting a fine lawn handkerchief between her fingers until the fabric began to shred.

'Sophia is a little over five years old,' she said, 'well grown for her age. A wiry child, for she is never still, yet quite strong and sturdy. Fair haired. Very pretty fair hair, in soft curls.' A sudden sob broke from her, and she pressed the torn handkerchief to her lips.

She turned to her son. 'Edward, was she still wearing the same clothes as she wore when I went out?'

Edward had stayed in the background all this time, listening, but saying nothing. 'Aye, Mama. Except that she put on boots, and wore her mulberry coloured cloak.'

Lady Bridget nodded. 'Then she was wearing a kirtle and overskirt of green velvet, embroidered at the neck and hems with gold thread and pearls. Her underskirt and sleeves were cream satin, also embroidered, in a pattern of green leaves and pink rosebuds. She had a girdle of gold cords, knotted.' She looked across at Nick. 'Does that help?'

'Aye. Excellent.' I knew him well enough to see what he was thinking.

'The child is an heiress, Nicholas,' I explained. 'That is why the money demanded for her release is so great.'

He made no comment on this, but it was plain to see from his face that he found it hard to believe that such a child should have been allowed to wander in the street with no more protection than a young girl.

'And there was nothing in the message,' he said, 'to explain how and where the money is to be paid?'

'Nothing.' Alchester took the scrap of paper out of his purse once again and handed it to Nick, who read it and passed it to me.

'You are an expert at judging handwriting, Kit,' he said. 'What do you make of this?'

He was right. In my work with Phelippes I had learned to recognise the different handwriting of several dozen agents, our own and our enemies'. Early in my time with Walsingham, Phelippes had taught me to forge them where necessary. When Alchester had first shown us the note, I had been so shocked by the contents that I had paid no attention to the handwriting. I now got up and carried the paper over to the candle on the table beside Lady Bridget.

'It has been written with a poor pen and worse ink,' I said slowly, 'but I think this is meant to deceive. What cannot be disguised is that this is a gentleman's writing, in educated secretary hand. This cannot have been written by either of the men the girl described. It must have been prepared beforehand and given to them to pass on through to the family by the maid.'

Nick and I looked at each other and exchanged a slight nod.

'Aye,' he said. 'This is not a random snatch by two ruffians. It has been planned in advance.'

'And they were employed to kidnap the child by some gentleman,' I finished.

It was time to discuss the possibilities.

I set the note down on the table and returned to my chair. 'Lady Bridget,' I said, 'Master Alchester has told me that Sophia Makepeace was consigned as a ward to your husband by her father, who was a lifelong friend. Is that correct?'

She nodded.

'And there is some distant cousin who tried to claim both the child's estates and wardship of the girl herself, but while he has been in London Sir Damian has confirmed that both the wardship and the inheritance are secure in law?'

Again, she nodded. 'The dispute over inheritance of the land even went before the Privy Council in Star Chamber, and the wardship to the Court of Wards. Both were adjudged valid and Sir Howard Wilcox's claim was thrown out.'

'Is it possible that this other claimant – Sir Howard Wilcox, you say? – having lost in the courts, might be behind this kidnapping of the child?'

She pressed the handkerchief to her lips and a stifled sob escaped from her.

'I pray not, Dr Alvarez! For I fear what he might do. He is a man of little property and many debts, who has always lived beyond his present means. Until the child was born, he expected to inherit the estates, although he is quite distant kin. I have never met him, but surely he can have little feeling for Sophia, except that she stands in his way. I know that my husband, who has met him over this matter of the court cases, neither likes nor trusts him. He has fought hard to keep

Sophia safe with us, for he feared what might become of her if this man gained the wardship.'

I wanted to shout out: *Then why did you not keep her safe?* But it would do no good, and only add to the poor woman's distress. She had forbidden the child to go out into the street before she left the house. She must have believed her orders would be obeyed in her absence. Cecilia had much to answer for.

'You understand the situation clearly now, Nick,' I said.

'Of course,' he said, trying to reassure Lady Bridget, who was now weeping openly, 'if this other claimant is behind the seizing of the child, the demand for five thousand pounds may be an attempt to compensate himself in part for the loss of the estates, and he means the child no harm. Most men would be more than content with such a vast sum. In possession of so much gold, he could easily purchase estates of his own.'

'Do you believe so?' She looked at him, painfully hopeful.

'I think that is what we must assume,' he said briskly. 'Now, I must go and brief my men.'

He rose from his chair and picked up his cloak. Rikki sidled out from behind my chair, where I had quite forgotten him, and Nick stooped briefly to rub his head. He glanced across at me and smiled. I knew he was remembering how the three of us had fled across the Low Countries together. Rikki had done us both good service then.

'He is quite healed of that sword thrust, Kit?' Berden asked, running his hand over the spot where a slight ridge in his coat was the only evidence now of Rikki's injury.

'Aye, fit and well, though he protected me from another attacker this very winter.'

Seeing the puzzled expression on Lady Bridget face, I explained. 'Rikki once saved my life from three villains in the Low Countries, and suffered a serious sword cut.'

'It is unfortunate,' Edward said grimly, 'that our little Sophia had no great dog to protect her.' He glowered at the door through which his sister had fled.

'When Sophia is returned to you,' I said, trying to strike a cheerful note, 'perhaps you should get her a dog for protection.'

Edward grinned at me. 'She would like that, the little miss.'

Lady Bridget held out her hands to Berden and said pleadingly, 'Do you believe you will find her, Master Berden?'

'My men know every corner and cranny in London, my lady,' he said, deftly avoiding any promises. 'Now, I will report to you here every noon and evening as we search. Do you think Sir Damian will have returned by tomorrow?'

She pressed her hands to her heart. 'I am sure he will return as soon as he is able, surely before noon tomorrow.'

'We must go also,' I said. 'Try to keep your spirits up, my lady. If anyone can find her, Master Berden will.'

'My friends and I will join in the search,' Simon said. 'We may not be as skilled as Master Berden, but a few more searchers will not go amiss.'

Lady Bridget gave him a vague smile. She must have wondered who and what he was, but was too preoccupied and too well mannered to ask. Indeed, if Simon recruited the other players in these days before they began their winter performances, they might lend considerable help, for their lodgings were scattered about in many different parishes. And the parishes of London, I had found over the years I had lived here, were like a cluster of individual villages, each with its own character, where all the neighbours knew each other.

We bowed ourselves out, Nick, Simon and I, escorted by Alchester, while Edward followed us, fondling Rikki's long drooping ears.

'He is a fine dog, Dr Alvarez,' he said longing. 'I miss our dogs now that I attend school in London. Did you say he was with you in the Low Countries?'

'Aye,' I said. 'He belonged to a brave soldier in Amsterdam, crippled in the wars with the Spanish. When he master was murdered, he followed me, and he has been with me ever since.'

'Murdered!' He opened his eyes in wonder.

'I will tell you the whole story someday.'

He laid his hand on my sleeve as the steward opened the door.

'Dr Alvarez,' he whispered, so that his mother might not hear through the open door, 'you do not think that Sophia will be killed, do you?' There were tears in his eyes. 'I should have stopped them. I knew they should not go out into the street alone, a child and that maidservant who is no older than I am. Or I should have gone with them for protection.'

'Edward,' I said, 'even if you had gone, what could you have done? These were big men and violent. You might have been killed or taken hostage yourself. There was no way you could have prevented what they were determined to do.'

'Cecilia should never have allowed it,' he said bitterly. 'She cares nothing for little Sophia, but I wish Sophia were my sister, instead of Cecilia.'

'Cecilia should not have given her permission.' I had no sympathy for the selfish, arrogant girl. 'Nor should she blame the little maidservant, who could no more have prevented what happened than you could. What you must do now, Edward, is offer up your most fervent prayers that Sophia will be found, and soon.'

He nodded, letting go of my sleeve, but as he turned away, he dashed his hand across his eyes.

'We are most grateful to you,' Alchester said, including the three of us in his glance. 'I did not know where to begin. I feared that if I went to the Sheriffs of London and they made a great to-do, we might never see the child again. That is why I came to you, Dr Alvarez.'

'Very wise,' Nick said. 'Best to go about this quietly. My men will try to discover first whether these two ruffians are known in London, and have not come from elsewhere. If they are known, their neighbourhood and cronies will be known. We will start from there.'

Alchester thanked us again profusely, and I think he might have gone on thanking us for some time, had not a few flakes of snow begun to drift down between us.

'Do not stand in the cold,' I urged. 'Go within and look after your mistress. Let us hope that Master Berden will have some news for us tomorrow.'

At last he stepped inside, drawing the door to behind him, and the three of us stood there in Cheapside, looking at each other less cheerfully than we had allowed ourselves to appear in the Fitzgeralds' parlour.

'Well, Nick,' I said, 'what do you think? Can you find the child?'

He shook his head. 'Difficult to say, Kit. I am tempted to think as you do that this is no simple snatching of a richly dressed child. That happens often enough in London, but the usual practice of those thieves is to strip off the rich clothes for resale and turn the child loose naked. Though that would be likely to be fatal in this weather.'

'It seems something much more carefully planned is at work here,' Simon said.

'Forgive me,' I said, 'I did not introduce Simon Hetherington in there, because I was not sure of Lady Bridget.'

Simon grinned. 'What Kit means is that the poor lady would have become even more hysterical, had she realised she had a common player in her parlour.'

I frowned at him. 'Simon is one of Lord Strange's Men. James Burbage's company.'

The two men bowed.

'Then I must have seen you perform,' Nick said, momentarily diverted from the matter in hand. 'At the Theatre.'

'Aye, but for the winter we will be appearing at the Cross Keys, from next week.'

'You are right, Master Hetherington,' Nick said. 'This was planned in advance. Kit has identified the writing of the note to be in a gentleman's hand. It seems likely that this other claimant to the estates may be behind the affair.'

'Sir Howard Wilcox,' I said. 'If he is, what a devil he must be, to treat a small child so. She must be terrified.' I did not voice my fears that she might already be beyond all terror, but I saw from the expression of their faces in the flickering light of the Fitzgeralds' door lanterns, that they feared the same.

'Well,' Nick said, 'I am off to instruct my men. They will make a start tonight, in the ale houses which keep illegal late hours. I will report back here, as I promised, twice a day.'

'My friends and I will be glad to help,' Simon said. 'Will you send word to the Cross Keys tomorrow morning? Tell us what you want us to do, and we will do it.'

'Aye,' Nick said, 'I will.'

'I have my duties at St Thomas's,' I said, 'but when I am finished for the day, I can search also.'

Nick considered for a moment. 'You might be best to make enquiries in Southwark, Kit. Amongst your poor patients and the servants and workmen at the hospital. Someone may have heard a whisper of a child where there was no child before.'

I nodded. Nick turned to leave, but I stopped him. 'While your men are searching, will you ask them to watch out for a group of pauper children, beggars?'

I described Matthew and his friends. 'They used to beg at the playhouse, but now that it is closed, they have disappeared. I fear for them in this terrible weather.'

Simon smiled. 'Kit collects waifs and strays. But if you see the little vagrants, tell them that the cook at the Cross Keys hands out leftover food to the poor at the kitchen door every night at ten o' the clock. I have seen him do it. They would be well to come and benefit by it.'

'I will,' Nick said. 'Good night, and God go with you both.'

'And with you, Nick,' I said.

He headed down Cheapside, which had now been partially cleared of the drifted snow, while Simon and I turned along one of the steep narrow streets which led down from Cheapside to the river. At

143

first we walked in silence, for it was hard going through the deep-lying snow, though the falling flakes were no more than a thin veil, compared with last night's blizzard. I had no idea what hour it was until the church clocks began to strike the hour.

'Eleven,' Simon said. 'You will be hard put to it to wake in time for the hospital tomorrow morning.'

I nodded, but saved my breath for the effort of ploughing on. At last we reached Salt Wharf where, to our relief, there was still one boat manned by a wherryman, who was fast asleep under his tilt cloth, wrapped in two blankets. Simon shook him awake and persuaded him to row us across the river, for three times the normal fare. On the way across we took possession of the blankets, thinking it only just when the man would be kept warm by his rowing, while we sat and shivered in the cutting wind.

At St Mary Overy Stairs we climbed out stiffly and paid the man. None of us had spoken a word as we crossed, and he merely grunted now, making himself a bed again under the tilt cloth. It seemed unlikely that he would get another fare that night, but perhaps he had nowhere else to go. At both wherry stations there had been thin ice, but not enough yet to bear out the warnings that the river might freeze altogether.

Still in an exhausted silence we trudged along the Bankside roadway toward our lodgings.

'Even the whorehouse is closed,' I said.

'Even whores must sleep.'

'Not usually before midnight.'

'I expect few of their clients are venturing out late in this weather. All sensible men are in bed, or seated by a good fire with a pot of ale.'

The steps up to our front door had frozen over treacherously. I slipped and would have gone down on my knees, had Simon not grabbed me by the elbow.

'I thank you,' I said breathlessly, for his touch always set off a lurch in my stomach that I could not control. 'That was timely.'

'You need studs to your boots in this weather.'

'I *have* studs to my boots,' I answered indignantly, and laid my hand on the latch of the door.

'Kit,' he said, 'do you think that child is still alive? I do not like the sound of this other claimant, this Sir Howard Wilcox.'

'Nor I.' I paused, and Rikki leaned against my knee, half asleep. He too had had a trying day. 'I suppose that, as long as the child can be used to bargain with the Fitzgeralds, she will be kept alive. That is, if we are right and it is Wilcox who is behind the kidnapping.'

'But once she is no longer of use,' Simon said, 'they may slit her throat, as they have threatened.'

'That,' I said, 'is what I fear.'

Chapter Eleven

$\mathcal{I}$ slept badly that night. For a long time I lay awake, staring up at the ceiling of my room. By now I knew every fine crack in the plaster, every patch of damp or mould, from which I painted fantastic pictures in my imagination. After the brief flurry as we were making our way home, the snow had ceased and even while we walked along from St Mary Overy Stairs we could see that a strong northwesterly wind in the high heavens was blowing the snow clouds downriver and out to sea. The sky had cleared and now the pale face of a wan moon shone down on London for the first time in many nights. The blanket of snow thrown over the land reflected the moonlight upwards, so that, between the moon and its sister image, a beam flowed in between my window curtains, which I had not drawn quite together, illuminating my chamber with a ghostly light. Huddled deep under my blankets and my thin feather quilt I could not summon the energy to climb out into the cold room – for I had not relit my fire – to pull the curtains together and shut out the light.

As usual, Rikki was curled up beside me on the bed and I was glad of his warmth, and even more of his company, but I could not settle, although I should have been ready enough to sleep after yesterday's blizzard and today's trials. Why is it, when we most crave sleep, that our minds will not give us rest?

I could not rid my head of the thought of that child, Sophia Makepeace. Five years old and gently reared, her father's only child and certainly dear to him, for he had taken great care to provide for her safety and welfare in the heart of his friend's family. Where was she now, even if she was still alive? I knew nothing of kidnappings. Working in Phelippes's office and undertaking missions for Walsingham, I had become familiar with the crimes of treason, conspiracy, and assassination, but this was a different kind of crime altogether, directed against a child. I had read the broadsheets hawked about the streets, recounting tales of the strange crimes, mysteries, and other wondrous happenings in the city of London. My friend Peter Lambert at Bart's had sometimes brought them in to read, where we discussed them, wondering whether they could be true, or mere invention, intended to earn a few shillings for the writer and printer. Cases of kidnapping were sometimes reported, but the only ones I could remember involved the capture of marriageable girls, who were then forced into a secret wedding against their will, so that a rejected suitor or some other undesirable man could lay claim to the girl's landed property or dowry. I had never heard of the capture of a child.

I turned over in irritation at my inability to go to sleep, and Rikki grunted in complaint. He was having no difficulty in sleeping, which was even more provoking.

Where had those men taken the child? It was my belief that the visit to the ale house was no more than a temporary pause. Their cart was probably hidden there in the yard, for it would have been too conspicuous for them to have had it with them while they lurked in Cheapside. They had then bundled the maidservant into it, driven it to Lothbury and thrown her into the alley. She had been sure Sophia was not with her. I should have asked why she thought this. It could well be that one man drove off with her in the cart while the other carried Sophia away somewhere else. But where? Did Sir Howard Wilcox own a house or have lodgings in London? That was something else I should have asked.

I turned over again, angry with myself, and with Nick Berden, who should have thought of it as well. Perhaps he had. He might have means to find out where Wilcox lodged when in London and did not want to cause greater panic in the Fitzgerald household by mentioning it. If Wilcox did have a London house, that would be the first place to look, more urgent than trying to trace the two ruffians. The more I considered, the more convinced I was that the two men had merely been hired to do the deed and might well have pocketed their fee and vanished from London by now. It was already many hours since the child had been snatched.

In case Nick had not had the same thought, I would send him a message tomorrow by one of the lads who ran errands at St Thomas's. I sat up in bed. I could write the message now.

The cold air hit me like a blow in the face. What was I thinking of? It was hours until morning. There was no need to write a message until then. Rikki raised his head and looked at me anxiously. Usually I fell asleep at once, tired after a full day on my feet at the hospital and

147

he could not understand what was amiss with me. I rubbed him behind the ears, his favourite spot.

'I'm sorry, lad,' I said. 'I did not mean to wake you. I will try to lie still, and then I will sleep. Perhaps.'

He thumped his tail and licked my face, so that I slid down again under the bedclothes, curled around his warm and protective form.

And perhaps my good intentions had some effect, for I found myself dropping into sleep, in that strange land between waking and sleep when you know that sleep awaits you like a dark, calm lake that you can somehow enter, and yet breath and live.

Except, that in that deep sleep, dreams come to torment you.

I was in a dark, windowless room. It was very cold, and damp, and I was very frightened. I was a child again. Was I Caterina, in the cell of the Inquisition in Portugal? Or was I Sophia, held somewhere – a cellar, an outbuilding, a prison – all alone, hurt, terrified, not knowing what was to be done to me? Whoever I was in my dream, I became more and more frightened. A man with black hairs on the back of his hands. A man come to drag my mother away to be tortured.

In my terror I tried to cry out. Again and again I struggled to make a noise, but my throat gagged and no sound came out. Something or someone was holding me down. I fought so hard to scream that the struggle woke me.

I was tangled in my blankets and hanging half out of the bed, and although the room was bitterly cold I was sweating with terror. Rikki was sitting up and whining anxiously. I gasped for breath and pressed my hands to my face. I could not stop shaking.

Slowly I pulled myself upright and put my arms around Rikki, burying my face in his fur. My face was wet with tears, but Rikki began to lick them away.

'Oh, Rikki!' I gulped and pushed my hair back from my sticky face. 'What would I do without you? I think you are the only one in the whole world who loves and understands me.'

I thrust my legs tentatively out of bed. This was doing no good. I was going to light a fire. I groped about until I found my flint and tinder to light a candle, then used the candle to light a spill. The hearth was quite cold, but I had a pile of kindling as well as firewood and a bucket of sea coal. Within a few minutes I had a fire going and had pulled my cloak round my shoulders. Sitting at the table with my candle, I wrote my note to Berden, then I found myself some bread and a scraping of butter, so I made myself some of the famous Cockney buttered toast. Rarely has it tasted better. I gave Rikki a bone I had been saving for him, and we sat together beside the fire, chewing contentedly. By the time I was warmed through, and no longer sweating in panic, I had heard the clock on St Mary Olave strike three in the morning. After the toast I was thirsty, so I warmed some ale with spices and drank that slowly, until a sluggish feeling of sleepiness began to steal over me. Perhaps now I could sleep.

I shovelled a layer of ashes, kept for the purpose, over my fire, so it would stay alight but damped down until the morning. My bed was a tangled heap, but by the time I had straightened it I was ready to fall onto the mattress like one barely alive. Resignedly Rikki jumped up again, making the ropes creak, and with a look that clearly said he hoped I would let him sleep in peace now. Lying on my side, I watched the dull glow of the fire and told myself firmly to think more pleasant thoughts. Mellie's face alight when she learned she could stay at Christ's with Hannah. Ellyn skipping off hand in hand with Moll, her long hair as bright as the Queen's.

When I arrived at St Thomas's the following morning, I was met just inside the door by Mistress Maynard, who quite clearly had been lying in wait for me.

'Dr Alvarez,' she began at once in exasperated tones, after barely giving me 'Good morrow', 'we cannot keep that imp Davy here any longer. He must be sent to Christ's Hospital or found a position before he does any more damage.'

With a sinking heart, I said, 'What has he done now?'

'Handstands or flips – whatever he calls them – all the way along the corridor outside the ward until he collided with one of my girls and made her drop a tray of breakfast dishes.'

'Oh.' I said lamely.

'Fortunately, most were pewter, but they are badly dented. Three earthenware bowls broken, and a waste of good food, while the mothers had to wait another half hour while the cooks made more. And the mess! I need not tell you!'

I could imagine it, but I could also imagine Davy, whom we had almost lost two weeks before from his lung infection, springing along the corridor, rejoicing in his restored strength and skill.

'I am very sorry he has been such a trouble to you, Mistress Maynard,' I said, 'but until this last week I was unsure that he would recover. We cannot possibly send him to Christ's. Think what havoc he would cause there! I have thought of someone who might take him on as an apprentice, and I will hope to see him today. In the meantime, keep all breakables well away from Davy and his antics.'

She looked very dubious. 'I cannot think who would take such a scamp on as an apprentice. He will wreak havoc wherever he goes.'

'Ah, but this is someone exceptional, who might be just the master Davy needs.'

When I reached the children's ward, I gave Davy a stern warning that he was to cause no more trouble.

'I may be able to find a place for you, but if you cannot behave as you should when there are so many sick people and young babies about, then I fear there will be nothing for it but a blue-coat uniform and schooling at Christ's Hospital. Where there will be no opportunity for acrobatics.'

'What sort of a place for me?' He attempted a frown through his tumble of thick hair, but only succeeded in looking anxious.

'You must wait and see,' I said. I did not want to raise his hopes, only to dash them again. 'In the meantime, I am going to ask Mistress Maynard to find some work for you to do. If you can turn handstands you are strong enough to do some useful tasks for her.'

I conducted a slightly sobered Davy to Mistress Maynard's parlour, where she thought for a moment, then said, 'You shall come with me to the old men's quarters. There is always work to be done there, fetching and carrying, for some of them are very feeble.'

As well as caring for the sick poor of Southwark, and the patients passed on to us from St Bartholomew's, which they believed incurable, St Thomas's also provided an extended almshouse for those too old and feeble to care for themselves, together with younger people who were blind or crippled or feeble minded. Bart's had made the same provision, for it had been part of the duty of both hospitals when they were established after the monasteries were dissolved. The monks had provided for both the sick and the helpless, and this had fallen as a legacy to both the restored hospitals. At Bart's I had had little to do with the permanent residents, except occasionally when one was ill. Here at St Thomas's I had so far had only one patient amongst the old men, a frail former wherryman who had an open sore on one calf which would not heal. I had been treating it with the same egg white preparation I had used in the summer on my own burned hand. Slowly, very slowly, it was beginning to draw together.

I walked across the courtyard with Davy and Mistress Maynard, to the separate building which was divided in half, the rooms to the right of the handsome doorway being provided for women, those on the left for men. The hospital servants had been hard at work, so that the centre of the courtyard was now clear of the worst of the snow, although there were great mounds of it heaped up against the perimeter wall.

Davy looked about him apprehensively as we entered the paupers' quarters. 'What shall I do, Mistress Maynard?'

'We will speak to Master Pilbury, who oversees the men's quarters, and he will find you something useful to do.'

I watched them go off in search of Master Pilbury with a smile. Davy for once seemed quite subdued. My patient, I was glad to see, was looking much better. The sore was no longer weeping and he swore he was in no more pain. Normally, this patient would not have come under my care, but Superintendent Ailmer, having observed the healing of my own injured hand, had allocated me the care of the old waterman.

Without Davy, the children's ward was quieter than usual, although it rang to the coughs of the many winter illnesses which always plagued Londoners. The thick coal smoke which hung in the air and the occasional Thames fogs did nothing to relieve them, though the recent clean cold air was easier to breath. The cold, however, brought its own burdens.

Soon after I returned from the almshouse, one of the hospital servants came into the ward carrying what looked like nothing more than a bundle of rags.

'A girl child,' he said, not without compassion. 'A beggar of seven or eight years old, I'd guess. The butcher just here-by found her in his doorway this morning. Frozen and starving. Still alive, but not for long.'

He deposited the bundle on one of the cots and went off again to his duties. One of the nursing sisters came hurrying over, her heels clacking on the floor in her haste.

'What was he thinking of, dropping that filth on the clean sheets! We have just made up that bed afresh.' And she went to drag the child on to the floor. Not all the women who work in the hospitals have much kindness for the dregs of the London alleys.

'Wait!' I said. 'The child is very ill. Take care!'

I leaned over the girl to examine her, though there was little to be seen, for the butcher or the servant had almost covered her face. All I could make out was a small snub nose covered with freckles. For a shocking moment I thought it was Maggie, one of the twins who went with Matthew, but when I turned back the threadbare cloth over her face, I saw that it was another child, of much the same age. Her eyes were sunken deep into their sockets and the fragile bones of her face poked up against the dirty skin as if they were trying to break through. I laid the back of my hand against her forehead, but her eyes did not open. I expected to find signs of a fever, but she was as cold as the frozen banks of the Thames.

The sister had brought a large basin of water, with soap and rags to wash the girl, something we always do with our new arrivals, who generally bear more than the normal burden of dirt, along with colonies of fleas and lice. She started to strip off the rags, but I shook my head.

'She is too far sunk in cold,' I said. 'Just remove the outer layer, but do not strip her to the skin. Wash her face and hands, and comb the nits out of her hair, then wrap her in two clean blankets.'

The woman's face showed what she thought of my interference with her routine, but she dared not contradict me. I left her to the task and sent a maidservant to fetch a hot stone wrapped in a piece of old blanket, so we could warm the child. As always in winter, we kept a good fire going in the ward, but the girl's flesh had felt colder than any living thing I had ever touched.

I checked on my other patients and when I returned the beggar girl was wrapped in blankets and covered with a feather quilt, with the hot stone at her feet, but she was still as cold as dead flesh. I pulled up a stool to sit by her bed. One hand had strayed outside the blankets and I took it in mine, chafing it to warm it. Her eyelids flickered, but did not open.

'What is your name?' I asked. 'You are safe now, as St Thomas's Hospital. Soon you will have some hot soup and then you will get better.'

I thought that she heard me, for her eyelids moved again, but she did not speak. For about an hour I sat there, rubbing her hands and talking quietly from time to time.

Then she was quite still, and I knew that she had died.

We had another loss that day. One of the new babies, whose mother was weakened with a congestion of the lungs, looked very frail from the moment of birth and died toward the end of the afternoon. The women in the lying-in ward, who were often quite boisterous, grew very quiet. They had first seen the small coffin of cheap wood carried past their open door from the children's ward, and now the baby was taken away in a box that could have held a rabbit.

The prostitute Meg, who had tried so hard to rid herself of her unwanted pregnancy, now seemed resigned to carrying the child to full term. As far as I could judge, the injuries inflicted on her by the abortionist had healed, but there was no way we could tell whether the unborn child was harmed. By my reckoning, it should be born around

Christmas Day, an auspicious time for an unloved child. Perhaps the blessing of the season would change the mother's mind.

All through that sad day I was restless, wondering how the search for Sophia Makepeace was proceeding. I had sent off my note to Nick Berden as soon as I arrived at the hospital in the morning, but had received no answer, though I had hardly expected one. Perhaps he was annoyed that I was suggesting what he already had well in hand. Since Simon and the other players were helping in the search, I thought that one of them might send me word, but the day passed and I heard nothing.

At last I was free to go. Davy had returned, in an odd frame of mind, quieter but slightly boastful, talking of how he had fetched and carried for the old men, even emptying piss pots (which I do not think was much to his liking).

'One of the men had an old lute,' he said. 'It wasn't much good, some of the courses were broken and I had to restring it. But when I had it tuned, I played and sang for them.'

He gave me a slantwise look.

'One of the men said my songs were shocking, but they laughed anyway.'

'I did not know you could play the lute and sing,' I said.

'I can play most instruments,' he said scornfully, 'though I like the trumpet best. And anyone can sing.'

The choice of trumpet did not surprise me. Still, it was useful to know this.

'I thought you went with a troupe of acrobats,' I said.

'A touring player must be able to turn his hand to anything,' he said, with all the air of a professional performer.

Aye, I thought. Steal a chicken. Cut a purse. Poach a salmon.

'Well, Davy,' I said, 'I am glad you were able to cheer the old men, however shocking your songs. I am off now to see the man who might have a position for you.'

Again he gave me that anxious look, but I was not prepared to tell him any more.

When I reached the Cross Keys in Gracechurch Street, the players were just coming in, cold, wet, tired and frustrated. They had spent the day searching London under Nick Berden's direction, but had found no sign of the missing child. Nick arrived soon after, having taken the news – or lack of it – to the Fitzgeralds.

'At least Sir Damian has now reached home,' he said, wearily stretching out his wet boots to the fire and accepting a pot of double beer from James Burbage.

Master Burbage alone had not been out searching. He was needed to supervise the continuing work on the indoor theatre, for the inn yard was too open to serve for a winter theatre. The innkeeper had agreed to the use of his great hall, the oldest part of the building. In shape, if not in decoration, it was not unlike the dining hall of one of the Inns of Court, so that it would serve the purpose well, with a new platform built at one end as a stage, where once there has been a dais. Like me, Burbage was anxious for any word of Sophia.

'The only thing we have achieved,' Nick said, after he had drunk deep of his beer, 'is to find out something of the men who seized her. The dark man, the Londoner, is one Ambrose Selby.'

'A grand name for a lowly villain,' Someone said. I think it was Will.

Nick nodded. 'He is well known to some of my men. Available for hire to anyone who pays well enough. Able for anything from petty theft to murder. He has managed to avoid the law so far, but he has skated very close to it. Once he was on trial for doing grave harm to another villain, but he managed to raise enough compurgators to speak for him. My men say people are so afraid of him that he did not even need to bribe them. His threats were enough to persuade them to bear witness to his good conduct and his innocence.'

'Murder?' I whispered.

'Aye, but he charges high for that, and he has not been seen flashing the chinks. So the word goes. It's said he demands half his fee in advance, or he will report his would-be employer to the magistrates, and when he has the chinks he throws them about. I do not think he was employed for murder this time.'

'What of the other man?' Dick Burbage asked. 'The Yorkshire man?'

Berden shook his head. 'Nothing. My lads have found no word of him yet. There was one innkeeper down by Billingsgate who said he might have seen him, but they have fishing boats from all along the east coast in and out there. It could have been another Yorkshire man, a seaman.'

He turned to me. 'Your lad brought the message. I had the same idea in mind myself, but it has taken me most of the day to discover where Wilcox lodges in London. I went off on a false trail at first, in search of a town house belonging to Sir Howard Wilcox, out on the north side of the Strand. The roads are still blocked out toward

Westminster. You would think, with all the great people who live along the Strand, that the roads would have been cleared, but it seems they have simply taken to their private barges and avoid the roads. I found the house at last, only to be told that Sir Howard sold it nearly two years ago.'

He took another long swig of his beer and Dick topped up his jar.

'I found the steward of one of the neighbouring houses, who said it was well known that Sir Howard was greatly in debt, so that he was obliged to sell his house to satisfy some of his creditors. The steward did not know where Sir Howard was to be found now. Eventually I tracked him down, not an hour since. He has rented a modest house in Wood Street.'

Wood Street? I thought. Where the Lopez family lived. I might have passed the man in the street while I was living with them a few months ago.

'So you will keep a watch on this house now?' Simon said, voicing my own thoughts.

'I have stationed two men on watch already.' Nick was being very patient with his unskilled assistants. 'Though I doubt whether they will see anything during the night.'

He shook his head. 'Sir Damian is anxious we should do nothing to alert or annoy Wilcox, for he fears if we are mistaken and the man has no part in this, then he will use our actions as weapons to attack Sir Damian at law, and overturn the decisions about the inheritance and the wardship. For the same reason he is reluctant to involve the city authorities, for fear it could be claimed that he is not a fit guardian for the little heiress. That he did not make proper provision for her safety.'

'Were you able to ascertain what kind of household Wilcox keeps?' I asked.

He flashed me a look which showed that I understood this business better than the players. 'Very small. He is unmarried. No children. It is very much a single man's household. A steward and a body servant, a cook, two maids to clean and wash.'

'So he has been obliged to retrench, being so much in debt,' I said. 'More and more it seems he must be behind this. Five thousand pound in gold would mean a great deal to such a man.'

'Aye, and the child's great estates would mean even more.'

I thought of those broadsheets telling the tales of girls kidnapped to be forced into marriage. I mentioned them hesitantly.

'Could a child this young be compelled to marry?' I said. 'I do not know what the law says, but if he married her, he would gain possession of her property.'

It seemed none of us knew whether a valid marriage could be forced on a child so young, without the consent of a parent or guardian.

'One other thing I have done,' Nick said. 'I have spoken to the city constables about any children taken up dead since yesterday, without mentioning Sophia Makepeace by name. There have been seven boys and eight girls found in the street, dead of the cold and hunger, but none answering the description of Sophia.'

For a moment I felt sick, remembering the little girl who had been brought into St Thomas's that morning and died. I had feared at first she might be Maggie. What if these other dead children included Matthew's little band? For a time I paid little heed to what was being said.

As if he guessed what was passing through my mind, Nick turned to me. 'You asked us to look out for that group of beggar waifs you know. Well, Tom Lewen met with them lurking about the Royal Exchange this afternoon, before being chased off. You remember Tom Lewen, you physicked him when he was attacked near the Italian merchant's house in the summer.'

'Aye, I remember him.' A wave of relief swept over me. The children had still been alive today. 'He spoke to them?'

'Spoke to them and gave them the message about the scraps at the kitchen door here. I'd not be surprised if they appeared tonight.'

At once I determined to speak to them, though it would be a long while yet. Burbage had once again bespoken a supper for us all, included Nick and me. At this rate he would beggar himself before he took any admission fees for the company's winter plays.

When we sat down to eat, I took the place next to Guy. 'There is something I want to discuss with you,' I said.

'Simon has told me that you may join me in a duet for lutes at Her Majesty's Twelfth Night Revels,' he said with a teasing smile.

I had been so caught up in the affair of Sophia Makepeace I had quite forgotten the grave matter of the fresh threat against the Queen.

'I may be obliged to,' I said, 'if there is no other way. It was another matter I wanted to raise. We had a boy brought into St Thomas's several weeks ago – Davy, his name is – who was found dying in a ditch just outside Southwark. He had spent all the life he can remember with a troupe of travelling acrobats, but has no memory of where he came from, or who his parents were. They trained him up in all kinds of acrobatic tricks. He is as lithe and flexible as a cat. They went about from fair to fair, both in England and the Low Countries, and sometimes performed at weddings or at rich men's feasts. Then there was a falling-out, a fight, one man was killed. He woke the next morning to find them all vanished, save for the body of the dead man.'

'A sorry tale,' Guy said.

I nodded. 'He tried to follow, but could not find them, made his way towards London, then eventually collapsed and was near death when he was brought in. Partly from starvation, partly from an inflammation of the lungs. Just when we thought he was recovering, his lungs grew worse and we nearly lost him. However, he is better now and I want to find him a place.'

Guy raised his eyebrows but said nothing.

'He is a little wild,' I admitted. 'I will not lie to you, but he is a very clever acrobat, plays several instruments and can sing. I wondered whether you would give him a trial, to train him up to be a comic actor and musician.'

There, I had laid it all before him.

Guy was rolling his bread into pellets, then raised his eyes to me. 'Simon has said that you have had a perfect orgy of rescuing children lately, Kit.'

'And where is the fault in that?' I was suddenly angry. Angry that Simon should say that of me, angry that Guy should react in this way.

'Nay, do not glare at me, Kit! I have been destitute and without hope myself in my day. Bring me this Davy lad. Tomorrow if you wish. And I will put him through his paces. If he shows some promise, I will take him on for, let us say, three months. He shall have food, lodging and clothes, but no wages. I will settle the matter with Master Burbage. He will be no expense to the company. If after three months I think we can make something of him, I will undertake to persuade Master Burbage to admit him into the company.'

'Thank you,' I said gruffly, grateful for his agreement, but still annoyed at what both he and Simon seemed to find amusing.

'Simon has also been telling me of this other matter,' Guy went on. If he sensed my continuing annoyance, he ignored it.

'Other matter?'

'About the Twelfth Night Revels.'

'Of course.'

There was no help for it. Phelippes had told me to find out all I could about the other entertainers and I could not do so without making the players aware that I was asking questions. I believed all the players of Lord Strange's Men to be trustworthy, at least I hoped they were. I knew little of the new man, Will Shakespeare, but he had played a stalwart part in helping Ellyn escape from her brute of a father. I knew even less of the young boys. Some were no more than lads who ran errands and hoped in return for food and a place to sleep. Others, with a talent for acting or music, were being trained up to play the women's parts, as Simon had once done, or to sing and dance in the musical entertainments that usually ended every performance.

'You want to know whether the other entertainers at the Revels can be vouched for,' Guy said. 'Master Burbage has been discussing the entertainments with the Queen's Master of the Revels, and all the companies he knows of are English and loyal. A consort of viols. They are London musicians and we know them. A troupe of Morris dancers from Essex. Our own Will Kempe, doing a song and dance of his devising. What the Master of the Revels keeps close secret is the more outlandish parts of the entertainment, and that is where your assassin is likely to be. He will be a foreigner, and most of them are foreigners.'

He sipped his beer and reached for a handful of nuts.

'Pass the nutcrackers, Christopher!' he called. When he had cracked a few and passed some to me, he went on. 'The Dutchmen are probably safe enough. I think it unlikely, even in the interests of novelty, that there will be any Spaniards. Or, after those puppeteers at Bartholomew Fair in the summer, any Italians. There may be a Turkish sword swallower. I have heard that there are some Polish jugglers. Are Poles dangerous to Her Majesty?'

I shrugged. 'That I cannot say.' I had had nothing to do with Poles, although I knew Phelippes sometimes received despatches from that far off country, and even from Muscovy.

'Now your Frenchman–' Guy chewed thoughtfully on a walnut which had proved difficult to crack. 'Your Frenchman is a slippery creature.'

I agreed. Over the past years our relations with France had swung to and fro. Once there had been the much talked-about possibility that the Queen might marry the Duke of Anjou, but it had come to nothing, despite good will on both sides. But on the other hand, there had been the horror of the massacre of Protestants in Paris and elsewhere in France on St Bartholomew's Day seventeen years ago. And of course, more recently, the Duke of Guise, cousin of the Scottish queen, had been implicated in the plot to assassinate our Queen and put his cousin on the throne.

'Aye,' I said. 'A Frenchman cannot be trusted. Have you heard that any are to be there on Twelfth Night?

'Nay, not to my knowledge, but that means nothing. As I have said, the Master of the Revels likes to spring surprises on the Court.'

All this had not taken me much further, but I would report back to Phelippes what little I knew.

'I am sorry we can be of so little help,' Guy said, 'but whatever we hear, we will pass on to you. And in the meantime, I believe Master Berden will be there, keeping watch?'

'He will.'

'He seems to know his business. And you will play a lute duet with me?'

'If I must,' I said gloomily. 'I must do it behind a curtain, or masked, for there are those in the Court who would recognise me, and that would be unfortunate in many different ways.'

'Indeed?' Guy was curious. 'Who would that be?'

I counted them off on my fingers. 'My lord of Essex, Sir Francis Drake, Lord Burghley, Lord Admiral Howard, Dom Antonio. Even Her Majesty the Queen herself, and they say she never forgets a face.'

Guy opened his eyes in astonishment. 'You have met the *Queen*?'

I nodded, remembering a room in Greenwich Palace full of courtiers as colourful and lifeless as a bouquet of artificial silk flowers.

'It was after I had been in the Low Countries. I am afraid I cannot speak of it.'

I was worried that Guy might press me to tell more, despite what I said, but the party at table was beginning to break up and I was able to escape.

'Do you walk back to Southwark now?' Simon asked.

'Aye, soon,' I said, 'though I fear we must take a wherry again. It is becoming costly, staying so late in the City every night, after the gates close.'

'But at least we are well fed,' he pointed out. 'And that saves us far more than the fare.'

'Certainly that is true. But before we set off, I want to see whether the children you call my waifs will come to be fed at the kitchen door of the inn.'

I spoke somewhat stiffly, for I still did not like the idea of Simon and Guy laughing at me behind their hands. However, Simon made no attempt to tease me now, but came quite willingly with me to the inn kitchen, where we found the assistant chef shovelling the leftover scraps of food all willy-nilly on to trenchers of old dry bread.

'Do you mix everything together?' I said, somewhat sickened to see him ladling a custard on top of a half chewed mutton chop.

'These beggars know no better,' he said indifferently. 'Let them be thankful to God and my master for what they get. And we cannot trust them even with platters of treen, for they make off with them to sell. We give them bread trenchers instead.'

He lined up the disgusting heaps on a large wooden tray, of the sort bakers' boys carry on their heads.

'Would you do me the kindness, Master,' he said to me, 'to open the door for me? It is as much as I can do to stop them knocking me over as they grab the food.'

I did as he asked and opened the door, stepping to one side to let him pass. The light from the kitchen candles and hearth flowed out over a miserable group standing patiently in the snow. None of them looked hearty enough to knock over the cook, who was very nearly as wide as he was tall, with a belly carried before him like a proud full-rigged ship with a following wind.

Matthew and the other children were there, elbowed to the back by the adult beggars, who were however strong enough to bully children.

'Bring something for the children,' I hissed at Simon, grabbing two trenchers from the tray before they should all be snatched. I passed them over the heads of those in front to Matthew and Katerina, then seized one more for Jamey as Simon passed a trencher each to the twins. There was some angry muttering amongst the other beggars, but there was plenty for all.

Matthew beckoned to his band and they backed away into the darkness beyond the reach of the light. I hurried after them, for I did not want to lose them. Besides, I wanted their help. Simon followed me.

The children were squatting down in the snow, gobbling the food as fast as any starving stray dog, but I was glad to see that they still had the warm clothes and blankets I had given them. I had feared they might have been forced to sell them to buy food.

'This was a good tip-off you give us, Master,' Matthew said, stuffing a last fragment into his mouth and wiping his lips on his sleeve. He addressed the air somewhere between us. I saw that every scrap of every bone-hard trencher had disappeared as well, even little Jamey's. They must have teeth like wolves.

'Have you managed to stay warm, Matthew,' I said, 'through these terrible blizzards? I have been worried for you.'

'We was well enough until two days ago,' he said. 'We had a cavey in a tenters' shed out on Moorfields. Then some upright man and his doxy turned us out.' He spat contemptuously on to the snow.

I was not sure precisely what he meant, but I caught his general meaning well enough. 'Where have you been since then?'

He looked shifty. 'Here and there. We don't stay in the same place twice, for fear of the constables.'

'You know that you could always go to Christ's Hospital,' I said, without much hope. 'They would take you in.'

'Them? There's like a prison. And me and Katerina, we'd be too old. We'd be sent to Bridewell. And that *is* a prison.'

'Not really.' I saw it was useless arguing with them. Surprisingly, Simon came to my support.

'Christ's Hospital is not at all like a prison, Matthew. You would have three good meals a day and warm clothes and a bed of your own to sleep in. It would certainly be better for little Jamey.'

'We stay together,' Matthew said firmly, and was about to turn away, but I laid my hand on his sleeve.

'Listen, Matthew, we need your help.' I could see he was astonished. I do not suppose anyone had ever asked for his help before. 'There is a little girl of five who has been stolen from her family, and money has been demanded, or her throat will be cut. People have been searching for her all day, with never a sign. I know you have sharp eyes and you know your way around the streets of London. Can you keep your eyes and ears open? You might hear or see something when others might not.'

'What's she look like, this girl?'

I described Sophia Makepeace as best I could, never having seen her, and mentioned the house in Wood Street which might be worth watching.

'If you learn anything, come to me at St Thomas's Hospital in Southwark – do you know where that is? Or tell any of the players here at the Cross Keys. You know them all. Can you do that?'

'Aye.' He looked at me gravely, suddenly seeming older and less disreputable. 'The streets of London a'nt no place for a girl who's not born to it.'

There, I thought, speaks the voice of wisdom.

161

Chapter Twelve

The next afternoon I took Davy to meet Guy. We had arranged that Guy would help in the search for Sophia during the morning, but would return to the Cross Keys in the afternoon. Mistress Maynard had found some respectable clothes for Davy, so that he walked at my side the picture of a well bred young London lad, save for the fact that he seemed to be containing a bubble of bursting energy with difficulty. It manifested itself only occasionally in a skipping step, quickly suppressed.

Guy was waiting for us and took us through from the parlour to the hall, where carpenters were hammering away at the new stage, overseen by James Burbage, who had begun his career as a builder. The main part of the hall was clear, so Guy began to put Davy through his paces, shouting quick orders to him to perform this trick or that. I had only seen Davy playing about in the hospital, when he thought no one in authority was watching. Now I was astonished at his skill. Instead of the wild lad he had always seemed, he was now concentrated and serious. When he turned a series of what he called flips – turning over and over from hands to feet to hands in a blur of speed – even the carpenters laid down their hammers and saws to applaud. Davy flourished a bow, breaking suddenly into a beaming smile.

'Now let us see how well you can juggle,' Guy said, tossing Davy five balls in quick succession, so that he was forced to begin juggling them as each new one came flying in. He managed up to seven balls before he dropped one.

'Not bad,' Guy said, 'but we will need to work on that. Can you handle skittles? Plates? Knives?'

'Of course!' Davy said scornfully, and proved that he could, though not as well as Guy.

When the acrobatics were over, Guy began to bring out musical instruments from a coffer, where they were wrapped in soft cloths. First a shawn, then a rebec, then his second lute (which I usually played), a cittern, a flute, and two recorders, a treble and a tenor. Davy could play them all, though not with great skill, yet with enthusiasm and a certain brash confidence. Guy also had charge of the company's trumpet, which was used to announce when a play was about to be performed, blown from the turret at the top of the playhouse. Davy reached for it eagerly, but Guy returned it to the coffer.

'Nay, we'll sound no trumpet. There are other guests in the inn and they will not thank you for deafening them with a trumpet blast. Now, let us hear you sing.'

Guy took up his own favourite lute and perched on a stool.

'Give me the melody first, and I will accompany you.'

Davy sang a line of melody, Guy picked it up and worked in a few variations, then nodded to Davy to start.

It was a strange experience, hearing the boy sing. His voice was as pure as a blackbird's, singing at dawn, so that the very sound of it wrenched at your heart. The carpenters ceased hammering and listened intently. Yet the words of the song were grossly indecent. The boy's face was untroubled, as near angelic as one could imagine that scamp's face to be. I wondered whether he had any understanding of the words he sang, or whether they were so familiar they had lost their meaning and all he heard in his head was the melody, which was sublime.

Guy looked astonished. The carpenters and James Burbage stared at one another, unsure what to make of him. After my first burning flush of embarrassment, I felt profoundly grateful that I had not taken Davy to sing for Mistress Wedderbury at Christ's Hospital. I had been told she was not easily shocked, but I think the words of that song would have shocked her.

'Well,' said Guy, after Davy had finished and he had rounded off the melody on the lute with a final flourish, 'you have some knowledge of the instruments and you have been gifted with a beautiful voice, but I think if we use that melody, we will write some new words. Perhaps one of our wordsmiths will do that for us. Can you read music?'

Davy frowned. 'What do you mean? I can't read words. How can anyone read music? You hear music, you don't read it.'

'I will show you.' Guy rummaged in a satchel lying beside the coffer and pulled out some sheets of printed music. 'Here, this is music.'

Davy looked suspicious, as though he were being tricked. 'That isn't music, it is just a lot of black squares on a piece of paper.'

'You don't believe me? Here, Kit.' Gus handed me a sheet. 'Sing that, so that we can prove to Davy that it is possible to read music.'

I do not have a strong voice, nor a voice of such soaring beauty as Davy's, but I can hold a tune. I would never choose to sing in public, but at the other end of the hall the carpenters had returned to their work. It was a simple enough tune, so to please Guy, and in the hope that he would offer Davy a place, I sang the song right through.

It was a success. Davy grabbed the music paper from my hand and stared at it. (He was holding it upside down.)

'Could I learn to do that?'

'Aye,' said Guy, 'if you will work hard.'

I was becoming hopeful. I had seen that Davy did not like to be told that not all of his skills were perfect, but Guy had probably encountered saucy lads before and would know how to deal with him.

'Well?' I said.

Guy replaced his lute in its case and laid it in the coffer, then held out his hand for the sheet of music, which Davy was still frowning over, as if he thought that by staring at it long enough he could puzzle out some meaning from it. He began to sing the song.

'You see,' he said triumphantly, 'I can read it!'

'Nay,' said Guy, 'you are holding the paper upside down. I grant you have a quick ear. Kit sang it and you remembered it at once, but if I were to give you this,' he handed Davy another sheet of music, 'could you sing that?'

Davy clutched the paper in his hand. This time it was the right way up. He glared at Guy, then threw the paper on the floor.

'You are just trying to trick me!'

'Be careful,' Guy said, picking up the paper and returning it the satchel. 'These are precious. I am not trying to trick you, only to show that to become a good musician, one who can make it his livelihood, it is necessary to work and learn and practice. Are you willing to do all that? Both for your acrobatic skills and your music? If you are not, then I will not waste my time on you. But if you swear to me that you will work hard, I will take you on for three months. And then we shall see.'

Davy was clearly struggling. He liked to believe that he had nothing to learn from Guy, slight and unprepossessing as the player was, but he was drawn to the possibilities opening up before him.

'While you are thinking it over,' Guy said, 'let me show you how you might learn to juggle.'

He caught up his balls and skittles and knives and began to juggle with so many of them that they seemed one unbroken arc of colour over his head. Then he performed a series of handsprings and tumbles which made Davy's efforts look simple, landing at last, light as a cat in front of the boy.

164

'What do you say, lad?'

'Aye,' Davy said slowly. Then he grinned from ear to ear and laughed aloud. 'Aye. I swear I will work hard and learn from you, Master Bingham.'

'Good lad,' Guy said. 'Now, see if you can find your way to the kitchen and tell the cook I sent you for a bite of cake and a pot of small ale.'

Davy ran off, and Guy winked at me.

'Very impressive,' I said dryly. 'I did not know you could do that, Guy.'

'It is wise to practice in order to stay supple,' he said modestly. Then he too grinned. 'I am not above a little showing off myself.'

Not long afterwards, the players who had been assisting in the search for Sophia joined us in the parlour of the inn. They were tired and discouraged, and I guessed they were losing their keenness for the search.

'Nothing,' Simon said, as he prised off his wet boots and examined his sodden hose. 'No sign of the child. Although the black-haired fellow, Ambrose Selby, has been seen out on Hackney Downs, riding a new horse. That figures that he has come into money, but he has been making a great show of going about openly. Nick Berden thinks he is doing it a'purpose, to draw attention away from wherever the child is hidden.'

'And no word of the Yorkshire man with the receding hair,' Christopher said. 'He seems to have vanished completely.'

'And perhaps the child with him.' Will finished the thought in all our minds.

'Those watching the house,' I said, 'they have seen nothing?'

They all shook their heads.

I was feeling frustrated. It had not often happened that I was on the edge, like this, watching others and unable to take part in the search myself. I knew that if anyone could find a missing child in London, it was Nicholas Berden, but I did not care for this feeling of being excluded. Originally my work for Walsingham had been forced upon me, but I had become accustomed to taking risks, venturing into danger. It was difficult to admit it to myself, but my life had become dull of late. Nick would certainly have told Thomas Phelippes about the stolen child. Perhaps Phelippes would authorise me to take my part. But to tell the truth, this matter of Sophia Makepeace had nothing to do with the work of Walsingham's office, however you looked at it.

In fact I was surprised that I had heard nothing from Phelippes for some time. Tomorrow, or at least some day soon, I would go to Seething Lane and ask what was afoot. I had never been so long without word from him.

James Burbage joined us soon after the searchers had returned.

'Well, my friends,' he said, beaming broadly and rubbing his hands together. 'The stage is complete. Tomorrow we will hang the rear curtains to simulate the entrances and exits of our playhouse stage. There is a door beyond, which will give us a way through to a servery, which we can use as a tiring room. So tomorrow we will begin rehearsals for *Friar Bungay*.'

Several of the players groaned.

'That old piece,' someone muttered, quite loud enough for Burbage to hear.

'Surely for an indoor audience we want something better,' Christopher said diplomatically. 'It won't be your penny groundlings coming here.'

'What, then?' Burbage asked.

'*Tamburlaine*!' Dick said, with a gleam in his eye. He was clearly hoping to play the dramatic leading part.

Everyone began talking at once. Davy, sitting on a stool in the corner, was listening with his mouth open.

I spoke softly aside to Simon. 'I will leave you to your disputes. For once I shall go home before the gates close.'

He nodded, but he was barely listening. I went out, signalling to Rikki to follow and closing the door quietly behind me.

My intention to visit Seething Lane was overtaken by events. Late the following morning I received a message from Thomas Phelippes, asking me to come to the office that afternoon and saying that he had also sent a message to Superintendent Ailmer, requesting my presence. It was an unwritten understanding, from the time that Sir Francis had first suggested me for the position at St Thomas's, that when he needed me, I was to be free to present myself at Seething Lane without question.

I had become so occupied by my work at the hospital in recent weeks, and by my studies for the examination at the Royal College, that my work for Phelippes seemed to be slipping away. I was glad, therefore, that instead of having to appear as if I were looking for work, I had been sent for.

In the early afternoon, I hung up my physician's gown and threw my cloak over my doublet, breeches and hose. During the bitter weather I had been glad of the extra layer of warmth, but there was no doubt that one moved more freely without a long gown trailing in the snow and gathering a frozen and heavy burden around the hem. I set off almost light heartedly and on my own, having decided to leave Rikki in the warmth of the gatehouse, for it was after this midday meal that Tom collected the bowls of scraps to feed both dogs.

The Bridge and the streets of the City were crowded. After the impediment to daily business caused by the heavy snow, it seemed every citizen was bustling about, trying to make up for lost time. No fresh snow had fallen, but a lowering sky darkened the day. The edges of all the streets were piled up with shovelled snow, forcing everyone to walk in the centre of the roadway, dodging hand carts and horse-drawn drays and the occasional gentleman's coach, whose driver whipped everyone out of the way. Horsemen too thrust those on foot aside into the drifts. In centre of the streets the snow was stained with horse dung and piss, and packed down hard with all the passing traffic. I twice saw someone slip and fall.

As I made my way along Tower Street, I saw a crowd coming toward me, some of them shouting. In the lead, one of the city constables had a rope over his shoulder, dragging along a man whose wrists were tied together with the other end of the rope. He was one of the familiar beggars seen about the City, a little cracked in his wits, perhaps, but harmless enough. His grey hair and beard were unkempt, his features gaunt. He had been stripped to the waist, so that I shuddered at the thought of the icy wind on his bare flesh, but I doubt if he felt it, for following behind him was another constable wielding a many-thonged lash, whipping the beggar's bare back until it was slashed into bloody grooves.

I stopped dead and caught hold of the jutting corner of a building to steady myself. The scars on my own back from that long-ago scourging in Coimbra throbbed with remembered pain, and I bowed my head at the remembered humiliation. People were leaning out of windows to watch them pass by. In the pursuing crowd, some yelled abuse at the beggar, and some at the constables.

He would be whipped out of town.

If he was caught again, he might even be hanged. The fellow howled in pain, stumbling over the rutted ice, but seemed not to understand what was happening to him.

This was what the future held for Matthew.

The disgraceful little procession was forced into the ditch as a messenger in red and gold livery came riding from the Tower and passed so close to me that I could smell the sweet, sickly scent of some pomade in his hair.

At Walsingham's house I went in as usual by the stableyard. I had no apple to give Hector, but hoped he would forgive me. I realised that the time would soon come when I would never ride him again. I slipped into his stall and put my arms around his neck, seeking consolation. I think he sensed my mood, for he blew softly into my ear and bowed his head on to my shoulder. He was as dear to me as Rikki, but he was not mine. I had ridden him often and believed he was as fond of me, in his equine heart, as I was of him. The thought that I would never see him again was hard to bear, and I pressed my face into the silky hollow where his neck met the curve of his strongly muscled shoulder. He smelled of hay and crushed oats and warm horse, and I found myself weeping into his brindled coat. Ashamed, I wiped my eyes on my sleeve. It would never do to arrive at Phelippes's office in tears.

When I came out of the stable, I saw that grey clouds were piling up again, threatening more snow. It was almost dark, despite still being early afternoon. I hoped that child Sophia was somewhere warm, if she still lived. The clothes Lady Bridget had described would be little protection on a cold night if she was held somewhere without a fire. The stableyard was deserted. Harry and the other lads were keeping warm in the room where the tack was stored and where they had a small fireplace to heat poultices for injuries to the horses and warm mash for them in cold weather. Some of the lads slept there as well, for it was probably warmer than the loft over the stables. I crossed the yard and began to feel my way up the back stairs, where no one had yet set a candle lantern to light the way.

At a turn in the stairs I became aware that someone was standing pressed against the wall. Something – an odour, a flicker of movement – warned me and I stopped, but too late. An arm shot out and grabbed me about the throat. My left arm was twisted up behind my back so that pain shot up through my shoulder, and I was pressed back against a hard body with an arm so tight across my throat that I could barely gasp for air.

Even before he spoke, I recognised the odour. Robert Poley had always been over fond of garlic and carried its smell on his breath and in his sweat. He was breathing hard now, and I knew instinctively that he was sweating as well.

'Damn you, you filthy whore!' His spittle hit my cheek as he leaned over me. He was taking care not to raise his voice, lest it should be heard upstairs or out in the yard.

'And good day to you, Robert Poley.' I was surprised that my voice sounded so calm. 'Returned to England, have you? After your little adventures abroad? Perhaps there was not such a profitable market for your traitorous secrets there as you had hoped.'

He twisted my arm more painfully, as I had known he would, but I would not allow him to intimidate me.

'What lies have you been telling Phelippes about me?' He shook me, so that the stiff braid around the cuff of his doublet pressed hard into my windpipe. There would be bruising there later.

'I have hardly seen Thomas Phelippes of late. If you mean your dealings with the Italian puppeteers and their plot in the summer, he has known that all along. You are not welcome in England, Poley.'

He shook me again, so that my teeth clattered together. 'You bitch! That was your doing. They can prove nothing against me.'

'In that case, why are you in such distress, Sweet Robyn?'

It was a deliberate taunt. Those were the words Anthony Babington had used when he suspected that Poley, despite posing as his friend, had betrayed him.

Poley removed his right arm from my throat, but before I could break away he punched me hard on the side of the head. The world dipped and spun. The pain was overwhelming. He wore a heavy ring on that hand. I could feel blood running down from my temple.

'You think you are clever, you Jewish whore, but you will not feel so clever when I have finished with you.'

He still gripped me with his left hand, but with his right he unlaced his breeches, then grabbed mine to pull them down.

My head was throbbing, but sheer terror gave me strength. I brought up my knee sharply into his exposed privates, twisted free of his hand and ran up the stairs.

When I fell into Phelippes's room I was gasping for breath and my legs were shaking so much I sank to my knees on the floor.

Phelippes leapt from his chair and Arthur rushed from his cubbyhole.

'Kit! What has happened?' Phelippes was staring at me helplessly.

Arthur sensed what to do first. He lifted me by the elbow and sat me on a chair, then poured me a cup of wine and held it for me to drink. I choked and sputtered, for my throat still felt constricted.

'Thank you, Arthur,' I said hoarsely.

'What happened, Kit?' he said.

'Robert Poley attacked me on the stairs. He was waiting for me, hidden in the corner where the stairs turn. How did he know I was coming? He accused me of something – I am not sure what.'

Phelippes stared at me in horror. 'He has been here looking for work. I refused him, saying we knew he was involved in that plot to blow up Drake's house, even if we could not prove it.'

'Did you mention me?'

'Nay, but he did. He swore that you had lied about him. I said–' Phelippes looked from me to Arthur in distress. 'I said that he could confront you with it if he chose to stay, because you were coming here this afternoon, but that I believed you. He stormed out, yet that was at least half an hour since.'

'He must have been lying in wait all that time,' Arthur said.

Phelippes walked back to his desk and sat down, burying his face in his hands. 'My fault, Kit. I am sorry I put you in danger. I never thought he would do such a thing, but I think I am beginning to fail in my judgement.'

One thing he could not have foreseen, I thought, was that Poley would attempt to rape me. I had seen it in the man's eyes before, as he nourished the secret that he knew my sex. Sooner or later he would blare the truth forth. I found I was shaking again.

Arthur busied himself pouring wine for all of us. I think they needed it as much as I did. Then Arthur noticed the deep cut on my temple and started to look for a cloth to staunch it, but I stopped him.

'I have all I need here,' I said, unbuckling my satchel.

There was a small round looking glass on the wall, which I used to see where to press a linen rag against the bleeding and then smear the place with a general salve of woundwort.

When calm had been more or less restored, I asked Phelippes, 'You wanted to see me?'

'Aye, and Nicholas Berden as well. And I think I hear him coming now.'

When Nick came in, he must have noticed something about us all, but then he was always a shrewd observer. 'What's amiss?' he said.

Phelippes explained, while I sat still and sipped my wine. After that blow on the head I felt muzzy. Drinking wine was not, perhaps, the wisest of actions.

Nick was concerned and insisted on examining the wound to my temple.

'That was done by a ring with a hard, sharp stone.'

'Aye. I fancy he wears that ring a'purpose.'

'And your neck is bruised.'

'Aye.' I ran my fingers tenderly over my windpipe. 'I think he would have enjoyed strangling me.'

'He can be a dangerous enemy, Kit. Best take care.'

I shrugged. 'I did not seek the encounter.' Then because I felt we had discussed it enough, and because I was afraid my wine-loosened tongue might spill the word 'rape', I urged Phelippes to say why he had summoned us. 'Does it concern the Twelfth Night Revels?'

'It does. I want to know from both of you what you have managed to discover so far. Twelfth Night is barely a month away.'

I nodded to Nick to speak first.

'I have been over all the ground,' he said. 'The Revels will be held in the Great Hall, just past the chapel, if you come from the direction of the river. It is likely that all the entertainers will arrive well in advance, in order to prepare. If by land, they will come through the Court Gate, and I will have men there, watching out for anything suspicious. Mostly, however, I expect they will come by the river, landing at Whitehall Stairs, unless the ice on the river grows worse. More men will be posted there for the like purpose. I, with four of my men, will be in the Great Hall itself, mingling with the entertainers, alert for anything out of the ordinary.'

'You have spoken to the Master of the Revels?'

'I have. I cannot say he was pleased at the prospect of his great court celebration being marred by me and my villains, but he agreed that we should be dressed as palace servants, apparently seeing that everything is arranged satisfactorily, providing food and drink for the entertainers during the evening.'

'Good, that was well thought of. And have you learned anything of what entertainers he has hired?'

Nick shook his head. 'He refused absolutely to tell me anything. I believe he feels it is more than his life is worth, to reveal his plans in advance. The man is a fool! I did not explain in so many words that we expected an attempt on Her Majesty's life, but he must surely have been able to guess that some such thing was afoot.'

Phelippes turned to me. 'What have you managed to discover, Kit?'

'Little enough,' I said regretfully. 'The players can vouch for all the English entertainers. At least, they do not personally know all of the troupe of Morris dancers from Essex, but they are long established and well thought of. It seems unlikely that a paid assassin could be concealed amongst them.'

'Unlikely,' Phelippes agreed.

'The only foreign entertainers they know of are some acrobats from Poland. Do we have anything to fear from Poland?'

Phelippes frowned. 'I cannot think so. Although I suppose that an assassin might be concealed amongst them who was not a Pole.'

'But he would have to be a skilled acrobat himself,' I said. 'Only the very best entertainers are employed to perform before the Court. And a skill in acrobatics cannot be faked.'

I was thinking of the performances I had watched the day before. Even Davy's level of skill would take several years to attain. Guy's was the product of a lifetime's training.

'And they knew of no other foreigners?'

I shook my head. 'They only knew that the acts the Master of the Revels keeps secret are generally foreign. I think you must demand that he reveals them to you, in the interests of the Queen's safety.'

Phelippes sighed. 'You are right. I had hoped that we might manage this affair without causing panic in the Court, and if the Master of the Revels knows the danger, who else will he tell?'

'Will you not warn the Queen herself?' Nick asked.

'I am not sure what is best to do.'

I had never known Phelippes look so unsure of himself. Without Walsingham's presence to support an approach to Her Majesty, Phelippes looked lost. Nick must have been thinking the same as I.

'Can you not suggest it to Sir Francis? Even if he is not well enough to see Her Majesty himself, he could grant you the authority to do so.'

'Or you could inform Lord Burghley,' I suggested.

'Aye, you are both right.' Phelippes rubbed his face with his hands, then ran his fingers up through the back of his hair in a familiar gesture. He looked as though he had not slept for a week.

'Now, there is this other matter,' he said.

I wondered what he could mean, but I saw that Nick understood him.

'It is the matter of the Fitzgerald child, Kit,' he said, turning to me. 'Or rather, the Makepeace child, the Fitzgerald ward.'

A sudden cold clenched my heart. Had she been found dead?

'You must understand,' Phelippes said, 'that Sir Damian is a wealthy and influential man, who has the ear of many at Court, including Lord Burghley. He and his family are former Catholics, but last year they converted to the Anglican church. He therefore represents something of a political as well as a religious success for the Cecils, who were instrumental in securing his conversion.'

172

Ah, I thought. Edward at Westminster School, and later to attend Oxford. Sir Damian has judged that the future lies with conformity.

'What has this to do with the missing child?' I asked.

'Sir Damian has been afraid to set in motion a public search for her on account of two things. First he fears that if the kidnapping were known, it could jeopardise his holding of the wardship.'

I nodded. I knew this already.

'Further, he fears that such a public search might cause her captors to panic, decide to abandon their plans, and cut the child's throat, as they have already threatened to do.'

'Of course the search must be carried out with discretion,' I said. 'That is what Nick has been doing. Has Sir Damian come here to you?'

'He spoke to Lord Burghley, saying he wished to discuss the next course of action with Sir Francis, and was told that at present that is not possible. Lord Burghley referred him to me. He came this morning.'

'What did he want you to do, other than what Nick is already doing?'

'For one thing, he wished to make sure that I was aware that the resources of our service were being used on his behalf.' Phelippes smiled. 'I understand that it was something of a private arrangement between you and Nick. Of course I explained to Sir Damian that Nick was keeping me informed each day.'

I had not known this, but it did not surprise me. Nick would not want to proceed without Phelippes's approval.

'Sir Damian also wanted to know whether we had any experience of such cases, which of course we have not. He is filled with anxiety that he may not be able to raise the very large sum of money in time.'

'But he does think he may be able to secure so much gold?' I found it almost impossible to imagine what such a sum would look like. It would surely be extremely heavy.

'He is pledging various manors against loans from certain leaders of the merchant community here in London, but naturally these things take time. No one man can lend so much, therefore a great many transactions must be agreed and formal legal papers drawn up. All this time, someone is holding the child.'

I shivered. 'And yet we do not know how the money is to be handed over or the child returned.'

'That,' said Nick, 'is the other news I bring.'

He reached inside the breast of his doublet and drew out a folded paper.

'I paid a visit to the Fitzgerald house in Cheapside before I came here. That is why I was a little past my time. Lady Bridget had just received this note, pushed under the front door of the house. No one saw who delivered it.'

He handed the note to Phelippes, who removed his spectacles, which only helped him to see better at a distance, and read the note, holding it close to his nose.

'So, Sir Damian has until the fifteenth day of the month. What is it today? The sixth?'

'Aye.'

'Nine days. I think he should manage to raise the money by then. Was he there when you saw Lady Bridget?'

'He was not, but he was expected shortly. She will tell him the terms. I thought it best to come here, as we had arranged.'

'The fifteenth,' I said impatiently, 'but does it not say where and how the money is to be handed over? Surely they will not risk being seen and taken when they collect the money.'

Phelippes raised his short sighted eyes to me. 'It is to be placed in two plain saddlebags and left in Paul's Walk, behind the fifth pillar on the left, counting from the west end. A note will be there to say where to find the child. If they have any suspicions that they are being watched or followed when they collect the money, then the child will be killed at once.'

I swallowed hard. It seemed these villains had thought of everything. 'Can you not keep watch, without being seen, Nick?'

'We must be very careful, until the child is safe,' he said.

'I think we all suspect that Sir Howard Wilcox is at the heart of this,' I said. 'Either he wishes to secure the money, or the inheritance as well. I would not give much for the chances that Sophia will survive. If she is dead, he inherits, does he not?'

'Unless he can be proved to be behind the crime,' Phelippes said.

'It would surely be possible to arrest him,' I said, 'after the money is handed over. Few men will have five thousand pound in their possession, in ready coin. To make it even more sure, could the coins be marked in some way? If the marking of the coins was witnessed by some responsible person, perhaps a judge, before the money is left at Paul's, and if the same is then found in Wilcox's possession, would that not be proof enough?'

They both stared at me.

'I believe you may have found a possible way to prove who the culprit is,' Phelippes said at last. 'If we can think of some way to mark the coins. It will not be easy. Not with coins of solid gold.'

'Also,' Nick cautioned, 'we are assuming that Sir Howard Wilcox is the culprit, but what if he is not? My men have been watching his house and he has stayed very quiet at home. Given what we know of his rakish habits, that in itself might be enough to rouse suspicion, but it is difficult to prove a man guilty by what he does *not* do. There have been no unusual comings and goings about the house, just the normal visits of the cook to the market, and his man went once to his tailor to collect a new doublet. All very quiet and innocent in appearance. If the child is there, she is well hidden away.'

'But surely the servants would know!' I said. The longer this inactivity dragged on, the more frustrated I felt. Yet we could not go rushing into the house, for fear of endangering the child.

'Do you truly believe it might be someone other than Wilcox who is behind this?' I demanded.

Nick raised his hands and let them fall in a gesture of hopelessness. 'How can we know? Perhaps Sir Damian has other enemies. He is not well known to us, but every rich man has enemies. Or perhaps he was chosen at random – a rich man, a vulnerable child. Perhaps it is no more than common thievery, and has nothing to do with the fact that little Sophia is an heiress.'

'But it seems they were watching the Fitzgeralds' house,' I said slowly. 'That does not seem like the random snatching of a child. It must have been planned.'

'Aye, it must have been planned, but it may be that our villains had noticed that the child was not always well guarded. We do not know whether she had been wandering the street before with no one but the little maidservant to protect her.'

'I do not think so,' I said. 'From young Edward's anger and Lady Bridget's shock, I do not believe it had happened before.'

'You are probably right. And I agree that Wilcox is most likely to be the culprit, but we must accept that if he is arrested after the gold has been collected, and he does *not* have it in his possession, then it may be lost and the true culprit with it.'

'It is a curious place to choose,' Phelippes said thoughtfully. 'Paul's Walk. Half London must pass through there every day. If the bags of money are left there, even if they are behind a pillar, what is to stop anyone picking them up and making off with them?'

'Very true,' Nick said.

'Then they will be watching,' I said. 'They will be waiting somewhere nearby, in the shadows, ready to leap forward and grab the saddlebags before anyone else.' I thought again about the weight.

'Surely it would need to be someone strong. Would not five thousand gold coins be very heavy?'

'They would,' Phelippes said, 'but I would not like to say how heavy.' He gave a short bark of laughter. 'It is quite outside my experience.'

All this time Arthur had been sitting quietly in the shadows, saying nothing. I think perhaps we had forgotten that he was there, but now he spoke.

'Does the note state merely a date on which the money is to be left at Paul's? Surely they would not risk waiting about all day long, for they would draw attention to themselves, would they not?'

'You are right,' Phelippes said, peering at the note again. 'I had not noticed. It is here, scribbled at the bottom. They too must have realised that they should specify a time. "When Paul's bell strikes noon." That is very precise. In that case they can be there waiting amongst the crowds for a short time only, and there are always crowds in the middle of the day. As soon as the saddlebags are left, they can make off with them.'

'Not quite,' Nick said. 'They cannot risk being seen by whoever leaves the money. They must wait at least until he is out of sight.'

'There is something else odd about the arrangement,' I said. 'A note is to be left where the saddlebags were, telling us where to find the child, so someone – one of us – will need to go back for it. Does not that risk their being seen?'

Nick shook his head. 'It is not for us to solve their difficulties for them. Perhaps they do not plan to leave the message at once. I will, of course, have men stationed in Paul's Walk, to watch for whoever collects the money.'

'You must not risk the child's life!' I cried.

'What would you have us do, Kit? We must catch the culprit, or Sir Damian is beggared. Besides, how much faith can we put in these villains, that they will even yield up the child? As you yourself have pointed out, with the child dead, Wilcox inherits the estate. If he is behind this, why should he return the child?'

The argument was unanswerable. All we could do was to keep to the terms and hope both that the child could be rescued and the money retrieved.

'To return to the question of marking the money,' Phelippes said, 'I cannot, as at this moment, think how it might be done.'

'Whoever collects the saddlebags,' Arthur said quietly, 'will surely not stop to count the money. Perhaps he will take a quick look inside, but he will want to be away from Paul's as quickly as possible.'

Nick nodded. 'He will have a horse ready, in the churchyard.'

'I wonder,' I said, 'we could smear some of the coins with something which is difficult to remove, and put those at the bottom of the bags, so that they will not immediately be noticed.'

'Could you supply such a substance?' Phelippes asked.

'I will need to think,' I said, 'but I think I might.'

'I have always wanted to try my hand at counterfeiting a coin,' Arthur said dreamily, 'merely to see if I could do it. Naturally, it is against the law. But if we were to get the permission of a judge in advance, or perhaps Lord Burghley, we might put one or two counterfeited coins in amongst the rest, and they would be easy to identify.'

'Do you think you could do it?' Phelippes asked.

'I could try. Making the die for a coin would not be so very different from making a counterfeit seal, I imagine.'

'Then I believe you should make the attempt.' Phelippes was beginning to look more optimistic.

It was agreed then that we would undertake our separate tasks. Nick would continue watching Wilcox's house and searching for Sophia. Phelippes would explain to Sir Damian what was planned and ask Lord Burghley's permission for the mock counterfeiting. He would also ask Burghley to examine the packing of the saddlebags before they were delivered. I would try to create some transparent but sticky substance which could be brushed over some of the coins. And Arthur, if he was given permission, would attempt to counterfeit coins of base metal, perhaps coated in gold foil.

As Nick left and I was about to follow, I turned to Arthur.

'I have always said,' I murmured, 'that you are a great loss to the criminal fraternity.'

Chapter Thirteen

Nine days. That was all the time we had before the money must be delivered to Paul's Walk, the long nave of St Paul's on Ludgate Hill. In some ways it seemed a strange place to choose, for all day long the nave was crowded with people – foreign visitors to London come to admire its vast roof, merchants meeting to discuss business, petty traders hawking their wares, women taking a shortcut to market, lovers stealing an illicit kiss, lawyers discussing legal matters with their clients, pickpockets, prostitutes, cutpurses, quack doctors, rich men, poor men, beggars. It was said that if you stood in the centre of Paul's Walk for a day, you would see every citizen of London.

So why there, with all the risk that someone else might steal the money before the villains themselves? On the other hand, it would be easy for the men to hide themselves amongst the crowds, which they could not do in some more lonely spot.

Nine days. Sir Damian would spend the time riding about London, seeking out his merchant friends in search of loans. Nick and his men would maintain a discreet watch on Wilcox's house, but would cease any overt searching for the child, although his men would continue to listen for any mention of the two rogues who had snatched her. Phelippes would solicit Lord Burghley's support for our schemes to identify the ransom money. Arthur would try his hand at counterfeiting coins. I supposed this meant carving the upper and lower halves of the die, which would be similar to his work with counterfeited seals. He would then strike false coins out of some base metal and cover them (I was not sure how) with the sort of gold leaf used by the makers of gilded gingerbread. Knowing his skills, I believed they would pass for real gold coins tumbled amongst the rest, if they were not examined too closely.

As for myself, it was my task to devise something which could be painted on some of the real coins, by which they could be identified and help to connect the possessor of the coins to the kidnapping of the child.

Fortunately my two hospital wards were fairly calm during the following week. The few births were uncomplicated and could be left to the competent care of the midwives. I was only needed in the lying-in ward when the women showed other signs of illness, or the birth was exceptionally complicated, or the new infant was sickly or in distress. The children's ward, now that Davy was gone, was remarkably quiet. I think the other children missed him, for they were constantly asking after him. The present period of peace meant that I could take myself off to the hospital stillroom to experiment with various mixtures, much to the displeasure of the stillroom maids, who resented my invasion of their little kingdom. When I had lived with my father in our cottage in Duck Lane, I had everything I needed to hand, but my present lodgings were bare of any equipment. I had, of course, requested permission from Superintendent Ailmer to use the stillroom, without explaining in great detail why I needed it. From time to time, I had made up salves and potions there on previous occasions, when I had not the patience to wait for the hospital apothecaries to do it for me.

Gum arabic, I thought, to provide an adhesive quality to my mixture, which would need to possess three qualities: stickiness to stay on the smooth metal surface of the coins, a colour which would reveal itself when the coins were rubbed, but at the same time would be virtually invisible to anyone glancing hastily at the coins. It would be an advantage if the colour rubbed off on the hands of anyone handling the coins, staining the skin. It would also be wise if the mixture did not smell too strongly, for a smell might arouse suspicions. Altogether, it was an interesting puzzle, one that would have interested my father. I am ashamed that I became so absorbed in the problem that I almost forgot the kidnapping which had made it necessary.

I felt like an alchemist as I began my experiments. The base of the mixture first, which would be the gum arabic. It would need to be thinned down until it could be applied to the coins with a paint brush, but must then dry out completely, or the coins would stick together. Water would not be suitable. I tried wine and ale, but neither mixed well, and when I coated some pennies with my mixture it was either too thick and lumpy or too wet and would not dry. It also smelled of the wine or ale, though perhaps that would fade with time. If we had enough time. Then I tried *aqua vitae*. First I ground the gum arabic much finer this time, then I pounded it in a mortar with some of the *aqua vitae*. Once the mixture was smooth I gradually added more and more of the *aqua vitae* until the mixture looked as thin as water, faintly yellowish in colour.

When I was satisfied with the consistency, I took it home with me in a phial, where I painted several coins and laid them out on the table to dry overnight. In the morning I was pleased to find that they were quite dry and only very slightly sticky to the touch, not enough to make the coins cling together. It had taken me four days to reach this stage, so I sent a message to Phelippes to report on my progress. He replied, with word that Burghley had given his consent to our proposals and Arthur had nearly completed the carving of his dies. Nick had observed nothing unusual happening about Wilcox's house.

What I needed next was something to tint my mixture. Something, if possible, that would stain the fingers of anyone handling the painted coins. I considered using wolfsbane, which leaves a brown stain, which would not be too noticeable on the coins, but I decided it was too dangerous. Even a small dose is fatal. Some innocent person might handle the coins, especially if we were not able to capture the man behind the crime before he spent some of the gold. I feared that even a finger put in the mouth might kill an innocent man.

Woad would stain the fingers bright blue, but would be too obvious amongst the gold. Madder was a possibility. We had none in the hospital stillroom, but I bought some from an apothecary near Winchester Palace. Although the best madder dye is a fine scarlet, in the earlier stages it is not so strong a red, so I purchased some of this paler colour. I thought that, thinned down in my gum arabic base, it might give no more than a slight reddish tint to the gold. The madder mixed satisfactorily with the base, so I applied a coating to a gold quarter angel, the highest value coin I possessed, and my only coin of gold. It dried overnight, but the coin looked decidedly red. When I handled it, a small amount of the madder adhered to my fingers, but it brushed away almost at once.

It was now the twelfth of December and I was growing worried that I would fail in my share of the business. It had been agreed that we would all meet at Seething Lane in the late afternoon of the thirteenth to pool all our efforts and prepare the money to be left at St Paul's two days later. I cleaned my quarter angel thoroughly, then paid another visit to the apothecary.

'Master Davis,' I said, 'I need a substance which will leave a yellow stain on the skin, which is not easy to remove. I am afraid I am not at liberty to explain to you the reason for this.'

He seemed untroubled by my request. No doubt he was often asked for even stranger items, such as love philtres, or a potion to ensure eternal youth. He ran his eye along the wall of shelves and drawers behind the counter, moved a stuffed crocodile – a very small one – and lifted down a glass jar containing a yellow powder.

'This is *turmeryte*,' he said. 'Very precious. Very expensive. First brought to England back in the days of the Crusades. Now it is imported by a few of our richest merchants, such as Master Dunstan Añez, along the trade routes from the far east to Venice, and then on by ship many miles to London.'

This, I thought, was intended to prepare me for the outrageous price he was going to charge me.

'It is used in exotic cooking,' he said thoughtfully, holding the glass jar up to the light. I could see that it was exactly the colour I wanted. 'But I believe it is also used as a dye, in those countries where it is readily available. I also understand that it is efficacious internally for the treatment of stomach ailments and externally for wounds and skin lesions. That is why I keep it, though I have no personal experience of its efficacy.'

This was interesting. When I had the opportunity I must look into its medical uses. For the moment, however, it was the use of *turmeryte* as a dye that occupied me. I paid Davis the outrageous amount of money he did charge me for a very small amount of *turmeryte*, and carried it back to the stillroom. To my relief, it blended well with my base liquid. Only one more night remained for painting and drying my coin before I must produce my effort at Seething Lane. One thing served to encourage me. I found that the yellow powder stained my skin after the slightest touch and despite repeated washing, a faint yellow tint remained.

When I arrived at Phelippes's office the next afternoon, I found Lord Burghley and Sir Damian Fitzgerald already sitting with him. I was grateful that Nick arrived at the same time as I, for the thought of that dark turn in the stairs frightened me, despite my reasoning that Poley was unlikely to attack me twice in the same place.

'Now that we are all gathered,' Phelippes said, 'Sir Francis would like us to go to his office, where he is waiting. My lord? Sir Damian? If you will allow me to conduct you?'

Sir Damian picked up a hessian sack which clinked. The gold.

As Nick, Arthur and I brought up the rear, I mouthed at Arthur, 'Sir Francis?'

He nodded and whispered, 'He has returned from Barn Elms and wished to take charge, under Lord Burghley, of course.'

I realised that Lord Burghley had not brought a judge with him to witness the preparation of the coins, as Phelippes had hoped, but both

Sir Francis and Sir Damian would be Justices of the Peace in their home county of Surrey, so perhaps two JPs would serve as well as one judge.

I was shocked at Sir Francis's appearance. Although he wore a voluminous fur-lined robe, it was plain to see that the body beneath was skeletal. His face had always had a gaunt look, but now the shape of the skull was plain to see beneath the greyish skin. There were yellow patches around his eyes, and the skin beneath them sagged. He rested his clasped hands on the desk before him, but even so I could see that they trembled. He half rose, but Burghley took a few swift strides over to him and laid his hand on his shoulder.

'Nay, Francis, do not get up. I am sorry to see you so–' It was clear he did not know how to continue.

'Thank you, my lord,' Walsingham said, in a voice that was surprisingly strong. 'Please, all of you, find a seat, and let us put our heads together over this dreadful business of the little heiress. I know that a case like this is not the usual business of those of us who work here, but such a crime against hereditary right is in a sense a case of petty treason, and treason has been my business for many years.'

I was suddenly aware of the irony that we should all be sitting here in the same room: Sir Damian Fitzgerald who had been suspected of treason against the state, Walsingham who had suspected him, and I myself who had been sent to spy on him. It was a strange turn of events that brought us – potential enemies – together, for the sake of one small child.

Walsingham looked at Nick. 'Have you any news of the child, or of the men who seized her?'

'Until today, I would have said you nay,' Nick answered, 'but now there is one small fragment of news. Nay, two. The bigger man, Ambrose Selby, who had been observed riding about up on Hackney Downs on a fine new horse, is returned to London, and was seen at the house rented by Sir Howard Wilcox in Wood Street. He entered by the kitchen premises and as far as we have observed – at least until I left to come here – he is still there.'

Sir Damian sat up and leaned forward. I saw that Phelippes looked suddenly more hopeful.

'You mentioned that there were two things, Nick,' Sir Francis said.

'It may or may not be relevant, but a fellow answering the description of the Yorkshire man was spotted in Paul's Walk this morning. I have one man there, in case anyone of interest might show up. The fellow seemed to pay some attention to the fifth pillar on the left from the west door.'

My heart gave a leap. If it *was* the man who had seized little Sophia, perhaps all would turn out as we hoped, the child rescued, the coins found in the possession of Sir Howard Wilcox. Unless, of course, this affair had nothing to do with him, in which case the recovery of the gold would depend on how skilfully Nick's men followed it from Paul's Walk.

'Good,' Walsingham said. 'It seems that at last matters may be shaping themselves satisfactorily. Now, Arthur, how well have you succeeded in your criminal activity?'

Like me, Arthur had taken a stool in a corner, away from the great men, but now he rose and walked across to Sir Francis's desk. For some reason I was sharply reminded of the first time I had been in this room. I had stood beside that desk, demonstrating my knowledge of codes to Sir Francis, while Thomas Phelippes watched silently from the corner where I was now sitting. Nearly four years ago, it was now. I wondered how many more times I would enter this room, and found myself filled with a great sadness.

Arthur opened a purse at his belt and tipped a small pile of coins on to the desk.

'I hope they will pass muster,' he said shyly, 'if they are not examined too closely.'

Everyone gathered about the desk. To my eyes they looked convincing, though I could not get very close. Lord Burghley had picked one up and was turning it over in his hand.

'Very good,' he said, 'very good. The only discrepancy is the weight.' He drew a good gold sovereign out of his purse and weighed the two coins against each other in his hands, the real and the counterfeit, then handed them to Sir Damian.

'Aye,' Sir Damian said. 'The true sovereign is noticeably heavier, but mixed in with the others, who is to say?' He passed both back to Lord Burghley. 'How many are there?' He stirred the pile with his finger.

'Twenty, sir,' Arthur said. 'I had to throw away my first three attempts. This was as many as I could make in the time.'

'Best not to have too many,' Phelippes observed, 'or they might be noticed. We can put ten in each saddlebag, at the bottom.'

'In that case,' Sir Damian said, 'I can withdraw twenty sovereigns of my real gold.' He gave a humorous grimace. 'Not that those will go far to repaying my debts.'

'Now, Kit.' Walsingham turned to me. 'How have you fared?'

I explained my various experiments briefly, and the result I had been aiming for, then I drew out from my own purse a small packet wrapped in a scrap of cloth.

'I am afraid I had only one gold coin to experiment with,' I said apologetically, as I folded back the wrapping, 'so I have coated a few silver coins as well.'

My small pile looked somewhat pathetic next to Arthur's. I had coated six silver pennies as well as my gold quarter angel. These silver coins had taken on a distinctly yellow tinge, but the colour of the gold was hardly altered at all. The cloth wrapping had picked up some of the yellow colour.

Lord Burghley reached out for the quarter angel.

'My lord!' I said warningly, 'I fear your fingers will be stained.'

He gave me a smile. 'Well, that is what we hoped, is it not?'

He picked up the gold coin, examined it closely, then passed it to Sir Damian, who passed it to Walsingham. Then they all looked at their fingers, which were stained bright yellow.

'Arthur,' said Walsingham, 'be kind enough to bring over that ewer and basin, and a towel.'

All three men washed their hands in the basin, tinting the water faintly yellow, then dried them, leaving stains on the towel. Their hands remained marked with yellow.

'I fear your washerwoman will have difficulty removing the marks from your towel, Sir Francis,' I said, and held out my own hands for them to see. 'The colour is very persistent. I must have washed my hands half a dozen times.' The yellow stains, though faint, were still clear to be seen.

'Well,' said Lord Burghley, studying his fingers with interest, 'I am satisfied that your various schemes will certainly help us to identify the man, if we can catch him, and that will be the difficulty.' He turned to Sir Damian. 'How long has the child been missing now?'

'Ten days, my lord.' His eyes were distressed, tears not far away.

I thought, He really does care for the child. It is not just a matter of money and honour.

'And she is healthy? Of a strong courage, would you say?'

'As strong and brave a heart as you could wish, my lord, in a girl child not much above five years old. As courageous as any boy, and a pert, saucy little madam,' but he said it fondly.

My heart sank. How pert and saucy would she be after all this time of terror?

'Well, I shall leave you to prepare the ransom,' Lord Burghley said. 'How many coins will you coat with Dr Alvarez's noxious paint?'

184

'I should say twenty, my lord,' Phelippes said, 'like the false coins. And we will place ten of each at the bottom of each saddlebag.'

'Good. Report to me regularly on your progress.'

Burghley bowed to the room in general and we all bowed deeply in return as Walsingham rang a small hand bell for a servant to show Burghley to the front door. No back stairs and stableyard for his lordship.

'We will take all this back to my office,' Phelippes said, gathering up the coins from Walsingham's desk. 'We can prepare everything there, ready to be conveyed to Paul's walk the day after tomorrow.'

'Very well.'

I saw that Walsingham was looking so tired that he was probably glad to be rid of us.

'Report to me also, at least as often as to his lordship.'

As we were leaving, he smiled broadly. 'You have done excellently well, all of you. I am glad I have trained up such a clever band of forgers and scoundrels!'

Sir Damian looked slightly shocked at this, but the rest of us laughed.

Back in Phelippes's office, Sir Damian rested his sack of coin on my table and withdrew twenty bright gold coins. I had never seen so much money in my life. As for what must be contained in the sack, my head reeled.

'Now, Kit,' Phelippes said, 'you had better set about painting your coins.'

'They will need to dry,' I said, placing a stool as close to the hearth as it was safe to put it and making up the fire. Then I found a sheet of our poorest quality paper and laid it on top of the stool. 'I would not want your future visitors to leave with the seat of their breeches stained yellow.'

'Do you need a brush?'

'I have brought one with me.' I set down my satchel on the floor and withdrew the brush I had used already, which was now dyed bright yellow. It was the one I used to paint the egg white salve on the leg of the old man in the almshouse, but it would be useless in future.

'Sir Damian,' I said, 'will you be kind enough to hand me twenty gold sovereigns?' As I spoke, I nearly laughed aloud at the absurdity of it.

He handed me the coins he had just withdrawn from the sack, then withdrew another twenty to put in his purse. They all watched as I laid out the coins in a circle on the stool, then crouched down and carefully painted the top surface and edges of each one.

'This side will need to dry before I can turn them over and paint the other side,' I said. 'I have been leaving them a good while to dry, but perhaps the fire will hasten the process.'

I got to my feet and laid the brush and the phial of the mixture on my table, stoppering the bottle in case it should be knocked over.

'I will need to clean my brush,' I said, 'else it will stiffen up before I can paint the other sides. I'll take it to the privy chamber.'

Walsingham's house was one of the few in London with a water supply. It flowed only slowly when the tap was opened, but piped water was a luxury few could afford. When I had cleaned my brush, I washed my hands, but still the yellow stains persisted. At least the *turmeryte* was achieving its purpose.

As I came back along the corridor to Phelippes's room, Sir Damian was just leaving. He gave me a polite nod.

'I thank you for all you have done in this matter, Dr Alvarez.' He gave me a quizzical look. 'When you came to us as a tutor for the children, I did not know that you were also a physician.'

My heart sank. Had he finally realised why I had been sent there? Yet he and Walsingham now seemed to be on amicable terms. What a changeable, shifting world we lived in!

'I am but an assistant physician, Sir Damian. "Dr" is purely a courtesy title. I have recently taken the examinations of the Royal College, in the hope of being awarded a licence, but I have not heard the outcome.'

'I wish you every success.' He began to move away.

'Sir Damian,' I said, 'I am so grieved about the child Sophia. I pray that we may find her safe and well in two days' time.'

He tried to smile, but his eyes were bleak. 'As I pray also. She is a courageous little maid. Too courageous, I fear, sometimes.'

'That will stand her in good stead.'

He nodded and turned aside to the servant who waiting to see him to the door.

Back in Phelippes's office, I peered at my painted coins, but it was clear they had not yet dried. The other three were counting out Sir Damian's gold coins into two piles on Phelippes's desk. The sight of it was enough to take your breath away.

'Where are your coins, Arthur?' I asked.

'Have no fear! They are in my own room, to keep them separate until we pack the saddlebags.'

'That is correct now,' Nick said, who had counted each pile twice. 'Two thousand four hundred and eighty pounds in each pile. To each of which we will add ten of Arthur's fakes and ten of Kit's dyed coins.'

We all looked at each other and laughed nervously. So much money! It was frightening.

'As we must wait until Kit can finish painting the coins,' Phelippes said, 'I will have some food sent up. That is, if you wish to stay, Nick, and you, Arthur.'

It seemed both were reluctant to leave until the task was finished, so Phelippes went out into the corridor and called to a servant to bring us food and ale from the kitchen. When he came back, he asked, 'Where is Rikki, Kit?'

'I left him with the stable lads,' I said. 'I thought it best not to bring him to confer with Lord Burghley and Sir Damian.'

'You may fetch him now. And ask them in the kitchen for a bone.'

Clearly Phelippes was feeling in an expansive mood, after the worry of the last few weeks. It was beginning to seem that the matter of Sophia Makepeace might be brought to a happy conclusion. However, there was still the alarm over the Twelfth Night Revels. And if the sight of Walsingham back in his office was a relief to him, I feared it would be short-lived.

I carried a candle lantern down to the stable yard with me, although it was not full dark. I wanted no surprises at the bend in the stairs. When Rikki and I returned with his bone, the others were settled with pewter platters of mutton chops, sausages and roast parsnips, washed down with double beer. I made Rikki lie down away from his favourite spot by the fire, lest he knock against the stool with the drying coins, then took my own platter and sat on my old chair.

It looked a peaceful scene, four friends and colleagues eating a meal while a dog gnawed noisily on a bone, but there was a jumpiness in the air, as one after another of us eyed those two piles of coin.

'Think of it,' Arthur said dreamily. 'With just a quarter of that gold, I could buy an estate in Kent and become a country gentleman.'

'I hope you do not think of taking up counterfeiting permanently,' I said, wiping my mouth on my handkerchief. The kitchen had not sent us up napkins, no doubt judging that we were not gentlemanly enough to need them.

Arthur laughed ruefully. 'Nay, but it was entertaining to try. I suppose I must now destroy my dies. I spent many hours working on them.'

'I would become a merchant,' Nick said decisively. 'With just one thousand pounds I could buy a sizeable vessel and a cargo of woollen cloth to make a start. Trade it with Scandinavia or Muscovy at a profit, buy furs to sell in London. In no time I should be a rich merchant venturer and it would be I who would be lending money to Sir Damian.'

Phelippes smiled. 'Well, while we are speculating – let me see. I am not sure I would want to move away from London, like Arthur. I would build a mansion on the Strand, with a water gate and a private barge. And I should have myself rowed up and down, from Greenwich to Oxford, pitying the poor souls who must work to earn their daily bread.'

'And you, Kit?' Arthur asked. 'What would you do?'

'Oh,' I laughed. 'I have everything I need. I would buy a new lute, certainly, for mine was sold. And I would buy books. But I need very little.'

'Poor imagination,' Nick said, teasing.

What I did not say was what I would really do. I would go back to Portugal and somehow buy my sister's life away from that evil man who held her virtually prisoner, but these were thoughts I could not share with anyone.

'I wonder what Francis Mylles paid Sir Francis for that manor,' Phelippes mused. 'I did not know he had so much money in savings.'

As they began to discuss this, I laid aside my platter and tested my painted coins. They were dry enough to turn over, I decided.

When I had finished painting the second sides of all twenty coins, I sat back on my heels. 'These can be left to dry overnight,' I said.

The others got up and stretched. Phelippes found two boxes for the two piles of gold coins from his desk and locked them in the cupboard where he kept the most secret documents.

'Tomorrow we will pack everything into the saddlebags,' he said, 'if you can all come here at the same time. It will be best to have as many witnesses as possible.' Perhaps he had been made uneasy by the expression of all those dreams of wealth. 'Sir Damian will be coming as well, to see that all is in order.'

'Will he deliver the money to Paul's Walk himself?' I asked.

'Nay. He wished to do so, but I persuaded him against it. It will be much safer if someone with experience does it. I will take the saddlebags myself, on horseback, for they will be extremely heavy. I will then deposit them in the appointed place and make a great business of walking away and mounting my horse.'

188

'Do you think he – whoever he is, who collects the money – will he have a horse in the churchyard?' I asked.

'It seems likely. Nick and some of his men will be waiting there, ready to follow him, and others in the church, in case he goes out another way.'

'But remember what was said about the child! If you are seen to be watching, her throat will be cut.'

'I think I am able to follow discreetly,' Nick said reprovingly.

'Someone must collect the note which will tell where Sophia is to be found,' I said. 'I could do that.'

'One of Nick's men will do it.'

But I was stubborn. I felt I had done little enough to help find Sophia Makepeace. At least I could do this. 'All of Nick's men are likely to have been seen, roaming about London looking for the child.'

Nick opened his mouth and I knew he was going to protest that his lads were too clever to have been noticed, but I forestalled him.

'I have taken no part in the search,' I said. 'I am quite unknown to them. I can be quite innocently in Paul's, just one of the crowd. Then as soon as the saddlebags are taken, and you are all chasing after the culprit, I can quickly pick up the note, so that we know at once where to find the child. She should not be kept in fear one moment longer than she need be.'

I had grown quite fierce by this point, so Phelippes nodded. 'Perhaps you are right, Kit. It would be as well to have someone there with the sole purpose of collecting the note. If they do leave a note.' His face was glum.

'That,' I said grimly, 'is the risk. It is possible the child is no longer even alive.'

We all knew it. All we could do was to hope and pray.

The next afternoon we gathered again in Phelippes's office, the same company as before, except for Lord Burghley. Sir Francis joined us, leaning on a stick, but clearly determined to supervise the packing of the saddlebags.

First we put a layer of ten fake sovereigns in the bottom of each bag, then a layer of ten of my dyed coins. Seeing them jostled there amongst the other coins, I was worried lest the coating should be rubbed off before it could be tested. Still, we had provided two means of detection. If mine failed, surely Arthur's counterfeits would reveal the culprit?

Phelippes lifted up one of the boxes containing half the genuine unmarked coins. As Nick held open the mouth of one saddlebag, he poured them in, a river of gold – Arthur's country manor house, Nick's merchant venture, Phelippes's mansion on the Strand, my sister. When it was full, Nick buckled it closed, then held up the second one. Phelippes locked both again into the cupboard, and someone sighed. I think perhaps it was Arthur.

'Now everything is in hand,' Walsingham said. 'Tell me exactly how you plan to proceed.'

So Nick and Phelippes between them explained every stage of the plan.

'And when you have found the note giving the child's whereabouts, Kit, what will you do then?' Walsingham asked.

In truth, we had not discussed this. 'If it is not too far away, I will go there at once and fetch the child,' I said.

'But it may *not* be nearby,' he said. 'What if she is held somewhere outside London? What then?'

To be honest, I had been sure that she would be in London or Southwark, or in one of the places outside the walls where more and more houses were being built. To the west there were the mansions along the Strand on the way to Westminster. I doubted that she would be there. To the north and especially to the east along the river there were the settlements that were growing like mushrooms, what the city authorities and the Privy Council called the 'suburbs', illegally built housing for the poor in places like Poplar and Wapping. Even to reach these places I would need to go on horseback. If she had been taken further afield, it might be a long journey.

'You are right, Sir Francis,' I said. 'If she is not nearby, I will return here, and Master Phelippes and I can decide who shall fetch her.'

'Aye,' said Phelippes. 'I should be back here by then, if I ride straight here from St Paul's.'

It seemed we had planned as far as was possible for every detail, but as in a battle, one cannot predict in advance exactly what will happen. However, there was nothing more we could do until the next day. We would each make our way separately to our positions in and around the church.

Walsingham had given me a note for Superintendent Ailmer, stating that I would be needed on business for him and would have to leave St Thomas's before eleven o' the clock. I handed this to Ailmer when I arrived the next morning, and also arranged for Rikki to stay with Tom Dean until I should be able to collect him. I had lain awake a good part of the night, partly in excitement that I should be doing something at last to help in a case where I had felt frustrated at being excluded, and partly in dread that something should go wrong. A number of things could go wrong, two in particular. The culprit might escape with the money before Nick could apprehend him. And we might not recover Sophia Makepeace. If Wilcox was behind the abduction, and if he would inherit the estates on her premature death, why should he restore her? Why keep her alive, once she was in his power? The promise to return her might be no more than a ruse to ensure the money was paid. The life of one small child would count for little to a ruthless man in pursuit of his own ambitions. Sophia would not be the first child heir to die in mysterious circumstances.

As I made my way across the Bridge shortly before eleven o' the clock, I felt the first soft touch of snowflakes on my face. I was unsure whether more snow would make the pursuit of the culprit more difficult, or whether it would be more of a hindrance to him. Probably the effects would be about equal. The wind was getting up again, as it had done the night that Simon and I had struggled through the blizzard, and it was certainly colder than it had been for several days. I was dressed in doublet and hose with only my cloak for warmth, since I felt my physician's gown would make me more conspicuous in Paul's, but I missed its warmth, particularly about my legs. Turning off the Bridge, I could see the wherrymen at Old Swan Steps smashing freshly formed ice with their oars to free their boats.

As I was on my way out that morning I had bumped into Simon on the stairs of our lodgings.

'You are up very early,' I said.

'Morning rehearsal,' he said. 'It is our first performance at the Cross Keys this afternoon and Master Burbage wants to ensure that everything is in place on the new stage. Where have you been? I have not seen you for days.'

I explained what I had been doing with the dyed coins, and how all was coming to a head that very day.

'I pray that everything goes well,' he said. 'That poor child, how frightened she must have been all this time. I will tell the others. We were all sorry that we failed in the search for her. Believe me, Kit, we will send up a prayer for her.'

Surely the strength of all these prayers must have some effect? I set off up New Fish Street now, then turned left on Eastcheap, leading to Candlewick Street, as the snow fall increased. I continued up Budge Row and Watling Street, quickening my pace, until I was almost running, the snow blowing into my face and lodging in my eyelashes. As I crossed Paul's churchyard toward the west door, I saw one of Nick's men, dressed as a stonemason, mixing a bucket of mortar near some repairs in the church wall. Two more, who appeared to be modestly prosperous tradesmen, were in earnest conversation no more than ten paces from the door. Nick himself was humbly dressed and crying his wares as a broadsheet seller. There were a number of horses in the churchyard, twenty at least, as those who could afford horseflesh tended to use it as a stableyard while they transacted business inside. Some of the horses were hobbled, some tied to trees or – sacrilegiously – to monuments. A few were held by gentlemen's servants or by one of the young lads who hung about the churchyard hoping to earn a penny or two.

Now if I were a man hoping to seize two saddlebags of money, I thought, and then escape pursuit, what would I do? That was easy enough to answer. I would pay some nameless urchin to hold my horse as close to the door as possible. There were three such horses, held by their reins within a few paces of the west door. One of them was almost certainly the culprit's. Nick had probably reasoned as I had. One of the other horses was most likely his. For a moment I regretted choosing the role I had in the business. If I had waited outside with the horse Hector, I could have outrun any of those three horses. Still, it was too late to change our plans now. I was here, on foot, and Hector was in his warm stable at Seething Lane, on the other side of London.

A gust of the freshening wind forced me to turn up the hood of my cloak. At least inside the church I would be warmer than those waiting outside, especially as the snow was falling very heavily now, clusters of snowflakes as large as silver pennies settling on the churchyard ground and the roofs of the nearby buildings. Well before noon I made my way inside and mingled with the crowds in Paul's Walk. Luckily, as so many people wander about, it is quite possible to linger here without drawing attention to oneself. I noted the pillar where the saddlebags were to be left, then found myself a place two pillars further up the nave on the right-hand side, and tried to look as if I were waiting for someone.

Precisely as the clock struck twelve, Phelippes entered the west door carrying the two saddlebags, strolled casually to the fifth pillar and slipped behind it. A moment or two later he emerged and walked firmly, but without haste, back to the west door.

My attention had been caught, a minute or two earlier by a clergyman, who was standing not far from me, a little further up the nave. The clergy in St Paul's are usually busy about something – replacing or lighting candles, trimming altar lamps, reprimanding the noisier citizens crying their wares. This clergyman simply stood still. And I felt he was watching the same pillar as I was. There was

192

something not right about his appearance. His bearing was too straight, too prideful. I do not mean that no clergymen are prideful. I have encountered a number of such men, particularly those of Puritan leanings, who are too apt to regard themselves as always right and the rest of the world as wrong. Yet there was something about this man's bearing that seemed out of place, though I could not have explained what it was. Moreover, his cassock was too short. He was a tall man and his cassock reached only halfway down his calf, revealing a length of white silk hose. Did clergymen wear white hose? I could not be sure, but I thought they wore dark woollen hose.

It was these oddities that kept my eyes on the man, so that I saw him move as soon as Phelippes was halfway to the door. He walked down the aisle past me and slipped behind the fifth pillar. Naturally no one in the crowd paid him the slightest attention. He was merely one of Paul's clergy, going about his business. As soon as I saw him emerge, carrying the saddlebags, I knew I was right. He headed at once for the west door, but moving slowly enough for Phelippes to be well away before he reached it.

I was torn. Should I rush after him and cry out to Nick: This is the man! Arrest him! But that might merely alert him to his danger before he could be seized. Nay, I must stay here and fulfil my own task. I crossed the central aisle of the nave as casually as I could, though my heart was pounding. I did not want to draw attention to myself. Just as I had been watching, someone might be watching me. I slid behind the seventh pillar, my hand on the cold stone, and waited. No one followed me. No one seemed to be looking in my direction. Softly I made my way along the side aisle behind the pillars, my heart beating so fast that I could feel the pulse in my throat.

Almost, I hardly dared to look, but there it surely was, a scrap of white paper showing clearly against the stone flags of the floor beside the fifth pillar. I bent and swiftly picked it up, moving on even as I did so, coming out into the central aisle again between the fourth and third pillars. There was no sound of a great commotion outside the door, so Nick had not arrested the man in the churchyard.

I unfolded the piece of paper with shaking hands. It contained just three words: *Behind Paul's Cross*. There had been no attempt this time to falsify the writing with cheap ink and a poor pen. It was the same educated hand as the first two messages. I turned and began to run up the aisle toward the east end of the church, where a door led outside to the angle between the choir and the north transept where Paul's Cross stood, the great open-air pulpit from which famous sermons were preached to the citizens of London. Even the Queen had her own royal pavilion, from which she could listen to some favoured preacher. The crowds in the aisle were thick and I had to dodge back and forth, sometimes losing patience and pushing my way through.

Behind Paul's Cross. That must mean the side toward which the preacher's back would be turned. While I had been inside, the snow had begun to fall much more heavily, as I had seen when the west door was opened. Was Sophia tied up? She must be, or she would surely not have stayed where she was put. How long had she been there? She would be half buried under the snow and frozen. I heaved open the heavy door and was met by a blast of icy air that made the nearby candles dip and send out streams of smoke sideways. I let the door fall to behind me. The number of people in the church had warmed it, so that the drop in temperature outside made me gasp.

I ran forward toward the pulpit. There was no sermon today and the weather had driven everyone indoors. The area was deserted. I thought some of Nick's men would be here, in case the culprit escaped this way, but perhaps they had already been summoned to the other end of the churchyard. Then I saw a fragment of cloth half hidden under the snow at the rear of the pulpit. I could remember clearly Lady Bridget's description of what Sophia had been wearing when she was seized:

> *'She was wearing a kirtle and overskirt of green velvet, embroidered at the neck and hems with gold thread and pearls. Her underskirt and sleeves were cream satin, also embroidered, in a pattern of green leaves and pink rosebuds. She had a girdle of gold cords, knotted.'*

It was a corner of green velvet I could see, the edge, embellished with seed pearls, was partially torn. Otherwise, there was nothing to be seen but a snow-covered mound, unmoving. I knelt beside it, feeling sick. Perhaps it was a cruel joke. It was the child's body which had been left here.

I began to dig frantically in the snow, calling out to Sophia, but there was no sound, no movement. At last the snow was cleared. A green velvet kirtle and skirt. An underskirt and sleeves of cream satin. On top, coiled like a snake, a girdle of gold cords.

But of the child there was no sign.

194

Chapter Fourteen

*B*y the time I had made my way back from St Paul's to Seething Lane I was cold, wet and in despair. The whole charade at the church had been a disaster. The false clergyman seemed to have escaped, although two of Nick's men who had remained behind said that Nick and three others were pursuing him. He had stripped off his cassock as he ran out of the door, threw it over Nick's head to hinder him, leapt on to his horse and ridden away in the direction of Aldersgate. By the time Nick had freed himself from the tangled cloth and the other men had gathered their wits together, the man was out of sight.

Phelippes was back in his office when I arrived, Sir Francis and Sir Damian sitting with him by the fire, waiting for news.

'They have ridden after him, and they had a good look at the horse,' I said. 'Nick caught only a glimpse of the man himself before the cassock smothered him, but he was fairly certain that it was Sir Howard Wilcox, going by his description, though of course the man has been lying low all this time, and hasn't been seen.'

'And the child?' Walsingham asked gently. He must have observed my distress.

I laid the bundle of clothing on the floor in front of them, where the remaining snow soon melted into a wide puddle. The clothes were sodden and stained, but unmistakable.

'These are Sophia's clothes, Sir Damian?' I said.

He nodded mutely.

'The child was not where they said?' Phelippes asked.

'The note was there, as agreed, behind the pillar where you left the saddlebags.' I took it out of my doublet pocket and handed it to him. 'I ran immediately to Paul's Cross and found these, under a mound of snow. I thought at first that Sophia was lying there dead, but when I dug them out, I found nothing but the clothes.' I paused. 'I have been thinking, as I walked back. There was so much snow on top of them, that I am sure the man concealed them there first, before coming into Paul's, heaping up the snow to make it seem as though the child was there. Then more snow fell, so they were even more deeply buried. He came into the church by the northeast door and either then – or perhaps before – donned the cassock. It was cleverly done.'

Phelippes nodded. 'No one notices a clergyman in a church.'

'I agree. I only took note of him because the cassock was too short, and I saw his white silk hose.'

'Let us hope Nick manages to overtake him. Clearly, although Nick did not know him, he knew Nick, else how would he have known to hinder him by throwing the cassock at him?'

'Probably he has seen him keeping watch on the house in Wood Street.'

Walsingham turned to Sir Damian, who was leaning forward, fingering the sodden clothes with a look of despair on his face.

'Do you know where Wilcox might be making for?'

Sir Damian straightened up. 'He owns a small manor in Yorkshire, about fifteen miles from the city of York. He could be heading that way.'

He turned to me. 'You believe Sophia is dead, do you not?'

'I thought at first she was dead under the snow,' I admitted, 'but now I am not so sure. Could Wilcox be intending to marry her, in order to gain possession of her estates that way? I am not sure how that stands in law, with a child as young as five.'

He shook his head. 'He could not marry her without my consent, as her guardian, but perhaps he could bring a case of neglect, since we did not prevent her abduction. If he were granted the wardship, then he could marry her. Even without that, he might force her into a pre-contract to marry. She would not understand. He could tell her any number of lies.'

'He has held her for nearly two weeks,' Walsingham said. 'In that time he may already have had her carried north. She may not have been in London at all.'

'Then we must pursue him,' Sir Damian leapt from his chair, clearly desperate to be taking some action. 'Or even overtake him. If we can reach his manor before he does, we may forestall him.' He turned to Walsingham. 'Sir Francis, can you lend me a body of men? I have none with me in London save household servants.'

'If that is the action you wish to take, then certainly.'

Walsingham got to his feet with difficulty and picked up his stick. As they left the room together, Arthur came out of his cubbyhole. I had not realised he was there, but he must have heard everything.

'Sir Damian might have given you a word of thanks, Kit,' he said.

I shrugged. 'The man is half out of his wits with worry. Let him go chasing up to Yorkshire, if that is what he wishes. What none of us here has said is that much the easiest course of action for Wilcox would be to kill the child. No legal wrangles, no child marriage. Once she is dead, he inherits.'

I sat down suddenly and covered my face with my hands, to hide my tears.

'Have you eaten anything today?' Arthur asked.

I shook my head, without looking up. Who could think of food at such a time? Ignoring my obvious indifference, Arthur went to the door to summon a servant. When the food came he stood over me and forced me to eat.

'You are become as fussy as a mother hen,' I said, half laughing, half crying.

'Arthur is right,' Phelippes said. 'You will need to keep up your strength if you are to be any good to Sir Francis or in the search for the child.'

'What is the point of searching?' I said despairingly. 'We all know she must be dead.'

'Then we must find her body and put an end to hope, otherwise the Fitzgeralds will never have any peace.'

I could not see how the child's body could bring them peace, but I said nothing.

'There is little more we can do today,' Phelippes said. 'We must hope that Nick overtakes Wilcox and arrests him. He will then bring him back here for questioning and that may lead us to the child. In the meantime, if we can gather Nick's remaining men together, we will comb every street and alley in London. There will be no need now for discretion. We can call on all the constables and the Watch to help. We are bound to find her, dead or alive.'

'You do not believe she has been carried off to Yorkshire, then,' Arthur said.

Phelippes shook his head. 'I do not. Let Sir Damian believe that if he will. He needs to take some action.'

I wanted to believe him but I said, 'We should remember that the Yorkshire man who was one of those who captured her disappeared for many days. He might have taken her away then.'

'He might,' Phelippes conceded, 'but I feel the answer lies in London.'

I did not argue with this. Phelippes's instincts had so often proved right in the past that I respected them.

'Sir Francis looks a little better today, does he not?' I said.

'He has his better days. But I fear this business will have drained his strength. It does not improve matters that my lord of Essex is constantly about the house, plaguing him and plaguing his daughter. Now, I do have some other news. I have interviewed the Master of the Queen's Revels. Under a certain amount of . . . pressure . . . he has given me a full list of the entertainers who will be present on Twelfth Night. He did not enjoy telling me, but I promised I would reveal nothing to the Court.'

He laid a paper on his desk and the three of us gathered round it. There were listed all those I knew of, together with several more innocent seeming English troupes, a Dutchman with a performing dog and a monkey brought from the far East, two Polish troupes, including the one Guy had mentioned, some French female dancers with their own musicians, a children's choir from Denmark, and – Guy had made a clever guess, or had he known all along? – a sword swallower from Turkey.

My mind was too much occupied with Sophia Makepeace to give much attention to this, and all I could say was that none of them looked a likely group to harbour an assassin. 'Perhaps the rumour was nothing more than a rumour,' I said. 'Perhaps there will be no attempt on the Queen.'

Phelippes looked at me sharply. 'You know we cannot ignore this, Kit. Go home. You are too tired to think sensibly. By tomorrow perhaps Nick will be back.'

Like Sir Damian I wanted to be doing something, anything, even though I knew that on my own I was useless. As for the matter of the Revels, Twelfth Night seemed a world away, though it was only about three weeks. Later, I would think about it. Later.

I made my way despondently back to Southwark and collected Rikki from Tom at the hospital gatehouse. He was clearly curious to know why I had gone off in such excitement in the morning and come back so mournful at night, but he said nothing. As usual, Rikki capered about me, as joyous as if I had been away for a week. Although a fresh layer of snow lay over everything, it had stopped some time ago, before I had reached Seething Lane. Ahead of me now the torches outside the whorehouse cast a cheerful light across the snow, as the silhouette of a client passed in through the door. I hurried past. Bessie Travis had not yet fulfilled her promise – her threat – to invite me inside, but I was always a little nervous passing the door during their hours of business.

The torchlight did not reach as far as the door to our lodging house, and a patch of dense shadow lay where a narrow alley ran up along the side of the whorehouse to some huddled shacks crowded in behind it. Rikki stopped his gambolling suddenly and stood with his head raised, his muzzle pointed toward the alley. He had either smelled or heard something. He tensed, as if he was about to spring, then relaxed and began to wag his tail.

'Simon?' I called uncertainly. I could not think why Simon would be standing out here in the cold, in the alleyway, so close to home, nor could I think who else would prompt Rikki to wag his tail.

A figure detached itself from the shadows and came towards me. I laid my hand on my dagger. The last time I had been accosted here, it had been the blacksmith, Ellyn's father, and he had intended me no good.

'Master Alvarez?' It was a young voice, husky, but one I knew.

I peered into the shadows. 'Matthew? Is that you?'

'Aye, Master. You said, if we needed help.'

'Of course. But how did you find me here?' I knew that I had told them to come to St Thomas's, but I had never told them where I lived.

'Oh, we've knowed where you lodged a long time. Followed you here once or twice, and you never saw.' There was a note of pride in his voice, but then he asked anxiously, 'Can you help?'

'Of course, but what is the matter?'

'See, we thought it was a dog,' he said. 'I've always wanted a dog. Why do they do that?' he demanded indignantly. 'Tie a dog in a sack and throw it into Houndsditch? If they just leave 'un alone they'd fare for themselves.'

I tried to make sense of this. 'You found a dog tied in a sack, thrown into Houndsditch?'

''Tis bad enough when it's a dead dog,' he said bitterly, 'but why throw in a live dog? Nay, I told you, it wasn't a dog.'

'You found something alive, tied in a sack, thrown into Houndsditch? You pulled it out?'

I was growing alarmed. Had one of the children been attacked? Some gentlemen enjoy collecting wild animals, like those kept at the Tower, and they do not always behave responsibly. Perhaps a tiger cub had grown too large for a pet, and Houndsditch (which had not earned that name for nothing) was an easy solution.

'I *told* you,' he said. We were both getting frustrated. 'We pulled it out and it was moving. Not much, but we could see it was alive. Too big for a cat. I thought I'd get me a dog at last. It was heavy, waterlogged, but it can't have been there long because it hadn't sunk. Anyway, there was that much blocking the ditch already. We saw a man run off. It was probably him did it. So I cut the sack open, and we found her.'

Her? I found myself guessing wildly, and grabbed hold of Matthew's arm.

'Who did you find, Matthew?'

'We think it's that lass you wanted us to find, only we're not sure. The right age and fair hair, but she don't look like some gentleman's daughter. She's got nothing on but a shift and she's very dirty.' He grinned suddenly, and I saw the gleam of his teeth in the edge of the light. 'She's even dirtier than me.'

I trembled between hope and despair. It might be Sophia, or it might be some unwanted pauper child. They were found dead every day in winter.

'Did you not ask her name?'

'See, we can't wake her up. She's alive. She's breathing. But she won't wake up.'

'Where have you left her?'

'She's here.' He jerked his head toward the alley. 'She don't weigh much, so I carried her.'

I thought of his thin arms, wasted with malnutrition, and I thought of the long, long walk from Houndsditch. It was a remarkable feat.

'Show me,' I said.

They were all there, Matthew's little family, squatting in a circle around a motionless figure lying in the snow. It was a girl of the right age, but I could tell little else in the dark. They had wrapped her in all their blankets and were shivering themselves in the cold. I made up my mind.

'Come with me, all of you,' I said. 'You may come to my lodgings, but you must be *very* quiet, not to disturb the other lodgers.'

I stooped and picked up the child, blankets and all. I realised at once that she was quite a well built child. In my arms she did not feel like a starving pauper. I had even more admiration for Matthew, carrying her such a long way.

The children followed me in total silence, something they had no doubt learned in their precarious lives. As we climbed the stairs to my room, I saw a thread of light under Simon's door. I would fetch him presently. I had to put the child down while I found my key and unlocked my door, and as I did so she gave a faint moan, but her eyes did not open. We all crowded into my room, where I laid the child on my bed and set about lighting candles and then a fire. The children sat on the floor and looked about them curiously. I wondered whether they had ever been inside a house before.

'You live here by yourself, Master?' Maggie asked, as I added wood to the fire to set it going quickly.

'I live in this room, but there are other lodgers in other rooms. You remember my friend Simon, the player? He has the room below this. Up above, there is a water-carrier.'

'But just you in this room? Nobody else?'

'Aye, just me.' This suggested Maggie had known the inside of a house, or perhaps one room, occupied by several families.

'Now, Katerina,' I said, 'if you look in that cupboard on the wall, you will find bread and cheese and some bacon. Matthew, there is pan for cooking the bacon, can you do that? Make a meal for all of us, while I see what is amiss with the little maid.'

The two older children set to excitedly, helped by Maggie, while little Jamey simply sat on the floor and stared. I noticed that Jonno's scalp was looking much better. He even had a slight fuzz of hair. I tried very hard not to notice how dirty were the hands that were handling the bread and cheese. I would probably find myself with an infestation of lice and fleas after this visit.

When I unwrapped the blankets from the motionless form of the child on the bed, I saw that what I had sensed was correct. This was not a starving pauper. My hopes began to rise. She had fair curls, though they were matted and dirty. There was a nasty bruise on her left temple, but otherwise she seemed unhurt. It might be that blow which had rendered her unconscious. I examined her shift carefully. It was dirty and torn, but it was made of the finest cambric, with delicate lace at the neck, cuffs and hem. Even more evidence that this might be Sophia.

I began to warm some water at the fire and saw that the children had laid out the food on the table and were looking at it hungrily.

'Do not wait for me,' I said with a laugh. 'Go ahead and eat, but leave a little for me.' They grabbed slices of bread, piled cheese and bacon on top and sat on the floor to eat.

When the water was comfortably warm, but not hot, I removed the child's shift and began to wash her all over, starting with her bruised face. Then I took a comb and teased the tangles out of her hair, before sponging it lightly. It did little to remove the dirt, but I thought it better not to leave her with wet hair. Once or twice she uttered those faint moans, but still she did not wake. I did not think the blow to her head could have caused such deep unconsciousness, and clearly the children had pulled her out of the water-filled ditch before she had inhaled water, though the filth of Houndsditch, London's common pit of rubbish, might cause her serious illness yet. I began to suspect that she had been drugged.

The most common drug is poppy syrup, which is not difficult to obtain, but it can be dangerous. Too large a dose is fatal, especially when given to a young child. Had they kept her drugged all this time? Or had they drugged her before throwing her into the ditch, to prevent her from struggling? If the children had not spotted her so quickly, she would have drowned before waking. They had seen movement from the sack, but it might have been no more than a convulsive spasm as she hit the water, which must have been very cold, even if it was not frozen. The full horror of what these men had done suddenly overwhelmed me and I closed my eyes, thankful that my back was to the children.

I was certain now that this was Sophia, but I laid the torn and dirty shift to one side; it would help to identify her if she stayed for long unconscious. Fortunately, when Sara had provided me with fresh clothes on my return from Portugal, she had included two night shifts. I warmed one now by the fire, before slipping it over the child's head and easing her arms into the sleeves. It was, of course, far too large, but it would serve to keep her warm until I could secure better clothes for her. Unlike her own shift, it was lightweight wool not fine cambric, but it would keep her all the warmer. Now that she was clean and warm, she seemed more like a child asleep and less like a half-drowned corpse. I could only pray that the dose of the drug would not prove too much for that young body.

I was startled by a sudden knock on the door, but then Simon's voice called out, 'Are you there, Kit?'

'Aye, come in.'

A look of blank astonishment came over him as he entered. 'From all the noise,' he said, 'I thought you must be having a party. I did not know you had started a rival to Christ's Hospital.'

'Shut the door, Simon,' I said. 'I do not want to disturb the rest of the house. You know Matthew and his friends. They have been extremely heroic. They have rescuing a drowning child from Houndsditch and carried her all the way here.'

Simon whistled softly and came over to stand next to me beside the bed.

'Is it?' he said.

'I think so. The right age, the right hair colour, but nothing else to identify her but a very expensive under shift. However, she will not wake.'

He pointed to the bruised temple. 'That?'

'Not serious enough. I think she has been dosed with poppy syrup.'

I turned to the children, who were licking the last of the bacon grease off their fingers. I shuddered at the thought of the dirt they were swallowing.

'Matthew,' I said, 'you saw a man running off. Can you describe him? Or was it too dark to see?'

'It weren't dark then.'

Of course not. Their trek carrying the child across London would have taken a long time.

'He was about as tall as you.' He pointed to Simon. 'Older than you, but not old. Only saw his face for a minute.'

'Would you know him again?' Simon asked. I knew he was thinking, as I was, about bringing the man to court.

'Of course.' Matthew was scornful. 'I don't forget faces.'

Probably not, I thought. These beggar children must learn many skills when they are very young. That is why this group has survived when so many similar children have died.

'Did you notice anything about him that you could tell us?' I said. 'Like his hair colour?'

'Brown. And he was going bald at the front, like this.' Matthew pulled his own hair back from his forehead on either side, leaving a tuft in the middle.

Simon and I looked at each other. The Yorkshire man.

'What time was it, Matthew, do you know, when you saw him?' I held my breath. This might help us to put the various pieces of the puzzle together.

'Near two o' the clock. I heard St Botolph's bell striking as we pulled her out of the ditch.'

Two hours after the saddlebags had been left in Paul's Walk. Wilcox – or whoever the mounted man was – would have been well away from London by then. Their plan must have been to deceive us into thinking that we would rescue the child in return for the money. The child would not be handed over, merely her clothes, so that we should know that these men did indeed hold her. Once the money was safely in their hands and on the way out of the City, the child was no longer of use and could be killed. It only remained for Wilcox to claim the estate once she was proved dead. Houndsditch was notorious not only as a dumping ground for dead dogs and other unpleasant rubbish. It was a constant nightmare for the authorities because it was frequently blocked, a stinking breeder of noxious vapours and insidious diseases. Once it had been a defence for the much smaller London. Now it was nothing but a blight. On their next frustrating attempt to clear the ditch, the authorities would have found the corpse of a small girl, who could be identified by that same shift that was now lying in a heap on my floor.

'What do you plan to do now?' Simon asked.

'I shall sit up with the child all night,' I said, 'so that I can attend to her and if she wakes, ask her name. The children had better stay here. I shall need Matthew to come with me to Seething Lane to tell all that he knows.'

'I hope you may not find it too difficult to persuade him. And will you take the child back to the Fitzgeralds' house in Cheapside?'

I had been pondering this before Simon arrived. 'Not yet, I think. Not until Sir Damian returns and as many of the culprits have been arrested as possible, certainly the three principals. At the moment there is no one at the Fitzgeralds' house but women, children, and household servants. If word got about that the child was back, someone might try to snatch her again, or the claim on the estate cannot be made.'

'You cannot keep her here. You would need to leave her alone when you are at St Thomas's.'

'Nay. I think I will take her to Christ's. Don't they say that the best place to hide something is in plain view? At Christ's she will just be one more child in a blue uniform amongst hundreds of others. Who would think to look for her there?'

'That sounds an excellent plan. Now, before all these brats fall asleep on your floor, suppose I take some of them to my room?'

'Are you sure? They are very dirty and flea-bitten.'

'What care I for dirt and a few fleas?' He made a comical face and began scratching himself like a mad dog. The children stared at him open mouthed, until Matthew, who was sitting with his arm around Rikki, began to laugh.

'Who is going to spend the night on my floor?' Simon asked. 'There are too many for this small room, and Dr Alvarez will be falling over you while he tries to care for your drowned rat. I think I might have an orange you can share.'

The twins found this an enticing offer and Jamey trailed after them. Matthew wanted to stay with Rikki, and Katerina wanted to stay with Matthew. As Simon ushered the children out of the door, his finger to his lips, I said, 'How did your performance fare this afternoon? Had you an audience?'

'Every seat taken! At sixpence a time! If this continues, we shall all grow rich.'

'And which did you play, *Friar Bungay* or *Tamburlaine*?'

'Oh, *Tamburlaine*, of course! Dick was bound to get his way!'

When they had gone, Matthew and Katerina curled up quite happily with Rikki before the fire, while I brought a chair close to the bed where the child still slept, and prepared myself for a long vigil.

It was shortly after the Watch had passed in the street below, crying, 'Two o' the clock and all's well', that the child began to stir. More than once my head had nodded and my chin dropped to my chest, but I had kept my hand on hers, so that as soon as she moved, I woke. The fire had died down and the candle was almost burnt out, so I lit two more. I did not want her to be frightened by the dark.

She struggled to sit up and looked around her wildly.

'You are safe now,' I said, speaking slowly and quietly. 'The bad men have gone away.'

'Who are you?' So soft a whisper I could scarcely hear.

'I am Dr Alvarez, a physician, and you are in my lodgings. Some kind children brought you here to be safe.'

She tried again to sit up and I put my arm round her shoulders to help her. At first she shrank away, but then she must have decided to trust me, for she leaned back against my arm and looked about her.

'It's a very small room,' she said.

'It is.'

'What am I wearing?' She was looking down at her arm in its over-large sleeve.

'One of my night shifts. Yours was torn and wet and dirty.'

Suddenly she shivered and her eyes widened in fear. 'They put me in a sack, and said they were going to drown me. They made me drink something nasty first.'

Two fat tears welled up in her eyes and spilled over.

'You mustn't be afraid any more,' I said. 'The bad men have gone and you are quite safe now, among friends. Would you like something good to drink, to take away the taste?'

'Aye,' she said. 'And something to eat.'

She looked about as though she expected a servant to appear. I had left some very weak ale near the fire to keep warm. I stirred a spoonful of honey into it now, and she drank it thirstily.

'I am not sure how much food your rescuers have left us,' I said, 'but I think there may be a little cheese.'

There were the remnants the children had left for me, which I had not eaten. I stepped over Matthew and Katerina to fetch them. The heel of the loaf, a small portion of cheese, and one slice of bacon. It was cold now, but a hungry child would probably not mind. I put it all on one of my pewter plates and carried it over to the bed. Matthew's little group appeared to be unfamiliar with plates and had simply used the slices of bread as trenchers. It saved the washing of dishes. I paid the water-carrier who lived upstairs to bring me two buckets of water a day from the conduit, but washing was never easy.

The child wolfed down the food, although she looked around as though she expected a tray and a linen napkin to be brought, but after her recent experiences it probably seemed like an improvement.

'Did they give you food, the men?' I asked casually, as I took the empty plate and cup away. We were both speaking quietly, for I did not want to wake Matthew and Katerina.

She wrinkled her nose. 'It was nasty. The bread was stale, and everything was cold and greasy.'

There was no need now to find out more about her captivity, but despite my own belief, I must make sure who she was.

'And what is your name?'

'I am Sophia Makepeace,' she said with dignity, 'and my guardian is Sir Damian Fitzgerald, and if he catches those men, he will kill them. The worst was that man who is a cousin of my father. He is called Sir Howard Wilcox and I hate him. He dragged me by my hair, and he hit me.' She touched the bruise on her temple with a chubby forefinger. 'And if my guardian does not call him out in a duel, then I *will*.'

'Girls do not usually fight duels.' My voice was matter-of-fact, but I glanced briefly to where my own sword hung on a hook beside the fireplace.

'I have practiced with Edward, Sir Damian's son. He says I am not a bad swordsman.'

'Edward has been fencing with you? With a *sword*?' I did not believe her. Edward was a sensible boy, and a sword would be almost as tall as Sophia herself.

'Nay,' she said regretfully. 'We used sticks, but he is teaching me the right moves. I never had a brother, you see.'

'I see.' I hid my smile. I hoped Sophia had given her captors a great deal of trouble. 'Now, it is the middle of the night and I think you should sleep until the morning.'

'I think that nasty drink made me sleep. I am awake now.'

'That may be true, but I have not slept, and I should like to sleep now.'

She looked around the room. 'Where is your bed?'

'You are lying on it.'

'If you do not kick, you may share with me,' she said graciously. 'That maidservant of mine shared with me when we travelled, and she kicked all the time. I had to make her sleep on the floor.'

So it was that instead of sharing my bed for the rest of the night with Rikki, I was allowed to share my bed with my unexpected guest, while Rikki slept on the floor between Matthew and Katerina. Later I was to discover that he had also shared their fleas.

The following morning we were all up early. I had no food left, and only a small flagon of ale, but Simon went to the nearest bakehouse and came back with saffron buns which we all ate hungrily. While he was gone, I wrote a hasty note to Mistress Maynard asking her to send me clothes for Sophia – an under shift, a plain dress and cloak, some woollen stockings and some boots suitable for wearing in the snow. I had Sophia stand on the paper while I drew round her foot, which all the children found highly entertaining. I also asked Mistress Maynard to inform Superintendent Ailmer that I would still be occupied on Sir Francis Walsingham's business today.

I folded the note, wrote the address on the outside and called Matthew over.

'I need you take this to St Thomas's. Give it to the gatekeeper, Goodman Dean. Then wait until the clothes are brought to his lodge.'

Matthew looked very doubtful. I suppose to him the hospital looked a formidable place, as intimidating as the prisons he so feared.

'Goodman Dean has an Irish wolfhound called Swifty,' I said cunningly. 'He's an old dog now, but ask Goodman Dean to tell you about some of his exploits when he was younger.'

Matthew brightened at this and went off willingly enough, while Simon set himself to entertain the children. Sophia, still draped in my night shift, looked out of place amongst the beggar children, to my eyes at least, but the children themselves seemed unconcerned. In fact I was so tired from my wakeful night that I stretched out again on the bed and fell asleep.

When Matthew returned with the bundle from Mistress Maynard, I helped Sophia to dress and ran a damp comb through her hair to remove a little more of the dirt. She had told us that she had been kept in a filthy cellar, but she had no idea where it was, which was of little help to us, save for the fact that Wilcox had visited her there several times and threatened to cut her throat if she tried to call for help. That might mean it was the cellar of the house in Wood Street.

'But I did not care. I was not afraid of him.' She spoke boldly, but I saw that her bottom lip quivered. With every passing minute, however, she seemed to be regaining what I could see was her natural courage. I could understand why Sir Damian had spoken of her spirit with admiration and some apprehension.

At last it was time to leave. I was unsure what to do about the beggar children. I was uneasy about leaving them here, for if my landlady discovered them she would be very displeased and might turn me out of my lodgings. Yet it seemed cruel to send them out into the snow-covered streets again. Matthew, however, settled matters for me.

'We got to be on our way, Dr Alvarez,' he said. 'Our pitch at the Royal Exchange – if we don't nab it soon, someone else will.'

'Don't they turn you away from the Royal Exchange?' Simon asked. 'That was what I heard. All those grand merchants and their wives.'

'You have to be nippy on your feet.' Matthew grinned. 'We got our ways and our hidey holes. Time we was at work.'

'What you did yesterday,' I said, 'that was very brave. You saved Sophia's life. And it was quite a feat, carrying her all the way here, but it was the right thing to do.'

He shuffled his feet, looking suddenly embarrassed. I don't suppose anyone had called him brave before. He was more used to being beaten and sworn at. He did not know what to say.

'Later,' I said, 'I will need you to tell some friends of mine what you saw at Houndsditch, and to describe the man. Will you do that?'

'Aye,' he said, though with some reluctance.

'Do you still come to the Cross Keys for food in the evenings?'

'Aye.' He grinned at Simon. 'That was a good tip, Master.'

With that they were off, leaving Simon, Sophia, Rikki, and me in a room which felt suddenly empty.

'I am going to take Sophia by wherry to Christ's Hospital,' I said to Simon. 'Will you come with us?'

'Aye. We have no rehearsal this morning, but I might as well cross the river now and share a wherry.'

'What is Christ's Hospital?' Sophia demanded. 'Why am I not going home to the Fitzgeralds?'

'Sir Damian is away at present,' I said. 'Christ's Hospital is a home for lots of boys and girls, rather like a country manor, with its own church and bakehouse and brewery and stables. There is even a school. You will like it there. Lots of other children to play with.'

'I own some manors like that,' she said. Then added wistfully, 'but I haven't ever had other children to play with, except Edward. And I do not go to school. I have my own tutors.'

'Can you read and write, Sophia?' Simon asked, as I locked my door and we started downstairs.

'Of course,' she said scornfully. 'And I know French, but I am not very good at Latin.'

Simon looked at me over her head and raised his eyebrows, but I only smiled. I too had started to learn French and Latin before I was five, and Italian at six, but then my father was an exceptional man, in believing that girls could learn as well as boys. Not that I had ever mentioned such a thing to Simon. As Sophia was to inherit great estates, it seems her father had seen fit to educate her too.

There was still ice around the wherry steps, but we were in no great hurry this time, escaping from an enraged father, as when we had taken little Ellyn to Christ's.

Simon must have been remembering that journey as well. 'I have never heard you say whether there has been any further trouble from the blacksmith.'

'He did come back,' I said, 'but John Haddon, the almoner, told him that Ellyn had left the hospital of her own free will when she was recovered, which was true. He intimated that we assumed she had gone home. It seems the blacksmith ranged all over Southwark hunting for her, getting more drunk and more angry, until he fell into a brawl, broke a man's nose and blacked another's eye. He was put in the pillory for brawling, then hauled off to Bridewell and given some honest hard work to do, as he appeared to be a sturdy fellow who had no useful employment. As far as I know, he is there still.'

On the far side of the river, we climbed up from Blackfriars Stairs and parted in Newgate, Simon heading for Gracechurch Street and the Cross Keys, while I made Rikki wait outside and led Sophia through the gatehouse and into the central quadrangle of Christ's Hospital. She seemed not at all intimidated by the place, but looked around with interest. As it was still early, I guessed that the children would be at their lessons and when we passed the petty school, we could hear the children chanting something, perhaps their counting sums for the day.

In Mistress Wedderbury's parlour, I explained who Sophia was and, rather obliquely, why I had come to Christ's. She sensed that I did not want to say more in front of the child, so called for her girl Moll to take Sophia down to the kitchens, to find a cup of milk and a sugar biscuit.

Once they were out of hearing, I recounted the whole story of Sophia's kidnapping and her rescue yesterday from Houndsditch.

Her hand flew to her mouth in horror. 'They left her to drown in that filth! What kind of men are these?'

'The paid servants of a man who will gladly kill a child in order to seize her inheritance,' I said grimly. 'So you see, until they are apprehended, and until Sir Damian returns home, it is safer for her to be kept out of sight.'

'Then you have brought her to the right place. I will gladly keep her here until you send for her. She will simply fit in with the other children.'

I laughed. 'Perhaps not too simply, for she has a strong will of her own. It must have stood her in good stead these last frightening weeks. And how are my other girls? Is Mellie proving satisfactory in the kitchens? And what have you decided about the baby? And how is little Ellyn?'

We talked for some while about the children, but I knew I must not linger.

'I will come and visit them all soon,' I promised, 'but I am expected at Sir Francis Walsingham's house. I thank you again for all your help, Mistress Wedderbury.'

Soon I was striding briskly east toward Tower Ward with Rikki trotting at my heels. I was the bearer of wonderful news, better than any of us could have hoped for less than a day ago. But what, I wondered, had become of the two parties of men riding north – Nick and his men following the trail of the gold, Sir Damian and his troop hoping to find Sophia in Yorkshire? I would not feel easy about Sophia's safety until Wilcox was brought before Sir Francis and made to answer for his crimes.

*P*helippes and Arthur were both in Phelippes's office when I arrived, but as soon as it was clear that I had something of importance to report, Phelippes insisted that we should go at once to Sir Francis, who was in a state of anxiety because all the might of his intelligence service, which could outwit the complex plans of enemy states, could not find one small child in London.

'The child has been found,' I said, without preamble, 'and not by trained agents or city authorities. She was found, and saved from death, by a group of ragged urchins not much older than she.'

I then recounted the entire story of the attempted murder of Sophia and her rescue by Matthew and his friends.

'We can only hope she has not caught some noxious disease from the filth of Houndsditch,' I said, 'but otherwise, she seems unhurt, except for a bruise on her temple, where Wilcox struck her.'

'Where is she now?' Walsingham asked. 'Have you taken her home to the Fitzgeralds?'

'Nay, I was not sure that she would be safe there. If word got about that she was in the house, with Sir Damian away, I feared she might be snatched again. She is quite safe.' I smiled at him. 'She is now disguised as a bluecoat orphan, doing her lessons at Christ's Hospital, where no doubt she will complain that Latin is not on the curriculum for the petties.'

I laughed aloud, for I was feeling elated and my mood soon communicated itself to the others.

'Is there any word from Nick Berden?' I asked. 'Or Sir Damian?'

'Nothing yet,' Walsingham said. He considered for a moment. 'I like your idea of placing the child amongst other children. She should be safe there until these villains are caught. We must contain ourselves in patience. Nicholas will send word as soon as there is anything to report.'

Three more days passed with no word from either of the parties which had ridden north. I was busy enough at St Thomas's with the usual crop of winter illness, and each evening I walked to the Theatre to practice with Guy, for Twelfth Night was drawing nearer, with still no more intelligence about the suspected assassin. I began seriously to wonder whether the conversation overheard all those weeks ago in the ale house was nothing but idle talk.

Guy and I had decided on a suite of lute pieces to play together, which would provide an interlude between the play and the final dance. It would give the players time to change their costumes and put the courtly audience in the mood for music after the comic action of the play, which was a light-hearted piece written by the new member of the company, Will Shakespeare. It seemed nonsensical to me – two pairs of twins, separated at birth, who are repeatedly mistaken for each other, to the utter confusion of everyone, including – I suspected – the audience. Simon and Christopher were to play the gentlemen twins, Guy and Will Kempe the servant twins. Guy said it was based on some Roman comedy, but it was not one I had ever read.

'No one could take Simon and Christopher for twins,' I objected. 'You and Will Kempe are more alike, at least you are the same height, but who could possibly mistake any of you for the other?'

'Ah, you have not the true feeling for the playhouse,' Guy said. 'You physicians, you must be able to give reasons for everything. In the playhouse you must work upon your imaginative forces. Each pair of twins will be dressed alike.'

'But that is even more ridiculous,' I said. 'They have been separated at birth. How could they end up dressed identically? It makes no sense.'

Guy shook his head regretfully and strummed a chord or two on his lute. 'No imagination,' he said.

Having discovered the quality of Davy's singing voice, Guy had decided that one of our pieces should be a song by Davy. Not one of the scurrilous songs he had learned while he was with the troupe of travelling acrobats, but one with music written by one of the Bassano brothers, with new words by Will. Under Guy's hand, Davy was changing. Having found his place for the moment amongst the players, he was determined to persuade them to keep him on. He no longer played the fool – except when he was asked to – and Guy said he was truly working hard.

All of the players had now been warned of the possible dangers at the Twelfth Night Revels and knew that they must keep their eyes open and their wits about them. There was little else any of us could do.

Although there was still no word from Nick or Sir Damian, there was one discovery that caused Phelippes to send for me, asking me to bring Matthew with me and to meet him at the church of St Botolph Without Bishopsgate. I left word with the innkeeper at the Cross Keys, and the following morning Matthew joined me at the church door. Phelippes was waiting for us. He looked Matthew over and seemed surprised that he was so small. Perhaps he found it difficult to believe that Matthew could have carried Sophia all that way across London.

'Matthew,' he said seriously, 'I want you to do something unpleasant. Have you the courage to do that?'

I could not see where this was leading.

'I hope so, Master,' Matthew said stoutly, though I could see he was puzzled. 'What do you want me to do?'

'Have you ever seen a dead body?'

'Oh, that!' Matthew laughed. 'What do you take me for, Master? Of course I seen dead bodies! We sees them all the time on the streets.'

Phelippes seemed relieved, and led us into the church and down some steps to the crypt. A man's body had been laid out on a stone slab. A man of medium height, perhaps between thirty and forty years old, with brown hair.

'I want you to look at this man, Matthew, and tell me whether you have ever seen him before.'

Without hesitation, Matthew walked over to the body and looked down at it. He nodded. 'That's him, that threw the lass into Houndsditch. Know him anywhere. Someone cut his throat, did they?'

He seemed quite unmoved, although I was shocked at his calmness. What other horrors had he witnessed in his young life?

'Aye,' said Phelippes, 'and we think we know who.' He turned to me. 'Ambrose Selby. That nursemaid identified him. A purseful of coin, he had, and blood on his clothes. Of course he will claim it was in a fair fight.'

'I wonder whether it was a falling out over the purse of coin,' I said, 'or whether Selby had instructions to silence the Yorkshire man, so he could not give evidence about who ordered him to kill the child.'

'But he didn't kill her,' Matthew interjected.

'Not for want of trying,' I said.

'It will make it more difficult to establish a case,' Phelippes said, 'but Matthew's identification of the man will help. We have Selby in hold. In Newgate.'

The following day, Nick Berden and Sir Damian Fitzgerald rode back to London together, with Sir Howard Wilcox tied to his horse and the saddlebags last seen in Paul's Walk fastened behind Nick's saddle. I was not present when Wilcox was brought before Walsingham, who was determined to question the man himself, but I was given a full account that evening by Phelippes.

'Sir Francis had asked Lord Burghley to come as a witness to opening the saddlebags. Nick caught up with Wilcox just beyond Banbury. He had already spent some of the coin on a night's lodging and a fresh horse. His fingers bore the stain of your yellow dye.'

'Good,' I said. 'Did Sir Francis reveal that we had rescued Sophia?'

'Nay, he preferred to make Wilcox sweat a little. He demanded to know where the child was, the child who had been promised in return for the gold, and Wilcox attempted to brazen it out. At first he swore he had nothing to do with the child's disappearance. Then when he saw that was useless, he claimed he had instructed his two servants – he called them his servants – to return the child, and swore they must have disobeyed his orders.'

'And what did Sir Francis say to that?'

'Told him we had the corpse of one. Nate Ollerby, he was called. And he *was* a servant from Wilcox's estate in Yorkshire. Then Sir Francis broke the news that we also held Selby, who has confessed to killing Ollerby on Wilcox's orders.'

'Sir Francis still did not mention Sophia?'

'Nay. He was enjoying himself, letting out the things we know, drip, drip. Next he asked Wilcox: Was this his own money in the saddlebags? Of course, says Wilcox, and I demand you return my money at once.'

Phelippes gave a grim laugh. 'He had the nerve of the Devil himself.'

He stretched out his legs. I could see that he too had enjoyed the encounter.

'So, Sir Francis says: Will he kindly count out the money on the desk, to make sure that Nick and his men haven't helped themselves to any. Of course, his fingers are soon covered with more of the yellow dye, and then Arthur's counterfeit coins come to light. Burghley swears this is the money handed over by Sir Damian in exchange for the child. Where is the child?'

He smiled complacently.

'They had him really frightened now, but he tried to bluster.'

'Of course,' I said thoughtfully, 'if he believed he could somehow escape the charge of inciting the kidnapping, and Sophia was dead, he would still inherit.'

'I could see that was what he was thinking. However, at this point Sir Francis said that Selby had confessed that he was told to silence Ollerby, because Ollerby had killed the child on Wilcox's orders. It seems once they explained to Selby in clear terms what Topcliffe could do to him with the instruments in the Tower dungeons, he couldn't talk fast enough.'

'So does Wilcox still believe that Sophia is dead?'

'Nay. Sir Francis saved that piece of information till last. Of course, coming straight in with the prisoner, Sir Damian also thought she was dead. When he heard that she was alive, rescued by someone who had since identified Ollerby as the man who threw her into Houndsditch, I though he was going to faint away. "I must tell my wife," he said. "Where is Sophia now?" But Sir Francis would not say, not in front of Wilcox.'

He leaned back in satisfaction. 'Despite all our fears at having failed, it seems everything has come to a satisfactory conclusion. Sir Damian has recovered his gold, all but the cost of a night's lodging and the hire of a horse. Ollerby is dead. Selby and Wilcox are in prison, and we can hand the matter over to the courts.'

'And,' I said, 'most important of all, Sophia Makepeace is alive, thanks to some beggar children that I don't suppose any of you would look at twice if you saw them dying in a gutter.'

I was annoyed, for it seemed to me that they were more pleased about the recovery of the money and the capture of the men than with the rescue of the child.

'That is a little hard, Kit,' Phelippes said. 'We knew the child was safe. We needed to punish the perpetrators.'

'I daresay. So has Sir Damian now been told where she is?'

'Nay. Sir Francis has said that she will be returned tomorrow. He wants you to fetch her from Christ's, as it was you who placed her there. They might be unwilling to yield her up to anyone else.'

'Very well,' I said. 'I will go tomorrow morning.'

Soon after nine o' the clock the following morning I was riding west along Cheapside on Hector. I had decided that Sophia should return to the Fitzgeralds in appropriate state, so I took with me Edwin Alchester, also mounted and leading Sophia's own stout little pony. We were both dressed in our best, and Alchester had a bundle strapped to the back of his saddle, containing a full set of Sophia's expensive clothing.

215

We met, however, with an obstacle.

'I don't want to go back to my guardian's house.'

Sophia stood with her legs braced wide apart and her hands on her hips. For one terrible moment she reminded me of the portraits of the late King Henry, Queen Elizabeth's father, and I nearly laughed out loud. I managed to cough instead, for laughter would have doomed my mission.

'But why, Sophia?' I said, genuinely puzzled. 'They have all been so worried. And Edward wants to see you.'

'Edward will go back to school after Twelfth Night. I have lots of friends here. And I am the top scholar of the petties. And,' at this point her voice began to tremble and tears spilled over, 'and tomorrow we are going a'Thomasing.'

Of course, tomorrow was the twenty-first of December, St Thomas's Day. Preparations for the celebration were already in hand at the hospital, but throughout England, children would go a'Thomasing.

'We have been making the sprigs of holly and mistletoe, tied together with wool. I made twenty myself. And I have been learning the song.' She began to sing:

Wassail, wassail, through the town,
If you've got any apples, throw them down;
Up with the stocking, and down with the shoe,
If you've got no apples, money will do…

Her voice trailed off and she looked anxiously at me. Mistress Wedderbury bent down and whispered in her ear. Sophia's face cleared.

The jug is white and the ale is brown,
This is the best house in the town.

'You see!' she said triumphantly. 'I know it all.'

She looked at me pleadingly, no longer the aristocratic heiress giving orders to her inferiors, but just another little girl, who was lonely, without friends or playmates.

'We carry a mumper's pot and they give us apples and money.'

She stamped her foot. 'I *shall* go a'Thomasing.'

I crouched down in front of her and took both her hands in mine.

'I am sorry, Sophia, but sometimes we must all do as we are told by the people who command us. I have been ordered by Lord Burghley and Sir Francis Walsingham to take you home. After the Queen herself, they are the most important people in England. I cannot disobey them. Nor can you. However, I have an idea.'

She looked at me with a faint flicker of interest.

'Why do you and Edward not prepare a feast for the Thomasers from Christ's Hospital? I will ask Mistress Wedderbury whether she might bring them to the house in Cheapside, and when they have sung their song, you can invite them in for a Thomas Day treat.'

Alchester looked at me in horror at the thought of dozens of bluecoat orphans invading the dignified premises of the Fitzgeralds' house, but I did not care. I thought the Fitzgeralds owed it to Sophia, after what she had endured. Indeed, they owed it to Christ's, which had taken her in.

Sophia was turning this idea over in her mind and decided that it appealed to her. She would be able to show off her new friends to the Fitzgeralds where, after all, she was an outsider, a valued ward but not part of the family. She would also have the pleasure of bestowing favours on those same new friends. At last she agreed to come with us, though we had one further struggle. She wanted to keep her bluecoat uniform, which she said was much more comfortable than her usual clothes, which it almost certainly was, but I pointed out that it belonged to Christ's Hospital, and would be needed for another little girl who, unlike Sophia, would have no clothes of her own.

Moll took her off to be dressed, and when she returned she looked like another child altogether. Boned and laced and confined in her beaded and embroidered clothes, she reminded me of a singing bird trapped in a cage. I had a shrewd idea, however, that this particular singing bird would break free when she was older.

Sophia kissed Mistress Wedderbury farewell, and as many of her new friends as she could reach as they clustered about her, promising them that they should all see her again on the morrow.

'I hope you will break the news to Lady Bridget,' Alchester murmured to me as we set off to ride back to the Fitzgeralds' house. 'I do not care to think what her reaction will be to this party you have promised.'

'I am sure she will be so grateful to have Sophia back unharmed, or mostly unharmed, and her husband's money restored, that she will be happy to entertain the children.'

I was not myself present at the Thomasing party, but I was told later by Alchester than it had been a great success, with only one precious Venetian vase broken.

'The Turkey carpet on the table will never be quite the same again,' he said, 'but I daresay we can cover the stains with dishes in future.'

On the Eve of Christ's Nativity, I arrived at the hospital as usual to learn that the superintendent wished to see me. As I walked toward his room, pulling off my gloves and unwinding the scarf with which I had protected my face against the increased cold, I wondered what he wanted. There had been no emergencies of late in either of my wards, just the usual chest complaints. My patient in the almshouse was recovered. I was anxious to reach the lying-in ward, for we had several women near their time, one of whom was Bessie Travis's friend Meg, who had grown very large and sluggish in the last few days. The baby had moved down. It would put in an appearance soon. All Meg would say was that she would be glad to be rid of it. Although its heartbeat was steady, I had no way of knowing whether the baby had been permanently harmed by the attempted abortion.

'Ah, Dr Alvarez,' Ailmer said, bowing me into his room and even offering me a chair. 'I trust you are well at this happy season?'

'Indeed, I thank you,' I said. 'And you, Superintendent?'

'Very well, very well.' He returned to his desk and picked something up. 'This has come for you.'

He handed me a thick packet of paper. The wax seal on the outside was stamped with a coat of arms I should know. Then, with a sinking heart, I recognised it. I will not say that I had forgotten that the President of the Royal College of Physicians was to write to me here, but so much had happened since I had faced that formidable row of black-robed examiners that it was not at the front of my mind.

I tried to slide my thumbnail under the edge of the wax, but it was very thick and I could not shift it. I did not want to tear the paper, which seemed somehow disrespectful. To my surprise, Ailmer silently handed me a thin-bladed paper knife, so I was able to lift the seal and unfold the paper.

There were, in fact, two documents, both written on the highest quality laid linen paper. In Phelippes's office I had learned to assess every conceivable type of paper, for it was part of our stock in trade. This was the best available in London. The outer document was a letter from the President, written in English, in a flowing secretary hand, saying, with much circumlocution and flowery phrasing, that after due consideration and careful debate he and the four censors had decided to award me a licence as a full physician, to practice under the authority of the College.

As if they belonged to someone else, I noticed that my hands were shaking.

I unfolded the inner document. This was beautifully written in black letter script, in Latin, authorising one Christoval Alvarez to practice as a physician throughout all the realms of Her Gracious Majesty Queen Elizabeth. Another seal, much larger and grander, was affixed to the bottom of the document.

I looked up at Ailmer.

'I have been granted a licence by the College.'

'Excellent. Congratulations.' He beamed, and I think he was genuinely pleased for me. He must have decided after all that the hospital funds would be able to cover my increased salary.

I stood up. 'Thank you,' I said, as I laid the paper knife back on his desk. 'I did not know whether to expect it, since I have no university degree.'

'Your work here merits it,' he said.

'I thank you,' I said again. I drew a deep breath. 'I only wish my father could have lived to see this.'

That evening a service was held in the hospital chapel for the Nativity of the Christ Child. Most of the physicians, surgeons and nursing sisters attended, save for those keeping a watch over the patients. In addition, most of the permanent residents came from the almshouse, and many of craftsmen who worked in the various trades attached to St Thomas's: masons and carpenters and carvers and printers and glass workers. I saw Adam amongst the glass workers and spoke to him briefly as we went in. A few of the patients who were able to walk came as well. Three mothers with their new babies, some men with minor injuries. Altogether we filled the chapel, and although it was cold when we went in, the press of people soon warmed it.

There was music and the clergy wore fine vestments, for the Queen approved of such things and resisted those of a Puritanical disposition, who would have stripped away all beauty from the Anglican church. I hardly heard the service, for I was preoccupied with my own thoughts. I gave thanks in my prayers for the children who had passed through my hands in recent months. So many young lives, from the poorest beggars on the streets to Sophia with her empty riches. I gave thanks for my recognition as a physician, though it seemed to me so much less important than the work itself. Looking back, I could hardly comprehend all that had happened to me in the last year, for only a year ago we were all recently recovering from the threat of invasion by Spain, and then my father and I had cared for the sick and dying soldiers and sailors smitten with typhus after the battle. It seemed a lifetime ago.

I prayed for my father's soul, and hoped he would forgive me for doing so in a Christian church. He had, after all, been baptised a

Christian himself. I no longer knew what I was, Christian or Jew. Perhaps it did not matter. If one tried to live a good life, and to care for others, to try to be worthy of this precious thing, a human life, why did theology matter? Could not God see into my heart?

As the chapel bell sounded the midnight hour the choir sang a Latin hymn glorying in the birth of the Christ Child. The choir was made up of Southwark men and boys, whose daily lives were hard, their work often unpleasant and thankless, but that night I thought they sang like the heavenly host itself.

As we came out into the snowy courtyard, lit by torches placed all around it, three times the usual number, I saw one of the nursing sisters from the main building hurrying toward me, clutching a cloak about her throat.

'It's Meg, Dr Alvarez. She's gone into labour, and the babe seems to be coming fast.'

I pulled my own cloak tightly around my neck, for it had begun to snow hard while we were attending the service.

'I am coming at once,' I said.

So Meg would give birth on the birthday of Christ. What a contrast in expectation of a birth!

The lying-in ward was in semi darkness when we reached it, but we always kept several candle lamps alight at night, for babies will demand to be fed at any time of the day or night, and women near their time may have need of a piss pot. When we have a night-time delivery (and they are not infrequent) we try to avoid disturbance for those who are sleeping by putting screens around the bed, but no one was going to have any sleep that night. Meg was in full cry, screaming and cursing by turns.

Our most experienced midwife was in attendance, Goodwife Appledean, with three others to assist her, more than enough for any normal birth. She gave me a worried look.

'I sent for you as you instructed, Dr Alvarez, because of what the woman Meg did, to rid herself of the babe.'

The midwives' sympathy lay almost entirely with the infants, so the activities of the abortionists who practised in the dark alleys of Southwark appalled them, for they had often to deal with the terrible consequences. Many women died as a result of the abortionists' cruel and filthy operations, and their babies with them. I had indeed instructed Goodwife Appledean to send for me, even in the night to my lodgings, once Meg's time had come, for I was determined this baby should have a chance of life. I did not question myself too closely on what I would do if the child proved to be grossly deformed, as the infants born after bungled abortions often were.

Meg was clad in a clean shift, one already bloodied cast aside on the floor. One of the midwives was bathing her face, although Meg swore at her and twisted away. On a stool beside the bed, herbs which relieve childbirth were burning, scenting the air sweetly, though they could not altogether hide the smell of Meg's sweat. She was perched on the birthing stool, with another midwife kneeling beside her, massaging her stomach with oil in which the relaxing herb lavender had been steeped. Meg was cursing her too.

'Now, Meg,' I said, when she paused for breath and I could make myself heard, 'there is no need to swear at these good women who are doing all they can to ease your pain. You will do better to save your breath for the necessary labour, and pray to God that he will help the pain to pass quickly.'

'What do you know of it?' she yelled. 'You b'yer lady men, you have all the pleasure and none of the pain.'

(I paraphrase. Her language was somewhat fouler.)

Goodwife Appledean beckoned me aside and we stepped out into the central aisle of the ward.

'It is a large baby, Dr Alvarez. She is a selfish woman and a coward, but I fear it will be a long and painful labour. Perhaps I should not have sent for you so soon.'

'Nay, you were right to do so. Otherwise I should have gone home, only to need to return again. And it is snowing heavily.'

'Is it?' She glanced vaguely toward a shuttered window. 'I did not realise.'

She came from a long family line of traditional midwives, and I knew she found the idea of a lying-in ward at a hospital strange, even now, a hundred and seventy years after it had been endowed by the benefactor Richard Whittington. In her eyes, the proper way to bring a child into the world was in a tightly sealed and darkened chamber, thick with the smoke of traditional herbal preparations. The fact that I allowed the small bowl of burning herbs was a concession to this practice, but in her eyes, no doubt, not nearly enough. I could concede that the thick traditional smoke might drug the mother effectively, so that she felt less pain, but I was certain that inhaling it, instead of good clean air, was highly dangerous for a newborn infant's first breaths.

'The position of the baby is normal?' I said. It had been so yesterday, and I saw no reason that it could have changed.

'Aye. But the head is large, as you yourself know.'

221

At that moment there was another scream from Meg and we heard a crash. Hurrying back, I found the midwife who had been smoothing Meg's stomach with oil lying flat on her back, with the bowl of oil smashed on the floor beside her, the oil spreading in a viscous pool around the midwives' feet and the legs of the birthing stool. I helped the fallen midwife to rise and summoned a servant to clear up the mess of oil and broken crockery.

'Are you hurt?' I asked the midwife.

She shook her head, glaring at Meg. 'Only my elbow.' She rubbed it and turned her back on Meg. 'She struck out at me.'

'That was foolishly done,' I said to Meg. 'Now you have lost what comfort that would have brought you.'

She spat at my feet, fortunately missing my robe. Before she could answer me back, another massive contraction seized her and she screamed again. I had attended many births, especially since coming to St Thomas's, but most women were more stoical than this. Of course, all brought forth in great pain, but I think Meg was outraged at having to endure this, when she had thought to escape it through abortion. She blamed me and everyone else in the hospital for her present agony.

'There is nothing I can do here any better than you,' I said to Goodwife Appledean. 'As soon as the baby is born, I will care for both mother and child. Call me when it is time.'

I left the midwives to their work – somewhat thankfully, it is true – and went to my room. I call it a room, but it was no bigger than Arthur's cubbyhole at Seething Lane. Probably intended for a cupboard or small storeroom, it served well enough, for I did not use it often, or for very long at a time. I kept some of my main salves, purges and strengthening potions here on a shelf. I had a small table and a stool. It was enough.

Even here, between the two wards and with the door shut, I could hear Meg's screams. I hoped it was not frightening the children in the other ward. I folded my arms on the table and leaned my head on them. It would probably be necessary for me to stay at St Thomas's all night. Rikki was alone at my lodgings and although he was learning to stay quiet there, I knew he would be distressed if I did not return until the morning. I would have left him with Simon, but Lord Strange's men were hired to perform at Lincoln's Inn as part of the Christmas Eve festivities. As these were certain to continue for most of the night, he was unlikely to return before I did.

With the lateness of the hour and the half dark, lit only by a single candle, I must have dozed, for the next thing I knew, the midwife who had been knocked to the floor was shaking me by the shoulder.

'Goodwife Appledean asks will you come now, sir.'

'The baby is born?'

'Any moment now.'

I followed her back to the ward, where most of the women were now awake, apart from two who had pulled their blankets over their heads to keep out the noise. Several of the babies were crying. I was just in time to see the newest citizen of London slip into the world. The baby was large, and not breathing.

Goodwife Appledean held the baby up by the heels while another midwife tied off and cut the cord. She administered several hard slaps to the baby's back, but there was still no sign of breath.

I reached out and took the baby from her. It was a boy and he looked healthy enough, with no obvious sign of deformity or sickness. I laid him on the bed and began to pummel his chest gently, then more firmly. I thought I could feel a flutter from his heart under my hands. Goodwife Appledean handed me a cloth and I wiped his nose and mouth, then turned him over and struck his back, over his lungs, with the side of my hand. The baby gave a snort, a gasp, and then a wail. I lifted him up. He was still slippery and bloody, but he was breathing. And as far as I could tell, a healthy boy, one of the largest newborns I had ever seen.

'Well, Meg,' I said, 'you have a fine boy, born on Christ's own birthday.'

I wiped away the blood and wrapped the babe in a small blanket ready laid out on the foot of the bed.

Meg refused to look at me. 'Take the foul thing away,' she said. 'I don't want it. Throw it away, and a blessed riddance.'

'There is nothing blessed in your words,' I said, suddenly furious with her. He was a beautiful baby, from a fine tuft of dark hair down to the perfect fingernails on the curling fingers which had slipped out of the blanket. Could she not see how wonderful it was to have brought forth such a lovely child?

She simply shrugged and turned away as the midwives tended to her.

I sat down on the edge of the bed, cradling the child. Even with those of the unmarried mothers who choose to give up their babies, we ensure that they feed them themselves for the first week or two, until arrangements are made to transfer them to the care of Christ's Hospital. It is best for both mother and child. However, I foresaw trouble here. One of the nursing sisters carried over a wicker cradle, and I laid the baby in it. He would not need feeding for a few hours yet.

By now Meg was delivered of the afterbirth, washed and returned to bed. Without thanks or apologies to the midwives, she turned on to her side and prepared to sleep.

'What will you call your son, Meg?' I asked.

'Call it what you like,' she mumbled through the blankets. 'Take it away or by God's bones, I'll wring its neck.'

Goodwife Appledean looked at me in horror. 'Do you think she means it?' she whispered.

I frowned at the lump in the bed. 'I fear she might. Best move him to the other end of the ward.'

'Shall you name him, Dr Alvarez?'

I looked down at the unwanted child. His long lashes rested on the tender flesh of his cheeks, and one hand had again crept out of the blanket. They are so vulnerable, these newborns.

'Let us call him Christopher, in honour of the day. And a blessed Christmas to you all,' I said, looking round at the tired faces of the women who had so lovingly and kindly attended this ungrateful mother.

They murmured their own Christmas blessings to me. There was no more I could do here tonight. I went home through snow and starlight.

The next day Christopher was wakeful and began to need feeding. Meg refused to touch him, so there was nothing for it but to take him swiftly to Christ's Hospital, where they would find him a wet nurse in London until he could be moved out to one of their cottages in the country when the weather permitted. I decided to take him to Christ's myself. One of the midwives could have done so, but I felt some kind of responsibility for this child, so cruelly rejected at the very beginning of life. So we dressed him in a warm woollen gown and wrapped him in several blankets, before tucking him into a sort of wicker carrying basket the women used for moving the babies in cold weather. Once more I took a wherry to Blackfriars Stairs, and handed over an abandoned child to the care of Mistress Wedderbury. This was one child who would have no memory of anything before this place. He would forever be a Christ's child.

Chapter Sixteen

$\mathcal{I}$t was necessary to explain to Superintendent Ailmer why I must be absent for the whole day on the eve of Epiphany. Phelippes had provided me with a letter, at the bottom of which he had forged Walsingham's signature, Sir Francis himself having been laid low again by another bout of illness and retired to Barn Elms for the whole of Christmastide. It was an excellent forgery (it was Phelippes, after all, who had taught me the art), but I knew Walsingham's signature too well to be taken in.

The letter, however, merely said that I was required for Sir Francis's service and nothing more.

'The entire day?' Ailmer said.

I could understand his irritation. One of the physicians on the men's wards was ill at home himself and I had been assisting there when I could. Moreover, Ailmer was now obliged to pay me the salary of a full physician, not an assistant. It was reasonable for him to get full value for the money he was paying me. However, it had been part of the original agreement negotiated by Sir Francis with St Thomas's, that I should be released whenever I was needed. When I worked at Bart's, I had often been required, in times of crisis, to spend half every day in Seething Lane. And when Sir Francis had sent me abroad, I had been away for weeks at a time.

However, when I thought of how the future was shaping itself before me, I suspected that my work would be here at the hospital and no longer in an intelligence service which was only kept functioning now through the strenuous efforts of Phelippes. This might be the very last task I undertook for Sir Francis.

'May I sit?' I asked.

Ailmer waved me impatiently to a chair.

'This is no light matter, Superintendent,' I said. I had decided to take him into my confidence. 'It is a matter of Her Majesty's safety.'

225

He looked startled. I am not sure what he believed the work of Walsingham's intelligence service to be. Perhaps he had some vague notion of thwarting the Spanish. I expect his every waking minute was occupied with the running of the hospital and almshouse. It was not only a matter of managing those of us who worked here, and the patients, both the sick and the permanently infirm and resident. The whole range of buildings needed constant repair. Some, which had been part of the original monastery, were very old. Just the previous week the heavy snow piled up on the roof of one wing had caused a whole section of tiles to slide to the ground and shatter. Men were repairing the roof now, while inside a row of buckets was catching the melting snow and tripping up every passer-by.

I sat on a chair facing him across his desk and leaned forward.

'This is a matter of the greatest secrecy, you understand.'

He nodded.

'We have word that an attempt will be made on the Queen's life during the Twelfth Night Revels at Whitehall Palace. More than that we do not know. There will be many entertainers present, about half from outside England. The assassin could be concealed amongst any of them.'

'Has Her Majesty been warned?'

'She has. She would not cancel the Revels.'

He smiled, half exasperated, half admiring. 'It is no more than I would expect.'

'Very true. She is a woman of great courage. However, it falls to others to protect her, and I am one of them. I will be there as part of Lord Strange's Men, as a musician. There will be others of Walsingham's men in the palace, and especially in the Great Hall, where the Revels will take place, but as one amongst a company of players, I will have a better opportunity than anyone to get close to the other entertainers and watch for anything – anything at all – which seems suspicious. As all the entertainers will be there from early in the day, preparing for the Revels, I must be there also. And during this time before the Court is present, someone may let something slip. It may prove the best time to catch the assassin. Better by far to forestall him from ever coming close to the Queen than to catch him in the act, with all the danger that involves.'

I remembered my discussion with Phelippes when the rumours had first been reported. A sword or a knife would be dangerous enough, but a gun, or gunpowder, could endanger many lives, even if we were able to protect the Queen.

226

'I understand,' he said slowly, then gave me a keen look. 'When Sir Francis first recommended you for a position here, I did not understand that I would be employing someone who might be engaged on such dangerous work.'

I laughed. 'Oh, most of my work has been very safe and dull. Code-breaking. Deciphering and transcribing and translating very dull documents, with only the occasional plum to pull out of the pie. Attending the confinement of the Winchester goose Meg was far more exciting!'

He joined in my laughter. The story of Meg had gone round the hospital, gaining in colourful details the more often it was repeated. Two days after giving birth and ignoring advice, Meg had taken herself off, back to Bessie Travis's bawdy house. We were all relieved to see the back of her.

'Well,' he said, 'I understand now why you must spend the whole day at Whitehall. And I thank you for allowing me into your confidence. However, I would ask you to take care of your personal safety. I would not wish to lose my newly licensed physician.'

It was the warmest thing he had ever said to me, and I realised I had been right to trust him.

The Eve of Epiphany dawned bright and clear. There had been no fresh snow for nearly a week, but it had been so cold that the fallen snow had a frozen crust that sparkled under the low beams of the early January sun. Ice had formed all along both banks of the Thames, reaching out two yards at least from the shore, and although the wherrymen constantly tried to break it up with their oars, they were losing the battle.

I had arranged to leave Rikki with Tom, for I wanted him well away from danger. Once he was settled at the gatehouse I made my way across the Bridge and on to the stables as Seething Lane. Phelippes had agreed that I should ride Hector today, and I also needed a final word with Nick Berden before we made our separate ways to Whitehall. He would be going directly there, meeting the men he was deploying and obtaining their palace livery from the Master of the Revels, so that they could blend in amongst the real servants. We rode as far as Eastcheap together, then he turned west and I rode along Gracechurch Street, in order to join the players at the Cross Keys.

'Here is your lute,' Guy said, handing me the lute case, which I slung over my left shoulder by its strap. As usual, I carried my satchel of medicines over my right shoulder. I would not consider going into a situation where people might be injured without taking it with me. Carrying both satchels, I felt a little like a packhorse.

'We make a fine sight, do we not?' Simon had ridden up beside me as we set out.

'Indeed we do.' I smiled at him.

The players were dressed in their best finery, led by James Burbage in a purple cloak and an extravagantly feathered hat. His sons Cuthbert and Richard rode on either side of him, almost as eye-catching. The rest of us followed behind, first the players, followed by the boys, some of whom were blowing trumpets and banging drums as they rode. Behind the boys, three carts containing costumes and properties brought up the rear. Even I wore a plumed hat, pressed on me by Guy.

'We are perhaps no match for the Lord Mayor's Procession,' I said, 'or one of the Queen's progresses, but we are certainly attracting attention.'

Indeed, as we made our gallant way along Cheapside, crowds gathered at the side of the road to watch us pass by, some of them waving and cheering. James Burbage scattered a handful of silver pennies amongst a crowd of small boys, who fell to chasing them as they rolled amongst the stalls and the feet of the shoppers. Once through Newgate we turned left down Shoe Lane to Fleet Street and on toward the Strand. Despite the cold, it was a glorious ride. I had never ridden thus through the City in such bold and brave company and it seemed strange, when so much of my life I had tried to be as inconspicuous as possible. There was a heady excitement about it that I had never experienced before. Perhaps this was what infected the players when they stood upon the stage, surrounded by all those people, watching their every move, intent upon their every word. For a brief time I could share in it, though I was not certain that I could live for long at such a high pitch of excitement.

We passed Charing Cross and saw the great Holbein Gate ahead of us, but before reaching it we turned left through the Court Gate, the shortest way to the Great Hall of the Palace. In the enormous courtyard we dismounted and our horses were led away to stables by grooms in palace livery, amongst whom I noticed one of Nick Berden's men, already well settled into his role as an accepted palace servant.

'This way.' James Burbage beckoned to us to follow him.

Ahead we could see the passageway leading to Whitehall Steps, and beyond, the river. A group of men who might be more of the entertainers were unloading bundles from a wherry, so some river traffic must be running, despite the ice. I looked about in confusion. I had never before been to Whitehall Palace. Guy was walking beside me, following Burbage.

'Where is the palace?' I whispered. There were buildings everywhere, but nothing that resembled Greenwich or Hampton Court.

He laughed. 'You're inside it.' He waved his arms around. 'All of this is the palace.'

I followed his gestures and frowned. 'It looks like a village, not a palace. All these separate buildings, scattered about. Different styles, different ages. It does not seem a very grand palace for our Queen.'

'It is the largest palace in Europe,' he said, 'but to tell truth,' he lowered his voice, 'it is an incoherent jumble. It started long ago, and bit by bit it has been added to. There is a tennis court, do you fancy a game? And a bowling alley. And a pit for cock fights. And a tilting ground. And I suppose it must be a grand place for exercise. Not only the servants but even the courtiers must walk miles every day, trying to get from one place to another. There is a huge pleasure garden in that direction.' He pointed upriver. 'And orchards beyond.'

'So it really is more village than palace,' I said.

Before he could say more, Burbage was ushering us into the Great Hall, while his elder son Cuthbert oversaw the unloading of the costumes and properties from the carts which had been drawn up near the door.

The palace as a whole might seem unimpressive at first sight, but the Great Hall was not. Far above our heads soared a magnificent hammer beam roof, from whose angles the carved and gilded forms of angels leaned out. Away at the far end, perhaps a hundred feet from where we stood at the door, there was a dais which stretched the whole width of the hall. When the Great Hall had been used for magnificent dinners, this was where the monarch and the most important guests would have sat, the senior courtiers, ambassadors, royal and aristocratic visitors. However, I had been told that our present Queen had built a new banqueting house, and that was where the Court would be dining before attending the Revels. We would use the dais here as a stage.

As for seating, palace servants were now carrying in chairs and arranging them in rows facing the dais. At the very front, on its own raised dais, a large object covered with a protective sheet had already been installed.

Simon poked me with his elbow. 'That will be the throne for the Queen.'

'She will be very close to the stage,' I said nervously.

'You need not worry,' he said. 'You will be hiding away behind a screen. She won't see you. I shall have to perform just a few yards in front of her.'

'That is not what I was thinking of,' I said. 'It would be very easy to launch an attack on her from the stage.'

'Oh,' he said, measuring the distance between the throne and the stage with his eyes. 'You are right. Do you suppose she could be persuaded to sit further back?'

I made a face at him. There was no need to say anything. We both knew the Queen would not move. She would never take any action which might pass for cowardice. It was one of the things that made protecting her so difficult.

However, we could not stand about gaping. We both hurried to help with carrying the wicker hampers of costumes to a safe place behind the dais, where there was a room entered by a door on the left, set aside as a tiring room. It would be shared by all the male entertainers who needed to change their clothes, though Burbage had ascertained that most would come ready dressed in their costumes, so it would be almost exclusively for our use. Fortunately, as I would be hidden, I could retain my best doublet and breeches, which I was already wearing. At the back of the stage on the right there was a smaller room allocated to the troupe of French female dancers. The men of our company were somewhat shocked at the idea of women performing in public.

'But they are French,' Christopher Haigh pointed out. 'The French have no shame about such things. I have heard that they even have women acting in plays, though I do not know whether that is true.'

The day passed remarkably quickly. I had thought there would be plenty of time to stroll about amongst the other entertainers, to see whether any aroused suspicions, but somehow the hours flew by in arranging the stage to Burbage's satisfaction, awaiting the outcome of his arguments with the Master of the Revels (which he invariably won), and dodging out of the way of the servants setting up first the chairs and then trestle tables along the walls to hold food and wine to be served to the courtiers throughout the Revels.

We met and talked to the London consort of viols and the Morris dancers, one of whom knew Will Kempe. They, and the Dutchman with the dog, and a few others, joined us when the palace servants brought us refreshment at midday. I was disappointed that the Dutchman no longer had the monkey, but it seemed it had died in the cold weather. Nick was amongst the servitors of the meal, so we managed a few quick words.

'Anything?' Nick asked me.

I shook my head. 'I've seen nothing suspicious yet. And you?'

'Nay, I noticed nothing, but there is such a mass of people. The Master of the Revels told Phelippes that all the palace servants are honest and long-serving, but who is to say whether one of them might have been waiting for a chance?'

'You do not really believe that, do you?'

'Not really.'

'I have not managed to speak to any of the foreign entertainers,' I said, 'except the Dutchman, who has good English. The Poles keep to themselves.' I jerked my head to where the two Polish groups were sitting together, warily eyeing the food they had been given. The Turk had joined them, though I did not know whether they had a common language.

'The sword swallower,' I said. 'I do not know how they perform the trick, but if it is a genuine sword, could it be used against Her Majesty?'

'I do not know, but I will take care to watch him.'

'Do you know how they do it?' I was curious. From my knowledge of anatomy, it seemed impossible.

He shook his head, but before we could discuss anything further, he was called away by the steward in charge of providing food for the entertainers.

The only group I had been unable to approach at all were the French dancers who, like the Poles, kept themselves apart. In my male attire, I would not be welcome making an approach, for they might misinterpret my intensions. They had pulled some of the chairs out of the carefully arranged rows and were sitting in a group, daintily picking at the hearty fare which had been provided – somewhat greasy beef pies and bowls of a vegetable potage. They quite refused to drink the ale brought in by the palace servants, although it was of excellent quality, but made a great to-do until they were given wine. I had lived so long in England now that I had forgotten that other countries did not have our appreciation of fine ales and beers.

Davy was larking about with the other boys, having bolted his food, as usual. He still ate every meal as if he suspected he would never see another. Now he began showing off his acrobatic skills. Some of the other lads could perform a few tricks, but none could compare with Davy. Even with my inexpert eye I could tell that he had already improved under Guy's instruction. Now he began to show off, performing a series of his flips very fast across the whole width of the hall along the floor in front of the stage. The French women were clustered at the far end and just as Davy drew level with them, one wearing a dress of scarlet satin stood up, turned and collided with Davy. Quick as a snake she struck out at him, punching him with a clenched fist on the side of his head, so that he fell to the ground and lay there quite dazed.

I ran over to him. 'Are you hurt, Davy?'

He simply stared at me, clearly stunned.

I turned on the woman, addressing her in French, 'Was that necessary? He is only a child, and it was as much your fault as his.'

She glowered at me. 'You should keep your brats under control. This is no place for foolish pranks.'

'It was not a prank. He is an acrobat. He was practising.'

She turned away, but not before she had given me a vicious look. The other women seemed embarrassed, and several began to apologise. From their rather confused remarks I gathered that the woman was not one of their own troupe, but a famous performer who had been sent to join them and had just arrived in London that morning.

I accepted their apologies as politely as I could and helped Davy to his feet. As I led him back to our fellows by the elbow (and none too gently), I muttered, 'Keep away from them, foolish boy. We want no trouble with the other entertainers.'

There were tears in his eyes, but that might only be because of the blow to his head. 'I did not mean to bump into her, Dr Alvarez,' he said. 'She suddenly stepped into my path.'

'I know.'

'She has a hard fist. And her busk felt like a fireback when I hit it.' He rubbed the opposite side of his head from where he had been struck.

'Some women torture themselves with busks of wood,' I said, 'instead of simple boning in their bodices.'

'It felt like iron,' he muttered, but ran off to the other boys, without any sign of permanent injury.

I wondered whether busks of iron inserted into the front of a bodice was a new fashion from France which, like so many French fashions, would be taken up by English ladies. Not for the first time I gave thanks that I was not obliged to wear such uncomfortable clothes.

At the hour drew nearer to five o' the clock, an atmosphere of tension grew palpable in the hall. This must be how the players felt as the time for a performance approached. Although I had little to do, other than play three duets with Guy, seated behind a screen, I found my own heart beating faster and the palms of my hands growing clammy. I told myself that this was sheer folly. I had been in the presence of the Queen before, the time Walsingham had brought me to Greenwich at the Queen's bidding, to receive her thanks. However, on that occasion I had only to remember courtly manners, bow, and withdraw. Now I was part of a company screwed up to a high pitch of nerves.

'This is much worse than simply performing before Her Majesty,' Simon confided. 'We have done it before, and then we had only to make sure that our own play went well. Now, there is all this rabble to perform before us. Who knows what they will do? They may annoy Her Majesty, or bore her. She may decide to walk out – she has done so before. I hate having to come last.'

I tried to console him. 'You will be so much better than everyone else, you will shine by the comparison.'

He shrugged, unconvinced. 'And now we hear that instead of our presenting the dance after the play, the French women are to do it, even though they will already have performed.'

I had no answer for that.

Because the temporary tiring room was so small, we could not await our turn there. Benches had been pushed back against the walls on either side of the hall, well away from the seats for the courtiers, so that the entertainers were at hand but inconspicuous. We took our places on the left with most of the others. The French troupe and one group of Poles were opposite us on the right, sitting a little apart from each other. The Turk was with us. Now that I was close to him, I noticed a distinct line on his neck where his golden brown skin ended and there was a strip of a paler colour. He had been using some sort of dye to give himself an eastern look. He wore a complex headdress, part turban, part hat, which sported an array of glass jewels. He was, I decided, no more a Turk than I was. He seemed nervous, plucking at his voluminous and baggy trousers with long, thin fingers.

I looked at Guy, who had taken the seat next to me as the courtiers began to file in. 'Clever of you,' I murmured, 'to guess that there would be a Turkish sword swallower.'

He grinned. 'Known him since we were boys. He's from Bermondsey. He's very good. Wait and see. He swallows fire as well, but he's Russian when he does that act.'

'Not a danger to the Queen, then?' I said.

'Henry Allinger? Suleiman the Unmatchable, I should say. Never in a thousand years. Worships the very ground beneath her slippers.'

So my most likely suspect was eliminated. However, we could speak no more. The entire Great Hall fell into silence except for the swishing of dozens of satin petticoats as every person rose and either bowed or curtseyed. Her Majesty the Queen was here.

I had, of course, never attended Revels at Court before, so I was not sure what to expect. Jugglers and acrobats I had seen at fairs, but these entertainments were much more elegant. Each was introduced by the Master of the Revels in flowery and extravagant terms. I suppose it was essential for the dignity of his office that everything here should seem to be of the best in the known world. He started by announcing the Essex Morris dancers, with an oblique but gallant reference to my lord of Essex, who was sitting at Her Majesty's right hand. The throne, uncovered now, was of gilded and painted wood, standing on feet shaped like the foreparts of lions and cushioned in red velvet. The Earl's chair was more modest, but not by much.

The dancers ran up the hall from the far end and leapt on to the stage, where they began their curious dance which involves much stamping of their feet, with the jingling of bells, and moving in and out of patterns. I had thought they carried sticks which they clashed together, but these men carried swords, so that the whole dance took on a much more menacing aspect.

'I had not noticed that they carried swords,' I whispered to Guy, although whispering was hardly necessary. The dancers were accompanied by a piper and a drummer, who beat out the time for their thundering leaps.

'They will have kept them wrapped up and hidden away,' Guy said, 'until they were needed for the dance.'

Here was another possible danger to the Queen, although the Morris men had been vouched for. They brought their eight swords clashing together in a sort of knot, then broke away to form another figure. The Queen seemed unconcerned. She had accepted a glass of wine from one servant and was now carefully selecting a plate of sweetmeats from another, kneeling before her. It was Nick, I observed. He backed away, crouched over to avoid blocking her view. It was clear he was staying as close to her as possible.

The Polish acrobats were next, performing feats of considerable dexterity, but without the seeming effortlessness that Guy showed. They were followed by the Dutchman with his dog, who had us all laughing, even the Queen. I wished Rikki could have seen that dog. He even seemed to hold a conversation with his master, conducted in English. Though it was all pretence, it was very funny. The Queen applauded loudly. The Dutchman, blushing with pleasure, nearly fell off the stage, whereupon the dog pretended to rescue him.

More entertainments followed. Juggling by the other Polish group. Some exquisite singing by the choir of Danish boys who had arrived late, their ship having been held up by the ice in the river. Considering how anxious this must have made them, they acquitted themselves very well. There was a Welsh conjuror, who made things appear and disappear by sleight of hand, and then the French dancers made their first appearance.

By now all the courtiers had been served with wine and comfits and were busy consuming them and chatting quietly amongst themselves. The Queen was saying something to Essex as the dancers appeared. I noticed that the woman in the red dress looked annoyed at this inattention, but the performance went ahead. It was a pretty thing to watch. The women had long trailing scarves of many colours which they wove around and about each other as they danced to the music of their accompanying flutes and citterns. The patterns of colour formed and reformed as they moved about the stage, while the woman in red danced by herself at the front. She was very supple and skilled, performing dance steps I had never seen before.

Then it was Guy's friend, the Turk from Bermondsey. I still could not see how the trick was done. I suspected that somehow the sword folded in on itself, sliding up into the pommel, but I could not be sure. The sword swallower was followed by both groups of Poles, who had arranged a combined performance which was an extra entertainment, and while it was going on, our company slipped behind the drapes at the side of the stage and into the tiring house, from which they would make their entrances for Will's play, *The Comedy of Errors*. I went with them to take my place behind the screen, where Guy and I would play our duets and Davy would sing, when the play was finished.

Our company's performance was, as I have said, a play in which confusion builds upon confusion, brought about by two sets of twins – unlikely as it may seem – separated at birth and then arriving in the same town at the same time wearing identical clothes. I hoped Master Burbage had made the right choice. What if the Court scorned all this silliness?

I was wrong and he was justified. The courtiers loved it. Peeping round the edge of the screen, I could see the Queen laughing heartily. When the players came to take their bows at the end, there was a great burst of applause, far greater than for any of the other entertainments. I sighed with relief, and realised that I had been clenching my hands nervously, so that my nails made half-moon impressions of red in my palms. I flexed my fingers to loosen them ready for playing my lute.

As the players ran past me and jumped from the stage, to take their places on the benches again, I whispered to them, 'Well done!'

Now Guy joined me and we quickly checked that the two lutes were in tune. The audience had begun to chatter again, so Guy warned me to wait until they had once more been served with refreshments. When he gave me the nod, we began. I was grateful for the screen. Sitting behind it, I could pretend that we were alone, practising as we often did at the Theatre. I forgot the courtiers in the hall, and the Queen, and simply enjoyed the music. They must have enjoyed it too, for they applauded generously.

It was time for the last piece. Davy walked out from the tiring room and stood in the centre of the stage, with his hands clasped behind his back. He looked very small. Then he began to sing and at the sound of that pure voice the last and faintest murmurs from the crowd were silenced. Will had written new words for the music, a simple song in which a shepherd boy longs for his lost love. You never know, in the end, whether it is another man or Death itself who has snatched her away, but the sheer beauty of the singing left that worldly-wise, sophisticated audience stunned.

As they applauded, Guy and I left the stage. Davy bowed and scampered after us. The Revels were nearly over. Surely the rumour of an attack on the Queen had been false, or the plot had been abandoned. There was nothing left now but the final dance by the French women, then we could all relax. It was a new experience for me to have joined, for a short time, the world of Simon and the other players. I understood better how they could become almost drunk on the exhilaration of performance, but for myself it was too public, too open to the vagaries of praise or censure.

To my surprise, the dancers were to perform on the floor in front of the stage, instead of on the stage itself. This must have been agreed in advance with the Master of the Revels, for he introduced them from the stage as they arranged themselves between him and the Queen. Most of their company had formed up in a double line along the front of the dais, carrying both their coloured scarves and garlands of fresh flowers. Their four musicians took their places behind them on the stage as the Master of the Revels stepped down off it. He looked pleased and relieved, as well he might. Everything had gone well. I saw him wipe his brow with a large handkerchief.

'Good.' Simon was sitting beside me now, as I laid my lute underneath the bench. 'All is well now. Just these elegant ladies to perform their dance and then we can go home. The story of an assassin must have been pure invention.'

'The play was excellent,' I said. 'I was almost fooled into thinking you and Christopher were twins. The Queen loved it.'

He flashed me a smile as the women began to dance. I wondered what had become of their principal dancer. Perhaps she had only agreed to give one performance. Then she came running lightly up from the back of the hall as the music began and the others moved into their first complicated patterns.

It was difficult to follow. The main dance was complex and lovely, involving the weaving of the garlands into a sort of carpet of flowers. It drew the eye. Yet at the same time I could not ignore the solo dancer, who seemed to be performing something quite separate. Where the other dance suggested some pastoral Arcadia peopled by youthful shepherds and shepherdesses, like those in Davy's song, the woman in red was like a violent flame. She whirled and leapt as the mystic Dervishes are said to do, and I could not understand how the two dances were meant to fit together, unless the red dance symbolised destruction of the innocent flower-filled paradise of Arcadia.

Something stirred in my mind. Davy had said that when he collided with the woman, her busk had felt like an iron fire back. Surely even the most extraordinary fashions of France would not demand anything more extreme than a wooden busk, above all for a dancer. I began to watch the woman more closely. Could this be a man, disguised as a woman, as I was a woman disguised as a man? It would be one way for an assassin to slip closer to the Queen. In which case, Davy had collided with a breastplate, not a busk.

Nay, that was impossible. The dancer's bodice was square necked and low cut. I could see the revealing swell of her breasts above the top of the bodice. This was a woman. Her frantic dancing was making her sweat, so that dark patches began to appear on her gown, which clung to her more closely. I seized hold of Simon's arm.

'The dancer in red,' I whispered. 'Look at the front of her gown. What do you see?'

'A very fine, buxom wench,' he said, 'with breasts as round as–'

'Between her breasts, you idiot!' I hissed.

'She does seem to have something stuffed down the front of her dress,' he admitted.

I sprang to my feet and ran forward, just as the woman whirled round, plunging her hand into the front of her dress and lunging toward the Queen. We collided at the Queen's feet. I grabbed the dancer's wrist, but she twisted away from me and slashed out at my neck with a slender dagger. I felt the sting of the blade as I hooked my leg behind her knees, in the move I had seen wrestlers use, and made another grab for her wrist.

I had the advantage of her, for I could move freely in doublet and hose, while she was hampered by her long skirts and the exhausting dance. Even so, she fought me like a creature possessed, spitting in my face and slashing at me again and again, even though I held her wrist.

'Berden!' I shouted.

I could hear cries of panic behind me, but I had the woman off balance now and she fell backwards to the floor, with me on top of her. Still we struggled for possession of the dagger. With a kind of cold disinterest, I watched blood dripping on to her face, and knew it was mine.

The struggle cannot have lasted more than half a minute before Nick was there, and two of his men, dragging the dancer away from me. I let go of her wrist and found myself being helped to my feet by Simon on one side and Guy on the other.

'It was a woman,' I gasped, looking at Nick.

'Aye.' He hauled the dancer to her feet.

One of his men had the dagger now, holding it loosely in his hand and staring at it in disbelief. None of us had suspected it could be a woman. But she was still as quick as a snake. Suddenly she snatched the dagger. Nick and I with one voice yelled a warning.

She turned the dagger on herself, plunging it into her stomach, below where the concealed sheath lay. She sank to the ground, slipping from the hands of her captors. Before anyone could question her, before we could even learn her name, she was dead.

An hour later, the Great Hall was almost deserted. The body had been carried away. All the other entertainers except the French women had been paid and dismissed. The courtiers had withdrawn, sent away by the Queen who had refused to leave, despite being urged by Essex and her ladies. He too had stayed, hovering solicitously in the background. The French dancers had been carried off by Nick Berden to be questioned, weeping and swearing they had never laid eyes on the woman in red until that very day.

I had lost blood from the slash in the side of my neck, and felt somewhat weak as a result, but no one might sit while the Queen remained standing.

'Dr Alvarez, I believe I owe you my life,' she said.

'Your Majesty,' I croaked, trying to bow, and wobbling as I did so.

'Will no one see to this wound?' she demanded.

'I have my satchel of medicines, Madam,' I said. 'It is not so grave.'

She gave an incredulous grunt and turned to the Master of the Revels. 'See that Dr Alvarez is properly cared for.' With that she swept out of the hall, with Essex hurrying off behind her.

'Just let me sit down,' I said. 'Simon, get my satchel.'

I made a pad to lay over the slash and Simon wound a bandage carefully round my neck to hold it in place.

'Not so tight,' I complained. 'I would like to be able to breathe.'

'We thought we had lost you then, Kit,' he said. I saw the fear and sorrow in his eyes and patted the hand that was fastening off the bandage.

'I'll recover,' I said, more cheerfully than I felt, for – if I was honest with myself – it was very painful.

Now, with everyone gone except our subdued company and the Master of the Revels, we made ready to leave. The costumes had been packed into the carts which had already left. The rest of us went out to the courtyard, where dozens of torches held back the dark, and waited for our horses to be brought.

'Where is my ridiculous hat?' I asked. 'The one with the feather?'

'Here,' Guy said, holding it out. 'Are you sure you want to wear it?'

'Of course.' I pulled it on to my head and smiled at James Burbage.

'Master Burbage,' I said, 'surely you wish to return from the palace in as fine a procession as when you arrived.'

He laughed and came near to clapping me on the shoulder, but luckily thought better of it.

'Kit is right. We have had a triumph here tonight, in more ways than one. Let us ride back to the City in our glory!'

We mounted. The young boys, tired as they were, revived at the thought of processing back to the City in our finery. They sounded off with their drums and trumpets again, which may have disturbed the rich folk who lived along the Strand but raised the spirits of all the company, which had been severely dampened by the last act of our drama.

As we rode out of the Court Gate, Simon leaned across from his horse and laid his hand on Hector's neck.

'I can play the hero on the stage, Kit, but I am not sure that I could have done what you did tonight. I thought you would be killed. I thank God you were not.' His voice was full of passion.

I could not speak, but only nodded. I was glad that in the dark he could not see my tears.

Chapter Seventeen

March, 1590

It was not yet spring, but the promise was there. The birds must have sensed that it was on the way, for I think I have never seen so many blackbirds and thrushes thronging the bushes that crowded the verges of the road through the Surrey countryside. The snow had vanished. Instead, the swathes of white, strewn like silk scarves beneath the trees beyond the hedges, were thousands of modest snowdrops, their heads inclined like obedient maidservants, and yet a mighty army in their number. So might the common folk of England seem, labourer and servant, herdsman and shepherd, aye, and even beggar, eyes cast down, but it was their unceasing labour which sustained the rich in their manor houses, the coloured butterflies in the Court.

I was filled with such pensive thoughts as I rode Hector, perhaps for the last time, south from London to Walsingham's country house at Barn Elms. Phelippes had sent me a message the previous evening. I was to carry a satchel of papers to Sir Francis, who was confined to bed again, and very weak, but determined to work as long as any strength remained to him. Phelippes could have sent any trusted servant to carry the papers, but Sir Francis himself had expressed a wish to see me. I did not know what this might concern, unless it was advice on what I should do when the intelligence service finally came to an end, for he had always treated me kindly, but whatever the reason I was glad to leave London for part of a day at least. The City had a tired, grubby look at the end of winter, and Southwark was no better.

It was barely past dawn when I had handed Rikki over to Harry in the stable yard at Seething Lane.

'I've Hector saddled for you already, Dr Alvarez,' he said. 'Master Phelippes is in his office.'

Phelippes passed me the satchel of papers, but had no more idea than I had why Sir Francis should want to see me in particular. He was looking glum, as he often did these days. The almost daily interference of Essex in his management of the service was a constant irritant.

Still, I thought all this would soon be of little concern to me. I took the papers, mounted Hector – who seemed as glad of the outing as I was – and rode off across the Bridge, heading for the country. I was wearing new doublet and breeches, and had left off my physician's gown. Since I had gained my licence, Dr Nuñez had handed over a number of his patients to my care, with their agreement. On the whole, they seemed satisfied with me. Most were well established merchants, Dr Nuñez having retained the aristocrats, who might have baulked at being treated by a newly licensed physician as young as I. For myself, I was happy with my new patients. I liked their practical approach to life, their hard work, and their general lack of arrogance. That is not to say that they did not take pleasure in their riches, in the expensive tapestries on their walls, the silver dishes on their tables, and the precious damasks on their wives, but it was pride in what they had themselves achieved, for many were self-made men. The reigns of the Tudors have brought many troubles to England, but they have also brought many opportunities for quite humble men to rise, through nothing more than their own hard work and acumen.

Some of these opportunities were opening up to me. Indeed I owed my new doublet and breeches to the fees from my private patients and my increased salary from St Thomas's. In my own modest way, I might rise above my humble status as a destitute Marrano refugee. More than ever, I knew I must reject Sara Lopez's opinion that I should abandon my role as a man and take on my true position as a woman. At twenty I had established myself as a physician, my abilities in medicine were recognised, and I had the kind of freedom no woman could ever enjoy, not even a woman of high birth and wealth. The Queen herself, although she had power, had not my freedom.

My life was changing, but I could not foresee what lay ahead. There was a shadow over the future of the intelligence service, and although Phelippes had hinted that he hoped I would continue to work with him, I was reluctant. He seemed certain that my lord of Essex would try to step into Walsingham's shoes, which in my eyes spelled disaster. Essex's ill-founded bravado, his conceit, nay, his *stupidity*, would surely destroy Walsingham's decades of service to Queen and State. I wanted nothing to do with him.

Still, there was little point in dwelling on these matters. It was a beautiful, almost warm, almost spring day, and I was mounted on the best horse in the kingdom. I did not intend to hurry. I leaned forward and caressed Hector's neck. I would make the most of this last ride. I was conscious of the vigour of my own body, and my pleasure in my youth and strength. The assassin's slash across my neck had healed cleanly, leaving nothing but a faint silver line of scar. The day after the Revels, the Queen had sent me a purse of gold as a reward. My friends had some wild suggestions on how I might spend it, but I had other plans.

Despite my dawdling, it was still morning when I reached Barn Elms, where I handed over Hector to one of the stable lads whose face was familiar, though I had forgotten his name. The door was answered by a servant who showed me into the office of Master Goodrich, Sir Francis's steward.

'Good day to you, Dr Alvarez,' he said, bowing and pulling out a chair for me. 'Sir Francis is not quite ready to receive you yet. Will you join me in a glass of wine?'

'I thank you,' I said. The wine in Sir Francis's houses was always of excellent quality. I thought Master Goodrich had aged since I had seen him last. His hair had been grizzled when I first met him. Now it was quite grey. The strain of Sir Francis's illness was clearly telling on him too.

'How is Sir Francis?'

He shook his head and I saw that his lip trembled. 'I fear it cannot be long now, Dr Alvarez. His spirit is so strong, it has sustained him when most men would have been felled long since, but even he cannot fight off Death's sickle for ever. He is in great pain.'

'Has he been given any relief?'

'He will take none. He says he is better able to withstand pain of the body than cloudiness of mind. It is almost unbearable to watch, for those of us who love him.'

I nodded. I realised that, in my own way, I too loved him. Unwilling as I had been at first to serve him, this was a man who had shown me respect from the outset and in doing so had given me courage and faith in myself. I owed him more than I could possibly express.

We drank our wine then in silence, each occupied with our own thoughts, until a servant knocked on the door and said that Sir Francis was ready to see me. I had expected to find him propped up on cushions in the small parlour, but instead I was conducted to his bed chamber, where he lay in a great curtained bed, with piles of documents covering the bedclothes.

I tried not the avert my eyes from his wasted form, but to look at him steadily. He was too shrewd to be deceived.

'You find me sadly depleted in body, Kit, but I have not yet lost the ability to work. You have the papers for me? Come, draw up a chair.'

I did as I was bid and laid the satchel I had brought on the bed. We were both silent as he drew the papers out and looked quickly through them, setting some down on the piles already on the bedclothes, retaining two or three to read at once.

'Good,' he said, when he had finished. 'Thomas Phelippes has indeed proved his worth during these last months. Most of the time he has run matters himself, and it has not been easy.'

I was tempted to make some mention of Essex, but kept my tongue behind my teeth. I was sure Walsingham knew exactly how much Essex had been interfering.

He laid aside the last of the documents I had brought and picked up a single sheet from a candle table on the other side of the bed.

'Now, Kit,' he said, 'I am sure you are curious as to why I sent for you specifically, but I needed to speak to you one last time. You are a physician, and no fool. You know that I have no more than weeks, perhaps only days, left on this earth.'

I opened my mouth to protest, but he raised his hand to stop me and smiled sadly. 'Do not try to deceive yourself or me. I am not afraid to meet my Maker. I hope I have lived a decent life and done my best in the tasks I was called upon to undertake. It has not always been easy or pleasant.'

'You have kept this land in peace, Sir Francis, and the Queen safe from her enemies,' I said. 'That is surely a life well lived. Many who know nothing of it owe the security of their own lives to you. Those of us who do know, respect and love you for it. We know that you have near beggared yourself that we may live in peace and prosper.'

He reached out and laid his hand over mine, where it rested on the edge of the bed. I saw there were tears in his eyes.

'I thank you for that, Kit. When you were very young, your first taste of what that peace can cost must have gone hard with you. The Babington case was a fearful affair, their punishment the cruellest.'

I nodded.

'However, that is not what I wanted to discuss with you. You have given me good service over these last years – four years it must be. As recently as Twelfth Night you showed your quick wits in averting a disaster. Now, I realise that you feel your true calling is that of physician, and you will be more occupied than ever with that now, but I also know that Thomas is anxious you should continue as his chief assistant. You must make your own decision, of course.'

'Sir Francis, my lord of Essex has seemed to take a great interest in the service of late.'

'So he has, so he has.' He sighed. 'I know that after the Portuguese expedition, you had no very high opinion of the Earl, but we must remember that he is the premier earl in England, beloved by the Queen, as much for his late uncle's sake, my lord Leicester, as for his own. In such a position, he could do much good for our intelligence service.'

I wanted to say, *And he could also do much harm.* But I did not.

'However, as I have said, you must decide for yourself, but I wanted you to know that you are greatly valued, both by me and by Thomas Phelippes.'

He struggled to sit up a little higher in bed, and instinctively I rose and straightened his pillows, then slipped my arm under his shoulders to help him.

'I thank you,' he said, a little breathlessly. 'There is, however, another matter.'

He lifted the paper he had taken from the table. I saw that it bore a wax seal at the bottom, like an official pronouncement, or a will.

'You are very fond of my piebald horse Hector, are you not?'

Surprised, I said, 'He is the finest horse in the kingdom!'

He laughed softly. 'Unlike many, you have seen through his strange appearance to the heroic heart beneath. I have watched the two of you together. I saw you ride in today.'

He gestured to the window just beyond his bed, and I realised he could see the comings and goings at the front of the house from here.

'Well, I am making a gift of Hector to you, Kit. This is the deed of gift.' He handed me the paper.

I could not believe what I was hearing. Hector was to be mine? Whatever his appearance, he was a very valuable animal, and Sir Francis had not much disposable property to leave to his wife and daughter. My hands holding the paper shook and I could not stop myself. I was weeping openly.

'Come now.' He patted my hand. 'You must not weep.'

'It is too much,' I whispered, but even as I said it I knew, fiercely, how much I wanted Hector. But how could I keep a horse? I had no stable, no stable lad. The cost of feeding a horse would be beyond my means, even with the increase in my earnings.

He must have read my thoughts in my face. 'When you read the deed of gift, you will see that it includes provision for Hector to have stabling and keep at Seething Lane or here at Barn Elms, for as long as you shall wish. I have also advised my wife and daughter of this, and they are in agreement. So you see, you have no need to worry about the expense.'

'It is too much,' I said again. 'How can I accept?'

He patted my hand again and I could see that he was growing tired, however hard he attempted to hide it.

'Do not force me to argue, Kit. The horse is yours.'

I lifted that frail hand to my lips and kissed it. 'I cannot find the words to thank you enough, Sir Francis,' I said.

'Fear not.' He gave a little smile. 'Your eyes speak it well enough. Now, go and find Mistress Oldcastle. She will be glad to see you, although we are somewhat at sixes and sevens here today. And perhaps you will take a meal with Edward Goodrich before you ride back to London. He has some estate papers to be delivered to Seething Lane.'

I rose from my chair, holding the deed of gift as if it were a vessel of fragile Venetian glass. With my other hand I picked up the satchel in which I had brought the despatches. I would need it if I was to take more documents back to London. At the door I turned and looked back. Sir Francis's eyes were closed, but he was not sleeping.

'And perhaps I should also say, Kit, how much I admire your courage. Few girls could live your life, with all its dangers, with as stout a heart as you do.'

I gasped involuntarily and he opened his eyes.

'Have no fear. Thomas Phelippes does not know. Or Arthur Gregory. Certainly not my lord of Essex.'

He closed his eyes and turned his face away. With a pounding heart I slipped quietly out of the room.

There was no one about. I leaned back against the door. I could barely breathe. How long had he known? How had I given myself away? Was it all those years ago when I had fled here from the Fitzgeralds' house and he had found me asleep by his parlour fire? Or after my father died and I found myself destitute? Had I at some time said or done something which gave me away? I hoped he was right, that Phelippes did not know, for I could not work with him again if he did. As for the Earl of Essex, it was a wonder if he had ever *seen* me, even when I was under his nose. He was a man so self absorbed, I imagined he barely took note of the Queen, except insofar as he could beguile her into giving him gifts and honours.

In a state of confusion I made my way downstairs, where I found the housekeeper, Mistress Oldcastle, who did indeed seem pleased to see me, although I could tell she was also distracted.

'Sir Francis is sadly reduced,' I said, in sympathy.

'Indeed he is, Dr Alvarez, but that does not hinder him. You would not believe what is afoot here today, but I must not speak of it.'

This was a strange remark, but I had little thought to spare for the mystery, still too occupied with the gift of Hector and Sir Francis's parting remark, that he knew my sex.

'I have laid a light meal for you and Master Goodrich in the small family dining room,' she said. 'You know where it is. And Sir Francis's secretary, Master Mylles, will be joining you as well. The family will be eating in the guest dining room, for my lord Essex is here today.'

With that she bustled off. Essex here – could one never escape the man?

I had a pleasant meal with the steward and Francis Mylles, despite the sadness which hung over the house. It seemed Goodrich knew of the gift of Hector, and Mylles congratulated me on it. I wondered whether he had yet taken possession of the manor he had bought from Sir Francis. One by one, Walsingham was disposing of his property.

After the meal, Goodrich and I went through the documents I was to carry back to Seething Lane, and Mylles instructed me where to store them with Phelippes, until he himself returned and could move the private papers to the family portion of the house.

After our meal I had sent for Hector and was waiting by the front door for him to be brought round from the stables, when Mylles came hurrying out of the house, looking distracted.

'You must not leave yet, Kit, after all. You are needed within.'

With that he turned back into the house and I followed him. To my surprise, I almost collided with Lady Frances, who was standing in the hallway, weeping openly, while her mother, Dame Ursula, had her arms around her daughter, clearly trying to comfort her. I hastened to pass, embarrassed at having seen them. As I did so, Frances lifted her face on which there was a look of bleak resignation.

'You know not how fortunate you are, Kit Alvarez,' she said bitterly. 'You have your independence and may live your life how you wish.'

Her mother hushed her, and hurried her away into the small parlour. What could be the meaning of this? It was clear that something was afoot in the house apart from Sir Francis's illness.

247

I quickened my steps to catch up with Francis Mylles. 'Where are we going? Why I am needed?'

'Through here,' he said. 'To the family chapel. You are needed to be a legal witness. One who was to have come has sent word that he has had a fall from his horse and broken his leg. That is his excuse, but it may be that he has thought better of being involved.'

With that he opened a door at the rear of the house and led the way across a formal garden to the small private chapel. I was more mystified than ever. We entered and took our seats at the side. Then we waited.

'What is this about?' I whispered.

'You shall soon see,' was all that he would answer.

Shortly after we were seated, Dame Ursula entered, watching over two strong servants who were carrying Sir Francis in a chair. Next Master Goodrich ushered in the Earl of Essex with much obsequious bowing, and led him to the front of the chapel, where a clergyman, whom I took to be the Walsingham's chaplain, stood waiting. Having seen her husband's chair also carefully placed at the front of the chapel, Dame Ursula hurried out again. At last I began to suspect what was toward here.

'Is this a forced marriage?' I demanded in a fierce whisper.

Mylles shook his head and frowned.

There was a long delay, then Lady Frances entered, led by her mother, with two of her ladies in attendance. She was heavily veiled, so that it was impossible to see whether she was still weeping, but she walked steadily forward to the altar. No one forced or dragged her. I saw suddenly in my mind the vivid image of her as she had walked into St Paul's on her father's arm, three years before, to attend the funeral of her husband, Sir Philip Sidney. Simon and I had stood outside on a freezing morning and watched. She had been pregnant with a child she had lost, and little Elizabeth, the only child of the marriage had followed her into the church, too young to understand what was happening. I wondered where Elizabeth was now. This time she was old enough to understand.

'She was weeping,' I whispered. 'She does not want this marriage. Essex is a notorious rake.'

Mylles frowned again. 'She will do as her father wishes. It is a great marriage for her, a knight's daughter, to marry the first earl in the land. She will be a countess. Her father only wants to provide for her before his death.'

'The Queen will not like it,' I said.

'She did not like the marriage to Sir Philip, but she accepted it in the end.'

'That was a love match. Besides, the difference in rank is much greater now.'

Mylles simply shrugged.

The ceremony had begun. If a marriage between such a distinguished couple could be said to be hasty and almost secret, then such was this marriage. The groom gave his answers with an air of indifference, yet there was somehow a certain self-satisfaction about them. The bride was subdued, but answered bravely and without hesitation. She must have resigned herself to her father's wishes. I could understand that he was anxious for her future welfare, a widow with a young child and a small inheritance, but could he not have chosen a worthier man? I remember then that Essex had been a friend of Sir Philip's, a friendship that had always baffled me. Sir Philip had left his sword to Essex. Perhaps he had bequeathed him his wife as well, but that was a long time ago now. It was Walsingham's impending death which had brought this about.

The ceremony was over. Mylles and I were summoned by the priest to sign as witnesses on the marriage document. As well as the bride and groom standing beside the priest, there were four witnesses: Sir Francis, Master Goodrich, Master Mylles and myself. I hesitated before I signed. Would the signature of a woman be valid, particularly a woman posing as a man? For all I knew of the law, it might invalidate the marriage. However, Sir Francis had just told me plainly that he knew who I was, so this was done with his approval.

The company filed out of the chapel, with none of the joyous chatter that usually accompanies such occasions. The family retired to the house.

I looked at Mylles. 'That was a strange business. Why the haste and near secrecy?'

He shrugged. 'Ours not to ask. I suppose if they had waited to gain the Queen's approval, it might have taken months, and Sir Francis could not live so long.'

'I feel nothing but pity for the Lady Frances. Essex is a boor and will treat her badly.'

'Do not speak so loud. Women from great families must accept the marriages arranged for them. It will give her a noble rank. Her father was not born a knight.'

'It is a cruel price to pay, merely for rank.' I sighed. 'I may return to London now?'

'Aye.' He gave a rueful smile. 'We too must do what is expected of us.'

I collected the satchel of papers from where I had left them beside the door when Mylles summoned me, and sent once again for Hector. I led him to the mounting block and swung myself into the saddle. Feeling his familiar back beneath me, I leaned forward and laid a hand on his silky neck.

'You are mine,' I whispered. 'Mine.'

It was one joyous outcome from a day of sorrows.

I did not hasten on the journey back to London, for I had much to think about. I would tell Phelippes and Arthur about the gift of Hector, but decided I should not mention the hasty marriage. I had been given no instructions as to whether it was to be kept secret, but the whole hasty business had left me uneasy, so that I thought it best to say nothing. The Walsingham family would announce the marriage when they saw fit.

When I told Harry that Hector was now mine, I showed him the deed of gift, but he shook his head.

'I cannot read, Dr Alvarez, but that is good news. We was afeared he might be sold when there wasn't need for so many horses.'

I understood what he meant. Walsingham kept more horses than were necessary for the family's use. He often also needed to provide mounts for his agents, which was how I had come to know Hector in the first place.

'And you say he'll be staying on here?' Harry said. 'That is good to know. Me and the other lads think he's a fine horse.' He looked at me sideways and said hesitantly, 'Do you know what will happen? I mean, if Sir Francis–'

I shook my head. 'Nay, Harry, I know no more than you.'

That was not strictly true. After what I had witnessed today, it seemed more than ever likely that the Earl of Essex would have some say in the future of the house and all its inhabitants, but I could not admit as much to Harry.

When I handed over the documents to Phelippes and gave him Mylles's instructions, he asked after Sir Francis's health. I shook my head.

'Not good. I fear it cannot be much longer.' I drew breath. I had never asked him outright before, but now it seemed best to do so. 'What will you do, after he is gone?'

'I do not know, Kit. Will Essex try to take over the service? He knows nothing about intelligence work, but if he does take over, he will need experienced men to work for him. This has been my life. I have no other skills. What else can I do? And you, Arthur?' He raised his voice. 'Will you stay, if Essex desires it?'

Arthur came through, peeling from his fingers some sealing wax which had dried there.

'Like you, I have no other trade. I have a wife and child to support.'

'You could always become a counterfeiter of coins,' I suggested.

He grinned at me. 'I value my neck too much. I would not put it in a noose.'

When I told them about Hector, I saw that they were truly happy for me.

'Now a horse is the last thing I should want myself,' Phelippes said, 'but I can see that it will be a fine addition to your collection – a stray dog from Amsterdam, a group of beggar children from London, a horse from the stables of Sir Francis Walsingham. I wonder what will be next?'

I laughed. 'I must collect my dog and visit my patients at St Thomas's before I go home. They have had to do without my care all day.'

Three weeks passed. My services were not needed at Seething Lane, but I made several visits to my new horse, though I had no excuse to ride him at present. It was truly spring now, so that Burbage's company were able to move back into the fair weather space of the Theatre. They could not charge as much for admission, but they would be able to accommodate much larger audiences than in their winter quarters at the Cross Keys, and with the passing of winter the citizens of London threw off their winter gloom and looked about them for entertainment. Davy was now officially a member of the company and improving daily under instruction from Guy, to whom he was apprenticed, though Burbage despaired of ever being able to train him to play women's parts.

Jamey had fallen very ill in February, and once more Matthew had appeared from the anonymity of the streets, carrying another child, although this time he had come to St Thomas's. He attempted to enter the hospital directly, by-passing the patient queue awaiting the attention of the almoner, and swore at anyone who tried to stop him. It was Mistress Maynard who calmed the angry shouting and sent Jamey up to me in the children's ward.

The little boy had a terrible fever and I had to fight hard to save him. All the time he remained at St Thomas's the other children came every morning and plagued Mistress Maynard for news of him. Once he began to show signs of recovery, I took Matthew aside.

'Jamey cannot go back to living on the streets, Matthew,' I said. 'He has been very weakened and will not survive such a life.'

Matthew opened his mouth to argue, but I raised my hand to silence him.

'I know you want to keep him with you, but if you do, you will be responsible for his death. Is that what you want?'

He tried to argue with me, but his heart was not in it. I think he had been truly frightened at seeing Jamey so close to dying. In the end he agreed, grudgingly, that Jamey should be taken to Christ's.

Since then, I had word of Jamey from time to time. He was beginning at last to speak. I knew he was not deaf, for he responded to sounds and knew his name. Why he had been mute, I did not know. He did not appear to be simple-minded. Whatever the reason, he had remained without speech while he lived on the streets, but within the sanctuary of Christ's Hospital he was at last shaping simple words.

As for the other children, they reappeared at the Theatre when Burbage's company returned there, and took up their old corner for begging. Nothing I could say to them would persuade them off the streets. Where they slept was still secret, but they were better fed now, and better clothed, thanks to hand-outs from the kitchen of the Cross Keys and from Mistress Maynard's store of clothes. As a result, they no longer depended entirely on begging. Katerina sometimes sold nuts and oranges to the playgoers. Matthew ran errands for Burbage and from time to time did a day's labour at one of the St Thomas's workshops. It was a fragile existence, but I had come to see that these four children would always live life on the margins. A mixture of pride and fear meant they could never accept a life under a conventional roof. Long ago, such children might have lived wild in the forest. I could never quite see the world through their eyes, but I had come to believe that for them the streets of London were another kind of forest, through which they roamed and carved a living as wild children would once have carved a living from the greenwood.

There were still unwanted babies to be delivered from St Thomas's to Christ's, and whenever I visited there I found Ellyn becoming a studious little maid, while Mellie worked hard to prove that she could be both cook's assistant and mother, so that Mistress Wedderbury had allowed her to keep Hannah with her.

At the beginning of April, the Fitzgeralds returned to Surrey, taking with them Sophia, who seemed to have forgotten her ordeal, though I judged, from my own childhood experience, that it would live on in her memory, to haunt her when she least expected it. Before they left, I took Edwin Alchester to see a performance at the Theatre. It was the same piece the company had played before the Queen on Twelfth Night, *A Comedy of Errors*, with those unlikely twins, Christopher Haigh and Simon Hetherington, involved in an even more unlikely tangle of misunderstandings and mistakes.

'But they do not look very much alike,' Alchester whispered to me.

'You must just pretend,' I said. 'You see that they are dressed alike. Imagine that their faces too are the same.'

'But–'

'Hush,' I said.

Then I received a message from Phelippes. Sir Francis had returned to Seething Lane, carried there in a litter, and the family had announced the marriage of Frances Walsingham to the Earl of Essex.

'And now we await the storm from the palace,' the message concluded.

I had gone to visit Hector on the evening of the fifth of April, my pockets stuffed with some late withered apples. As I approached the house, I saw Master Goodrich hastening down the steps from the front door. I had not realised he had also come up from the country.

'Dr Alvarez,' he said, as startled at seeing me as I was at seeing him.

'Something is amiss,' I said.

'Aye. I am sent for a priest.'

'It has come, then. Can I be of any help?'

'Nay, though I thank you. He has said he needs no physician now, other than a priest to give him the last rites and see him on his way.'

I nodded, suddenly too grieved to speak as he hurried away. I stayed a long while in Hector's stall, talking to him, for nothing is more comfort at a time of sorrow than the presence of a loving animal. Eventually, I went home, just managing to slip through the gates on the Bridge before they closed. The light was shining from Simon's room, so I thumped on his door and went in. Simon was sprawled half sitting on his bed, with a pot of ale in one hand and a half-eaten pasty abandoned on his knee. Rikki looked hopefully at the pasty, then threw himself down in front of the fire, which was nearly out.

As I made up the fire, I said, 'You are too tired to eat?'

'Aye. We have spent all morning rehearsing a new play of Will's, then a performance of *Tamburlaine* this afternoon, which is always exhausting. Too much high drama! Here, Rikki.'

He held out the remains of the pasty and Rikki took it neatly, retiring back to the fire to enjoy it. I slumped down on a stool and sat looking into the fire, my clasped hands dangling between my knees. Simon swung his legs over the edge of the bed and sat up.

'What is the matter, Kit?'

'Sir Francis is dying.'

'He has been dying for weeks.'

'He has sent for a priest to give him the last rites. He will not last the night.'

I put my hands over my face and began to weep. Of late I seemed to be forever in tears. In a confused way, I was weeping for a man who had been more that simply the master of the service to which I had belonged; I was also weeping for my father who had died alone, while I was away in Portugal, less than a year before. Somehow the two deaths had become fused in my mind.

Simon put his arm briefly round my shoulder, then fetched me a pot of ale and pressed it into my hand.

'Drink,' he said.

I sipped a little, but I had no desire for ale, though I appreciated his kindness.

'What will happen now?' he said.

'I fear the Earl of Essex will seize control of the intelligence service and ruin it.' It was public knowledge now, so I added, 'Essex was married to Frances Walsingham three weeks ago, in a private ceremony at Barn Elms.'

'Wasn't that when you were sent there?'

'Aye. They asked me to be a witness, but it has only now been announced.'

He whistled softly and said, as I had done, 'The Queen will not like it.'

'She will not.'

'Could it mean trouble for you?'

'I hope not. There were three other witnesses. Sir Francis will be gone before any storm can break. The others were Francis Mylles and the Walsingham's steward at Barn Elms, Edward Goodrich.'

'You know,' he said thoughtfully, sitting down on the floor beside Rikki, 'we hear much gossip in the playhouse.'

'I know.' I gave a sad smile. It was an old joke, and I did not feel like jokes or gossip at that moment.

'There is a general expectation that the Cecils will assume control of the intelligence gathering once Walsingham is gone. Lord

Burghley is said to have been grooming his younger son to take on the role of Principal Secretary to the Queen after Sir Francis.'

'Sir Robert Cecil? He is very frail, is he not? Crippled by disease as a child.'

'He has a formidable mind.'

'Well, that makes him the perfect opposite to Essex, who is formidable in body, but weak in mind.'

'If it comes to a battle between the two,' he said, 'I wonder which of them will prove the victor?'

I went to my work in the hospital as usual the next morning, but before noon a letter was brought to me. It was in Phelippes's minute handwriting, so I carried it near a window, the better to make it out.

> *Sir Francis went to his Maker at about one o' the clock during this last night. He is at peace now and free of pain. The funeral will be a night service tomorrow, at ten o' the clock in St Paul's. Dame Ursula has asked me to extend her invitation to you to attend. At Sir Francis's wish, it will be a simple ceremony, with no procession, no heraldry, no black draping of the church, only torches to light the church and a brief sermon. He is to be buried next to Sir Philip Sidney. If you will come, I will meet you at Paul's west door one quarter of an hour before the ceremony.*
>
> *Thos. Phelippes*

I wrote a hasty reply and sent it back by the same messenger.

> *I shall be there.*
>
> *Chr. Alvarez*

As so often in April, the weather had turned from spring back to winter, with a bitter wind blowing up the river from the east. I possessed no mourning clothes of my own, but I had appealed to Master Burbage for something suitable, and he was able to equip me with decent black, over which I wore my black physician's gown and cap. I carried my battered small Bible which had travelled with me to Portugal and back. The spine was beginning to tear, but I had a certain affection for it. I had not much cared for our old rector at St Bartholomew-the-Great, who had given it to me, but it had brought me comfort in dark moments of personal grief and times when I struggled to understand my own confused faith.

Heavy clouds scudded overhead, driven by the wind, so that the light from the moon came and went like an illumination from some ghostly visitation. Where there were torches mounted as house doorways, their flames streamed sideways like horses' tails. I took a wherry across the river to Blackfriars Stairs, then walked up to St Paul's, carrying a candle lantern that rocked and tossed in the wind, casting fearful shadows dancing all about me in the street. I was glad to see Thomas Phelippes and Arthur Gregory standing together beside the west door. A few people passed into the church, but there were no great crowds. This was to be a small private funeral, not the great public affair which a man of such importance to the State should have merited. It was inevitable that I remembered the huge crowds, the panoply, the vast procession of mourners at the funeral of his son-in-law, just three years before. How like the man, I thought. Out of love and respect for Sidney, he near beggared himself for the sake of a man whose fame he was determined should last forever, while he decrees that he shall slip away in the night, like this.

In the vastness of that great empty nave, our funeral party seemed lost. Church wardens ushered us forward until we formed a pathetic cluster in front of the altar, where the modest coffin lay, covered with a mortcloth of black velvet on which a posy of spring flowers had been placed. I looked about me covertly. The members of his family and both households were there, from Seething Lane and Barn Elms. A few gentlemen who were his closest friends: Lord Burghley, leaning on a stick, his son Sir Robert Cecil, Dr Nuñez and his wife, Dunstan Añez and his, several distinguished merchants. At the back, where I stood, those of us who had worked in his intelligence service, including Nick Berden standing with the retired agent Titus Allanby, together with the lesser servants, like Harry and the other stable lads.

Dame Ursula looked very pale, but held herself upright with great dignity. Lady Frances – or the Countess, as she now was – leaned on the arm of the Earl of Essex. She looked drawn and ill, but he did not seem unduly distressed. He wore mourning black, but his clothes were sewn with silver thread and there were diamonds in his cap.

The Dean of St Paul's conducted the service, reading the rubrics from the Queen's new prayer book. We sang a psalm. He delivered a brief sermon, extolling Sir Francis's virtues, but with no overblown phrases. We sang another psalm. Somehow the wind had found its way into the church, thrashing the flames of the torches so that our monstrous shadows leapt and cavorted about the walls of the nave and were lost in the high shadows of the roof.

Several flagstones had been lifted alongside the grave of Sir Philip Sidney, and now the pall bearers lifted the coffin to lower it into the hole. I shuddered and tried not to think of that damp dark prison closing round a man of such wide vision and understanding. What must Frances Walsingham be feeling, holding the arm of the man she had been obliged to marry, and looking down at that dark hole which had swallowed up both the love of her young life and her beloved father?

The flagstones were lowered again into place with a scraping of stone on stone that set my teeth on edge. And it was over.

Outside the wind blew even more fiercely, so that I was obliged to retreat into the shelter of the doorway to relight my lantern.

'You do not want to travel back to Southwark tonight, surely?' Arthur said. 'It is past midnight. Why do you not come home with me? My wife will be glad to welcome you.'

'That is kind,' I said, shivering as the wind cut through my clothes, but I have left Rikki shut up in my lodgings. I cannot leave him all night.'

'We will walk with you to Blackfriars Stairs,' Phelippes said decisively, 'then if there is no wherry to be had, you must accept Arthur's invitation.'

'I will welcome your company,' I said, and indeed I was glad of it, for the funeral had left me in a deep melancholy, which was not eased by the dark and the wind and the loneliness.

Fortunately or otherwise, there was a wherry, and I bade them goodnight.

'Come to Seething Lane tomorrow morning,' Phelippes said, 'before you go to St Thomas's. We must take counsel what is to be done.'

'I shall come,' I promised, as I stepped into the wherry.

Rikki was overjoyed to see me, and I managed to stay calm as I removed my borrowed funeral wear and laid it carefully in my clothes coffer, but when I had crawled into my bed, I put my arms around my dog for comfort. The world seemed a dark and lonely place, as dark and lonely as that hole beneath the flagstones of St. Paul's.

The next morning I arrived early at Seething Lane and went up the back stairs to see Phelippes. The house appeared to be in a turmoil, but the corridor leading to Phelippes's office was silent. There was something unsettling about that silence. I opened the door and went in, to find Phelippes and Arthur standing helplessly in the centre of the room. The secure cupboards with their heavy locks had been broken open, their doors hanging from shattered hinges, their shelves empty. Phelippes's desk – always so precise and neat – was covered with torn paper and spilled ink. Mine was the same. The shelf above my chair, where I kept my code sheets had been ransacked.

257

'What has happened?' I whispered. I could hardly believe the devastation before me.

'The house was broken into during the night,' Phelippes said. 'While we were all attending the funeral. By someone who would know that, though it was not public knowledge. My lord of Essex is like to run mad.'

I made a helpless gesture at the open cupboards.

'The files?' I said. 'Those that were kept here? Those in Sir Francis's office?'

'All the secret papers are gone. All.' He said it in a tone of utter disbelief.

The very earth seemed to totter beneath our feet.

I remembered what Walsingham always used to say: 'Intelligence is power.'

Into whose hands, I wondered, would that power now fall?

Historical Note

When Henry VIII dissolved the monasteries in 1536-41, he was intent upon seizing their lands and riches for himself, although reports of corruption and the break with Rome provided the excuse. What he overlooked – or given his character, perhaps he did not care – was the immense contribution to social welfare by the religious institutions. Not only did they offer safe lodging for travellers, they provided permanent homes for the aged and infirm and for those incapable of looking after themselves, they took in orphans and foundlings, and they supplied medical care for the sick who were too poor to employ a private physician.

When this service collapsed, the multiple problems of the poor became acute. In London above all, the ever-growing number of inhabitants meant that the situation was a cause for serious concern. There were many religious houses in London, one of the largest being St Bartholomew's, founded as an Augustinian priory in 1123 and incorporating a hospital (the oldest surviving hospital in the world). The church of St Bartholomew-the-Great was in large part pulled down at the dissolution, but fortunately some survives. The hospital building remained, but without any income. Henry VIII was persuaded to hand the hospital over to the Corporation of London, who managed to save it and continue its work for the sick poor north of the river.

In Southwark, south of the river, was St Thomas's, an Augustinian monastery of monks and nuns, also founded in the twelfth century, also providing care for the poor, and also dissolved by Henry. Its hospital was closed and only reopened in 1551, when the city obtained the land and a charter from Edward VI. Both hospitals figure in my series of novels about the young physician, Christoval Alvarez.

As a result of these humanitarian actions by the city authorities, medical care was restored for the poor. A further serious problem, however, was the vast number of abandoned and orphaned children. The crowded conditions in London meant that epidemics spread quickly and killed large numbers of the inhabitants. Best known are the recurrent episodes of the plague, but there were others – the sweating sickness, dysentery ('the bloody flux'), typhus, typhoid, cholera, tuberculosis ('consumption'), smallpox – quite apart from all the common illnesses we know today – influenza, measles, mumps, chickenpox, pneumonia, and many chest infections. Venereal diseases also took their toll, especially syphilis, which reached Europe after the invasion of the New World.

These killer diseases meant that many children were left orphans. Unwanted babies were abandoned on doorsteps and in public privies.

Children were exploited by beggars who used them to illicit sympathy. In times of hardship and starvation, such as the famine years of the 1590s, poor families simply could not feed their children. What was to be done about this growing problem of destitute babies and children? Those who managed to survive swarmed in the streets as beggars and potential criminals. It was an acute crisis.

King Edward VI wrote to the Lord Mayor of London, asking him:

> to take out of the streets all the fatherless children, and other poor men's children that were not able to keep them, and bring them to the late dissolved house of the Greyfriars...where they should have meat, drink and clothes, lodging and officers to attend upon them...the sucking children and such as for want of years were not able to learn should be kept in the country...
> [John Howes, 1582, quoted in Liza Picard, *Elizabeth's London.*]

Remarkably, Greyfriars, located in Newgate, across the street from Newgate Prison, had not been torn down, though it was in a derelict state. The Lord Mayor assembled a committee of thirty solid and benevolent citizens who immediately set to work to raise funds, repair the buildings and appoint a large staff. The first children were admitted in November 1552, before winter set in.

The site, which can be seen on the Agas map of London, was huge, incorporating a church, dormitories, quadrangles (like an Oxford or Cambridge college), and numerous outbuildings, which provided everything necessary for this model orphanage: bakery, brewery, laundry, and so on. Moreover, there were to be two schools, a petty school for the small children and a grammar school for the older ones. These children were not to join the unskilled and indigent paupers of London when they left Christ's. They were trained in basic clerical skills, some were later apprenticed to craftsmen, some very clever boys would even go on to university and rise to high positions in the church.

The numbers were initially to be limited to 250, then 300, but they frequently rose to as many as 700. From the outset it seems to have been a kindly and humane home, for cases are recorded where children apprenticed to cruel masters ran away and came home to Christ's Hospital. At a time when life could be unbelievably brutal, Christ's was an extraordinary exception.

Many of the buildings were destroyed in the Great Fire of London in 1666 (though no children died), and Christ's was obliged to move out of London to Hertfordshire. However, the children returned to London when the school was rebuilt in the eighteenth century. In the twentieth century Christ's made its final move to Horsham in Sussex, where it continues to this day, known more commonly as the Bluecoats School. Recently the pupils were allowed to vote on whether or not they wished to retain their Tudor uniform of long blue coats and yellow socks. The vote was overwhelmingly in favour of retention. It is believed to be the oldest, and probably the first, school uniform in the world.

Today Christ's Hospital is purely a school, but it retains much of its charitable funding and great pride in its origins. Those benevolent citizens of London who opened their purses and their hearts to destitute children in the sixteenth century set in train a truly remarkable institution.

In 1601, the Elizabethan Poor Law was introduced, a refinement of an earlier act of 1597, which (with modifications) provided general relief for the poor until the new act of 1834. But that is another story.

The Author

Ann Swinfen spent her childhood partly in England and partly on the east coast of America. She was educated at Somerville College, Oxford, where she read Classics and Mathematics and married a fellow undergraduate, the historian David Swinfen. While bringing up their five children and studying for a postgraduate MSc in Mathematics and a BA and PhD in English Literature, she had a variety of jobs, including university lecturer, translator, freelance journalist and software designer. She served for nine years on the governing council of the Open University and for five years worked as a manager and editor in the technical author division of an international computer company, but gave up her full-time job to concentrate on her writing, while continuing part-time university teaching. In 1995 she founded Dundee Book Events, a voluntary organisation promoting books and authors to the general public.

Her first three novels, *The Anniversary*, *The Travellers*, and *A Running Tide*, all with a contemporary setting but also an historical resonance, were published by Random House, with translations into Dutch and German. *The Testament of Mariam* marked something of a departure. Set in the first century, it recounts, from an unusual perspective, one of the most famous and yet ambiguous stories in human history. At the same time it explores life under a foreign occupying force, in lands still torn by conflict to this day. Her second historical novel, *Flood*, takes place in the fenlands of East Anglia during the seventeenth century, where the local people fought desperately to save their land from greedy and unscrupulous speculators. *This Rough Ocean* is based on the real-life experiences of the Swinfen family during the 1640s, at the time of the English Civil War.

Currently she is working on a late sixteenth century series, featuring a young Marrano physician who is recruited as a code-breaker and spy in Walsingham's secret service. The first book in the series is *The Secret World of Christoval Alvarez*, the second is *The Enterprise of England*, the third is *The Portuguese Affair*, the fourth is *Bartholomew Fair* and the fifth is *Suffer the Little Children*.

She now lives in Broughty Ferry, on the northeast coast of Scotland, with her husband, formerly vice-principal of the University of Dundee, and a rescue kitten.

www.annswinfen.com

Printed in Great Britain
by Amazon